$\mathcal{D}$ARK $\mathcal{L}$EGACY

F. HAYWOOD GLENN

Ambiance Publishing Company
Philadelphia, Pennsylvania

Printed by CreateSpace
Charleston, SC

Cover Art by LaReine M. Nixon
Author Photo by D. Scott

ACKNOWLEDEMENTS

Thank God for the World Wide Web. We now have the ability to visit digital libraries across the nation with the click of the mouse.

Special thanks to my Editor Alicia (Adlals) James, who did a phenomenal job. Words cannot express my sincere admiration and appreciation for her professional attention to this work.

DEDICATION

For my family.

We are all products of our families. I am blessed to come from a long line of intelligent, creative, strong black women.

"You don't choose your family. They are God's gift to you, as you are to them." *Desmond Tutu*

I never stop being amazed at the awesomeness God.

"Thanks be to God for his inexpressible gift!" 2Co 9:15

Forever rejoicing in the memory of my parents,
Francis Thomas Haywood, Jr. and
Jessie Marie Witherspoon Haywood

Dark Legacy

F. HAYWOOD GLENN

CHAPTER 1

JUNE 1839
PHILADELPHIA, PENNSYLVANIA

Born Again

Slave or free, Negros were only allowed a few seats at the back of the train car. Beth sat in the middle of the car with other whites. There were four other Negros on that train, all traveling with their masters. Lillian paid them no attention. All around them, people were laughing and talking but the three Vance women were mournfully silent. Under more favorable circumstances, Lillian and Rebecca would have been in awe of their first train ride. But the circumstances that led to this train ride were hardly favorable. Instead, few words passed between them as they each tried to come to terms with the events of the past few months.

All three women had loved David Vance but each love was different as was their grief. Rebecca mourned the father that had never given her the attention that she craved. Beth mourned the husband that had saved her from a life of degradation in a waterfront brothel only to endure the misery of a loveless marriage. Lillian loved more and longer than her former mistress and her daughter. David Vance was the only man Lillian had ever loved though he was both her master and lover. Her grief was somewhat ambivalent, mourning her loss while wanting desperately to celebrate her freedom.

The train rocked backward and forward and Beth glanced back at Lillian. She couldn't help but notice how different Lillian looked now. The usual smug expression and haughty attitude that had become all too familiar to Beth over the years, had vanished. Lillian's shoulders slumped and her head hung low. Her somber expression marked her grief and her fear.

Beth knew that Lillian hated her and would likely never trust her but she did not hate Lillian. Of course, with all that Lillian had done to come between her and David, no one could blame her if she did hate Lillian. She no longer blamed Lillian for her failed marriage, finally admitting to herself that it had been a farce from the very beginning. Beth now knew that Lillian and David were the true victims of Big Bill's deception. She even wished that she could take back every hateful thing she'd ever said or done to Lillian.

Now that they had left Virginia and all the hurt and deception was behind them, Beth only wanted to help Lillian to move on with her life. She wanted a normal life for herself, with a man who would love her and she didn't want anything less for Lillian and Rebecca.

Beth neither mourned nor missed her husband of seven years. So surprised was she at her own feeling that she now questioned if she had ever loved David. There were no tears and no regrets. The only thing she felt was an overwhelming sense of relief. Her mind wondered over the years she spent with David, as it had many times since leaving Gloria. She thought of how many times she should have just packed her things and left him.

The first time she actually caught David and Lillian in the throes of lovemaking should have been the end of it all, but instead it only increased her determination to have David to herself. What a fool she'd been. Even though David had never promised to love her, he did promise to be a good husband; a promise he was emotionally unable to keep. Beth realized now that everything she had wanted and every act from that moment until David went off in search of Lillian and Rebecca had been wrought by her own selfish pride. She just couldn't accept the fact that her husband was in love with his slave. Beth knew now that David had always belonged to Lillian just as Lillian belonged to him. There was no way she could have competed with that kind of twisted love.

Beth just wanted to put it all behind her now however, she really did want to do all she could do to help Lillian if only Lillian would allow her. Seeing Lillian and Rebecca safely to Philadelphia was her first attempt at mending their fractured relationship. In spite of everything, they would all have to learn to live with the past.

The last stop was just outside of Philadelphia and Beth had to hire a carriage to take them into the city.

One by one, the other passengers disembarked until there was only Beth, Lillian, and Rebecca. As the carriage rocked forward, Rebecca leaned wearily on her mother while Lillian concentrated on the passing landscape. Her head ached from the tangle of emotions in which her mind whirled. She not only grieved David's death, but the realization that the love of her life was actually her brother had soiled their relationship beyond redemption. The memory of their love was now sinful, sordid, and dirty and she couldn't help but cringe when she thought of it. She also could not stop reliving her failed escape from Gloria. Her mind relived the nights she and Rebecca spent sleeping in the wilderness on wet ground; their nightly watching for the North Star, and eventually being captured and taken to Richmond for auction. The memory was as vivid as if it were only yesterday. The memories kept coming, no matter how hard she tried to keep those disturbing thoughts from her mind. She leaned her head on the side of the carriage and closed her eyes in an effort to stop the pounding at her temples. *I'm free now,* she thought. *Rebecca and I are free of it all and I don't want to think about it anymore.*

Lillian had never been a religious woman. She had listened to the sermons of the white minister who came to Gloria but had not really given any of it much thought until the night she and Rebecca tried to escape to the north. Now she prayed for the second time in her life. *Lord, I know that I ain't been one of the good people and I'm sorry. People say you love everybody so if you love me, Lord, forgive me, and help me to be a good person and a good mother to Rebecca. Help me to forget the past. Amen!*

Lillian had no preconceived notions of freedom. She was both happy and afraid of her newfound freedom, even though, she had no idea of what to expect or what freedom felt like for a black woman. She didn't know anyone who had been freed that could tell her what to expect. Even Miss Beth could not tell her what to expect. She tried not to think about it, telling herself that she would just have to learn to deal with whatever came her way. She was determined to be strong for Rebecca. However, Lillian was well aware that their freedom was fragile. Rumors of freed slaves being captured in the northern states and returned to the south in chains to be sold were rampant on Gloria. They often captured freed slaves while in pursuit of runaways. Slave catchers and kidnappers were known to travel as far north as Canada tracking runaway slaves. Lillian knew that she or Rebecca could be snatched off the street and taken back to Virginia or some other southern state and sold back into slavery. The thought made her reach into her dress pocket to feel for the envelope that contained the freedom documents signed by David before they left Virginia. The papers were folded into a small soiled square but Lillian felt a measure of comfort as her fingers slid over the textured paper.

Another disturbing thought crossed her mind several times since leaving Gloria. Why had Miss Beth agreed to let her and Rebecca travel with her to Philadelphia? She and Beth had hated each other for so long that it was hard to believe that Beth could now just put her hatred aside and offer to assist her former slaves. Lillian still harbored a generous amount of distrust and jealousy toward her former mistress but she could not help feeling a begrudging amount of gratitude for Beth's help. She knew that this journey would have been far different had she attempted such a move on her own. Lillian knew that traveling with Miss Beth and pretending to be her slaves was far safer for her and Rebecca then traveling alone.

The Vance women arrived in Philadelphia at a most unfortunate time. Though the city was experiencing a period of relative calm, tempers of recent racial unrest still simmered below the surface. It had only been a matter of months since the city had experienced two incidents of racial conflict. The first was the result of two murders committed by black men against white men, even though one of the black men was known not to be in his right mind. As mourners attended the burial of one of the victims, a mob of angry white men began to gather. Fueled by hatred and revenge, the mob marched down Fifth Street from Passyunk Avenue. However, before any real violence took place, the mob was dispersed by city police.

The second incident was at the dedication of the newly built Pennsylvania Hall, built by abolitionists as a place where they could enjoy freedom of speech. The first meeting in the new building was held by the Anti-Slavery Convention of American Women. Blacks and whites met peacefully to discuss abolition activities and sometimes black and white women walked arm and arm in front of the building. This aroused the tempers of the larger white community to a fever pitch and soon a riot ensued. It happened during the dedication ceremony in May of 1838. The hall was burnt to the ground along with the shelter for colored orphans at Thirteenth and Callowhill Streets. Bethel Church on

Sixth Street suffered some damage. Black people were pulled from their homes and beaten. Many homes were set on fire with the residents still inside. The riot was too large and widespread for the city police to put down and it lasted for two days before the Pennsylvania Militia put an end to the violence.

Beth, who had lived just outside of Philadelphia all of her life before moving to Virginia with David, had never experienced such violence and now found a very different and confusing city. Philadelphia had entered the Industrial Revolution and the growth of factories, textile mills, and railroads led to an influx of foreigners from Ireland, Cuba and freed and run-away slaves from the south. The city inevitably experienced a tremendous population growth. Though there was a growing middle class of blacks who owned houses and businesses, there was also a large underclass living in squalid conditions in the southern area of the city. The severe poverty of the underclass blacks was a direct result of the arrival of foreigners. Domestic employment and other unskilled labor jobs, which had traditionally been available to free blacks, now went to the Irish. These circumstances stoked the fires of racial tension in the city.

Upon arrival in the city, Beth took rooms at the City Hotel on Market Street until she could find a suitable home for renting. As she stood in the lobby waiting for the hotel clerk, she had a sudden feeling of deja'vu. She was reminded of the hotel where David had brought her the first night they met. This was the place where David had first broached the possibility of a marriage of convenience. *What a fool I'd been,* she thought now. She was reminded again of what a travesty David's so called marriage of convenience turned out to be and how it was his lust that had ruined all their lives.

Beth glanced over her shoulder at Lillian and Rebecca who stood there looking as out of place in this grand hotel lobby as a hog at a wedding. Both of their heads were covered with dirty rags as they had been on the plantation. Their faded calico dresses and mud-covered boots looked extremely worn.

As expected, the hotel clerk assumed that Lillian and Rebecca were Beth's slaves and she saw no need to correct him. He rang a bell and a black man seemed to appear out of nowhere. He was dressed in a blue suit with gold braiding around the shoulders and cuffs, and large brass buttons down the front of his suit. Both Lillian and Rebecca stared in awe. Though it was just a uniform, neither Lillian or Rebecca had ever seen a black man wear such finery. The man bowed deeply from the waist, then picked up Beth's bags. "Follow me, Ma'am," he said as he headed for the grand staircase. He smiled at Lillian and she smiled back, but he made no move to pick up her tattered bags. Several seconds passed before Lillian realized that the young man did not intend to help her with her bags. She then instructed Rebecca to pick up one of the bags while she gathered the other two and ran to catch up with Beth and the young man. They were led to a large suite of rooms, which included a small room for her slaves.

The man put the bags in the room and then politely waited until Beth placed a couple of pennies in his palm. "Thank you," he said, nodding his head and bowing from the waist again. "My name is Benjamin. If you need anything, just ask for Benjamin."

"Thank you, Benjamin," Beth said. "I have just one question, Benjamin. Will my slaves be allowed to dine with me in the hotel dining room?"

The look that came over Benjamin's face let Beth know just how foolish a question she'd asked. "No Ma'am! Free or slave, Black folk ain't allowed in the hotel dining room."

"Then where do they eat?" Beth asked with sarcasm.

"There is a small room by the kitchen where slaves, whose masters are guest in the hotel, can eat the day's left-overs."

Several silent moments passed, as neither Beth nor Benjamin knew what to say. Finally, Beth said, "Thank you Benjamin. You have been very helpful."

No sooner had the door closed then Lillian and Rebecca assailed Beth with questions.

"Is he a freeman?" Lillian wanted to know. "You gave him money. Negros get money for their work here in Philadelphia?"

"Where did he get such fine clothes?" Rebecca wanted to know.

Beth smiled realizing that their encounter with Benjamin, the first free black man they'd ever seen, had somehow broken the ice. She began to unpack. "Yes, Lillian, Benjamin is a freeman and I assume he is working here at the hotel, a job for which he is paid money. Those fine clothes, Rebecca, are his uniform for working here at the hotel."

They were all three exhausted. Beth ordered food brought to the room and after they'd eaten, they all went to bed. Rebecca slept like a baby. It was not as easy for Lillian or Beth. Both had brought ghosts from Gloria that would haunt their new lives for many weeks.

Lillian was still finding it difficult to put David out of her mind. She dreamed of him. Her body relaxed as her mind placed her safely in the cradle of his strong masculine arms. The smell of him filled her nostrils and she breathed in his essence. She felt as if she were suspended in time as she relived the recent past and reveled in the glory of her life-long love. She could feel his breath on her skin and his lips as they kissed every inch of her body. Yet, the dream ended in terror. When the lovemaking was over, David's words came back to her as clear as if he were standing right before her. "Lillian I am the child that Big Bill took from Mamie and my father tried to keep us apart not because you were a slave but because you are my half-sister." The words would repeat over and over and then she would suddenly see her beloved swinging from a tree. She awoke with a jolt as her mind slowly brought her back to the present. Would she ever be rid of these visions, she wondered.

Beth's sleep was also fitful. She had gotten Lillian and Rebecca safely to Philadelphia, but what was she to do now? How would they survive in the city? She didn't even know where the free Negro people of Philadelphia lived and even if she had known, she knew that Lillian didn't know anyone. Beth tossed and turned most of the night but she awoke with a plan. The first thing she needed to do was to rent a house. She would give Lillian and Rebecca the opportunity to live with her as her live-in servants and she would pay them a fair wage. She knew that Lillian was a prideful woman and would likely refuse. If she did indeed refuse, Beth vowed to do the best she could to help them find a place of their own.

The three women spent the next couple of days walking the crowded streets of Philadelphia. Beth wanted them to get a feel for the city. It seemed cleaner than she remembered. The sidewalks were wider and there were new buildings and homes throughout the city. Market and Chestnut Streets had become the premier shopping district. New Market was a bricked in structure known as the Shambles on Second Street where vendors sold everything from boots to fruit. The waterfront was just a few blocks away. Beth remembered the dirt and decadence of the waterfront during her brief stay at Madam Renee's Pleasure Chateau. The brothel had apparently been torn down. There was still evidence that the waterfront was the seedier section of the city but it seemed to have been cleaned up somewhat or maybe just well hidden.

Lillian stared wide-eyed at the many free Negros in the city. She was stunned to learn that many of them actually owned businesses. There were bakers and caterers, hat shop owners, and clothing stores. When they passed a Negro man or woman on the street, they would always nod their heads or tip their hat as they smiled a silent greeting. Lillian was also shocked that most of the black women she saw did not wear their hair tied up in a rag. They wore their hair in different styles or they wore fashionable hats or no head covering at all.

The difference between the city dwelling Negros and Lillian and Rebecca did not escape Beth's notice. She decided that Lillian and Rebecca needed new looks to accurately represented their new lives as free people of color. Beth suggested that they shop for a few new dresses and shoes. Lillian was predictably skeptical.

"Why do you offer such kindness?" she asked Beth.

"Because Lillian, we have the opportunity to start again. Whatever mistakes that we've made in the past are far away. Here in Philadelphia, we get to start again. You and Rebecca are free women now. Why not shed the rags of bondage?"

For a moment, Lillian just stared at Beth. She couldn't believe what she was hearing. This really didn't sound like the Miss Beth that she had known on Gloria. Lillian didn't know this new Miss Beth but she was beginning to like her. "Alright," she said with a slow smile. "I ain't ever had a new dress."

Rebecca was quiet but she listened to both her mother and Miss Beth.

Beth also bought a daily newspaper so she could look for a small house to rent.

It was a warm Saturday and the women had been shopping all afternoon. Beth bought Rebecca her first pair of button-up boots and she was absolutely thrilled. Not only did Miss Beth buy her a dress, but with some of the money David had given her, for the first time in her life, Lillian was able to buy new dresses for herself and Rebecca. "I ain't ever had a dress that wasn't stitched together from some left-over scraps of fabric," Lillian said.

Rebecca paraded around the hotel suite with her new boots. Every couple of minutes, she would stop and look down as if she expected them to disappear before her eyes. "These boots make me look like a proper lady, don't they Mamma?"

"Yes. You look very proper Rebecca." Lillian said.

"Thank you again Miss Beth. I just love them."

"You are very welcome Rebecca."

Both Lillian and Beth were tired when they returned to the hotel. They both went to their rooms for a short nap, leaving Rebecca with nothing to do. At first, she just stared out of the window and watched the crowded street below. Then a collection of dolls in a toyshop window on the other side of Market Street caught her attention. She quietly slipped out of the room and headed down the grand staircase. No one seemed to even notice as she moved quickly through the lobby. She was almost to the front door when Benjamin spotted her. He took two long strides and stood before Rebecca in seconds. His quick movement brought the attention of the hotel clerk, who looked up with a frown. "Miss," Benjamin whispered. "You shouldn't be here. Colored ain't allowed in the lobby."

"I was just leaving," Rebecca said brazenly.

"You should come and go by the back door unless you're with your mistress."

"I don't have a mistress!" Rebecca said.

Their conversation was gaining the attention of other guest and employees. A man dressed in the same uniform as Benjamin came up and said, "Benjamin, you gone get yourself in some trouble. Why you standin here jawin with a white girl?"

"She ain't white, Robert. She's colored and I'm trying to stop *her* from getting into trouble."

At that moment, Benjamin saw the hotel clerk come from behind his desk. "This way, Ma'am," he said a little too loudly as he took Rebecca by the elbow and steered her to the back of the hotel. Rebecca allowed him to show her to the back door. Once they were out of sight of the hotel clerk, Rebecca pulled her arm away and turned on the young man.

"I told you that I don't have a mistress."

"Look girl, I don't care if you are free or slave. You can't be in the lobby without your mistress. Where you going, anyway? You running away?"

"Of course not, I just wanted to see those dolls in the window across the street."

He smiled at that, realizing that she may look like a woman but she was really just a girl. "Maybe you ought to talk to your Mama about that before you go and get yourself into some real trouble. Come on. I'll show you how to get back to your room from the back stairs."

Rebecca followed quietly. Just as she mounted the narrow staircase, they heard a loud crash and suddenly people were running in every direction. The same black man she had seen in the lobby came running up to Benjamin. "Riot!" he yelled as he ran pass them both.

"Go!" Benjamin said to Rebecca. "Get to your room as fast as you can and lock yourself in. Tell your mama and that white lady not to leave the room cause there's a riot outside." Then he ran off before Rebecca could say a word.

Rebecca didn't even know what a riot was, she didn't know what was happening but the noise coming from the street was alarming. People were screaming and yelling and she could hear glass breaking. She did as Benjamin told her and got to the room as fast as she could. "Mama, Miss Beth," she called as she came through the door. She turned and locked the door as she continued to scream for her mother.

Beth was the first to hear her and came running from the bedroom. "What is it Rebecca?"

"Benjamin says there's a riot on the street. I don't know what that is but folks is running and hiding and screaming. It must be something really bad."

"Oh my God!" Beth said.

"A riot? What's a riot?" Lillian asked then they all heard the screams and yelling of what sounded like a mob.

Lillian tried to go to the window but Beth stopped her. "Stay away from the windows!" she yelled as she quickly closed the curtains of each window facing the street. She then wedged the back of a chair under the door to the suite so no one could get in from the corridor. With Lillian's help, she slid the long bureau in front of two windows just as the glass was shattered by a flying rock.

Rebecca began to scream and Lillian grabbed her in an embrace while covering her daughter's mouth with her hand. "Quiet," she whispered.

The three women were terrified as the riot lasted well into the night. Once the sun began to go down, Beth and Lillian peeped around the bureau and down into the street. What they saw was horrifying. Two of the black men who owned businesses along Market Street, a shoemaker and a toyshop owner, had been hung from their shingles while their businesses were burned to the ground. The dolls that had so enticed Rebecca were now piles of black ash.

On Sunday morning when the Pennsylvania Militia was finally able to quell the violence, the riot was over. The remnants of the riot had left the pristine streets of the City of Brotherly Love strewn with bodies, both black and white. Buildings that had been set on fire now smoldered. Armed men patrolled the streets and people were still wary of leaving their homes.

Rebecca finally slept but Beth and Lillian paced the small space of their suite while occasionally taking a peep into the streets below. Sometime close to mid-day, someone knocked on the door. Both Beth and Lillian did not move or answer the knock. "Miss Vance," Benjamin called through the door.

Beth rushed to let in the young man, removing the chair that had secured the door closed. "Benjamin," she said. "What happened? Is it over?" she asked.

"Yes Ma'am," Benjamin said. "It's over for now. I just wanted to make sure that you all were doing all right. Sorry, but I couldn't come before now."

Beth let out a breath of relief. "Thank God," she whispered.

Rebecca woke up and came to stand by her mother. "What happened?" she whispered.

"Well," Benjamin said while scratching his head. "I don't rightly know but the rumor is that it all started on Dock Street when a Negro who was unloading produce would not move his wagon when a white man told him to move. The Negro speaks his mind, the white man hits him over the head, and the next thing you know it's a riot. This ain't the first, Ma'am, and I know it ain't gone be the last."

"Thank you Benjamin," Beth said.

He tipped his hat and backed out of the room. The three women just stared at each other for a few minutes. Neither said anything and Beth was glad for that. She couldn't have explained any of it because she didn't understand what happened any more than Lillian or Rebecca.

Later that day Rebecca told Lillian what happened in the lobby on Saturday afternoon when she was trying to go to the toy store across the street. "The man thought that I was white but Benjamin told him that I was colored. Can you believe that, Mama? He really thought that I was white."

Lillian was getting ready for bed. She leaned over the washbowl and splashed some fresh water over her face and arms. Water dripped from her face as she stood and reached for a towel. "Becca, don't let that go to your head. You *are* colored but that makes you no different than Black or Negro." She eyed her daughter as she dried her face and noticed that there was a spark in Rebecca's eyes. She seemed happy that someone actually thought she was white. "Enough of this nonsense," Lillian said as she pulled a nightgown from their bags for Rebecca. She threw the garment to Rebecca and turned her back as if to say that the conversation was over.

Rebecca just would not let it go. "Do they call me colored cause my daddy was a white man?"

Lillian sighed loudly, her frustration evident in the tone of her voice. Through gritted teeth she said, "I know that all of your life you been made to think you were mixed white and colored, but we know now that that ain't the truth. I'm colored, cause my daddy was white. Now we know that your daddy was also colored, but that don't make you better than any other Negro. You got more black blood than either me or your daddy, so please stop thinking that your daddy was white, cause he wasn't. Just cause you lighter than most coloreds, it don't make you better. We are all Black people."

"I know, but look at me, Mama. I look as white as any white girl," she said eagerly. "Do you know what that means, Mama?"

Lillian had put her nightgown on and was turning back the covers on the bed. "It don't mean nothin! You are a Negro and that's all there is to this."

"No Mama. This means that when I grow up, I can move away from you and Miss Beth and just be white."

Lillian turned with a jerk and slapped Rebecca hard across the face. The girl fell backward in disbelief. "Don't ever say that again. You are not white and the sooner you get that into your head the better." Lillian's anger quickly faded as she saw a red welt rising on Rebecca's cheek. She pulled her daughter to her and embraced her as Rebecca sniffed back tears. "I know that you don't understand, baby, but trying to be white can only get you into trouble. No matter how fair our skin might be, the black is in our blood. We can't wash it away and we can't ignore it. You are not white, Rebecca. I want you to get that thought out of your head. You are not white!"

Rebecca shook her head as if she understood even as she thought, *'If I look white, I can be white.'*

CHAPTER 2

GLORIA PLANTATION
RICHMOND, VIRGINIA
JULY 1839

The Burden of Guilt

The 150-year-old Live Oak sprawled its strong branches across the road leading to Gloria Plantation. Its limbs, adorned with a lacy covering of Spanish moss, leaned across the road to intertwine with its sister tree, creating a sun-filtering canopy. James had ridden or walked under this canopy his entire life with little thought. At the beginning of the road, there was a ten-foot tall iron gate, which was usually open. Now, this familiar path held only sorrow. More times than he liked, his mind's eye could still see David's limp body hanging from a low branch on that tree.

The subtle pangs of guilt began on the day David was buried. Of course, James was grief stricken, but what he was experiencing was much more than grief. At first, he couldn't understand his feelings. There were no words to describe the anxiety and depression that seemed to overwhelm him. As time moved on, his grief eventually lessened, which helped him to more clearly understand what he was feeling. He understood now that what he felt was guilt but why? He had no hand in the deception his father had wrought on his family. In fact, it began long before he was even born, so why should he feel any responsibility for the events that led to his brother's suicide? These were the thoughts that consumed James since David's death and he just could not find a way to relieve himself from the shroud of depression that came with his remorse.

After spending two days in Richmond on business and it was early evening when James arrived at the gate. He reined in his horse at the base of the tree. The air was heavy with heat and humidity and you could almost smell that a storm was brewing in the density of cloud cover. James sat in his saddle gazing up at the tree and wondering, as he had so many times in recent months, if he should have the tree cut down. It was such a stark reminder of everything that had destroyed his family, and most of all, David's life. But then again, he knew that to fell this tree, a long symbol of southern strength, would do nothing to assuage his guilt or bring his family back. He would continue to see the image of David hanging from that tree every time he closed his eyes.

He tugged on the reins, pulling his horse away from the tree and moving slowly up the road toward the main house. Jacob came out and immediately took the reins. "Evenin Massa James," Jacob said.

"Good evening Jacob."

Although it was early evening, the heat of the day lingered, as is often the case on summer evenings in the south. James headed straight for his study. He was in no mood to talk to anyone. His head ached and he felt stifled by the heat. He shut himself up in the study with the French doors that led to the garden open to let in a breeze if one should happen by. He ordered Nan to bring him a bottle of red wine before he opened the collar and cuffs of his shirt and dropped into the leather chair behind the desk.

After a couple of glasses of wine, he felt more relaxed, however his mind would not leave the past. He was thinking of the day he found Big Bill's journals, and how he had been astonished to find that his father had meticulously spelled out the circumstances of David's birth. Since that tragic day, James would read those pages again and again, as if by the mere act of reading, the words on the page might somehow change, but of course, they were the same each time he read them. James thought now that if he had known that David would take his own life, he might have kept those journals secret forever. He could not explain why he felt so guilty. None of it was his doing but he felt somehow responsible.

Big Bill's sins and his obvious disregard for the consequences were meticulously penned as if he were detailing the most mundane circumstances. His journals gave an account of a frightened young female slave, who had been forced to lay with her master and conceive a son. His slave Mamie and his wife Gloria endured the pangs of labor at the same time. After many hours of labor, Gloria delivered a stillborn baby boy. Big Bill could not bear the thought of telling his beloved

Gloria that her child had not lived. But when he saw that Mamie's son was as white as any white child he'd ever seen and his eyes were as green as his own, he knew what he must do. He stole the son he'd conceived with Mamie his slave, and presented him to his wife as if he were a trophy for her long suffering labor. David was the firstborn son, but he was not Gloria's son.

However, James knew that nothing could ever be secret forever. If he hadn't found those journals, David would have eventually found them and the outcome could have been even more disastrous.

A soft knock on the door brought him back to the present. He had no idea how long he'd been in the study but the wine bottle was now empty. "Yes," he called out.

Nan came in. "Supper is ready, Massa."

"I'll eat in here," he said. "And bring me another bottle of wine," his tone was unusually harsh.

"Yes sir," Nan said before she backed out of the study.

David may have escaped his demons by taking his life, but his death could not undo the carnage he left behind. Had David even considered his wife, Beth? She knew that her marriage to David had been little more than a farce but now she knew that there was nothing she could have done to make David love her any more than he'd promised. And what of Lillian? They had loved each other from the time they were children and now she was left with the knowledge that their love was not only taboo because she was a black woman and a slave, but it was something sinful, sordid and dirty because she was his half-sister. James wondered if David gave any thought to the daughter, he left with the stigma of being the product of incest.

James had done his best to assure his brother that the information contained in those journals need never become public. In fact, no one would ever know of their contents if David chose to continue on as if they had never existed. They both knew that Beth would divorce him and James promised him that he would see Lillian and Rebecca safely free in a northeastern city.

Unfortunately, that was not enough for David. He just could not accept this new reality. The knowledge of his birth would torment him so, that he chose to take his life. Was it the incest that he could not live with or the knowledge that he had lived his entire life as a privileged, white, southern gentleman before learning that he was a black man? No one would ever know exactly why David chose to end his life. James and David both had witnessed black men tied to a tree and lashed until their backs bled and they had also seen black men hanged from trees. James wondered now if his brother thought that his birth was somehow an offense deserving such a penance as hanging. James would never know. What he did know was that the demons that David was able to escape through death, were now with him. Since the day of David's death, James had been tormented by visions of the hanging. His brother spoke to him in his dreams and though he knew that he bore no responsibility for the events that led to David's death, he felt an overwhelming responsibility to those that were forced to live with the new reality left in David's wake.

His feelings of responsibility were only part of the burden he was left to shoulder. There was also the business of running the plantation. He had long ago learned to run the plantation alone. David was gone for over ten years and a good many of those years his father was convalescent. But this was an entirely new environment for Southern Planters.

After Nat Turner's revolt, the Virginia legislator sought to restrict the interaction between slaves. More laws were enacted against slaves. They were forbidden to congregate for any reason. Preaching by free black ministers was also forbidden. Allowing a slave to travel freely over the roads of Virginia was now unsafe. Free black families, slave owners themselves, had enjoyed relative peace until the Nat Turner raids. The raids had instilled a new kind of fear in whites and they became distrustful and hostile to all blacks causing many to leave their family homes and flee to the safety of northern states and some went as far as Canada. Tensions were high for both slave and master.

One of the Overseers James hired turned out to be a cruel taskmaster causing the slaves to become restless and agitated. He'd had to fire the Overseer in the middle of the year causing that season's harvest to be paltry compared to previous years. Without an Overseer, the slaves became even harder to manage. Most of slave holding states were experiencing more run-aways and Gloria lost a couple of slaves every quarter.

Nan brought in his supper but he was in no mood to eat. However, he consumed another half bottle of sherry.

If only there were someone he could talk to, he thought, but there was no one. He was the only white man on the plantation. He couldn't very well talk of family business with his slaves and he didn't want to share the sordid details of his brother's life and death with neighbors. These burdens, no matter how substantial, were his to endure and his to resolve.

James could not explain his feelings any more than he could explain David's feelings. He only knew that it was a lie, a secret, that had destroyed his family and he felt an inexplicable compulsion to right the wrongs of the past.

As the effects of the wine caused his awareness to ebb away, James' last thoughts before passing into unconsciousness were of Beth, Lillian, and Rebecca. He wondered how they were fairing in Philadelphia and if they were still together.

CHAPTER 3
Unbound

Finally, after looking for more than two weeks, Beth was able to rent a small but elegant home on Walnut Street between Eighth and Ninth Streets. It was their last night in the hotel and after Rebecca went to sleep, Beth told Lillian that they needed to have a talk. She ordered a pitcher of lemonade and waited for Lillian in the modest parlor of her suite. Lillian appeared at the door. Apprehension was written in the lines across her forehead. She was remembering the last time Beth had summoned her in the late evening. At that time, Lillian had suspected that her mistress was up to something that could cause her and Rebecca harm, so she took her daughter and fled. She knew that this summons was something much different but even knowing that did little to lessen her trepidation. Though in the past few days Miss Beth had been kind to she and Rebecca, she still didn't trust her. "You want to talk with me, Miss Beth?"

"Yes, come and sit with me." Lillian's defenses were immediately on alert. Beth handed Lillian the glass of lemonade, a gesture that she hoped would put Lillian at ease. The two just sat quiet for a few moments. "I'll be moving into my house tomorrow," Beth said.

"Yes Ma'am."

"Lillian, I know that our relationship is a strange one, to say the least, but things are different now. You are not my slave and you are not sleeping with my husband anymore. There is no reason why we can't be friends."

"Blacks and whites ain't ever friends, Miss Beth."

"Yes, I know that but we can at least be something close to friends." Lillian did not answer. "I mean, well, we don't have to be enemies. We could still need each other just as we did on the journey here to Philadelphia."

"Why do we need each other?"

"Well," Beth said again. "We are both new to this city and the only people we know are each other." Lillian smiled. She knew that Beth was right. "As I said, I will be moving into my house tomorrow. What will you and Rebecca do, where will you go?"

Lillian took a sip from her drink and leaned back to reflect a moment. Her usual impertinence was absent. Then she put the glass on the table and turned to face Beth. "You have been very generous, Miss Beth and I am grateful for your help in getting me and Rebecca here to Philadelphia," Lillian hesitated as she searched for the right words. She didn't want to offend Beth but she didn't want to be with her any more than was necessary.

"I'm sorry but, I am free now. I want to feel my freedom. I want to live as a free woman."

Beth eyed Lillian suspiciously. "Lillian, believe me, I understand but do you realize just how hard life will be without a protector? A young woman alone in this city could be very dangerous."

"I know," she said. "Miss Beth you know that I will protect Rebecca with my life."

"Yes, but what about you?"

"I can take care of myself."

"Yes, well I'm sure that I can make that a little easier for you, Lillian. You know that once I've moved into my own house, I'll need a housekeeper."

Lillian didn't know what Beth was trying to say. She couldn't believe that Miss Beth would ever really want her for a housekeeper. "Yes," she said as she eyed Beth wondering at her sincerity.

"You and Rebecca could move in with me, come and go as you please," Beth said. Lillian didn't act as if she understood anything Beth was saying. "Lillian," Beth said. "I am offering you a job as my housekeeper."

Lillian sniffed back her tears and stiffened her spine. "You mean your slave?" She accused.

"No! I mean my housekeeper. Of course, you will be doing the same things you've always done except that I will pay you a wage."

"A wage? What is that?"

Beth laughed. "Money, Lillian. You will make money by working. That means you will have money to buy clothes and shoes and anything else that you might need for you and Rebecca. I promise to pay you a fair wage. David left me a generous amount of money and

James promises to send me an allowance. We will all be just fine."

Beth waited a few moments for Lillian to absorb all that she'd said. "Let us just try it for a few months. If you decide that you want to move out and get your own place, you are free to do so."

Lillian was quiet and thoughtful for several minutes. Beth could see that she was hesitant. "Think about it, Lillian. This could be the right thing for both of us."

"I don't want to seem ungrateful Miss Beth, but I don't want to work for you. David gave me money too. I think I have enough to find a place for Rebecca and me to live. I'll find work somewhere. I just want to be on my own. I want to feel free." Her eyes filled with tears as she spoke and she sniffed trying to hold them back. "I hope you understand."

Before Beth knew what was happening she had taken Lillian in her arms and held the woman as she cried into her shoulder. "Yes, Lillian. I do understand." She stroked the long dark hair that streamed down Lillian's back. The two women were quiet for a few moments and Lillian was able to sniff back her tears. "Just promise me that if you ever need anything, you will come to me."

Lillian sniffed. "I promise."

"I'll write the address down and you will keep it with your documents of freedom."

"Yes, Ma'am."

⁓

Since Benjamin was the only person Beth and Lillian had met since their arrival in Philadelphia, as

Beth prepared to move, Lillian went down to the lobby to speak with Benjamin. She was certain he could tell her where she could find housing for rent and she was right. He readily directed her to the Bethel Church, where he said she could find a list of properties available for rent. Lillian was too embarrassed to tell the young man that she couldn't read, so she just thanked Benjamin and hurried back to the room to pack.

As Lillian and Beth prepared to move out of the hotel, Rebecca slipped out again. This time she didn't try to go through the front of the hotel but went to the back door. It was a beautiful day, the sun was high, and there was a slight breeze. The fresh air felt good after being shut in the room for a couple of days. Rebecca walked a few paces past the back of the building where there were trash cans and stacks of wood. Hotel workers rushed in and out of the back door but seemed not to even notice her as she walked around. She had no idea where she was going or what she was looking for, so when she reached the street she just stood there on the sidewalk looking about.

Benjamin saw Rebecca through the window as she rounded the side of the building and stood there looking lost on the street. Robert walked over to see what had Benjamin's attention so riveted to the window. "Oh," he said with a chuckle. "It's that girl that tried to walk through the lobby a couple of days ago. Take it from me, young man. That girl ain't nothing but trouble. You had better keep your mind on your duties and leave that girl be."

"Yeah," Benjamin acknowledged. "But she sure is fine. She's damn near white and uppity to boot, but she has got to be the prettiest girl I ever seen." He continued to watch for a few moments. "Hey, Robert!" Robert raised an eye brow in answer. "I'm gonna take my break now. I'll be back in a little while." Benjamin slid out of the door before Robert could answer.

"Can I help you find something?" The voice startled Rebecca and she turned around with a jolt.

"Oh, Benjamin, you scared me."

"I didn't mean to scare you. I saw you from the window and wondered why you were here on the sidewalk."

"I just wanted to get some air. It was so stuffy in the hotel room."

"Would you like to take a walk with me?"

Rebecca thought for a moment. "Yes, not too far though. Mama and Miss Beth will be looking for me soon."

"All right," he said. They walked down Market Street for only a few blocks before they turned and headed back to the hotel. "Do you mind if I ask you a question," he said as they walked.

"No, I don't mind."

"How old are you, Miss Rebecca."

"Seventeen. Miss Beth says I'm close to being a woman but Mama says I am already a woman."

Benjamin smiled. Her lax of sophistication had led him to believe that she was much younger. "Once you and your mama have settled, do you think I might call on you?"

Rebecca stopped and turned to look at Benjamin. He stood there, tall and dignified in his uniform. His big brown eyes and an easy smile were attractive. He smiled now as he looked down at Rebecca but her look was serious as she considered his question. To Rebecca he looked just like Walker on the plantation. If they were on the plantation, Benjamin would have been a field hand. She found nothing pleasing about him. He was nice and she didn't want to hurt his feelings but he was hardly the type of man she wanted to court her. "Well, I don't know," she said shyly.

"Well, maybe I should be asking you mama, anyway."

Rebecca said no more as they slowly walked back to the hotel but she was thinking about Benjamin and the other hotel worker who had thought she was white. If he thought she was white, maybe a white boy would also think she was white. She just couldn't see herself ending up with a man like Benjamin.

Benjamin was also silent on the walk back to the hotel. He was thinking that he knew he'd never have a chance with a high yellow woman like Rebecca. Even though she was young, she was already thinking that she was better than him just because he was darker.

Benjamin was a nineteen year old free man. He was the youngest of four siblings born to Henry and Mary Bowman. Henry was raised on a plantation in Maryland where he learned to cook while helping a French chef who worked for the Bowman's. He and Mary married young and quickly bore three sons one right after the other. By age twenty-five, Henry's master had let him take jobs cooking for the elite of Maryland society. Henry saved his money and eventually bought his freedom when he was thirty. He left Mary and his three sons in Maryland while he moved to

Philadelphia where his mother had moved years earlier. With a keen business sense and superior cooking skills, Henry was able to save enough money to buy freedom for his wife, and three sons. Once they were all in Philadelphia, Henry started a catering business run by he and his wife. Mary bore him a fourth son in Philadelphia, Benjamin. Benjamin was the only son born free and the only son to survive the cholera epidemic of 1832.

Thomas was the eldest son and the first to contract the deadly disease. Mary left her husband to run the business alone while she cared for her son. In a matter of months the entire family, except Benjamin, had perished from the deadly disease. Benjamin was sent to live with his free grandmother but he never forgot that his parents had been prominent members of the community with a well-established and respected business. It had always been his dream to one day reopen the Bowman Catering Company and he had been saving his money toward that end from his very first job.

Now as he thought about Rebecca's polite rejection of him, he consoled himself with the thought that it would be her loss because he knew that he would soon be able to provide a comfortable living for a deserving young woman who would not reject him because of the color of his skin.

༄

Lillian found the church easily. A young man sat at a desk in the foyer when she and Rebecca entered the church. It was dark, the only light coming from a round stained glass window above the door. The young man did not look up immediately and she and Rebecca just stood and waited until he finally noticed them. "I'm sorry," he said. "May I help you with something?"

"Yes," Lillian tried to sound dignified. "I was told that the church might have a list of properties for rent."

"We do," he said as he began to rummage through a stack of papers on the desk. "Here is one list," he said as he handed her a paper on which she assumed was a list of available houses for rent. He walked away and Lillian just stood there staring at the paper, embarrassed again that she could not read.

After a few minutes, the man came back. "Oh, you're still here. Is there something else I can help you with Madam?"

"I, ah . . . I can't read this paper," she stammered.

"Oh," the man said as he took the paper from her hand, but he didn't even seem surprised. "Well, there is a living quarters over the stable at the end of Fourth Street," he read. "I'm sure you aren't interested in that property, the smell would sicken you. Well now, there is a house on North Fifth Street, and . . . ."

"Excuse me sir," Lillian interrupted. "I'm new to Philadelphia and I don't know where anything is in this city. Would you please just tell me where I should go?"

"I'm sorry," he said as he glanced down at the list. Lillian just waited patiently. "Well, this one might be right for you, Miss."

"Miss Vance," Lillian put in. "If you don't mind my asking, what is your name sir?"

"My name is William Gilbert, Ma'am. Folks just call me Willie."

Lillian put her hand out and Willie took her hand in his lightly. "Happy to meet you Willie."

"Pleased to meet you too, Miss Vance."

They both smiled, immediately taking the formalness out of their meeting. "I believe I know a place that might be perfect for you." Willie said. "Mrs. Althea Brown, she's a member here at Bethel and she has a house for rent on Lombard Street."

Lillian and Rebecca were in the church office for a couple of hours. Willie also told her about an available job and helped her and Rebecca sign up for classes for reading and writing held at the church in the evenings. He then patiently gave Lillian directions to Mrs. Brown's property.

By the end of the day, Lillian had rented a small house in the ten hundred block of Lombard Street and she had the address of a home in Overbrook where a job as housekeeper was available.

It was a small house, scantily furnished, but very clean. The owner, Mrs. Althea Brown, was a very tall, big boned woman with fair skin and she lived right next door. Lillian thought Mrs. Brown looked like the Iroquoian natives seen in Virginia. Mrs. Brown said that it was a quiet and peaceful neighborhood of free blacks. She walked with Lillian and Rebecca through each room. There were two bedrooms but only one had a bed. In the front room on the first floor, there was an old wooden rocking chair and one small table. The kitchen had an old cast iron cook stove, a table, and two rickety old chairs. "I had two more chairs for the kitchen but they were damaged by the last tenants. I ain't had time to replace them. I got another bed too. I'll have someone bring it over for you. You'll need some firewood for that stove. I can give you some to get you started, but you'll have to buy your own soon. There's a man down on Dock Street where you can buy wood scraps for cheap." Mrs. Brown said. "Oh, and don't worry about that back door. It's boarded up because it's broken. I'll have a carpenter fix it in a couple of days." She placed two keys in Lillian's hand and started toward the front door. "Rent is due on the first of the month and if you have any problems, you just knock on my door anytime."

"Yes Ma'am," Lillian said.

"Are you new to Philadelphia?"

"Yes Ma'am."

"Where you from?"

"Virginia," Lillian said.

Althea eyed Lillian suspiciously. They both knew the question Althea wanted to ask, but was maybe too polite to give voice to her question. "We were slaves in Virginia," Lillian offered. "But we free now," she said proudly.

"I see," Althea said as she made her way to the door. "Look, we don't usually see white folks in this part of town. If you see a white man, he's either collecting or he's a slave catcher. Most black folks got a good eye for what sort of white man they come across. You and your girl better be careful. If you come across one of them slave catchers, you be a slave again before the next sunrise."

"Thank you, Mrs. Brown," Lillian said slowly.

"Honey, don't call me Ma'am or Mrs. Brown. Althea is my name. That's all that's necessary. Althea."

"Thank you, Althea."

37

When Althea left, Lillian locked the door behind her and then she leaned her back against the door and just looked around. She had such a strange expression on her face that Rebecca thought something was wrong with her. "Mama," she said. "You alright?"

"I am just fine," Lillian said. She lifted her arms high in the air and began to twirl around. "Now, this is what freedom feels like," she said. Then she grabbed Rebecca by the hands and began to twirl her around. Round and round they went, laughing and laughing until they were both dizzy and out of breath. "Oh baby girl, I never even dreamed of being free. When Massa David handed me them papers, I was so torn up about everything that happened, that I couldn't find no joy in being free. Then he went and hanged his self. That about ripped my heart out, so I still couldn't find no joy in them papers he gave me. But now, I'm here with no Massa and no mistress; I am truly free and I'm just about ready to burst with joy."

"Yes, Mama," Rebecca said. "We free, but how are we gone take care of ourselves? We need money to get food and what are we gone do all day?"

"It's like Miss Beth said, we gone work and get paid money for working. With our own money, we can buy what we need. It's like; we got a chance to start all over again. We gone be all right, baby. I promise you, everything is gone be fine for you and me. You'll see."

Early the next morning Lillian knocked on Althea's door to ask her how to get to Overbrook. "I bet you ain't eaten breakfast yet," Althea said. Then not waiting for an answer, she went on. "Come on in, make yourself at home. I got bacon frying and I can whip you up some eggs real quick."

"Thank you," Lillian said as she moved into the house while looking around. The house was exactly like the one she was renting but it was furnished with heavily stuffed chairs, a sofa, and tables. There was a rug on the floor of the front room which added to the warm and cozy feel of the house. "Your house is lovely," Lillian said.

"Thank you. I've been living in this house since I was born. My mother and father worked very hard to buy these two houses and they were very proud to be among the few black folk that actually owned property. My father died ten years ago and when I got married, I moved into the house next door but my mother died five years later and I moved back here. I've been renting out the house next-door ever since. Coffee?"

"Yes, thank you. You're married?"

Althea was moving around the small kitchen quickly. She barely stopped to answer, "Yeah, but he ain't here no more."

Lillian and Rebecca sat down and ate the wonderful breakfast Althea prepared while she talked about the neighborhood, Bethel church, neighbors, and schools. Lillian and Rebecca said very little as Althea talked on endlessly. They were both content to just listen. There was something very real about Althea Brown and Lillian liked her from the moment they met. Although she knew that she was a stranger to this young woman, Althea treated her as if they were long-time friends and Lillian appreciated her kindness. By the time they had finished eating; Althea seemed to have talked herself out. She leaned back in her chair with a contented look on her face. For the first time, the room was actually quiet for a moment.

"I learned about a housekeeping job in Overbrook. Can you tell me how to get there?" Lillian asked.

"Course I can," she said with a smile. "There's a man from St. Thomas African Episcopal Church who carries domestic workers to and from Overbrook. His name is Briggs, George Briggs. He doesn't do it for the money but he'll charge you two cents for the trip there and back. The little money he gets pays for the keep of the horses and upkeep of the wagon. He leaves at seven in the morning and returns at seven in the evening."

"If he doesn't do it for the money then why does he do it?"

"Mr. Briggs is a kind soul. He use to work for a family in Overbrook and he got into the habit of carrying folks along who didn't have their own horse and wagon. Then one day, his white lady just up and fires him. She says she caught him peeping at her through the window." Lillian raised an eyebrow. "It wasn't true, of course, but he was too old to get another job and too young to take to a rocking chair and wait for God's call. He says he got the idea of shuttling folks back and forth from Reverend Douglas. He's been doing this near about three years now and I never heard one complaint from him or his riders."

"Where is St. Thomas Church?"

"Oh, it's just a few blocks away on Fifth and Adelphia Streets. If you like, we can take a walk there and I'll show you where the carriage waits for folks."

"Would you? Oh, thank you Althea."

The next day Lillian rose early. She left Rebecca at home to do some cleaning and finish unpacking. Althea promised to look in on Rebecca a couple of times through the day. Lillian walked the few blocks to St. Thomas Church and a carriage waited just as Althea had said. "Mr. Briggs?" Lillian questioned.

"Yes Ma'am, at your service. How far are you going?" Lillian fished in her bag for the address and handed it to Mr. Briggs. "Wallingford House? Are you the new housekeeper?"

"Don't know yet. I hope so."

"I'll say a little prayer for you. Hop on up. That will be two cents."

Lillian handed him her fair and settled herself on the wooden bench that had been installed in the back of the wagon. Mr. Briggs waited a little while for other riders to arrive before he headed out.

Mr. Briggs sang, hummed, or whistled for the entire ride. He was not only a nice man, Lillian thought, he was a genuinely happy man. In a short time, they had ridden out of the city. The road became narrow and the trees and foliage became denser. Soon, the road became steep as they traveled uphill. Lillian noticed that the other passengers chatted on about their work. They were all domestic workers and many of the women referred to the mistress of the house where they worked as "my lady" or "Ma'am." For a moment, it took Lillian back to the plantation. For most of her life there hadn't been a mistress at Gloria and when Miss Beth came, Lillian flat out refused to call her "Mistress." Though David and James were referred to as Massa, Beth was simply, "Miss Beth."

"You see that big white house on the top of the hill?" Mr. Briggs said to Lillian.

"Yes."

"That's where you get off. That's Wallingford House." He dropped Lillian at the gate of a huge house. "Honey," he said. "Go round to the back door. I know the Wallingford's and they be real big on manners and such. I'll be right here about seven this evening. Good luck."

"Thank you," Lillian muttered. "But what if I don't get the job?"

"You will."

"How do you know?"

"I just know, now go on. You don't want to be late your first day."

She made her way around to the back of the house and knocked softly on the door. A young black man answered the knock. "Yes," he said stiffly. The young man was very formally dressed, almost as if for a funeral, Lillian thought.

"I'm here about the housekeeping job."

"Come in," he said as he held the door opened and Lillian stepped inside. "Your name, please."

"Lillian Vance," she said as she thought, this boy looked far too young to wear so serious an expression.

He left her standing in the kitchen and went off to find his mistress. Lillian looked around as she stood waiting for the boy to return. This was the largest kitchen she'd ever seen and it looked so modern. Smoke wafted up from the cast iron oven and pots and pans hung from an iron grate on the wall. Two women were busy cooking and neither looked up or even acknowledged Lillian's presence. In fact, they weren't even talking with each other.

When the boy returned, he stood at the doorway and announced, "Madam will see you now. Follow me."

Lillian followed without a word. She was lead to a lavishly decorated parlor. Though it was a warm day, a fire burned in the hearth and a shawl was draped around Mrs. Wallingford's shoulders. Two over-stuffed chairs faced the mantel, above which was a painting of Mrs. Wallingford in her younger days. "Come," she said in a slight voice. Lillian stepped forward. "Have a seat Miss Vance." As Lillian stepped forward, she caught sight of Mrs. Wallingford, a slight woman of about fifty who looked Lillian up and down with a critical eye before she brought her eyes up to face her directly. Have you worked as a housekeeper before, Miss Vance?" Mrs. Wallingford sat opposite Lillian.

"No," Lillian said without thinking. "I . . . I mean, Ma'am, I was a slave in Virginia, a house slave," she stammered.

Again, Mrs. Wallingford eyed her suspiciously. "Are you a fugitive, Miss Vance?"

"No Ma'am," Lillian said somewhat indignant. "I am a free woman."

"And, I guess you have papers to prove this claim?"

Lillian's ire was rising and she straightened her back and said, "It ain't a claim, Mrs. Wallingford." She presented her papers and waited while Mrs. Wallingford scanned through the document.

"Do you have a husband or children?" She asked without looking up.

"I have a seventeen year old daughter."

"Can both of you read and write?"

"No Ma'am."

Mrs. Wallingford folded the document and handed it back to Lillian. "Have you any interest in learning to read, Miss Vance."

At first, the question puzzled Lillian. *What has that to do with housekeeping*, she thought. "Yes Ma'am," she said slowly. "My daughter and I are taking classes at the Bethel Church a few days a week.

"Good," Mrs. Wallingford said excitedly. "As housekeeper of the Wallingford Estate, you will be expected to hire, fire, and supervise all other house staff. You will also be expected to shop for the household and keep meticulous records. Unless you learn to read, write, and do basic arithmetic that will be impossible."

"Yes, Ma'am," Lillian said. Because she thought she was being dismissed, she stood and reached for her bag to leave.

"I have not finished, Miss Vance. Please remain seated." Lillian dropped into the chair, puzzled again. "Our current housekeeper, Mrs. Byrne, has been ill of late and desires to return to her family in Ireland. She has agreed to stay on until the new housekeeper has learned how to run the house properly. Mrs. Byrne will be leaving us in the spring. By that time, I expect you will have learned to run the house and to read and write sufficiently for the task." She paused briefly to see if Lillian would react to her words. "Have you any objections, Miss. Vance?"

"No Ma'am."

"Have you any questions?"

"Yes."

"Well, what is it?" Mrs. Wallingford said impatiently.

"How much will I be paid and do you have a job for my daughter?"

"I will pay you two dollars a week and your daughter, one dollar, until you both can read and write. After you have assumed your full duties as housekeeper, I will pay you four dollars, and your daughter, two dollars and a half. As I said, as housekeeper, you will be responsible for the house staff so it will be up to you to find a suitable job for your daughter."

"Yes, Ma'am."

"Very well, you will start with the new week. I expect breakfast by eight in the morning and you may leave any time after dinner, which is at six." With some effort, Mrs. Wallingford stood up and reached for her cane. Lillian stood too. "I will introduce you to Mrs. Byrne, who will show you around the estate and answer any more questions you might have."

"Yes, Ma'am. Thank you Ma'am, I mean Mrs. Wallingford."

Mrs. Byrne was a large woman with rosy cheeks, snow white hair, and she spoke the weirdest English Lillian had ever heard. Lillian didn't understand half of what she said but it didn't matter because Lillian was so excited, she could hardly pay attention anyway. She couldn't wait to get home to tell the good news to Rebecca and Althea.

The Wallingford Estate was even larger than Gloria plantation. Mrs. Byrne talked continuously as she ushered Lillian through the house. On the second floor, there were six rooms and an additional two rooms on the top floor. The master bedroom included a water closet and a sitting room. Lillian had never heard of a water closet. The next room, according to Mrs. Byrne, was the nursery.

"Oh," Lillian said. "Do the Wallingford's have children?"

It was an honest question and it did not take Mrs. Byrne by surprise as she rattled on, but she did stop talking long enough to give Lillian a stern look. "No," she said emphatically. "There are no children but you will see to it that this room is kept clean and dust free."

"But if there are no children . . . ," Lillian began.

"Miss Vance, there are many things about this family that are just unexplainable. They are not open for discussion today or any other day. Is that clear?"

"Yes Ma'am," Lillian said as *she wondered why Mrs. Wallingford would have a nursery in the house at her age.*

"However, they are some things that I will eventually explain and others that you will learn on your own and still not discuss with another living soul." Mrs. Byrne did not wait for Lillian to respond. She moved quickly on to the next room. "This is Lindy's room, she's Mrs. Wallingford's personal maid." Mrs. Byrne threw open the door and allowed Lillian a glance inside, then she quickly moved on. "The next room is a guest room, and this my room. As you don't intend to live in, it will become another guest room after I've moved back to Ireland.

"The room at the far end of the hall belongs to Charles, the Wallingford's son. He is usually away at university, but he will be home next week." By now, they were at the far end of the hall. There were two narrow doors just before the last door. "This is a linen closet," Mrs. Byrne continued. She swung open the door and closed it quickly. "And this, my dear, is the back stairs." She opened the door and moved quickly down the very narrow and steep staircase. "Follow me," she said. The back stairs led to a hall behind the dining room.

Lillian was introduced to the rest of the house staff. She learned that the tall, very dignified, but stoic young man, who'd answered the door, was Gabriel Dubai. He had escaped from a Haitian sugar plantation and stowed away in a cargo ship bound for America. Mrs. Wallingford's brother was captive of that ship and willingly took charge of the ten-year-old boy. Gabriel was now twenty and had grown up on the Wallingford estate.

Lillian was also introduced to a young woman named Hillary, whom everyone called Hilly. She was a slight little thing with big brown eyes and a bright smile. She was a chambermaid and spent much of her time with Mrs. Wallingford's personal maid, Lindy. There were other staff who worked the grounds of the estate, but Lillian would meet them at a later time.

The house tour ended in the kitchen. "What time is it?" Lillian asked Mrs. Byrne.

"After six, you'll be going soon enough," she said flatly.

Lillian was introduced to the cook, a tall thin woman named Della, who spoke very little. Mrs. Byrne called her a Geechee. "Does that mean she come from some place across the water?" Lillian wanted to know.

Mrs. Byrne gave Lillian a curious look, as if she was surprised that Lillian didn't already know what a Geechee was. "No," she said slowly. "The lass don't speak much cause folks have a hard time understanding her. She comes from the lowlands of Georgia. Her English is mixed up with African words."

"Oh," Lillian said.

"Don't worry. You'll get on just fine. Gabriel and Hilly seem to understand her well enough." She eyed Lillian again. "All right now sit down to the table. Mrs. Wallingford says to let you eat a good supper before you head back into the city. Della will fix you a plate to take home to your lass too."

Mrs. Byrne sat at one end of the big wooden table while Lillian sat at the other end. Lillian watched as Della moved about the kitchen giving directions to Hilly and Lindy as they shuffled back and forth between the kitchen and the large dining room where Mrs. Wallingford dined.

Even with the aromas of the food wafting through the kitchen, Lillian didn't realize how hungry she was until Della placed a plate of roast chicken, creamed potatoes, string beans, and corn bread before her. "teurkofe?" Della said. Lillian didn't answer right away and that seemed to annoy Della. With one hand on her hip, the tall dark woman looked down on Lillian and said, "Don yon know' um wanton? Teurkofe?" She spoke very fast and her eyes never left Lillian's face. It was almost as if she were speaking with her eyes as well as her mouth. Her eyes said, *'you know you know what I'm saying.'*

"Oh," Lillian said as she realized she did understand Della.

"She means . . ." Mrs. Byrne tried to translate.

"No," Lillian said. "I understand her," she said to Mrs. Byrne. "Coffee, Della. I'd like to have a cup coffee."

Not only was it a delicious meal that warmed Lillian inside and out, but her encounter with Della seemed to have forged and understanding that was far more profound than the language they spoke. Whatever it was, Lillian knew that it was more than the fact that both women had once been slaves.

Lillian left the Wallingford House feeling happier than she had in a very long time. She was optimistic, feeling that she and Rebecca didn't need to lean on Miss Beth or James for support. She was sure that with her freedom, she could make it on her own.

Mr. Briggs was there with his wagon stopped just beyond the Wallingford gate. He jumped down from his seat as soon as he saw Lillian. "Hello Mr. Briggs," Lillian called when she was still a few feet away.

George Briggs removed his dusty old hat and bowed from the waist in a mock gesture of formality. "Hello Miss Vance and congratulations. I told you that you were gonna get that job, didn't I?"

"How do you know that I got the job?"

"The look on your face says it all."

"Yes, you were right. I got the job and one for my daughter too," Lillian said as he helped her into the wagon.

There were three other ladies and one man already in the wagon and Lillian spoke to each of them. She was quiet on the ride home, content to listen to the others chatter on about the people and the goings on where they worked. Lillian only looked up when she felt the wagon slow. The wagon was just about to cross the bridge over the Schuylkill River when Mr. Briggs pulled on the reins as he whispered, "Woe," to the horses.

"What is it?" Lillian asked.

"Could be nothing at all, or it could be trouble."

Everyone was quiet now as they all peered through the trees with the moon as the only light. You could barely make out three figures on the bridge but their voices carried on the wind. Mr. Briggs jumped down and quickly pulled the wagon off the road and deeper into the foliage on the west side of the bridge. All six of them quietly got down and crouched in the bushes as they quietly watched in horror. A young black man had been captured on the bridge. Two white men were beating him with their fist, until he fell to the ground and then they began to kick him. The young man folded his body with his knees pushed into his chest as he screamed in anguish. "I told you, my name is not Samuel. I don't know Samuel!" the young man screamed.

"Well," one of the men said before he spat a stream of tobacco juice. "You look a lot like Samuel to me, so from now on we'll just say you're Samuel." He laughed loudly then the other man joined him in laughter. They shackled the young man's arms behind his back. The other man tied him by the ankles, before throwing him into the back of their wagon. The man with the tobacco stuffed into his jaw said, "How long you figure it will take us to get this nigger back to Mississippi?"

"We'll be home by the end of the week," the other answered before he leaped into the wagon.

"I'm telling you, I am not Samuel," the young man continued to scream as the wagon lurched forward.

Mr. Briggs kept his wagon hidden in the bushes until they had been gone for a few minutes. "Slave catchers," he said.

"Shouldn't we do something? The boy said that he wasn't this Samuel that they were looking for. Why would they take him?" Lillian asked.

"Because they can, Miss Lillian," one of the men said. Then they were all quiet for a while.

"I feel like we should do something," Lillian said again.

"The best thing we can do is keep quiet before one of us is tied up and thrown into the back of that wagon," another man said.

"But he said he wasn't Samuel," Lillian said again.

"Hell, it don't matter to them. One slave is as good as another."

The ride home was quiet from then until they arrived in the city. The incident had shaken Lillian and Mr. Briggs noticed it as soon as he looked into her face. "Good night Mr. Briggs. I guess I'll see you in the morning," she said.

"Good night. Lillian," he said. "Try not to be too upset. There are always slave catchers in and around the area. You don't see them much in the city but you can't be too careful."

"I guess you're right. Good night," Lillian whispered. She had been so shaken by the incident and now she realized more than ever that Philadelphia was a dangerous and unpredictable city.

CHAPTER 4

IN SEARCH OF HAPPINESS

Philadelphia's growing population had spurred a building frenzy within the city. Single homes were being built at an alarming rate. The most elaborate structures erected were of marble and sandstone, complete with functioning water closets. The area of Walnut Street, west of seventh was quickly becoming the most fashionable section of the city, catering to the upper echelon of Philadelphia society. Beth was lucky to be able to rent one of these elegant homes. It was a two-story home with small gardens in front and back on a quiet tree lined street with wide sidewalks. The street was cobblestoned and illuminated at night by gaslights. Although spacious for a city home, it was far smaller than the mansion on Gloria.

In the weeks that followed, Beth furnished the house with attractive but modest furniture. The kitchen was spacious and equipped with all the conveniences of the day. After hiring a brash young Irish girl, Bethany, as housekeeper, Beth filled the pantry with food.

An easy comfortable lifestyle was emerging for Beth and she was content, if not happy. With Lillian and Rebecca gone, there were no reminders of her failed marriage to David Vance. At first, she could think of little else but lately, she thought of David less every day. After she was settled into her comfortable home, she realized that she was utterly lonely. She had not made any friends yet and there was no man in her life. Although her marriage failed in Virginia, it had not made her reject the possibility of falling in love again. She realized that she *did* want a special man in her life and she wanted to be romanced, and to fall in love again. She wanted to build a future with someone who would love her as much as she loved him. She longed for a man to hold her in his arms and kiss her neck while she snuggled closer to his warmth. She never doubted that she would one day meet someone who would put an end to her lonely days and nights.

It would be almost a month before Beth would meet her neighbors, Mr. and Mrs. Nottingham who lived adjacent to the Vance house. Mr. Stuart Nottingham owned the city's only sugar refinery. The Nottingham's had two sons and a daughter and to Beth, they all seemed to be very nice people. They did not own slaves and all of their servants were white except the nanny, Mary.

Mrs. Nottingham, Ellen, and Beth quickly became friends. Beth was grateful to have someone with whom she could talk. They began to attend the Presbyterian Church together and had tea or played cards in the afternoons. Beth was introduced to other women of all ages who resided in the same neighborhood and she was grateful for her new friendships but she still longed for a special companionship.

Thanks to Ellen, who was quite active in social and charitable circles of Philadelphia, Beth had become fairly social over the rest of that year. Ellen belonged to a group called, The Women's Benevolent Society whose mission it was to care for the needy of Philadelphia, both black and white. They collected used clothing from their more affluent neighborhoods and had the clothes laundered and packaged. They then arranged give-away events in the poorer neighborhoods to give the clothing to needy families. Beth was very active in this group and she enjoyed the work.

Ellen had also invited Beth to join various other groups and though she had not joined any of them, she did attend some of the functions. It was through these various functions that she met several gentlemen who were interested in spending time with her and although they were nice and respectful, none of them provided the spark that would ignite Beth's interest.

It was a warm September afternoon and Beth and Ellen were shopping along the east end of Chestnut Street where exclusive dress shops lined both sides of the street. Beth caught the glimpse of a tall mulatto woman who she was sure was Lillian. "Wait here," she said to Ellen as she pushed through the throngs of shoppers. The woman moved quickly with her head held high. She wore a lavender shawl and straw bonnet. Beth would lose sight of her and then a sliver of lavender would appear and spur her forward again. She must have followed behind the woman for nearly an entire block before she caught up to her. "Lillian, Lillian," she yelled but the woman did not turn around.

Finally, when she was close enough to touch the woman on the shoulder, the woman turned to face her. It was not Lillian and Beth was disappointed and embarrassed. "I'm sorry," she said softly. "I thought you were someone else." The woman smiled and nodded her head and Beth turned to make her way back to Ellen.

"My God Beth, what on earth were you looking for?"

"Oh, I thought I saw an old friend."

Beth's disappointment seemed to put an end to the cheerfulness of the day. When they had finished shopping, she declined an invitation to dinner and went home. She ate dinner alone and retired to her bed early. She was not only disappointed, she was sad and she couldn't understand why. After all, she and Lillian had never really been close. From that day forward, Beth found herself thinking about Lillian often. She wondered how she and Rebecca were faring in the big city. She also wondered if Lillian was able to find work and if Rebecca was able to go to school? She just couldn't stop thinking about them both.

༄

The Nottingham Sugar Refinery gave an annual Thanksgiving Dinner a couple of days before the actual holiday and Ellen invited Beth. The company had rented a large ballroom at the city's town hall. The hall was aptly decorated for the holiday with round tables seating eight at each. The event had been catered with all the traditional thanksgiving foods and a local entertainment group would provide the music.

Beth was excited to be attending her first big social event. Ellen shared in her excitement and helped her shop for a new gown and shoes. When the day finally arrived, Beth spent the better part of the day having her thick auburn hair curled and piled high on the crown of her head, with a few ringlets left loose to frame her round face. When she was finally finished dressing, she looked in her full-length mirror and smiled. Though she could see that she had aged some, she smiled knowing that she was still attractive for a woman close to her fortieth year.

Beth was somewhat disappointed that she would not have an escort but Ellen assured her that she would not look out of place arriving with Ellen and her husband. Mr. and Mrs. Nottingham were seated at the head table as host and hostess and Beth was seated at a table right in the front of the ballroom. She was introduced to so many people that she knew she would hardly remember most of them. However, she would certainly remember a gentleman seated at a table behind her. He was Mr. Jefferson Miller, a wealthy textile man from Manayunk. He watched Beth from the time she entered the ballroom but he did not approach her until the meal was done and the floor was opened for dancing.

Beth watched as young couples began to fill the dance floor. Suddenly this handsome gentleman was standing before her. He introduced himself with mock formality, bowing deeply as he asked Beth to dance. She could not help but laugh as she presented him with her gloved hand. Before she knew it, he swept her onto the dance floor and whirled her round and round and she laughed even more. "Stop, stop! You will have me so dizzy that I won't be able to stand."

He immediately stopped and began a proper waltz. "Forgive me. I just wanted to make a lasting impression on the most beautiful woman in the room. Do you think that I have accomplished my goal?"

"Most certainly," Beth said. "Are you always so happy, Mr. Miller?"

"Yes, for the most part; except of course, if I am being rebuffed by a beautiful woman."

They talked and danced with each other for the rest of the evening. Beth was immediately attracted to Jefferson. He was handsome, charming, and had an amazing sense of humor. He made her smile, even laugh as she had forgotten she could. And so began the dawn of a new relationship.

Jefferson began to call on Beth on a regular basis. He escorted her to the theater and weekend rides near the river. He was very forthcoming regarding his life and told Beth anything she wanted to know. She learned that he owned two textile mills, one, spinning cotton, and another producing wool. He lived in a renovated farmhouse in Overbrook, just outside of Philadelphia, not far from where Beth had grown up. His home was a beautiful Victorian style mansion, which he had inherited upon his father's death. He still cared for his aging mother who lived with him. Though he had once been married, he lost his wife to pneumonia after only five years of marriage and there were no children. He was forty years old and had been widowed for three years.

Beth told Jefferson very little of her background. She told him that she'd grown up nearby, had married a wealthy Virginia planter who had died a year ago. Jefferson never asked why Beth had chosen to return to Philadelphia and Beth never felt the need to tell him more.

She eagerly awaited every visit and she was happier than she had been in years. Though Beth's experience with men was limited, she thought that Jefferson was different. He was ruggedly handsome with skin darkened by many hours in the sun. He had dark brown hair with streaks of blonde but he wore it longer than Beth thought attractive for a man of his age. She guessed that he must have been blonde as a child and age had obviously darkened his hair. Though it was apparent that he came from wealth, he looked as though he was no stranger to hard work.

Beth liked that he escorted his mother to church every Sunday morning but he readily confessed to Beth that he was not a very religious man. She liked Jefferson and had high hopes that their relationship could last and develop into something meaningful.

An incident that happened in the beginning of December would change her mind. Jefferson would reveal a side of himself that Beth had not previously witnessed. After they had returned from the theater, Beth offered Jefferson a glass of wine. He made himself comfortable on the sofa and Beth made herself comfortable beside him. After a few sips of wine, he pulled her close to him, as he had often over the few months that they had been acquainted. He kissed her passionately and Beth returned his passion. She had no reason to fear, as this was not their first kiss. He'd kissed her many times. Sometimes his kisses were playful little pecks on the cheek and at other times, they were more serious. Beth always got the feeling that he was exercising self-control and she appreciated his discipline. But this time was far different. There was urgency in his mere touch. After the second kiss, Jefferson began to press his body forward, pushing Beth down on the sofa. She began to feel uncomfortable and she tried to pull away, putting the palm of her right hand on his chest, in an attempt to push him back. All the while, he kept whispering affectionate compliments. "You are the most beautiful woman I've ever known. The smell of your hair makes me weak for you. I love you Beth. I know we haven't known each other long, but I know that I love you."

It wasn't as if she did not feel the need for physical intimacy, but she had promised herself that if she were blessed to fall in love again, she would make wiser decisions. She wanted a man to love her, not just want her physically. She didn't expect to abstain until marriage, only until she felt the time and the man were right. This not only did not feel right, it felt sordid.

Jefferson continued to press forward. His breath was hot on Beth's neck and her hand did little to hold him back. She put her forearm against his chest and pushed him backward with all of her strength. "You are right, of course. We've only known each other a couple of months," Beth said. Then she felt his fingers fumbling with the snaps of her bodice as if he meant to take her right there. "What are you doing," she said.

"I can't help myself. I have to have you," he said breathlessly.

"Stop," she yelled. But Jefferson had no intention of stopping. With her one free hand, Beth slapped him hard across the face and that seemed to bring an end to his pleasure seeking.

He pulled back from her and looked down as if in shock. "I'm sorry, Beth. I don't know what came over me." As soon as the weight of his body was lifted, Beth jumped to her feet and began to adjust her clothes.

"I think there may be a misunderstanding between us, Mr. Miller," she said while taking a few steps away, wanting to be out of his reach before she continued. "I should like to clarify the nature of our relationship, if I may?"

Jefferson repositioned himself on the sofa. He looked both surprised and wounded. "Please do," he said somberly.

"Mr. Miller, I am very fond of you and I am not unfamiliar with passion, after all, I was a married woman. But I am also not a woman with questionable morals. In time, I may very well desire to return your passion, but if that happens, it will be on my terms, at a time of my choosing. I am just not ready for this and I will not be forced."

At first, an eye brow rose in surprise, then his face seemed to melt as if it were made of candle wax. He dropped his head to his chest and said nothing for several seconds. When he finally stood and took a step toward Beth, she stepped backward. "I'm sorry," he said again.

"I want you to leave," she said.

"Please forgive me. I didn't mean to hurt you. It's just that it has been so long and I *do* love you."

"Your actions had very little to do with love. After all, we are not teenagers, Mr. Miller." Beth retrieved his hat and coat, and then walked to the front door. He realized that Beth was serious about him leaving so he stood and began to slowly follow her to the door.

After pulling on his coat, he turned to face her again. "Will you ever forgive me, Beth?"

"Only time will tell. Good day, Mr. Miller."

Later, Beth would recount the entire incident to Ellen who did not hide her shock. "Why do you look so dismayed?" Beth wanted to know.

"I can't believe that you felt so injured. After all, you aren't a virgin. You were married for several years and Jefferson has made no secret of his love for you."

"Oh," Beth said. "Does his love for me give him the right to disgrace me?"

"Of course not," Ellen said. "But he has been widowed for several years now. Can't you understand his desire to be with you?"

Beth chuckled a little. "Oh Ellen, you are so naïve. I've learned that men always find a way have their physical needs meant. You don't really believe that Jefferson Miller has been celibate since he lost his wife, do you?"

Ellen was thoughtful for a few moments. "Maybe you're right."

"I know I'm right. I made so many mistakes with my first marriage that I'm not willing to just go headlong into a relationship that will leave me scorned in the end. This time, everything will be on my terms. He may think that he loves me, but I want to be sure. If he is at all serious, he'll do the right thing."

"I suppose you're right but I haven't heard you say anything about how you feel about Jefferson."

Beth was thoughtful for a moment. "I really hadn't given it much thought. I like him. He's charming and fun but I'm not in love with him."

"Well, I'm no expert in these matters, of course, but I think your own feelings should figure into your decisions at some point." Ellen was forever the practical one and Beth appreciated her friend's candor and advice even if she thought it was sometimes old fashioned.

"Ellen, I didn't love my husband when we married but I grew to love him. When I realized that he cared for me but did not really love me as a man ought to love his wife, I became obsessed with making him love me. This time I really want to be sure that I am loved before I invest my own feelings. I don't want to be hurt again."

"I understand," Ellen said but she sat stone faced or a while. She had never heard a woman speak so frankly about love and relationships. She knew very little of Beth's life before Philadelphia but she now thought that whatever had happened to Beth during her time in Virginia, had certainly given her a different perspective on life and love. Beth was the first woman she'd ever met who was actually living on her own, which was something unheard of in her circles. Ellen had become somewhat in awe of her new friend.

∽

It had been nearly six months since Beth said goodbye to Lillian and Rebecca. She told herself that they must be doing fine or she would have heard from them by now. She tried to console herself by thinking that they were part of her past, a time that she wanted to put behind her. However, those thoughts did little to ease her mind and now she wasn't so sure that they should be relegated to a forgotten past. Beth was convinced that not seeing Lillian these past months helped her to forget David. He hadn't crossed her mind in a really long time but she never stopped thinking of Lillian and Rebecca.

There was a strange connection between she and Lillian and she missed her more than she was willing to admit. It didn't make any sense that she should miss Lillian. After all, the woman had been the source of her unhappiness for many years. But Beth couldn't let go of the fact that they had both been wounded by David. Beth had always felt a searing distain for the entire institution of slavery but it wasn't just that Lillian was a slave. It was much more than that. Even though Beth couldn't explain it, she was now convinced that she and Lillian would be strangely linked for the rest of their lives.

CHAPTER 5

The Wallingford Estate

The Wallingford's were adept at hiding the dysfunction of their very complicated family. However, a skeleton or two was bound to fall from the closet from time to time, shocking any who had unwittingly put the Wallingford's on a pedestal. This would become so for Lillian and Rebecca.

Edward Wallingford was the son of William Wallingford, a poor Englishman who at age fifteen had been sentenced to exile in America for a series of petty crimes and general debauchery. William was orphaned at ten years old and most of his crimes were a means of survival on the streets of London. His exile to America would turn out to be a blessing rather than a sentence. He was lucky enough to be in the service of Lawrence Brown, a local sea merchant who treated him more like an adopted son than an indentured slave. His benefactor saw to his education and also taught him the shipping business and the importance of importing and exporting. At eighteen, he took over the business, which was eventually bequeathed to William's only son Edward.

When Edward and Ella first married, he ran the business from an office on High Street, hiring captains and seamen to oversee his fleet of merchant ships. However, after their first daughter died, Ella seemed to change right before his eyes. She became a very different young woman. Her grief consumed her, leaving her void of any other emotion. When the second daughter died three years later, Ella became extremely depressed and spent most of her time in bed. Inactivity soon transformed her svelte figure into one of considerable girth. She eventually developed painful joints and difficulty breathing. She was no longer the beautiful, vivacious young woman he'd fallen in love with years earlier. Though Edward still loved his wife dearly, it became more difficult to be at home. He needed time away from the gloom that had enshrouded his home. Taking one or two trips a year not only saved his marriage, it likely saved his sanity.

Ella seemed to rebound some after the birth of her only son Charles but as he grew older and needed his mother less, Ella sank back into depression. Now, he was a student at University and like his father, Charles found it difficult to spend too much time at home.

Mrs. Byrne introduced Lillian and Rebecca to Charles Wallingford on their first Monday and he appeared to be a shy reserved young man. But, from the moment Mrs. Byrne introduced him to Lillian and her daughter, he was struck by Rebecca's beauty. He thought her exquisite but knew that he should keep a respectable distance from so desirable a young woman. Oh, he'd had his share of free loving servants from time to time but always with young Irish girls. He never even had the desire to lay with any of the colored help, but then he had not seen any so appealing as young Rebecca.

Lillian got on well with the other members of the house staff. Mrs. Byrnes was very thorough in teaching Lillian her role as head housekeeper. In their reading classes at the church, Rebecca learned quickly with little effort. It was not so easy for Lillian, but she was so grateful for the job and the opportunity to learn to read and write that she gave it her best effort. By the fall of 1839, Lillian was confident that she could run the Wallingford house with ease.

Mrs. Wallingford had instructed her to find a job for Rebecca within the household and Lillian chose to install her daughter as a second chambermaid. Once the upstairs rooms were cleaned, the chamber pots had been emptied, and the beds made, Rebecca would help in the kitchen.

Early one chilly morning in October, while Rebecca was preparing a basket of linens to be washed, a loud scream shattered the early morning quiet. Startled, Rebecca dropped the heavy basket of linens. As she bent down and scrambled to gather the linens from the floor, another scream brought her attention to the room at the far end of the hall. In the few weeks that Rebecca worked for the Wallingford's, she had only seen Mrs. Wallingford on two occasions. Both times, the woman acted as if she hadn't even noticed Rebecca. But now, her bedroom door was wide open and there was no one else around. Rebecca could hear the woman panting as if she couldn't breathe and every couple of second, she would scream again. It was a horrible scream, as if she were in some kind of severe pain. Rebecca left the basket and slowly approached the opened door. Inside, Mrs. Wallingford was sitting on the edge of her bed and tearing at the fabric of her nightgown. She had already ripped the sleeves off and was tearing the gown down the middle. In seconds, she was stark naked, screaming, and panting continuously now. Rebecca stood there wide-eyed and motionless for a couple of seconds. She really didn't know what she should do, but then Mrs. Wallingford started pounding her head and chest with her fist. She was lashing out so violently that Rebecca thought she would surely injure herself.

"Mrs. Wallingford, no," Rebecca said as she quickly went to the woman. She grabbed Mrs. Wallingford by her wrist, in an attempt to stop her from punching herself. "No, no," she pleaded. You don't want to do that. What is it? Are you hurt?"

Mrs. Wallingford stared at Rebecca as if she were an apparition. She jerked her wrist away from Rebecca's hold and began to pull away, crawling over her bed on her knees. She started to tremble while shaking her head as if she couldn't believe what she was seeing.

In the next moment, Lindy was there. "It's all right, Mrs. Wallingford," Lindy soothed. Rebecca watched as Lindy drew a vial from her apron pocket. "I have your medicine, Mrs. Wallingford. Just open your mouth. You will feel much better in just a little while." She helped Mrs. Wallingford to her feet and she complied without objection. Once she was seated on the edge of the bed, she opened her mouth wide and Lindy dropped a few drops of the liquid from the vile onto her tongue. In seconds, she was as docile as a babe.

Lindy quickly dressed Mrs. Wallingford in a clean nightgown and helped her into bed. "Thank you, Lindy," she said.

"You're welcome," Lindy said. "Now, close your eyes and get some rest. I'll check on you before lunch."

Mrs. Wallingford was asleep before Lindy finished the sentence. She ushered Rebecca out of the room and closed the door behind them. "What's wrong with her?" Rebecca wanted to know. "Is she crazy?"

Lindy smiled. "That old woman is out of her mind when she doesn't take her medicine. Sometimes she just doesn't take it as she should. I keep a vile in my pocket for days just like this. When she starts acting crazy, I know she hasn't taken that medicine for a while." Lindy spoke as if Rebecca should have understood what she was talking about but Rebecca had never seen anyone act that way before.

Having Rebecca work in the upstairs rooms was an arrangement that seemed to work well for the first few months. However, Lindy made a habit of shrugging many of her responsibilities and assigning certain of her duties to Rebecca. When she was in her right mind, Mrs. Wallingford was not one to ignore the goings on in her own household. Lindy getting out of her duties did not go unnoticed.

One morning Mrs. Wallingford sat reading in the small study adjacent to her bedroom, while Rebecca was busy changing the bed linens. "Lindy," she called out, but there was no answer. "Lindy," she said again.

Rebecca walked to the sitting room door. "Mrs. Wallingford, Lindy isn't here right now."

"Oh, good morning, Rebecca." It was the first time the woman had addressed Rebecca directly. "Where is Lindy?"

"I don't know, Ma'am."

The older woman contemplated for a moment. "Is she ill? Why isn't she here?"

"I don't know," Rebecca said again.

"Come here, Rebecca," she said sweetly. "Sit with me for a while."

"Ma'am, I still have a lot of work to do. I am changing your linens."

"That can wait. Come now, sit with me."

Rebecca moved further into the room and sat down warily. "How do you like your job here?"

"I like it just fine," Rebecca said.

"And what of your studies?"

"I've already learned to read and write pretty good, and I like reading."

"Well, well, Rebecca. I am happy to know that you like to read."

"Yes. I've already learned to read very well."

"Really? Well you must be a good student to have learned so quickly." Mrs. Wallingford reached behind her and took a book from the bookcase. She handed it to Rebecca. "Here," she said. "Read to me for a while."

Rebecca reluctantly opened the book and began to read. She stumbled over some of the words but Mrs. Wallingford helped her to sound out each syllable. She spent more than an hour in the small cluttered sitting room with Mrs. Wallingford.

During the next couple of weeks, Rebecca spent a great deal of time with Mrs. Wallingford. She told

Rebecca of her participation in equestrian contest when she was a girl. She talked of books and authors, art and artists, and the many places around the world that she'd visited in her youth. Rebecca understood little of what Mrs. Wallingford said and even less of this strange new relationship. Rebecca didn't mind though, after all, reading was far more fun than changing beds and empting chamber pots.

One morning when Lindy came to tidy up the room and change the bed sheets, Mrs. Wallingford calmly told her that the master bedroom was no longer her responsibility. She was now just one of the chambermaids and her salary would reflect the change. Lindy was furious, but could only say, "Yes Ma'am." She didn't exactly blame Rebecca because she knew that she should not have neglected her duties, but the friendship that might have developed between the two girls would never grow.

Rebecca became more than a personal maid to Mrs. Wallingford; she was more like her companion. Rebecca helped her to dress every day before reading to her for sometimes hours. Mrs. Wallingford had even requested that Rebecca accompany her on the occasional outing.

Mrs. Byrne thought there was something strange in the way Mrs. Wallingford had taken so quickly to Rebecca and she mentioned this to Lillian one evening. "Don ya think it strange that the Missis has taken such a liking to your lass?"

"Well," Lillian said as she paused to think this over. "The Missis is just a lonely old woman. I think that Rebecca may be good for her."

"Do ya, now?" Mrs. Byrne said.

Lillian detected a note of sarcasm in her voice and she turned to face her. "And what do you think, Mrs. Byrne?"

"Oh, I'll tell you girl. There are some things about Mrs. Wallingford I think you should know." Mrs. Byrne sat down at the kitchen table and motioned for Lillian to do the same. "She had two births early in her marriage. Both were girls and both died before they reached their first birthday. She was so broken by their deaths that it was a full ten years before Charles was born."

"Oh," Lillian whispered. "That *is* very sad."

"No," said Mrs. Byrne. "Sad is what it would have been for most women. For Mrs. Wallingford, it was a tragedy from which she has never fully recovered. I think your lass reminds her of the daughters she loss."

"That's ridiculous."

"Why, because your Rebecca is a Negro? If I didn't know she was your daughter, I would think she was a white girl, especially with those green eyes."

"So what if Rebecca reminds her of her daughters? Where is the harm in that? Do you see some problem with Mrs. Wallingford taking so kindly to Rebecca?"

"Could be, who's to say? But, if I were you, I'd keep an eye on the situation."

Lillian was quiet on the ride back to the city. She couldn't stop thinking about the things Mrs. Byrne said, but she also couldn't think how or why Mrs. Byrne thought this could be a problem. Rebecca had adjusted well to all of the new changes in their lives and she was proud of how easily she'd learned to read. She had learned so much during the time she spent with Mrs.

Wallingford and Lillian could see how she was maturing. However, Lillian could not have suspected the extent of the trouble brewing right under her nose.

Later that evening while they were both getting ready for bed, Lillian brought the subject up to Rebecca. "So honey, how are you getting on with Mrs. Wallingford?"

Rebecca laughed. "Mama, why do you keep calling her '*Mrs. Wallingford*'?

"Everyone calls her Mrs. Wallingford. That's her name."

"Not me. I call her Ella, that's her Christian name."

"Oh, Rebecca," Lillian was shocked. "You can't go talking to white folk like you are their equal. You just can't call her by her first name, it's disrespectful."

"Mama, she told me to call her *Ella*."

"Why on earth would she tell you such a thing?"

Rebecca bounced down on the bed, shrugging her shoulders as she began to brush her hair. "She says that I look exactly like she thinks her second daughter would have looked if she were my age. She told me that I was beautiful and with the right clothes, I could look just like a princess."

"Oh Rebecca," Lillian was in disbelief. "I'm sure she said no such thing."

"But she did, Mama. She's always telling how pretty I am. I think that's why she likes me."

"All right, I don't want to talk about this anymore. Just go to sleep." The house was warm and cozy and usually Lillian was so tired that she fell off to sleep as soon as she blew out the candles. But tonight, she just couldn't stop thinking about Rebecca and Mrs.

Wallingford. Although she couldn't exactly see how this situation could cause trouble, after learning about the Wallingford's daughters, she was not at all comfortable with Mrs. Wallingford's attachment to Rebecca. She felt that she should at least speak to the woman about it, but what could she say. She couldn't very well tell her that she was uncomfortable with the kindness she has shown her daughter. She decided to just wait and see where this was going before she said anything that could possibly get her and Rebecca fired.

With the money she earned, Lillian was able to comfortably furnish her small house. She and Althea had become fast friends. She even counted some of the Wallingford house staff among her friends. Along with Althea, Lillian and Rebecca had begun to attend the Bethel Church and Lillian was friendly with several of the women in the congregation.

∽

On the plantation, Lillian found friendships difficult. Her relationship with David had always made her feel that she was above the other female slaves and she was resented for that lofty attitude. In Philadelphia, things were different. She met both free and slave Negro women and most of them liked her from the start.

The Winter Reception of Bethel Church, a social event for the young people in the congregation, was usually held in July. For reasons that were not explained to the congregation, the Reception was scheduled for October 5, 1839. The big hall adjacent to the sanctuary was decorated with purple streamers; tables and chairs had been set up and covered with purple table cloths, and flowered centerpieces. Rebecca was excited to attend her first social function.

She would, of course, have to learn to dance and Althea was happy to teach her what she could. "The waltz is the most popular dance and it's really easy," Althea said to Rebecca.

"There are only three steps and I can show you. Watch me," Althea said excitedly. She put one hand on her midriff and held the other in the air as if held by a gentleman. "The first step is a long step, followed by two short steps, like this," Althea demonstrated. "One, two, three; one, two, three, you see. You'll be waltzing in no time."

Lillian worked feverishly to create a beautiful green evening gown. Althea and Lillian shopped for days looking for affordable fabric. They finally found a remnant of a bold of green silk, which the merchant was eager to sell. With expert hands, Lillian was able to fashion a gown that would rival any bought from the most exquisite dress shops of the day. The gown was off the shoulders and the waist gathered to form the fashionable V-shape. It had full puffy sleeves and a full skirt accentuated by layers of petticoats. The green gown made Rebecca's eyes sparkle like emeralds. Her dark hair with its natural auburn highlights was piled high on her head while ringlets of curls framed her strawberry shaped face.

At seventeen, Rebecca was far past the age when young girls first start to notice members of the opposite sex. The complicated social hierarchy of the plantation had forestalled this inevitable stage of her life until now. She had gained the attention of several young men from the church but none seemed to peak her interest.

Rebecca still thought herself socially above her peers, a mindset that disturbed Lillian because she knew that such an attitude could lead Rebecca into trouble.

It was customary that young ladies be escorted to all social functions and Althea knew of a young man from the church that was without and escort. Even though they had never met until he arrived that evening, Rebecca agreed to be escorted by Robert Brown. The young man was short and stout with thin lips that he moistened with his tongue more than necessary. His suit seemed a little small for his size and he was constantly tugging at the vest to pull it over his considerable girth. The sight of Rebecca standing in the door rendered the young man wordless and he stood there staring as if she were a ghost. After they exchanged pleasantries, the couple left for the Reception.

Robert was acquainted with a good many members of the Bethel congregation. He was chided by his peers and more than one expressed their surprise at Robert being able to get such a beautiful young women to agree to accompany him. He was clumsy and uncomfortable and Rebecca could hardly keep the look of disdain from her face. She consoled herself with anticipation of the wonderful meal she would enjoy. They were served a catered meal of roast duck with wild rice, cranberry jelly with buttermilk biscuits, mixed greens, candied yams, and corn pudding. Once the prayer was said and everyone began to eat, Robert seemed to have forgotten that he wasn't alone. He attacked the meal as if it was his last and Rebecca found it hard to enjoy her own meal while watching Robert cram food into his mouth with alarming speed. The room was warm and though the food was delicious, Rebecca found it difficult to eat. She suddenly felt as if she needed some air. "Excuse me," she said softly as she rose from the table and headed for the balcony.

The evening breeze was refreshing but she couldn't shake the image of Robert eating. His smacking and chomping as if this was his last meal made her laugh out loud. "What's so funny?" a voice came from the shadows.

The realization that she wasn't alone startled her and she jumped as she swung around. A very tall, slim, and dark young man stood nonchalantly leaning against the far wall. He had big brown eyes framed by full dark brows. His smile was radiant as he now smirked at Rebecca as he slowly came toward her. "A private joke?" he asked.

"Yes. I didn't know anyone was here."

"The hall was getting stuffy so I came out here for some air, and you? Why are you out here instead of enjoying your meal with the others?"

"It was getting stuffy for me too."

"You came with Robert Brown, right?"

"R-i-g-h-t," Rebecca stammered. "But we aren't a couple or anything."

Now, he laughed. "I didn't think you were. Robert is well known. Believe me, we've not seen Robert with woman before now, let alone, a woman as beautiful as you Miss . . ."

"Rebecca Vance."

"Rebecca," he said her name again as if to try it out. "My name is Jonah Mason." Jonah was the son of a deacon in Bethel Church who was also a prominent figure and organizer in the Negro community and an undertaker. "So are you a new member of Bethel?"

"Not exactly, I'm not a member. I just come to some of the Sunday services with my mother and her friend Althea." She didn't want to tell him that she was also taking reading and writing classes in the evenings.

"Oh, so you know Miss Althea?"

"Yes, do you know her?"

"Yes."

Silent moments passed as Jonah stared at Rebecca in awe of her green eyes. Rebecca began to feel uncomfortable under his gaze and she turned away from him. That too did not escape Jonah and he softly said, "Am I making you uncomfortable?"

"You're staring at me."

"I'm sorry, it's just that I've rarely seen a woman as beautiful as you are and I've never seen eyes that color."

"Thank you. My father's eyes were green."

"Look Rebecca, I know that Robert was your escort tonight but I would really like to call on you one day, if I may."

Rebecca turned to face Jonah but she didn't answer, which was more than a little confusing to the young man. "Should I ask your father for permission?"

"He's dead," she said bluntly.

"Well, your mother, would you like me to ask your mother for permission?"

"Why do you want to call on me?"

This question stunned Jonah. At first, he didn't know what to make of it. Was she toying with him? He didn't know. "That is what is customary when a young man wants to spend time with a young lady. Did I say something to offend you?"

"No. I just don't want you getting any ideas about us. I'm not looking to pair up with anyone. I'm not one of those girls always looking for a husband."

This was even more outrageous to Jonah. He'd never heard a young lady speak about such things so openly. Rebecca appeared to be a respectable young woman but in the space of a few moments, he began to question that assumption. He didn't even know how to respond to such a statement. He waited for a few uncomfortable moments while Rebecca stared back at him defiantly. "Rebecca," he began softly. "We have just met. I'd say friends are all we could possibly be at this point. Now, if you'll excuse me, I think I'll return to the hall now." Without another word, he turned on his heels and left Rebecca standing alone on the balcony.

Rebecca returned to the hall to find Robert stuffing his face with pie, both apple and sweet potato. His vest was undone and the front of his white shirt was stained with cranberry jelly and a few stains that Rebecca could not identify. The musicians began to play a waltz and couples migrated to the center of the room for the dance. "I don't dance." Robert announced.

"I'm not surprised," was Rebecca's snide remark. "Robert, I'd like to go home now."

"But the party is just starting. Did you know that there is chocolate pudding on the dessert table? I'll take you home as soon as I've had some chocolate pudding."

Rebecca sat back in her chair and crossed her arms in disgust. As she looked toward the dance floor, she couldn't help noticing Jonah dancing with a young woman who looked to be about her age. She was also fair skinned but she had big brown eyes and curly brown hair. The girl laughed and smiled up at Jonah as if she were in paradise as he glided her around the dance floor. A few moments later Jonah took to the dance floor with another young lady who was also pretty but not nearly as fair. Rebecca couldn't understand why, but she felt a twinge of jealousy. She had rebuffed Jonah's attention soundly and had no logical reason why she had done so, but seeing him with the other women made her feel slighted. She did not want to watch the dance floor anymore and turned her head only to find Robert licking chocolate pudding from his lips.

"Robert, please take me home now."

"All right, all right," Robert said.

No sooner than the carriage came to a stop, Rebecca hopped down. She did not wait for Robert's help. "Thank you Robert," she said before lifting her gown and walking briskly to the front door.

"Don't you want me to see you to the door?" Robert yelled after her.

"No. I'll be just fine. Good night."

Lillian was surprised to see Rebecca home so early. She was sitting near the stove reading and having a cup of tea when Rebecca closed the front door. As soon as she heard the door close, she came to see why Rebecca had returned so early.

"So how was it?" she asked. "Did you dance? Why are you home so early?"

"It was very nice. I danced and we ate a wonderful meal."

"Then why are you home so early? Did Robert do anything to upset you?" Lillian wanted to know.

"No, Mother." Rebecca said. "Robert was the perfect gentlemen," she lied. "He wasn't feeling well so we left a little early.

Lillian was not so easily persuaded but she said no more on the subject at that time. Lillian went back to her reading and Rebecca said good night and went to her room. Lillian waited until she thought Rebecca was in bed, and then she climbed the stairs and went to confront Rebecca.

"Alright, what happened tonight?"

"I already told you.

"You lied, now tell me the truth this time. What happened? I know something happened. I could see it in your face," Lillian whispered.

"Alright Mama. That Robert is a disgusting fat pig and I never want to see him again."

"Is that all?"

"No. I met a boy, a really nice boy who asked to call on me but I was rude to him and I rejected him."

Lillian glanced down at Rebecca, surprised at this new attitude. "Why would you reject him if he was such a nice boy?"

"Because mother, I didn't want to like him."

Lillian took her by the hand and sat down on the bed with her. "Why, Rebecca?"

Rebecca's eyes became moist as she fought to hold back her tears. "Because, he's a Negro Mama. They were all Negros. I don't want to fall in love with a Negro." Tears streamed down her face now. "Mama I don't want to be a Negro or Colored. I want to be white. Look at me, Mother. I look white. Why can't I fall in love with a white man and be married and live in a big house with my own servants."

"Rebecca! Stop this nonsense!" Lillian said in the sternest voice she could muster. She was both angry and afraid. "You are not white and you will never be in a position to meet a white man who doesn't know who and what you are. You have to stop dreaming of something that just isn't going to happen. You will never find happiness if you don't accept who you are."

"No Mama, you're wrong. I could walk away from this house tomorrow and just be white. No one would ever know."

"And you would not find happiness, Rebecca. You will spend your life trying to hide who you really are and no one can live that way. Tell me, have you thought of what would happen when you find this white man and marry him and your baby comes along with brown skin and kinky hair? You and your baby will be thrown into the street if he doesn't kill you for tricking him into a marriage he wouldn't have dared chose for himself."

"I won't have children."

"This is foolishness, Rebecca." Lillian stood. Her frustration with her daughter evident in the clinched fist she held at her side. "I warn you that if you don't forget this foolishness and remember who you are there can only be trouble in your future. That kind of thinking can get you killed." Lillian was at her wits end. She didn't know anything else she could say that would show Rebecca how dangerous it was for her to think of such things. "You do know that I was in love with your father, don't you?"

"Yes."

"You also know that I wasn't his wife. Miss Beth was his wife and I could never be more than his lover and his slave. You know these things, don't you?"

"Of course, mother, but you don't look white. You're colored. Everyone can see that but I don't look like you."

"I'm telling you for the last time Rebecca, you are not white no matter how white you look." Lillian wanted to strike Rebecca again but she knew it would do no good. Instead, she pulled Rebecca to her and hugged her tightly. "Besides, if you leave I will be heart sick."

"I know."

Lillian held her daughter a few moments longer. After Lillian released Rebecca from her embrace they were both quiet for some minutes, as they made ready for bed and they were both left to their own private thoughts on the matter.

"What is the young man's name anyway? I hope you didn't hurt that young man's feelings too much," Lillian finally said.

"His name is Jonah but I really don't think he will call on me."

"We'll see."

Rebecca was wrong about Jonah. Being the respectful young man that he'd been brought up to be, Jonah came to Lillian's door to ask permission to call on Rebecca about two weeks after they met. Over those two weeks, he had repeatedly asked himself what he'd done to raise Rebecca's ire. He could think of nothing but he also could not get Rebecca out of his head and decided that he had to see her again. Rebecca was not at home that afternoon and Jonah presented himself to Lillian asking Lillian's permission to court her daughter. Lillian was very impressed with Jonah and she happily gave consent. The next evening when they returned from the Wallingford House, a note had been placed under the door for Rebecca. It was a small white envelope with her name neatly written in the center of the envelope.

Lillian picked up the envelope. "Look Rebecca, it's for you. I think it might be from your young man," she said. Rebecca had already sat down. She opened the letter quickly and began to read.

> *To Miss Rebecca Vance,*
> *Greetings,*
>
> *I would like to call on you this Sunday after church service. I have already taken the liberty to ask permission of your mother, Miss Lillian Vance, who granted my request without hesitation.*
>
> *I await your response.*
> *Respectfully, Jonah Mason*

"Well," Lillian said impatiently. "Is it from him?"

"Yes."

"What does he say?"

"He wants to call on me this Sunday after church. I can't believe it. He actually came here to ask your permission. Why didn't you tell me?"

Lillian was more excited than Rebecca. "Never mind that, are you going to say yes?"

"I suppose. I can't believe he still wants to see me."

"Well, I think he's a very nice young man. If you give him half a chance you might actually like him."

Reluctantly, Rebecca did give Jonah half a chance. At first, she sent no reply to his message but in a few days, another arrived. He apologized for not considering that she may have already made plans for Sunday afternoon and asked her to consider the next Saturday. At the urging of her mother, Rebecca finally agreed to see Jonah.

Jonah had some experience with courting. He had taken out quite a few of the young women from school or the church but he had never met a young woman like Rebecca Vance. He was completely taken with her from their very first encounter. Her beauty often left him speechless. Besides being beautiful, she was petite and graceful with an uncommon elegance in her mannerisms.

He came on a cool November evening. Lillian invited him into her small front room and offered him a cup of tea. "No, thank you Miss. Vance," he said. Rebecca took her time coming downstairs but once she had, Jonah's eyes lit up as if he were seeing a vision from heaven. "Rebecca," he whispered her name as he got quickly to his feet.

"Hello, Jonah," Rebecca said flatly.

Lillian made an excuse to leave the two young people alone for a time while she went next door to visit with Althea.

"I can hardly believe that you still want to court me after I was so rude to you the night of the Church

Anniversary." She plopped down next to him on the small sofa in front of the hearth.

"Well, you *were* pretty rude, but I forgave you that same night. The funny thing is, I just couldn't stop thinking about you. It's like you put a hex on me or something."

Rebecca laughed. "A hex? Why, that's crazy talk. After all, I'm not one of those root doctors or anything." She laughed again then Jonah laughed too. "Jonah," she said in a softer tone. "I am so sorry I was rude to you that night. I don't know why I acted so disgracefully."

The awkwardness of their first meeting passed easily and they began to talk of all sorts of things. Jonah only stayed for little more than an hour but that was enough time to leave him completely smitten and for the first time wondering if this was the woman with whom he could spend the rest of his life.

Jonah called on Rebecca often though his many invitations were seldom accepted. It seemed that the more she rebuffed him, the more determined he became in his pursuit of her devotion. His invitations came so regularly that Lillian began to expect them on Saturday evenings and Sunday afternoons. On the few occasions when Rebecca reluctantly accepted his invitation, Jonah was always the gentlemen. He was charming, attentive, and witty. He often made her laugh with his quirky sense of humor. When he was more serious, he would speak about his plans to apprentice as a mortician in the coming months, assuring Rebecca that such a profession was both profitable and secure. He wanted her to know that he would be able to give her a respectable and comfortable life.

No matter how much Rebecca wished it not to be so, she could not deny that she actually enjoyed Jonah's company. But Jonah was not what Rebecca wanted in a suitor. Even with all of Jonah's obvious attributes, he was still a Negro and could have no place in Rebecca's future plans. She could not let go of her obsession to deny her heritage and enter into the white world. She had visions of a white man falling in love with her just as David Vance had fallen in love with her mother.

Completely unaware of how futile his attempts to win Rebecca actually were, Jonah continued to court Rebecca with the vision of a long-lasting future relationship.

CHAPTER 6

Holiday Spirit

The Christmas spirit was a relatively new concept in Philadelphia. The constant influx of European immigrants and ex-slaves was making the Christmas holiday a more popular celebration in the city and thus, ushered in a more peaceful spirit to the city. Mrs. Wallingford, though not a Quaker, felt much the same as the Quakers about the holiday. She believed that every day was the Lord's Day and should be celebrated as a wondrous gift from God. She made no special preparations for Christmas, though she did not begrudge those in her service their wish for celebration.

On Christmas Eve, the Wallingford House was eerily quiet. After supper, Mrs. Wallingford summoned Rebecca to her room. There she presented her with a small leather bound Bible as a gift. The Bible was wrapped in white tissue paper and tied with a red ribbon. Rebecca was so shocked that she didn't immediately reach for the small package.

"Well, go on. Take it," Mrs. Wallingford said.

"This is for me?" Rebecca questioned.

"Yes Dear, I thought you might want to read God's word on your own sometimes."

"Thank you," Rebecca said. "Thank you," she said again.

Ella Wallingford was in an exceptionally good mood, but her mood had little to do with the Christmas holiday. After more than six months abroad on business, Mr. Wallingford was coming home. His letter said that he would be home by December 25th and Ella could hardly wait.

After the house staff had finished preparing for Mr. Wallingford's arrival, the servants, with the exception of two, were given time off for the holiday. Lindy would stay on. Lillian would have three days off. However, Rebecca was the other exception. Mrs. Wallingford chose not to give Rebecca time off. She explained to Lillian that she had become so dependent on the girl that she could not bear to be without her for even a day.

Because the Wallingford's now employed a large amount of servants, most of which Edward knew celebrated the Christmas holiday with relish, he expected to see a bevy of activity and decorations. But to his surprise, there were no decorations and no servants in the house that he knew except Lindy. He came through the kitchen door because he wanted to surprise Ella. Even before he opened the door, the aroma of roast duck assailed his senses. It gave him the warm, welcome feeling of finally being home.

It seemed to Lindy that Edward just appeared in the kitchen. She was startled as she turned away from the sideboard and almost bumped into him. He put a finger to his mouth so that she would not announce his arrival. "Mr. Wallingford," she whispered. "The Mrs. has been anxious all day. She's been expecting you since early afternoon."

"I know Lindy. Where is she now?"

"I believe she's in her sitting room with Rebecca."

"Rebecca? Who is Rebecca?"

"She's the daughter of the new housekeeper, Lillian. She was supposed to be a chambermaid but Mrs. Wallingford took a real liking to the girl, now she's more like a companion to your wife than a maid." Lindy wiped her hand on her apron while shaking her head from side to side, as if in disbelief. "No disrespect, but I ain't seen that girl do any work yet."

Edward just smiled. As he made his way to the master bedroom, he noticed that there were no decorations and the house was virtually empty. Once he had entered the bedroom, he could hear the tender voice of a young woman as she read one of Ella's favorite poems, *On a Honey Bee,* by Philip Freneau. Ella was lying on the lounge chair with her head back and her eyes closed but the young woman immediately looked up at Edward. Again, he pressed his finger to his mouth to signal that she should not announce his arrival. For several moments, Edward just stood there staring. He was struck by this young woman's beauty.

A fire burned in the hearth and more than a dozen candles blazed, illuminating the room in a tawny glow. Edward knew that this young woman could be no older than her early teens but she was exquisite. A single moment of complete awe lasted far too long and the young woman looked up from her reading again, questions written in her bright green eyes. Edward shook his head, disturbing the vision and bringing him back to reality.

"Philip Freneau," he said in a deep voice.

Ella immediately jumped to her feet. "You're home," she said gleefully as she ran into his outstretched arms.

Rebecca glanced at Mrs. Wallingford's cane that stood in a nearby corner. She hadn't seen Mrs. Wallingford take even one step without that cane since she and Lillian had come to Wallingford House. Rebecca guessed that this man, who looked much younger than Mrs. Wallingford, must be her husband. He was a tall man with skin darkened by the sun. He had short cropped, dark hair and when Rebecca first glanced up at him, she thought of her father. With the exception of Edward's dark brown eyes, he looked very similar to David Vance. "And, who is this beautiful young lady?" Edward said. Ella took Rebecca by the hand and pulled her forward. "Edward, I'd like you to meet Rebecca Vance."

"Well now," Edward said. "I'm happy to meet you Miss Vance." He extended his hand as if he meant to take Rebecca's hand, a gesture that instantly told Rebecca that he thought she was white. Rebecca made no move to present her hand and Mrs. Wallingford quickly intervened.

"Edward," she said a little awkwardly. "This is my lady's maid." Silent, uncomfortable moments passed before Ella said, "Rebecca, you may go now. Lindy will show you where you are to sleep."

"Yes, Ma'am," was all Rebecca said before she quietly left the master bedroom.

Once Rebecca was gone, Edward said, "That was awkward. Lindy led me to believe that the girl was your companion."

"Really, Edward, the girl is a Negro, for God's sake."

Now it was Edward's turn to be surprised. "She doesn't look like a Negro."

"Well," Ella said as she groped for her cane in the corner of the sitting room. "Looks are often deceiving. Her mother is mulatto and I'm told that her father was also mulatto."

"She not only looks white, she is absolutely beautiful." His wife gave him a peculiar look at that remark but she said nothing for several minutes as she thought about his comment. "Are you hungry?"

"Famished."

"You know Edward," Ella said as she rang for Lindy. "I thought the same thing the first time I saw her. She's not only beautiful, she remind me of Amy."

"Amy?" Edward said as he sat on the edge of the bed and began to remove his boots. "Ella, that's ridiculous. Amy was only ten months old when she died. This Rebecca must be at least fifteen." He paused for a moment to study his wife. "Ella, have you been taking your medicine?"

Before Ella could answer they were interrupted by Lindy's light tap on the door before she entered the room. She brought Edward a dinner tray and a glass of their best sherry. All conversation stopped until she had finished serving Edward and quietly left the room.

Ella got into bed. "Of course I'm taking the medicine," she lied. She did not always take the medicine prescribed by Dr. Moore because it made her feel sluggish and sleepy. "As for Rebecca," she said. "I know that she is seventeen Edward, but when I look at Rebecca, I see Amy all grown up. Besides, she is a very sweet young woman and I just like her."

Edward said nothing but the danger in such a relationship, did not escape him. His wife had been depressed for so many years, to see her without the melancholy that had defined her in recent years, was a welcomed sight, and may have been why he did not question Ella further about taking her medicine. Had she not, she would not have been in such high spirits. He thought that it was maybe the combination of her relationship with this Rebecca and her medication. However, he worried that this new state of mind could only be temporary and the fall, which he was sure would come, could well be worse the second time. "It's quite obvious that you like the girl. Why else would you have her reading poetry to you?"

"Oh, Edward," Ella said excitedly. "It is much more than you think. She has only been with us a few months and she couldn't read a word when she arrived. I offered her mother a job, provided she learned to read and write. They were both taught to read at the Bethel Church but the girl was exceptional. She is a very smart girl and it seemed that she just took to learning. She loves to read and she gets better day by day."

"Really?" Edward said between bites.

"Yes. I was so impressed with her that I took it upon myself to further her education in a few areas."

Edward finished his meal and took a long drink of wine. "And what, my dear, do you suppose a young Negro girl will do with this education? I'll tell you, Ella. She is going to be a domestic for the rest of her life. She will be able to do nothing with your fine education. The only thing you will succeed in doing is making that girl think too highly of herself, which will hardly be beneficial to her in the long run."

Ella was quiet for several minutes while Edward pushed his tray aside and went to relieve himself. She rang the bell again for Lindy to come and remove the tray. Once Lindy left the room and Edward climbed into bed, Ella turned to face her husband. "I hadn't thought of it that way Edward. It's just that I like Rebecca and teaching her made me feel needed again. Spending time introducing her to literature and geography was as much rewarding for me as it was for the girl. Maybe I was doing it more for myself than for Rebecca."

Edward took his wife into his arms and kissed her soundly. "I know you meant well, Ella," he said in a softer tone. "But now you've got to fix this situation. You have to ease her back into the position she was hired for before she gets the idea that she is above her station."

"You're right, of course. I'll see to it, I promise."

Edward tossed and turned for more than an hour. He didn't know why, but he couldn't fall asleep. He was certainly tired enough, but he just couldn't shake the image of Rebecca from his mind. He was curious about this new maid. *What a petite little woman she was, and so beautiful that she was sure to seize the attention of any man in her presence,* he thought. He decided to get a book from the study to read until he fell asleep. Once Ella was fast asleep, Edward left their bed with the intention of going to his small study on the first floor. He told himself that he was just going to choose a book to help him to relax. However, when he passed the door to the room where he knew Rebecca slept, he stopped. He stood there outside of her room for several minutes, willing himself not to open the door that was certain to lead to trouble. His curiosity got the best of him and he quietly opened the door. For a moment, he just watched her sleep from just inside the door. A moment later, he abandoned caution and went further into Rebecca's room. He softly closed the door behind him. As he stood over her bed, gazing down at her, he marveled at the long chestnut colored hair that was tussled in the top while the rest fell down her back and over her pillow in deep waves. Her long dark lashes, fanned beneath her eyes on the creamy complexion of youth, all seemed to stir something in him. He walked closer to her and in a moment of complete weakness, he reached down and ran his calloused fingers down the side of her face.

Rebecca stirred and wiped a hand over her face, but did not wake at first. She turned, pushing her hair from her face. Suddenly gripped with the feeling that she was being watched, she opened her eyes. It took a moment for her eyes to adjust to the darkness. She blinked to clear her vision and then she saw him. Edward Wallingford was standing above her as still as if he were made of stone. She didn't know why, but she was not afraid. She sat up, pulling the covers up to her chin to cover her exposed shoulders and breast.

Edward put his index finger to his lips in a plea for her not to scream. "Don't be afraid," he whispered. "I am not here to do you harm."

"I am *not* afraid but why *are* you here, sir?"

Edward could not give her a suitable answer. He could not tell her that their briefest encounter had left him yearning to see her again. He could not tell her that her beauty had rendered him weak and wanting. He could not tell her of the tightness he felt in his loins when she looked up at him with her moss colored eyes.

"Is there something I can get for you, sir?" Rebecca asked even as she knew that he was not standing in her room in the middle of the night to ask for some domestic service.

"No," he whispered then walked quickly to the door. "I should not have intruded on your privacy and I do apologize." He paused, unsure of what else he should say. "It would be better for both of us if you did not speak of this meeting to anyone. Do you understand, Rebecca?"

"Yes, I understand," she said with a smile. "I will not speak of this to anyone, sir."

When he was gone, Rebecca lay awake for a long time thinking of Edward Wallingford. This was a new awareness for her. It was obvious that he was attracted to her. She knew that she looked white but until that moment in her short life, she had not known that she was desirable to men. The look in his eyes said that he wanted her and Rebecca could not help feeling a little bit pleased at the effect she was having on Edward Wallingford. Of course, she had no attraction to him, but she now thought that if he desired her, she could certainly attract a younger, maybe even richer, white man. The entire incident only served to strengthen her resolve to leave the life she was born into and assume a white identity at the first opportunity. She now felt sure that she would be able to easily find the right man who would fall in love with her and marry her, thereby allowing her to enter into the world that she so desperately coveted.

The next morning Rebecca dressed and went down to the kitchen to eat breakfast. "Morning, Lindy. Merry Christmas!" she said cheerfully.

"Morning," Said Lindy, who was usually cheerful and talkative, but today she seemed exceptionally quiet.

"Is something wrong?" Rebecca asked.

"Not for me. Sorry I can't say the same for you."

"What are you talking about?"

"You'll find out," was all Lindy said.

Rebecca chose to ignore Lindy's comments and finished her breakfast quickly. She then went to Mrs. Wallingford's room as usual. She tapped lightly on the door and waited for Mrs. Wallingford to tell her to come in. The first thing she noticed was that Mr. Wallingford had already left the room. The second thing she noticed was that Mrs. Wallingford seemed somehow different.

"Rebecca, you're late. I thought I informed you that I'd like you here before nine," she said as she pushed her breakfast tray aside. "The linen needs to be changed and the water closet needs a thorough cleaning. Of course, you will have to assist me in getting dressed first."

For a brief moment, Rebecca just stood there staring at the woman. She didn't even seem like the same person. "Rebecca," Mrs. Wallingford said sternly.

"Yes Ma'am, right away Ma'am." She went to the closet and pushed the curtain aside. "Which dress would you like to wear today, Mrs. Wallingford?"

"The red velvet, it is Christmas after all."

"Yes Ma'am."

"When you are done here, you will go down stairs to Mr. Wallingford's study. He's been away nearly six months and I'm sure that room needs a thorough cleaning as well."

"Yes Ma'am," Rebecca said.

Rebecca realized that her comfortable position at Wallingford house had ended with the arrival of Mr. Wallingford. She wasn't even sad about the changes. She knew her special relationship with Mrs. Wallingford would end eventually. She did as she was told without complaint.

The study was a room on the west side of the house. It had tall windows on one wall and floor to ceiling bookshelves on two other walls. There was a big desk in the middle of the room and several tables with stacks of papers. It was cluttered and dusty and Rebecca looked around wondering where to begin. She walked slowly into the room, drawn to the scads of books that lined the walls. She ran her fingers along the dusty spines, reading each title carefully, wondering if she would be allowed to read any of these fine books. There was one book bound in red leather. The words on the spine were in gold. *"The Canterbury Tales,"* she read aloud.

She was startled by the booming voice of Mr. Wallingford who was slumped in a chair in the corner of the room. "You read well, Rebecca."

"Thank you sir," she said as she hastily pushed the book back into its place on the shelf.

"Well, go on with your cleaning. I won't disturb you. You'll need to have one of the lads carry this rug out back and give it a sound beating. I can almost smell the dust it has collected."

"Yes sir," she whispered as she quickly left the room.

From that day forward, Rebecca dusted that room every day. She made sure that it was thoroughly cleaned. After a time, she began to know when Mr. Wallingford would work in the study. She made sure that there was a fire burning, a hot pot of tea with cup, sugar, and lemon was placed on a small table next to his desk, and the candles were lit. If he appreciated her efforts, he never gave any indication.

∼

It had been eight weeks since Beth spent time with Jefferson. He continued to write her letters and send cards. Occasionally, he sent flowers, but Beth held out, hoping that time would convey her seriousness in the matter. However, times when she felt her loneliest, she began to think that she had been too hard on him. After all, they were both single adults pursuing the possibility of a long-term relationship.

It was Christmas Eve and Beth had never felt more isolated. She'd spent a lovely evening with the Nottingham's but being surrounded by a loving family full of the holiday spirit, only served to make her feel even more alone. The Nottingham house was illuminated with hundreds of candles. A seven foot decorated spruce tree stood in the corner by the hearth. The Nottingham children were aglow with anticipation and the atmosphere was full of holiday cheer. Beth half expected to see Jefferson as one of the Nottingham's dinner guest and she mentioned this to Ellen at the first opportunity.

"He declined our invitation," Ellen said. "I'm sure he thought that you would not be happy to see him here."

"Oh," was all that Beth said but she was somewhat disappointed. She was also sorry that she had been the cause of him missing the opportunity to celebrate the holiday with his friends.

When the evening ended, Beth went home to her lonely house. She poured herself a healthy glass of wine and went right to bed. On Christmas day, Beth didn't even have the urge to leave her bed. She lay there for hours staring out of the window as a light snow gently covered the city. As she had many times in recent months, she wondered what had become of Lillian and Rebecca. She also thought about James. It had been nearly six months since she'd gotten a letter from James.

She got up and prepared to start her day. Once she was dressed and went down stairs, she noticed that a card had been left at the door. She immediately recognized Jefferson's carefree scrawl.

My Dearest Elizabeth,

These past eight weeks have been some of the worst I've spent in recent memory. I understand that you considered my actions on that August afternoon as being too presumptuous. Though I have previously expressed my apologies, there are really no words to convey the depths of my despair at having wronged you. I never intended to dishonor you in any way.

To think a thoughtless moment of weakness has taken from me the one woman

DARK LEGACY

*with whom I could spend the rest of my life,
is almost more than I can endure. If God
would grant me but one gift this holiday, I
would ask that you reconsider and allow me
the chance to make amends. Why should we
both be lonely during this holiday season?*

*I love you Elizabeth and would do
anything to have you back in my life.*
Yours Sincerely,
Jefferson

By the time Beth came to the end of the letter, she
was almost in tears. She realized that it was her fear of
another failed relationship that led her to such
unrealistic expectations of Jefferson. She also realized
that if she took this too far, or too long, she would risk
the possibility of Jefferson losing interest in their
budding relationship.

Beth folded the letter with a smile as she walked
to the front window and gazed out at the snow-covered
street. The snow had stopped and the dense gray clouds
were moving eastward across the sky, promising a
brighter day. It seemed to Beth that those dark clouds
had also carried away her dark mood.

She made up her mind to answer Jefferson's
letter as soon as possible. She also decided that she
needed to write James and find out how things were
going on Gloria and she would find Lillian and Rebecca,
if for no other reason than to make sure that they were
both doing well.

It seemed that making up her mind to make
contact with the people she cared for, especially those

who had been so much a part of her life for the past eight years, was all that was necessary to lift her spirits.

Feeling resolute, she sat down to her small desk in the front room and began to write. With each stroke of her pen, her spirit lifted a little more. By the time she'd placed her letters in their respective envelopes, her mood moved from the depths of despair to such an elevated state of peace and contentment. She couldn't wait to tell Ellen about Jefferson's letter.

∽

Bernie, Althea's estranged husband, had inexplicably returned to the house on Lombard Street. He had been gone for more than a year and Althea had no way of knowing, if or when, he would return. It was an evening two days before Christmas and she and Lillian had just returned from prayer meeting at the church. Each stood in front of their respective front doors saying their goodbyes when Althea's door suddenly swung open. At first, both women were stunned into silence. "Bernie," Althea whispered as she took several steps backward. Bernie was a large man, over six feet, with a broad back and muscular arms. He seemed to fill the entire doorframe as he looked down on Althea with a smirk on his full dark lips.

"Merry Christmas," he said huskily.

Althea looked from Bernie to Lillian. The look on her face was a mixture of surprise and fear. When Lillian glanced up at Bernie he quickly, almost defiantly, turned to face her.

"Hey," he said as he flashed an unattractive smile of rotting teeth.

103

"Bernie," Althea spoke softly. "This is Lillian, my neighbor and tenant." Bernie just stood staring at Lillian with dark, unfeeling eyes. He had the look of a man very use to intimating people and Lillian looked away from his probing gaze.

"You gone be alright?" Lillian whispered to Althea.

"Come on in here woman and welcome your man home," Bernie said.

Althea didn't answer Lillian but the look she gave her as she mounted the three marble steps in front of her house, was one of fear. Lillian stood on the sidewalk watching Bernie and Althea until they disappeared into the house.

Mrs. Wallingford had given Lillian time off until the day after Christmas. However, she elected to keep Rebecca with her so Lillian would be spending the holiday alone. It would be the first Christmas that she and Rebecca would not be together. Although Lillian was happy that Mrs. Wallingford had really taken to Rebecca, she was not happy that she and her daughter would be separated for the holiday.

She had hoped that she and Althea would spend some time together, but now that Bernie was home, she didn't know if she would see Althea at all. She lit the stove and filled the kettle with water. As she waited for the water to heat for a cup of tea, she pulled her chair close to the stove and pulled off her boots to warm her feet. Then she pulled out the cold chicken and biscuits that she'd brought from the Wallingford house for her dinner.

As she sat munching on her cold chicken and sipping hot tea, Lillian began to think about Mrs.

Wallingford's peculiar affection for Rebecca and Rebecca's foolish wish to be white. Maybe spending so much time with Mrs. Wallingford was somehow contributing to Rebecca's foolish dreams. She finished her chicken and tea and went up to bed.

The rickety old wooden windows did little to keep out the chill. Lillian put her heavy wool socks back on with her flannel nightgown and snuggled into bed. She lay still under the heavy blankets listening as the wind whistled through the gaps around her windows. Sometimes, the gusts were so strong, that the glass windowpanes shook in their frames. Again, she thought about Rebecca and Mrs. Wallingford. Still, Lillian didn't know exactly what she could do about the situation without causing a problem. I will just have to speak with Mrs. Wallingford, was her last thought before falling off to sleep.

Hours later, she heard loud voices through the wall. She knew the man's voice was Bernie's, but the female voice, which she assumed to be Althea, was little more than a whimper. Bernie yelled and screamed at Althea most of the night and Lillian finally left her bed to escape the sound.

The next day Lillian waited to hear from Althea until nearly noon before she decided to knock on her door. Bernie opened the door. "I'd like to see Althea, please," Lillian said.

"She don't want to see nobody. She ain't feelin too well today."

"I don't believe you," Lillian said as she stared defiantly. She slowly walked up the three steps, coming face to face with Bernie. He was over six feet tall and a burly man. "I want to see Althea, right now."

Bernie threw his head back and laughed. "You planning to walk right through me lady?"

"Look, I don't know you but Althea is my friend and I'm not leaving until I see that she is all right, so step aside and let me pass."

He laughed again. "And what if I don't?"

Lillian glared at him. "Oh, I think you will let me pass, cause I promise it ain't gone be good for either of us if you don't let me see that Althea is alright. Do you get my meaning Mr. Bernie?" Bernie knew she meant to go for the constable if he didn't let her see Althea. He smiled, bowed, and stepped aside with mock chivalry. Lillian moved into the house, all the while keeping a watchful eye on Bernie. Althea was sitting at her kitchen table and she jumped, startled at the sound as Lillian entered. She immediately hid her face with her hands. "What are you doing here, Lillian?"

"I needed to make sure you were alright." Lillian went to Althea and she turned away. "Let me see your face," Lillian whispered. She gently pulled Althea's hands away from her face. She gasped when she saw her blackened eye and swollen jaw. "Oh my God," Lillian whispered. "Why would he do this?"

Bernie strode into the kitchen. "See," he said. He took a drink from a jug that was on the table and wiped at his mouth with his sleeve. "I told you she was feelin poorly." Lillian could smell the liquor on his breath. He laughed as he walked away.

A bitter loathing simmered in Lillian and she wanted to strike him, but there was nothing she could do. She knew that had she lashed out at him, he would have surely beaten her down just as he'd done to Althea. What sort of man would beat on a woman he hadn't even seen in over a year, she thought. Lillian wet a cloth and began to wipe the dried blood from Althea's face. "Why?" she whispered. "Why, why?"

"He hates me, that's why." Althea said.

"Why?" Lillian asked again.

"I don't know. I think he loved me a long time ago. I loved him too. I'm not sure when he began to hate me but I know he hates me now. Once he's full of whiskey, the hate just comes out."

"How long you been with Bernie?"

"When he was young, he was a good boy. His Mama died when he was a boy, so him and his daddy ran away from Mississippi and came here. He and his daddy did loading and unloading at the docks until his daddy got caught stealing crates of whiskey. White man hanged him right there on the spot. Bernie ain't been the same since."

Lillian didn't understand but she didn't question Althea more. They both heard the door slam and knew that Bernie had gone. "Althea, you've got to get away from this man."

"Where would I go, Lillian? This is my home. I know that these two houses ain't much but they belong to me. My mama and daddy worked hard to own something. It's mine now and I can't just walk away."

"I know all that but maybe one day you can rent both houses and you move someplace where Bernie won't be able to find you."

Althea chuckled. "Yeah, but that ain't today," she said. She could see the worry in Lillian's eyes and knew that her friends concerns were real. "Oh, don't worry about me, Lillian. I been through this time and time again. Old Bernie gone stay a few days, get what he needs from me, then he'll be gone again. I'll be alright, Lillian."

Lillian looked at her friend. She hadn't known just how much she cared for Althea until now. Althea was her first and best friend and she hated to see her hurt. "Alright, she said. " But, I'll be back to check on you later today. Is there anything I can get for you?"

"No. Go on now. He'll be back before long and he won't like finding you here. Just go. I promise you, I'll be alright."

Lillian did not see Althea the rest of the day and that night was quiet. She felt as if she should be able to get a good night's sleep, but sound sleep eluded her again. The two women who meant the most to her were in peril and there was nothing she could do. She worried about the relationship between Rebecca and Mrs. Wallingford. She also worried for Althea. When would Bernie decide to beat on Althea again? There were no ready answers but after at least an hour of thinking, Lillian finally fell asleep.

It was Christmas morning. A light powdery snow fell over the city with an insulating quiet. The fire in the stove had burned out and the house was cold. Lillian wrapped herself in her bed covers and went to the window. As she stood there looking out at a snow-covered city and thinking how beautiful the snow looked, she was shaken from her thoughts by a loud noise and a thump. Then she heard a loud, piercing scream. "Althea," she said aloud.

She dressed quickly and went to Althea's door. She pounded on the door, all the while calling Althea's name. No one answered, but she could hear a commotion on the other side of the door and knew that her friend was once again in danger. Lillian didn't know what she could do. She only knew that if she didn't find a way to stop Bernie, he may well kill Althea. Her first thought was to elicit the help of another neighbor, but it was early morning and the streets were deserted. It suddenly occurred to her that she once saw Althea put a key above the door jam. She reached for the door jam, but couldn't reach it. Even jumping didn't give her enough lift to reach the key. Still, Althea continued to scream between Bernie's occasional loud curses. The sound of glass breaking and furniture being moved was heard from the street. Lillian turned toward the street, her eyes searching up and down the block. She didn't even know what she was looking for until she spotted an old fish crate that someone had abandoned. Lillian retrieved the crate and placed it on the top step. She climbed on top of the crate and got the key down from the door jam. It was easy to break the crate apart with her foot. So she tore away a large piece of wood before opening the door.

The inside of the house was dark. It took a moment for her eyes to adjust from the brightness of the snow-covered street to darkness indoors. What she saw first was overturned furniture and broken picture frames. As she moved further into the house, she saw Althea huddled in a corner of her kitchen. Her face and shoulders were covered in blood. Bernie was standing above her with the hair from the crown of Althea's head in his left hand. His right hand was balled into a fist as he raged, hitting Althea's head again and again.

So intent was he in his brutal attack on Althea that he didn't hear Lillian enter. As Bernie drew his arm back to strike Althea again, Lillian swung at his head with the piece of wood she'd torn from the fish crate. The blow landed on the side of Bernie's head. It was so unexpected, that it sent him reeling sideways.

Althea began to scream again, "No Lillian. He'll hurt you," she said. "Run, Lillian. Run!"

Bernie regained his bearings and tried to struggle to his feet, but Lillian hit him again, sending him back to the floor in a heap. She stood over him with the wood held high above her head. "Get up," she whispered.

"No," Althea pleaded.

Bernie got to his feet with both hands balled into fist. "You should have minded your own business, lady," he said through clenched teeth. In one large stride, he was only an arm distance away from Lillian. She swung her stick again. This time she hit him across the knees and as he buckled over, she raised the stick again and plunged it into his groin. He groaned as he fell, bringing his knees up to his chest he rolled over. "You bitch!" he mumbled.

"Ain't it enough that we have to worry about white men using and abusing us that we got to also be worried about our own men?" Lillian stood over Bernie, glaring down at him.

"Bah," he said. "The white man's got his foot on my neck same as you. What do you know about it? You might be tough with a big stick in your hand, but you ain't a black man."

"Oh, so that's it. You can't fight the white man so you get full of whiskey then come here and beat the hell out of Althea? If you think that will solve your problem you are a bigger fool than you look. I don't know how hard your life has been or what will make life better for you, but I do know that I ain't gone let you hurt her no more. I want you to get up and get whatever you think belongs to you and get out." Lillian could hear Althea softly crying from the corner.

Bernie got to his feet, all the while, keeping an eye on Lillian. "I'll go," he said. "But I'll be back. You can't keep a man from his wife."

"From what I can tell, you don't have a wife cause you sure as hell ain't no husband. You're no more a husband than an old dog and Althea don't need the likes of you."

He put his coat on and began to grab things from the kitchen and stuff them into his pockets. Lillian continued to hold her stick high in the air, ready to strike him again if necessary. As he stumbled past Lillian toward the door, she could smell the liquor. As soon as he closed the door, she went to the window and watched as he stumbled down the street. When she was sure he had gone, she went to help Althea.

Besides the many cuts and abrasions on her face and forearms, Althea's left eye was black, her nose and her right arm were broken. Lillian spent most of Christmas day nursing Althea and helping to get her house back in order.

CHAPTER 7

House of Secrets

Gabriel was given permission to drive Rebecca home in the carriage late afternoon on Christmas Day. A single candle that burned in the window of the small house on Lombard Street and a crudely twisted wreath tied with red ribbon hung from the front door. Inside Lillian and Althea sat in the front room sipping hot tea. A malnourished evergreen stood in the corner by the hearth. A few brightly colored glass balls hung from its sparse branches and a tin star was perched on the top of the tree. There were three gifts under the tree, wrapped in brown paper and tied with twine. "Merry Christmas," Rebecca said as she came through the door.

"Merry Christmas," both Lillian and Althea said. Althea kept her head turned toward Lillian. Her chair was in the corner of the room in the shadows and she never even glanced in Rebecca's direction. The bruises on her face and arms were now a deep purple and she was too embarrassed to show her face to Rebecca.

"How was your stay with the Wallingford's?" Lillian wanted to know.

"Mr. Wallingford came home."

"Really?" Lillian said as she left her chair and headed for the kitchen. "I've kept a plate warming for you. I hope you're hungry."

"Thank you."

"Why don't you open the gifts under the tree? They're all for you, honey."

Rebecca threw off her coat, got down on her knees in front of the tree. She began to quickly open the packages. The first was a beautifully knitted white shawl with hood, from Althea. "This is lovely. Thank you, Miss Althea."

In the next box was a new pair of brown leather boots, from Lillian. Rebecca went to the kitchen and kissed her mother on the cheek. "Thank you."

"There should be another package. That small box is for you too."

Rebecca opened the box and saw a silver chain with a tiny little heart-shaped locket. The engraving on the outside of the locket read, *'You have my heart.'* Inside the locket was the word, *'Forever.'* There was no name on the packaging and no card. Rebecca gasped, "This is beautiful, mother. Thank you."

"Oh, that isn't from me."

Rebecca just sat there examining the locket. "This must have cost a fortune. Who would give me such a thing?"

"It's from Jonah, Rebecca. He brought it here last night. He was hoping to see you and he was very disappointed when I told him that you were spending the night at the Wallingford's. I told him that you would be back today."

"Jonah?" Rebecca was more than a little surprised. She quickly got to her feet and turned toward Lillian. "Why would he buy me something like this?"

"I guess he cares for you, honey. Why do you seem angry about it?" Lillian wanted to know.

"Jonah is nice enough Mama, but he wants us to be a couple but I just don't feel that way about him. I'm not interested."

Lillian sat down in her chair and began to sip her tea. "Jonah is a nice young man. He's studying the undertaker business with his father and he will one day be a prominent member of this community. He likes you, Rebecca. I can't see the harm in that." Lillian watched Rebecca's face but she had gone blank. She went to the kitchen and began to eat as if Lillian hadn't said a word. "If you don't want the locket, give it back to him." Lillian said. She couldn't keep the annoyance she felt at Rebecca's ungratefulness from her voice.

After more than five minutes with absolutely no conversation, Rebecca said, "Alright Mama! But I promise you, there will never be anything between Jonah and me. He's a Negro. He has nothing to offer me that I want. I'm not interested in being the wife of a prominent Negro in this community. I don't even want to be in this community."

Althea gasped and put her hand over her mouth. She couldn't believe what she was hearing from Rebecca, but Lillian didn't seem surprised to hear her daughter saying such terrible things. "Lillian, I think it's time I go home," Althea said.

"No," Lillian put her hand up. "You don't have to go, Althea."

Althea sat back down but she felt uncomfortable listening to mother and daughter in this unpleasant conversation.

"Oh, let's not start that again, Rebecca," Lillian said. "I don't even want to talk about it anymore. Do as you please with Jonah."

Rebecca finished her plate and went straight to bed. When Lillian and Althea were alone, Althea pulled her chair closer to Lillian and said, "What is she saying?"

"My daughter thinks that because she looks white, she can somehow marry a white man and live happily ever after in a white world."

Althea was thoughtful for a few moments. "You know, I heard stories of folks trying to pass for white but none of them stories ever have happy endings. Your girl is playing a dangerous game, Lillian."

"I know and I've been trying to tell her just how dangerous this could be for her." Lillian said. "What happens when her white man finds out he's been tricked. He'll kick her out; beat her up, or worse. Rebecca has to get these ridiculous notions out of her head. If we were still on the plantation, no one would let her forget who she was or that she was a slave. But here, where she has freedom, she's been able to dream of a different life. Besides all of this nonsense, that boy Jonah is really a nice boy. He's going make some young girl a fine husband but Rebecca just can't see that."

The day after Christmas was a Thursday and Jonah came by to see Rebecca. She was alone because her mother and Althea had gone to the market. When the knock came at the door, Rebecca assumed that it was her mother returning and wondered why she would knock. "That was quick," she said as she opened the door. Her face registered surprise at seeing Jonah standing on the top step. "Jonah?" she said. "Come in." She looked him up and down and decided that he looked very distinguished in his black overcoat and hat.

"Merry Christmas, Miss Rebecca."

"Merry Christmas, Jonah. I didn't expect you. Come in, please. Would you like to sit down? Let me take your coat."

As soon as he stepped through the door, he removed his hat. He handed his coat and hat to Rebecca and then took a seat in Lillian's favorite rocker. Rebecca sat across from him. "I trust that your mother gave you my gift?"

"Yes, thank you. It is a beautiful locket, though I'm not sure that I should accept such an expensive gift."

"Why wouldn't you accept my gift? It is given in love."

Rebecca didn't answer right away. She didn't want to hurt Jonah's feelings but she didn't want to encourage him either. "You see, Jonah, that's just it. I don't love you. I really hope that you didn't give me this gift expecting me to fall in your arms and confess my love?"

Jonah looked surprised at first but he quickly recovered. "Look Rebecca, I think that you are a very special girl and I like you. Of course, I'd hoped that we would eventually be a couple. You may not love me now but who's to say what the future holds for us? If we spend more time together, maybe one day you will love me."

"Would you like a cup of tea?" Rebecca asked, not wanting to address the things Jonah said.

"Yes," he said and Rebecca went to the kitchen to fix his tea.

Moments later, she came back with a tray with two cups of tea. Jonah sipped his tea, all the while sneaking looks at Rebecca. Finally, he said, "I like you, Rebecca."

"I like you too," she whispered.

"Then what could be wrong with the two of us spending time together?"

"Nothing, we're spending time together right now."

"And so we are," he said then he threw his head back and laughed heartily. "So tell me, how do you like working for the Wallingford's? I hear that they are a strange family."

For the next hour, they talked about the Wallingford's. Rebecca told him of how Mrs. Wallingford had taken a liking to her and wanted her to read to her every day. Jonah told Rebecca about his apprenticeship in the undertaker business. They laughed and talked and Rebecca almost forgot why she did not want to spend time with Jonah. When he left, he promised that he would see her in church on Sunday and asked if she would like to go out for something to eat after the morning service. Rebecca accepted. At the door, after Jonah said goodbye, he bent down and gave her the sweetest, softest kiss on her cheek.

Lillian's time was divided between work, church, and Althea. In fact, Lillian spent so much time with Althea that Rebecca began to feel a tiny amount of jealousy. Rebecca had begun to notice that when she was not at the Wallingford's, she saw very little of her mother. Althea was always around. Rebecca brought the subject up one evening after Althea had gone home to her own house. "Mama, what's wrong with Miss Althea?"

"Why would you think something is wrong?" Lillian said as she went about tidying up their small kitchen.

"She's always around and she always looks so sad. Doesn't she have her own family?"

Lillian chuckled. "No, she has no family. Her parents died and she had no brothers or sisters."

"What about cousins or aunts and uncles?"

"I don't know. She's never mentioned any family other than her parents. Why do you ask such questions?" Rebecca didn't answer right away and Lillian stopped sweeping the floor and turned to face her daughter. "Miss Althea is my friend, Rebecca. I ain't ever had a friend and this friendship is special to me. She's been good to me and that's something I never experienced before meeting Althea. Don't you like her?"

"I like her well enough. I just wish she wasn't here all of the time."

Lillian went back to sweeping up the dust from the floor. She bundled it with other trash and handed it to Rebecca to put outside the back door. After Rebecca came back into the kitchen and closed the back door, she went into the front room and plopped down in one of the few chairs. When Lillian came into the front room, she could see a scowl on Rebecca's face. "You don't like her, do you?" Lillian said as she sat across from Rebecca. "I'm sorry you feel that way Rebecca, but you do know that my friendship with Althea has nothing to do with how much I love you. For a long time, we had no one but each other. Now, there are other people in our lives and I guess that takes some getting used to. You're growing up Rebecca and I suspect that very soon, there will be other people that you love and it won't mean that you love me any less. You are going to fall in love with a young man and leave your old mother behind and I'll understand because that's the way life is supposed to be."

"I understand," Rebecca said.

"I spent so much time thinking about my own problems, that it was a surprise to me to find out that other people had problems too, maybe even bigger than my own. Althea is one of those people Rebecca, but her problems didn't stop her from being kind to us. I hope that she will always be my friend."

As Rebecca listened to Lillian, she realized just how much her mother had changed since they'd left Virginia. The mother she had grown up with was unhappy most of the time. This new Lillian was completely different. She was happy and nice and even cared for others. Could leaving Virginia have caused Lillian to change so, or was it because they were now free? The more Rebecca thought about it, the more she realized that the reasons didn't really matter. She decided that she liked the changes she saw in her mother, in fact, she was even proud of her. She had always known that Lillian was a strong woman, but this was a different kind of strength and Rebecca admired her even more for this new strength.

It was just two weeks into the New Year when Rebecca, after finishing her chores upstairs and helping Mrs. Wallingford to dress, that she approached her about their reading sessions. Mrs. Wallingford was in her room sitting in a chair facing the window. Rebecca did not know that Mr. Wallingford was in the adjoining sitting room. "Mrs. Wallingford, do you think we might read together soon?"

Mrs. Wallingford looked as if Rebecca had uttered something blasphemous. Her eyes widened and the color seemed to drain from her face. She just stared at Rebecca with cold gray eyes that seemed as pale as ice crystals. Thinking that the woman must be ill, Rebecca took a step forward, but she was halted by the thunderous, angry voice of Mr. Wallingford. "That will be all, Rebecca," he yelled.

Rebecca ignored him. "If we are no longer able to read anymore, could I please borrow one of your books?" she asked. Rebecca knew she was being insolent and she didn't care. She had done nothing to cause the Wallingford's to be displeased with her and she refused to act as if she were guilty of something. Although she suspected that Mr. Wallingford did not agree with his wife spending so much time with her, she didn't believe that she should be treated as if she'd done something wrong. "Please, Ma'am," she added a moment later.

Before she had finished speaking, Mr. Wallingford was on his feet and storming out of the sitting room. "Now, that is enough!" he shouted. "You are out of line girl. Mrs. Wallingford has no obligation to provide you with books or reading sessions."

Rebecca glanced at Mrs. Wallingford, hoping that she would speak up and maybe even defend them both from her husband's unprovoked verbal assault. One look at Mrs. Wallingford's face and Rebecca knew the she was afraid of her husband. Her eyes held a silent warning for Rebecca to leave the subject be or just leave the room.

"I'm sorry," Rebecca said. "I just thought . . .," Tears welled in her eyes and it took every ounce of restraint she could muster to keep them from spilling onto her cheeks.

"I don't want to hear what you thought. There will be no more reading sessions. Do you understand? You are paid a salary. If you want books, you will have to buy them yourself. Now, if you want to continue to receive that salary, I suggest you get to the work you are being paid to do."

"Yes, sir," Rebecca whispered then she turned and left the room. As soon as she closed the door, the tears that she'd tried so desperately to hold back, now spilled from her eyes as she ran down the corridor. She didn't want any of the other servants to see her crying so she went toward the back steps, which lead to the kitchen. She intended to go straight through the kitchen and outside, but she ran into Charles at the end of the corridor.

"Rebecca? You're crying. What's wrong?" he asked as he stopped and took both of her hands in his. "What has got you so upset?"

"Nothing," she said, retrieving her hands and wiping at her tears with the hem of her apron.

"Well, it must be something. You're crying."

"I'll be fine," she said as she looked up into his face.

"You know Rebecca, you can talk to me." He draped his arm over Rebecca's shoulders and she spun away from his grasp.

"I'm fine," she said again.

This time when she looked at him, she recognized the look in his dark eyes and the sultry smile on his timid little face. His secret desire shone on his face. It was the same look his father had on Christmas Eve when he stood over her bed. Rebecca couldn't help wondering if this desire that the Wallingford men held for her could be of some use, but she decided that now was not the time to use their weaknesses against them. She would wait until the time was right. "As I said, I'll be fine. May I go now, sir?"

"Yes, of course," he said as his smile faded from his face.

Again, she wiped at her tear stained face as she proceeded down the back stairs to the kitchen.

Lillian was in the kitchen and Rebecca was unable to move quickly enough for her not to see her distraught daughter. "Oh, my God Rebecca!" Lillian said as she enveloped Rebecca in her arms. "What happened?"

"It was nothing."

"Don't tell me, nothing when your face is as red as a beet and I can see that you have been crying. What is it? Who hurt you?"

"It was Mr. Wallingford. He yelled at me."

"Huh," Della said from the stove.

Lillian knew that Della would listen to every word, and then spread it around the house like an infection. She grabbed their coats from the hooks on the door and then ushered Rebecca outside. The two of them walked the narrow red brick path that lead to the garden. Again, Lillian asked her daughter what happened.

"I asked Mrs. Wallingford if I could maybe borrow a book. You know, since her husband came home, she doesn't let me read to her anymore. I think she's afraid of him. Anyway, he heard me and came screaming from the sitting room to tell me that there will be no more reading sessions and if I want books, I should buy them myself."

"Oh, so he hurt your feelings?"

"He didn't have to yell."

"Well maybe that is just his way. He may have hurt your feelings sweetheart, but he was right. You have no business asking for anything. We aren't slaves but we are servants. We work for these people. They don't owe you anything."

"But Mama, she was so nice to me before he came. She treated me as if I were a relative."

"Yes, a situation which I felt would soon lead to trouble. I think that Mr. Wallingford feels as I do, that you are not a relative. You will never be a relative. You are a servant Rebecca, nothing more. Now, wipe the tearstains from your pretty face and get back to your duties. Never let them see you cry. If it's books you want, we will find some for you. I promise." Rebecca didn't bother to tell her mother of her brief encounter with Edward Wallingford on Christmas Eve or young Charles just moments ago.

Rebecca never stayed over at the Wallingford House again. She left with Lillian every night after the evening meal was served and they returned before breakfast. Her mother was genuinely pleased that Mrs. Wallingford's peculiar interest in her daughter had come to an end. Lindy had resumed her duties and Mrs. Wallingford's ladies maid and it now seemed to Lillian that Rebecca was doing well in her duties as one of the Wallingford's maids. Lillian was also pleased with her daughter's interest in books. She was proud that Rebecca, not only read well, but she loved reading. As she promised, whenever she found books for sale, new or used, she bought whatever she thought would please Rebecca.

Most days there was no time for reading while at Wallingford House, but Rebecca always brought a book along just in case she was able to steal a few moments for reading. Late one January evening after all the house chores had been done and Lillian and Rebecca waited in the kitchen for the time Mr. Briggs would come with the wagon to carry them back into the city, Rebecca pulled a tattered, used book from her bag and began to read while she waited.

Della glanced at first at Rebecca and then Lillian. "Dos ur girl more harm den good to be readin dem books," she said to Lillian.

"She said," Lindy attempted to translate but Lillian cut her off.

"I know what she said, Lindy." Lillian got up and walked slowly to the stove to confront Della. "Why on earth would you say something like that? What you say isn't true."

"Ya keep lettin her read, she gon get big ideas. Start dreamin bout a world she ain't neber gon git to. Better to teach her to be satisfied wit da lot Gawd give her."

Lillian didn't want to make a scene but she needed to put Della in her place. "Lindy, would you wait with Rebecca outside for me?" Lindy and Rebecca quickly obeyed. They both grabbed their coats from the hooks on the back door and quickly slipped out.

"Della, we need to agree on some things." Della was a big woman and she stood at least a head taller than Lillian did, but that hardly mattered. Lillian spoke softly so no one would hear what she had to say except Della. "Rebecca is my daughter and whatever you think about her, you should keep it to yourself. I will not have you question me about what I allow her to do or not. It's not your business." Lillian waited for a snappy response but none came. Della rolled her eyes toward the ceiling and went back to the stove to continue cooking.

"Della may have had no right to say what she said," it was Mr. Wallingford standing just inside the door. Lillian swung her head around at the sound of his voice. His tall, thin body leaned casually against the doorframe with his hands thrust deep into the pockets of his trousers. "But she is right, of course." His shirt was unbuttoned almost to the waist and his dark hair was tussled, as if he'd just awoken.

Lillian just froze. It wasn't just what he said, that struck Lillian. It was the casual way he said it, as if she should have known these things. She didn't want to dispute her employer for fear of being fired but she also didn't want his advice when it came to Rebecca either. "The underclass is much happier with their station in life if they believe that is where they belong. Reading only serves to make them unhappy with who they are and sometimes makes one aspire to be greater than is possible."

"I don't believe you," Lillian whispered.

"It matters little what you believe, Miss Vance. Just tell your girl to leave her books at home." He turned and sauntered away as if he'd won some moral victory.

"Yes, sir,"

Lillian hadn't noticed but Gabriel had been standing on the landing of the back steps where he couldn't be easily seen. Lillian grabbed her coat and slipped out the back door. Gabriel was right behind her. She was so angry that she could hardly contain herself and she swore and cursed the Wallingford's as she made her way down the path to the road. "The nerve of that bastard," she whispered into the cold night air.

"Welcome to the house of secrets," Gabriel said.

Lillian stopped and turned to face him. "What?"

"I said, welcome to the house of secrets. Look, Lillian, maybe you expected something different because you aren't a slave here, but working for the Wallingford's' isn't much different from being a slave."

"That ain't it, Gabriel."

"I know you expected these northern whites to be different than the whites in the south but the Wallingford's' are a strange family. I call it the house of secrets because this family is full of secrets. Captain Wallingford, he walks around like God made him captain of the whole world, but the secret is that he's nothing but a poor drunk, with more bad habits than most people could think of. And Ella Wallingford," he smiled, as if he knew more than he was willing to say. "She wants folks to think that she is a dignified Christian woman. Maybe feel a little sorry for her cause she's cripple. Truth is she's a mean old woman that holds on to the young captain with her money."

"Why are you telling me this?"

"Because Lillian, if you know who they really are, you'll know just how to deal with them. I've been around these people all of my life. I've seen servants come and go. No one stays very long. The Wallingford's' are two lonely and unhappy people and they will spread the unhappiness to as many folk as allows them. Do you understand?"

"Yes, I think so." They both heard the hooves of Mr. Brigg's nag and the wagon as it approached. "Thank you Gabriel."

He nodded then turned and ran back up the road to the house. Lillian watched him go, grateful that he had taken time to talk with her, which did much to ease her anger.

Once she and Rebecca were in the wagon, she said to Rebecca, "No more books at the Wallingford's."

"It's all right, Mama. I just won't bring books with me anymore."

"It really isn't about you anymore, Rebecca. It is the nerve of them to think that learning could do anyone harm. That kind of thinking is just as bad as being a slave."

Lillian didn't mention any of this to anyone, not even Althea. That brief conversation with Edward Wallingford and Gabriel changed everything she thought about the Wallingford family and how she felt about working for them. Althea had once told her that if she or Rebecca were fired, word would spread to the other wealthy families and they would have a hard time finding other employment. She would just have to find other employment before she was fired by the Wallingford's.

From that day on, whenever Lillian had questions or needed to know more about the goings on in the Wallingford house, she spoke with Gabriel or Lindy. She learned that Edward Wallingford was a womanizing alcoholic. He was known for trying to seduce the female help. If they were willing, their employment would last until the tryst was discovered by Ella Wallingford. If the poor servant was unwilling, and if given the opportunity, Edward would take what he wanted and then fire the young woman to keep her quiet.

Lillian learned from Lindy that Charles, the young university student, spent as little time at home as possible because he hated his father. Charles had known that his father was unfaithful to his mother since he was a young boy. When he was no more than ten, he accidentally came across his father and a young white girl in the carriage house. He believed she was the daughter of an associate of his father's. Charles never told anyone what he saw but when he returned to the house, he was so shaken that Lindy wanted to know what was wrong. "Where were you," she asked.

"In the carriage house," he replied

"What happened in the carriage house?"

Charles just shook his head and turned and walked away. Lindy draped a shawl over her shoulders and went to the carriage house to see what the boy had seen that had him so shaken. As she approached the door she heard the unmistakable moans and groans of a man and woman in the throes of sexual intercourse. Lindy hurried away from the carriage house but she now knew what young Charles saw that had upset him so.

A few years back, Charles had come home for spring break with a young woman that he was courting. Charles was in love and planned to ask the girl to marry him after presenting her to his parents. However, during their short visit, his father, in one of his alcohol induced periods of incoherence, wondered into the girl's room, and fell into bed with her. He intended to rape the girl but he was so drunk that he just passed out on the bed with his trousers down around his ankles and his manhood complete exposed. The young woman was terrified and woke up screaming. Charles, Lindy, and Gabriel came running at the sound of those horrific screams. Gabriel pulled Mr. Wallingford's trousers up and helped him back to his room while Charles and Lindy tried to console the terrified young woman. She left Wallingford House the very next morning and refused to see Charles again. She wanted nothing to do with Charles Wallingford or his family.

Both Lindy and Gabriel thought that Mrs. Wallingford knew more than she would admit. She had to know that her husband no longer loved her and were it not for her owning seventy-five percent of his company, Edward Wallingford would have left her years ago.

Now Lillian knew that none of them were who they seemed to be. The entire Wallingford family was a sham and they were all actors, playing their given roles for the world to see.

CHAPTER 8

January 1840
Gloria Plantation, Southampton County, Virginia

Nan left the back of the main house on her way to the kitchen house. She wrapped her shawl around her shoulders tightly to ward off the crisp winter winds. Master James would be home soon and not a morsel of food was on the table. Tiny ice crystals stung her cheeks and her breath made puffs of white smoke in the cold air as she walked the few yards to the kitchen house. She pushed the door open and stood there taking in the scene before her, a look of impatience on her pretty brown face. The conversation between the two women inside the kitchen stopped at the sight of Nan. Inez had taken over cooking when Nan became the housekeeper. Her helper was a young girl named Sally. "Masta James will be comin through the door in minutes and you two still in here millin round," Nan said.

"Now, Nan," Inez said indignantly. "That ain't the truth. We been cookin just like we's posed to be doin. Just cause you heard a little chatter, that don't mean we ain't got these pots hummin in here. Sally, go on over and set the table. Masta James say he be havin a guest tonight."

"Yes, Ma'am," Sally said as she scurried past Nan and out of the door.

Nan had taken over the running of the house after Lillian left without ever being told to do so. Master James was grief stricken and of no mind to make house staff adjustments at the time. After several weeks, Nan did complain to James that she needed more help in the house. He said that he would consider it, but Nan knew that he would give her complaints little thought. Inez was already working in the house doing laundry and cleaning. She assured Nan that she could cook and after James agreed, which took very little convincing, Inez became the cook. Denny and Nan still did most of the housework. No one was sure where Sally came from. Masta James just showed up one day with the girl and told Nan to put her to work.

"Nan, sometimes I swear, you is harder than the Masta," Inez complained.

Nan laughed at that statement. "I'm sorry, Inez. It's just that things is so different now. Before Bell died and when Lillian was still here taking care of the house, things just worked out better. And you know Masta James really ain't been his self. Seems like the man is so down all the time."

Nan began to help Inez fill the serving dishes. "Maybe he just misses his brother?" Inez offered.

"Maybe. All I know is that I don't want anything to send him into another rage. Before all that mess started, the man was as cool as he could be; now the slightest little thing sets him off. If he ain't raging on bout something or other, he's so down he won't even leave the study. That's why I'm so hard on you and Sally. Come on, I'll help you get the food on the table."

It had been six months since David's death and Beth, Lillian, and Rebecca left for Philadelphia, but James was still shrouded in grief. Because of David's addictions, James had considered himself to be the stronger of the brothers and he fully expected to get over the loss and just get on with life. However, he was finding that his feelings could not be so easily assuaged. His feelings of grief went far beyond the loss of his brother and were inexplicably connected with the entire sordid matter.

He couldn't help himself. His thoughts were centered around all of the lives destroyed by his father's actions on the night of David's birth. Memories and regrets whirled in his mind during every waking moment. He couldn't sleep at night and when he was awake, he couldn't concentrate. He drank more than he ever had in his life. No, he couldn't exactly just put it all behind him and move on with his life as he'd planned. He knew that his life would never be the same unless he took some action, though he had no idea of what he should do. He could not turn back the hands of time. He could not bring David back or help Lillian resolve her feelings of guilt and shame for loving her brother. His apologies to Beth were hollow and empty. Most of the time he just felt helpless.

The things he'd learned from his father's journals had changed everything he thought he knew about his family. James had grown up being proud to be a Vance. After all, the Vance's were one of the wealthiest families in the county. They were owners of the largest tobacco plantation in the county and they had enjoyed the respect and admiration of their neighbors for years. Even with Big Bill's reputation for cruelty and womanizing, he was still considered a respected businessman. The family was known in and outside of Southampton County. Even though no one knew the wretched details contained in Big Bill's journals, James was no longer proud.

That fourth journal contained information that James originally thought should be kept secret forever. He hadn't shared all he learned from those journals with David or Beth. He kept it all to himself but he just couldn't stop thinking about what he'd learned. Four years after Gloria died giving birth to James, a third son was born to a slave girl named Martina. There was very little information about Martina. Once she gave birth, she and her son were sold to a planter in New Orleans by the name of Bissette.

James could not shake the feeling that he should do something to make amends for all the devastation. The one thing that kept coming back to him was this unknown brother. He spent a lot of time thinking about Martina and the half-brother he did not know.

After about a month of just thinking it over, he decided to do some investigating. He scoured his father's files for any business dealings with the planter Jon Bissette. When he came across a bit of information that he deemed creditable, he wrote a letter to Bissette inquiring about the slave Martina.

It took nearly six weeks before he received a return letter.

February 20, 1840

Dear Mr. Vance:

Your request for information concerning Martina is curious to say the least. However, Jon Bissette, my father, passed some fifteen years ago. Martina served as his nurse during his long illness and in gratitude; he set her free upon his deathbed. Her son Louis is also a free man.

However, I am sorry to report that Martina, while living with her son and his wife, died in a suspicious fire not long ago. Louis had been married to a free Negro woman and they had two small daughters. His wife, Marianne, had been accused of slapping a white child in her care. Though she vehemently denied the charge, she was quickly arrested. The law found no evidence to support the charge against Marianne and she was soon released.

However, two days later, under the cover of night, kerosene was doused around the small farmhouse and it was set ablaze. Louis tried with every ounce of energy and desperation he possessed to put out the flames and save his small family. There were two rooms at the back of his small house where his daughters and his mother slept and where the fire had been set.

By the time he and Marianne smelled the smoke, the back of the house was burning ferociously. Marianne was so intent on saving her girls that she could not even hear Louis as he tried to convince her that it was too late. She plunged through the burning archway but before she could even get close to where the girls slept, she was engulfed in flames. Louis tried to save her but the fire burned too hot. He sustained burns to his back, arms, hands, and eventually gave up and ran from the house. When it was over, and the house was no more than a pile of smoldering embers, Louis sat on the ground looking in disbelief at the charred remnants of his life and family.

If you need any additional information about Martina, I am including an address where you might reach Louis Bissette.

I hope this information will be helpful to you.

Cordially,
Christophe Bissette.

Though it was a very sad letter, James was elated at the possibility of meeting Louis Bissette. He immediately sent a letter to Louis to offer him the job of Overseer.

∾

In her short life, Martina had lived on five plantations, none long enough to have been given a last name. Every master had been mean in one way or another, but Big Bill Vance had been the cruelest. He bought her from Martha Givens, an old woman in North Carolina. He and Miss Martha had negotiated the terms of sale as Martina stood nearby with her hands folded and her eyes fixed on her bare feet. They spoke as if she weren't even there, couldn't hear, or even understand.

Miss Martha sat in her rocking chair on her old rickety porch. Big Bill sat upon his large stallion, not bothering to give Martina even a glance. Miss Martha's property could no longer be considered a farm. After her husband died and her sons went off to seek a new lives for themselves, the farm fell into ruin. Now it was just an old house and a patch of parched land surrounded by waist high weeds.

"I want a Christian burial," the old woman demanded. "I got no family, no work, and no use for the girl."

"I got even less use for a girl like this." Big Bill said. Martina was a slim girl of average height. It was obvious by her almond colored complexion and big brown eyes that there was some Caucasian in her lineage but how far back, no one knew. If anyone had ever bothered to talk with the girl, her intelligence would have been obvious for she was quick-witted, observant, and resourceful.

"She's a bit too lean and narrow for the fields and I don't need no more house slaves," Bill said with a smirk.

Miss Martha spit a stream of brown tobacco juice between her decaying teeth. "Come on now Bill. I been knowing you for near twenty years and I know that you know exactly what this girl is good for, now don't you?

Bill smiled giving credence to the old woman's assumptions. "Hell Bill, you ain't even got to give me the money. Just pay the undertaker in town for my burial. Then you can just take the girl and go."

Bill did as Martha asked. Martina was fourteen and a virgin when she arrived on Gloria. Bill put her in a shack down by the river, far away from the line of shacks that housed

Gloria's field slaves. That in itself was odd. A young girl living alone so close to the woods was hardly common. The closest shack was nearly a half a mile away.

For the first couple of days Martina was left alone in that old shack. She was so scared that she barely ventured even a couple of yards from the straw packed fabric that served as a bed. At night, the sounds of the woods seemed to come alive. Animals, for which she knew no names, howled, chirped, and squealed through the night, each increasing her terror.

On the third day, an old woman came to the door. The woman just threw open door and sunlight flooded the inside of the darkened shack. Martina looked up in alarm and saw this woman dressed in rags with her head wrapped in brightly colored rags and adorned with bones, teeth, and pieces of twisted metal. The woman walked with a heavy branch, which she used as a cane. "You ain't but a wee thing, a child," she said. "Gad is surely gone send dat man to the hell fire," she said as she moved into the shack. "I be Miss Jubba. I am the healer for our people." Miss Jubba could see that the girl was afraid. "Everything is gone be all right, child." She moved close to Martina and patted the girl on the head. "You must be hungry. You been in here for two days now. Don't worry. Jubba brought you something to eat."

From under the mounds of rags, she produced a basket full of cold chicken and buttermilk biscuits. "Here child. You eat up."

"Thank you," Martina whispered as she took the basket from Jubba. "My name is Martina," she whispered.

"Martina?" the old woman questioned. "How you get a fancy name like that?" Martina shrugged. "Well, you eat up. I be back to check on you later."

"Thank you," Martina said again.

That night Martina learned why she had been housed so far away from the main house and the other slaves. Big Bill came in the middle of the night. He didn't say a word as he dropped his trousers and stole the sacred core of Martina's womanhood, her only gift to the man she would one day love, her virginity. The girl's meager protest was met with a hand held over her mouth while he grunted and humped until he finally relieved himself and dropped his exhausted dead weight onto her fragile frame.

When he had regained his breath and composure, he stood and adjusted his clothing while Martina tried to cover herself and tears streamed down her face. He left her bruised and bleeding.

Early the next morning, Miss Jubba came with a tin basin. She hauled in buckets of water and helped Martina to clean herself as the girl's tears continued to flow. "Ain't no use in crying child? This is just how things is for black women folk. Don't complain and don't fight him. I know this man and I know that he will soon tire of you and be off to different one."

The old woman's word did little to ease Martina's bodily bruises and emotional wounds. Miss Jubba didn't want to be cruel but she also didn't want to watch this child wallowing in self-pity either. "Look here girl!" she said more harshly than was necessary. "I know that he hurt you but what he took was his for the taking. You are a slave, just like me. He owns us both. The part of you that matters most is your soul and he can't take that from you. Stop your weeping. Don't give that devil the satisfaction of knowing that he hurt you. Won't make a bit of difference anyhow."

At first, Big Bill came every night, then there were times when there were days between his visits. Sometimes he smelled of alcohol, cigars, and sweat. Most times, he just smelled of tobacco and sweat. He never said anything. He just did his business and left but on a few occasions, he was so impatient that he couldn't wait until she got to the pallet on the floor. He would kick the door closed and just roughly bend her over the table.

In the months that followed, Martina spent her days helping Miss Jubba make her medicines and asking questions about everything under the sun. Miss Jubba proved to be a good teacher on most subjects and she was kind and patient with Martina.

One day, nearly six weeks after her arrival, Martina became violently ill while helping Miss Jubba pick herbs from her small herb garden. Miss Jubba gave Martina a potion to drink that she said would settle her stomach. "When was the last time you bled?" she asked Martina.

"I don't know," she said honestly.

"I think you got little one growing in there, girl," she said as she pointed to Martina's belly.

"Oh, no. What shall I do?"

"Do? Ain't nothing to be done except tell Masta Vance."

Real terror shown on the girl's face.

"Don't be afraid, child. I'll tell Masta Vance. You go lie down until you're feeling better."

Miss Jubba did tell Masta Vance and he made arrangements that same day to sell Martina. As soon as the child was born, she was gone.

For the first time in her life, Martina was given a last name, Bissette. Jon Bissette was a kind and patient man. Once he learned that Martina had some knowledge of healing herbs, he allowed her to further her knowledge and practice her healing with the other slaves on the Bissette plantation.

Louis was born and raised on the Bissette plantation. His earliest memory was of following his mother, as she gathered the necessary herbs, plants and roots for healing.

∾

Louis was devastated. He had never experienced such lost and hopelessness in his life. Everything and everybody he had ever loved was loss in the fire. He tried to pick up the pieces of his life but he found that the memories were more than he could bear. He had been staying with friends, Daniel and Kyrah Sims, and hoping to find work. Each day it became harder and harder for him to rally enough energy to prowl the streets of New Orleans looking for work. He couldn't stand the sympathetic expressions on the faces of his friends and associates, for how could he move on when their sad faces brought every memory vividly to mind. After a few weeks, he began to feel that he had worn out his welcome. He needed to move on and decided to leave his beloved New Orleans. He didn't at first have a destination in mind. He only knew that he wanted to be as far away from New Orleans as possible. Besides the clothes on his back, his buckboard wagon was his only possession. He borrowed a nag from Daniel, promising to send him payment for it as soon as he could. It was as he was hitching the nag to his wagon that Daniel came running from the house with a letter in his hand. Louis just stood there not quite sure of what could have Daniel so excited. Louis secured all the leather straps and climbed up onto the seat.

"Wait!" Daniel called. "Here's a letter. Just delivered by the postman."

Louis took the letter and noticed a Virginia postmark. He slowly opened the envelope as he wondered who in the world would be writing to him. As he read the few lines, the corners of his lips began to lift and in the next moment, he was smiling from ear to ear.

"What is it?" Daniel wanted to know.

"A job offer. Seems a man in Virginia heard about what happened and he's offering me a job as Overseer."

Daniel cocked his head to the side in a questioning stance. "Don't you think that is a little odd? Do you even know this person?"

"Well, yeah! It is odd, but I ain't ever been one to question God's benevolence." Louis said. He was hardly able to contain his happiness. "The man's name is James Vance. He says we're related, though he doesn't say how. He wants us to meet at a tavern in Richmond in a couple of days."

Daniel was thoughtful. "I don't know, Louis. This all sounds pretty suspicious to me."

"Maybe, but what have I got to lose?"

"I guess you're right."

"You'll hear from me, I promise," Louis said as he snapped the reins and the nag slowly moved forward.

He had been in Richmond for a few days when he decided to have a drink before going to the boarding house room he had rented. As he sat at a corner table nursing the foul tasting beer, he noticed another young man sitting at the bar. As bad as he felt, the look on that young man's face seemed just as dire. He could tell that the young man was of considerable means just by the clothes he wore, and he wondered what could make a man of means so disheartened.

Louis moved to a seat next to the man. "Hello," he tried to sound cheerful.

"Hello," James said without even lifting his head to look at the man who spoke.

"This is about the worst tasting beer I've ever consumed," was Louis' attempt at small talk. At that, James turned to look at him. Green eyes stared back at him and James was momentarily speechless. "It tastes like piss or gut rot."

James burst into laughter. "Yeah," he said. "If you are looking for more refined ale, why not choose one of the establishments on the other side of town?"

"You might have noticed that I ain't exactly white, which means they ain't likely to let me into those establishments. Besides, I'm more partial to a glass of red wine," Louis said.

James didn't answer. He was still staring at the young man in complete disbelief. His skin was a little darker, his hair much longer but he was looking at the same mass of charcoal colored waves and curls as he remembered David to have. "Really," James said slowly. The Louisiana accent did not escape him and he knew that this must be Louis Bissette.

Louis began to wonder why this man was looking at him with such a strange expression on his face. "Is there something wrong, Mister?"

"Oh no," James said. "It's just that you don't look old enough to be drinking either wine or beer."

"Oh, I'm old enough, all right."

"Where are you from?" James asked.

"New Orleans."

"Well now, you must be Louis Bissette. I was expecting to meet with you later today. It is fortuitous that we should meet like this," James said with a smile.

"Mr. Vance?"

"Yes. I'm happy to meet you, Louis." The two men shook hands heartily.

Louis at first amused James but after the two had talked for a couple of hours and consumed a couple of pitchers of the gut rot beer, James decided that he liked the young man and invited him to spend the night at Gloria.

The two arrived at Gloria for supper a little after seven in the evening. The first thing Nan noticed was that Masta James was in a good mood. The second thing she noticed was that the young man who sat with him at the table was not a white man. In all of Nan's forty plus years, she could not recall ever seeing a person of color sit at the Vance table. As soon as she got over that shock, she noticed the uncanny resemblance this young man had to the deceased Master David.

She was both shocked and curious. Who was this handsome young man? Where had he come from and what was he doing here? He was tall with a light complexion, dark curly hair, and thick unruly eyebrows. All these questions and more ran through Nan's head as she helped Inez and Sally serve supper.

By morning, Louis was the talk of the plantation. Nan overheard bits and pieces of the conversation between Louis and Masta James, and knew that Louis was free, a widow, and looking for work. Nan also noticed that he smiled a lot, showing beautiful white straight teeth. Sally, at eighteen, and Denny at nineteen, were both smitten. Inez readily admitted that Louis was a handsome man, but she showed no other interest. Inez was in love with Tim, one of the field slaves. "Do you think Masta James is gone hire this man?" Denny wanted to know.

"Now Denny, since when does the Masta discuss his business with me?"

"I know, but I thought you might have heard."

"Well, I ain't so keep your mind on your chores and not on business that ain't got nothin to do with you."

The conversation between Louis and James continued in the morning at breakfast. "So," James said while munching on a crisp bacon slice. "What kind of work do you do?"

"Well, I owned a small farm in Louisiana, but I left it and all the bad memories behind. I'm looking for something new." Louis wanted to ask how they could possibly be related but he figured it might be better if he waited until James was ready to tell him.

By the time breakfast was over, Louis had told James all the sordid details of his life and the loss of his family and James formally offered him a job as overseer of Gloria.

James and Louis spent many hours together. They toured the entire plantation. When James took Louis to the Overseer's cabin, the look on his face indicated that the space was not to his liking. Louis walked around the small one room cabin. Streams of light filtered through the uneven wooden planks that served as a wall, making the cabin drafty. There was a dirt floor, a small table sat in the center of the room and the stone fireplace was covered in soot and missing several stones. The cabin's only redeeming quality was that it had a real bed with four short post and a spring mattress.

"This cabin has been the same for as long as I can remember," James said.

"Your previous Overseers lived in this cabin?"

"Like I said, it's been the same for as long as I can remember. Every Overseer on Gloria has lived in this cabin."

"Looks like it needs some work," Louis said.

The condition of the Overseer's cabin had never even occurred to James. He followed Louis' eyes and he looked around and realized that Louis was right. This was little more than a hovel, James thought. "Maybe it's time we made some improvements? I'll tell you what," James said. "Since we've got a couple of months before we start plowing and getting the fields ready for planting, I'll give you permission to do whatever improvements to the space that you feel necessary. As long as your work here is done before the end of March."

"Thank you sir," Louis said. "I'll need some wood."

"You'll find all the wood you need down by the river. I'll send a couple of field hands to give you a hand. If you need anything else just let me know."

"Thank you sir," Louis said again.

"I'll have Nan bring you some sheets and other necessities and I'll come down and check on you tomorrow."

Louis nodded and James was gone.

He found some wood stacked on the front porch and began to bring it inside too get a fire going. By the time the fire burned, Nan was knocking on the door. He opened the door to see Nan and a large older black man. They both stepped inside quickly. "Mr. Bissette, this is my husband Jacob," Nan said.

"Louis," he corrected. "You don't have to call me Mr. Bissette. Just Louis will be fine."

"Louis, my husband Jacob came down to bring some candles and a couple of pots, a washtub, and some other things. Here are your sheets and some towels too."

Jacob just tipped his hat but said nothing as he deposited the supplies on the table then went back outside to drag in the washtub. "Once a week, you bring your sheets and towels to the kitchen house and they'll be washed for you," Nan said.

"That's very nice but what I really need now is a broom. There is enough dust in here to choke a rat."

Nan snickered at that. "Well, I'm sure there is one around here somewhere." Without a word, Jacob went to the porch and came back with a broom.

As Nan and Jacob walked back to the big house, she said, "I ain't never seen a person of color as a guest in the big house and I ain't never seen the Overseer as a guest either."

"You right about that," Jacob said. Massa James must really like this young man because they seem more like friends than boss and worker."

"Yeah. Things round here sure is changing and Massa James most of all."

"He ain't been right since his brother went and killed his self."

"Yeah, he sure has been acting real strange."

Over the next couple of weeks, Louis met all of the house staff and a number of the field slaves. He wore dusty blue overalls and a plaid flannel shirt. His long curls were pulled back and tied with a string and he wore an old John Bull felt hat. When James summoned the house staff to the drawing room to formally introduce the new overseer, they were all anxious to meet Louis. He smiled handsomely and nodded as James introduced him to each of the women.

"And this is Denny," James said. Louis smiled and Denny looked as if she would pass out right on the spot. It was as if her tongue was stuck in place. She opened her mouth, but no words came out. Nan stood directly behind her and nudged her hard.

"Hello," Denny whispered. Louis smiled as if he knew the effect he was having on the women.

The hiring of Louis Bissette as Overseer was no different from the hiring of any other Overseer. They had gone through this many times but what was different this time was that Louis Bissette was not a white man.

This was an arrangement that was more beneficial than James could have imagined at the time. Of course, not much work was to be done until planting season, but Louis was a fast learner; he was personable and took to his new job with vigor. He was just and sympathetic, qualities that would help to develop a special bond with the field slaves.

With the running of the plantation now safely in the hands of Louis, James wanted to discuss his feelings with the only one person, he thought could possibly understand how he felt, Beth. He decided to write her to inquire about Lillian and Rebecca and to tell her some of the things that were on his mind.

CHAPTER 9

THE ABSENCE OF PEACE

"Peace . . . can only be obtained through
understanding."
Ralph Waldo Emerson

Philadelphia continued to be a tinderbox of
social unrest. While the inner city was crowded and
dirty and presented numerous sanitation problems for
poor whites and blacks, the neighborhoods surrounding
the city were a hodgepodge of different ethnic groups,
with different social structures and religions, which
often lead to hostilities between groups.

In the city of brotherly love, violence continued
to simmer just below the surface and the slightest
confrontation could result in a riot. Blacks were often
the targets of frustrated whites who called themselves
the natives, because they claimed an advantage for
being among the first arrivals to America. They
completely disregarded the fact that the true natives
were the people here before Europeans began to settle.

The Lenape Tribes, sometimes called the

Delaware Indians, were displaced with the influx of Europeans and the Revolutionary War. Many moved to other territories in Canada and Midwestern states. In Philadelphia, there were hostilities between Protestants and Catholics, Irish immigrants and natives and they all hated blacks and white abolitionists.

Lillian learned of a small shop in the Kensington section, just outside the city proper, where they sold used books. On one of the rare occasions when both Lillian and Rebecca had the day off, Lillian hired Mr. Briggs to ride them to and from the bookshop in his wagon. Rebecca was excited. Thanks to Mrs. Wallingford, she had come to love books and reading. She was very happy at the prospect of being able to buy a couple of books.

Mr. Briggs waited outside the shop while Lillian and Rebecca went inside to shop for books. The streets were teeming with people. Workmen, shoppers, and little children running up and down the narrow sidewalks. Then, without warning, Mr. Briggs noticed a crowd gathering in the middle of the intersection. The crowd was mostly white men, but a few women were included. They carried sticks and clubs and the closer they came, the louder their voices rose. Mr. Briggs, sensing that some violent confrontation was eminent, went into the bookshop to hurry Lillian and Rebecca along.

"What's the hurry?" Lillian wanted to know.

"I'm not sure," he said. "But I think something is about to go down out there. We don't need to be anywhere near this place if there's a riot. Let's go, ladies."

As soon as Lillian had paid for her purchases, the shop owner walked behind them to the door. As they climbed into the wagon, Lillian watched as the shop owner poked his head outside and looked up and down the street. A look of alarm creased his brow and he immediately began to close his shop. Shades were pulled and doors were locked in a hurried pace.

Kensington was one of the communities known for violent civil unrest. The residents and business owners were currently protesting the building of a railroad. The proposed rail line would run right down Front Street. Most of the homes and businesses along Front Street, between Girard and Montgomery, were wooden structures and people believed that the sparks, ashes, and soot from the trains would put these structures in jeopardy. The residents also felt that a train running right through their neighborhood would put their children in danger. Then there was the matter of the disruption of business by impeding cross street traffic. The residents and business owners of Kensington had protested the building of the rail line for months but on this day, in early March of 1840, the highly protested work on the Philadelphia-Trenton rail line finally resulted in a calamity.

Mr. Briggs tried desperately to move his wagon through the intersection, but he was much too late. The mob descended on the intersection intent on forbidding the railroad workers from working. At first, they were yelling and screaming their aversion the rail line. It was as if they hadn't even noticed Mr. Briggs and his wagon. One man grabbed the reins of the nag pulling the wagon. "Get the hell out of here!" he screamed.

Mr. Briggs was still trying to move through the crowd when someone hurled a bottled into the crowd and that seemed to ignite the violence. The crowd surged forward and Lillian screamed. "We've got to get out of here," she yelled. Rebecca just sat wide-eyed and trembling.

Mr. Briggs had no choice but to jump down and pull the wagon into a nearby alley. They all watched as the protest escalated to a full blown riot. The crowd grew as people came to join in the mayhem. The rail workers were beaten, property was damaged, and many other people were injured. At least two buildings were torched. Eventually, Mr. Briggs was able to maneuver through alleys and behind buildings and homes until he came to a street that was clear of protesters. Embers of burning buildings floated in the air and the stench of burning wood was evident for miles as they made their way back into the city. The Sheriff, with the help of city police, finally put down the violence.

It was in this violently charged atmosphere that Rebecca, in all her naivety, still saw the possibility of assimilation into white society as not only possible, but essential for her future happiness.

∽

It was late in an unusually warm April and the first signs of spring were everywhere. A robin chirped while perched on the kitchen window ledge of Lillian's small house on Lombard Street. Nature had begun to redress the chestnut and beech trees in lush shades of green. Though a cool wind gently wafted through the growing foliage, flowering weeds that had lain dormant over the cold winter months were already pushing through the soft earth.

Althea seemed to be healing both physically and emotionally. She no longer jumped at the sound of a door closing or walked down the street as if she were being followed. There had been no sign of Bernie since Lillian had chased him away, but they both knew that it was only a matter of time before he showed up again, and again, Althea would be in danger.

Rebecca never stayed over at the Wallingford House again. She left with Lillian every night after the evening meal was served and they returned before breakfast. Her mother was genuinely pleased that Mrs. Wallingford's peculiar interest in her daughter had come to an end. It now seemed to Lillian that Rebecca had learned a valuable lesson and now performed her duties in silence.

Also, Lillian rarely saw either Edward or Ella Wallingford. Even though everything seemed to be going well, Lillian still searched for other employment. It had become obvious that Ella Wallingford was unstable. She was aware that the peace that she now enjoyed could be shattered on the turn of a word or a careless expression or comment. She and Rebecca would tread lightly in the Wallingford House until she was able to secure employment elsewhere.

It was Palm Sunday and Lillian was looking forward to attending services at the Bethel Church. Rebecca was also looking forward to this Sunday, as she and Jonah had planned an afternoon picnic in the park. Rebecca was dressed in a lightweight yellow cotton dress with a low squared neckline, accentuated with white a ribbing on the sleeves. The dress was cinched at the waist and flared over her hips. She wore the top of her hair pulled back and held with yellow and white ribbon while the rest was allowed to flow down her back. Lillian thought she was absolutely lovely.

As they waited for Althea on the sidewalk in front of her house, Lillian noticed that Rebecca was happier than usual. "You look almost cheerful, Rebecca. Could it be that you are excited about the outing you have planned with Jonah today?" Lillian joked.

Rebecca thought for a moment. "I guess you could say that, but it isn't so much Jonah as it is this wonderful weather. I'm just happy to get out of the house and Jonah's offer of a picnic in the park seemed as good a reason as any to enjoy the weather."

"I think you're starting to like Jonah," Lillian said.

"I like him well enough, Mother," was Rebecca's noncommittal response.

When the service was over, Lillian and Althea stayed to enjoy the early dinner that the church offered. As planned, Jonah waited outside the church in a buggy for Rebecca. As soon as he saw her, always the gentleman, he jumped down to help her climb into the buggy. "Miss Rebecca, you are the prettiest woman I've ever seen. Every time I see you, it seems that you are more beautiful than the last time."

"Why, thank you, Mr. Mason," Rebecca answered with mock formality.

As they rode toward the edge of the city Rebecca could smell fried chicken and freshly baked biscuits packed into the basket at her feet. "Oh, this basket smells heavenly, Jonah. Did you fry the chicken?"

"Yeah! Cooked all morning," he said with a smile.

"I don't believe you, Jonah," Rebecca giggled.

"Well, I was going to but my mother wouldn't let me in the kitchen. She did all the cooking."

"Ah ha," Rebecca said with some surprise. "You must be a very spoiled boy."

"Why, because my mother loves me." He didn't give her a chance to answer before he rushed forward. "Speaking of my mother Rebecca, my parents want to meet you. When do you think you could have dinner with my family?" He waited a moment for Rebecca to answer, but she immediately stiffened and said nothing. "I want you to come to dinner at my house one Sunday after church," he continued.

"I can't think of one reason why your parents are so interested in meeting me, Jonah. After all, we are just friends."

"I know we're friends but you know that I am very fond of you Rebecca and I can't help hoping we'll be more than friends one day soon. So what do you say? When will you come to dinner?"

"Soon," was all Rebecca had to say.

They chose a spot under a large tree a few yards back from the river's edge. It was a lovely day and other couples obviously had the same idea. The riverbank was unusually crowded. Some people were walking their dogs while others were also enjoying a picnic. Jonah carefully spread a white tablecloth over the grass and began to unpack the food. Rebecca tried to help but he wanted to do it all himself. "No, no," he said. "All this is for you. It's a celebration."

"A celebration? What are we celebrating?"

"Oh, I don't know—spring, Palm Sunday, or just being together."

"Oh, I see," Rebecca, said and she laughed, throwing her head back.

"You are so beautiful," Jonah whispered. "Your eyes are the most gorgeous shade of green. I've never seen eyes that color.

"You're pretty gorgeous yourself, Jonah," she said as she swung around and laid her head on his lap with her dark hair falling in the grass beside him. He stroked her hair a few times before he bent his head down to kiss her. Rebecca raised just enough to meet his lips with her own. It was a short, sweet kiss but then Rebecca sat up so that she could give him the full measure of her kiss and he quickly slid his arms around her small waist, pulling her to him in a crushing embrace. They kissed several times before Jonah pulled back and looked into Rebecca's eyes. "I think I'm falling in love with you, Rebecca."

The spell was broken. Rebecca put her hands in his chest and pushed him away. "Jonah, I like you. I like you a lot but I'm not ready to call it love."

Jonah quickly spun around and faced her on his knees. He took her hands in his. "I'm sorry if you think I'm rushing you, but it's alright, I understand that you want to take it slow."

Something rustled in the nearby foliage, which caught both of their attention. Jonah quickly got to his feet but Rebecca just froze where she sat. Jonah walked slowly toward the sound. When he came close to where the woods became more dense, he saw a young white boy who looked to be about ten or eleven years old. Jonah parted the bushes with his arm. The boy looked up in fear and scrambled away before Jonah could speak with him.

"What is it?" Rebecca wanted to know as she stood.

"Oh, it's nothing," he said and in a few long strides he was at her side again. "It was just a young white boy watching us through the bushes."

The couple went back to their picnic and once settled onto the tablecloth, Jonah kissed Rebecca again. She did not push him away or resist him this time. With one arm around her waist, he slide her down until she was lying face up on the grass as he pressed forward with the most passionate kiss they had ever shared. He began to kiss her neck, down her throat, and the part of her breast that rose from the neckline of her dress. Rebecca threw her head back and wrapped her arms around his neck. But again, they heard the rustle of someone in the bushes. This time, Jonah heard the heavy thudding footsteps of someone much larger than the boy he'd caught watching. Jonah was very still, listening and waiting.

"What is it?" Rebecca asked.

"I don't know but I think someone is watching us."

"Oh, it's probably that same boy again. He'll tire of his peeping game soon. Don't look so worried." Rebecca was unruffled.

A moment later a man's voice commanded, "Get off that white lady, boy!" Two large white men, one with a shotgun, stepped through the trees. "Did you hear me, boy!" the man said as he aimed the gun at Jonah's head. Jonah got slowly to his feet and Rebecca sat up in terror.

"Mr., she's not a white lady. She's my girl, a Negro girl."

The man with the gun stepped forward and before anyone knew what was happening, he hit Jonah with the butt of his gun, knocking him to the ground. Rebecca screamed then pressed her hands to her mouth, but she said nothing.

"Thought you were going to have your way with a white girl, didn't you boy?" The other man said.

"No, no sir. She ain't white. I swear it!" Jonah screamed. "Tell them Rebecca.   Tell   them   that you're mixed. Tell them that you're a colored girl." Jonah was pleading with Rebecca but she just stood there. She wanted to tell them as Jonah said, but the words just wouldn't come out. "Tell them," he screamed again.

A crowd began to form as other people came to investigate the commotion. The two white men began to beat Jonah with their fist. Jonah struggled to get to his feet and move away from the blows but once on his feet again, the assault took a more brutal turn.   He was hit in the face with the butt of the gun again, making blood sputtered from his nose. He soon went down to the ground again and they began to kick him. Women, both black and white, began to scream at the horrific scene while Rebecca just stood there with her hands covering her mouth. After the beating went on for several minutes and Jonah was battered and bloodied, Rebecca finally found her voice. "Stop," she yelled. "Please stop. You're going to kill him."

But, they didn't stop. Other men stood watching and no one offered to help. "Help," Jonah whimpered as he spat up blood. "Rebecca, help me!" Jonah could hear a bell in the distance and knew that the constable's wagon was coming with the city police.

One of the men went to Rebecca. "Are you all right, Miss?" he wanted to know.

"I'm not white," she whispered, almost as if she didn't want anyone else to hear. Her voice was so low that the man could hardly make out what she was saying.

"What?" he yelled. "You're not white?"

At this point, his cohort had Jonah by the neck and was still punching him in the face as Jonah sputtered blood and his body flopped around like a rag doll. "She's not white?" his cohort yelled.

"What?" The man suddenly stopped, with his fist in mid-air.

"That's what she says."

He dropped Jonah and stepped over his battered body. "Uh, she sure as hell looks white," he said.

By that time, the constable wagon was there and two police officers began to disperse the crowd while trying to find out what was happening. The larger of the two white men stepped forward and calmly explained that they beat the boy because they thought he was raping a white woman.

The older, and much taller of the two officers, took in the entire scene. "How often have you seen a black boy having a picnic with a white lady? Seems to me that they were just enjoying this good weather like everyone else. What would make you two knuckle heads think this girl was white?"

"Look at her," one of the men said.

"Um," the officer said. "Maybe she does look white, but she ain't. I could arrest both of you for assault."

"It was an honest mistake," one of the white men pleaded. "Look at her! She's as pale as any white woman and those green eyes. I ain't ever seen a Negro with green eyes, have you?"

The older of the two officers walked up to Rebecca as if to see for his self if she really had green eyes. Rebecca stared back defiantly. "Umm," he said as he pondered the situation. "I guess you're right, she does have green eyes. I can see how she might be mistaken for white."

"You see," the man said. "It was all just a big mistake."

"All right," the older officer said. "You boys just get out of here before I change my mind." The two white men were gone in seconds. They parted the bushes and left just as they had come. Once they were gone, the police left too, leaving Jonah's bloodied body in a heap on the grass.

Rebecca still stood trembling with her hands covering her mouth. A young black boy, who recognized Jonah from church, pushed his way through the crowd. He knelt beside Jonah. "Can you walk?" he asked. Jonah just shook his head. "Put your arms around my neck," the boy said. "I'll help you get to your buggy."

When Rebecca noticed that Jonah was being helped to the buggy, she immediately began to wrap up the tablecloth and repack the food into the basket. She climbed into the back of the buggy with Jonah. The boy, whose name neither of them knew, said, "I'll get you home Jonah."

"Thank you," Jonah whispered.

Through swollen eyelids, he peered at Rebecca. "Why didn't you help me, Rebecca?"

"I'm so sorry, Jonah. I wanted to help you, but I was just so scared."

"All you had to do was tell them that you weren't white."

"I did."

"Yeah, after they beat the hell out of me." She didn't answer but the look on her face told him all he needed to know. "You really didn't want to tell them that you were a Negro. You didn't care if they killed me out there as long as they thought you were white."

"Oh now, that, that just isn't true, Jonah." Rebecca stammered. "I was in shock. I was afraid. I tried to speak, but I couldn't."

"It's all right, Rebecca. You don't need to explain anymore."

He directed the young boy to Rebecca's house on Lombard. "Good bye, Jonah," Rebecca said after she jumped down from the buggy. "I truly am sorry you were hurt."

"I'll heal," was all he said before the buggy lurched forward leaving Rebecca standing on the sidewalk in her new yellow dress stained with Jonah's blood.

Rebecca was grateful that Lillian had not yet returned from church with Althea. She didn't want to have to explain anything so she quickly changed out of her blood soaked dress. She washed her face and tried to compose herself so that Lillian would not suspect that anything was amiss.

By the time Lillian came home, nearly an hour later, Rebecca had collected herself and sat comfortably reading in the front room. "Hello, Mama. Did you have a good time?"

Lillian was surprised that Rebecca was home so early. "It was good. What about your picnic with Jonah?"

"Oh, we came home early. He wasn't feeling well."

"Oh, what a shame to feel unwell on such a beautiful day. I hope it isn't serious."

"He'll be fine, Mama."

Lillian went to bed that night not knowing anything about the horrific beating that Jonah suffered. Rebecca said nothing of the incident to anyone but there were too many people in the black community who had witnessed the scene for it to stay hidden for long.

It was nearly four days later when Althea learned of the incident while working in her small garden behind her house. Bess, a woman that Althea had known for many years from the neighborhood, stopped by her small fenced in garden. "Hey Althea, you planting tomatoes again this year."

"Hello, Bess," Althea said. "Yeah, you know I am. I don't usually plant this early, but the weather has been so good, I just couldn't wait to get the plants in the ground."

"Well, I'll be looking forward to some of them beautiful tomatoes at the end of the summer."

"I'm planting so early, that you might not have to wait until summer's end. Some of these tomatoes may ripen by August. I hope so, anyway."

"Did you hear what happened to Jonah Mason?" Althea stood up and wiped her hands on her apron. "No Bess, what happened to Jonah?"

"Rumor has it that he was with your new neighbor's daughter and some white men thought she was white and that Jonah was raping her."

"Really? Jonah?"

"Yeah. They beat him really bad. Broke his nose and cracked a few ribs. One of his eyes is still swollen shut. They say he may never see out of that eye again."

Althea was stunned. "What?" She couldn't believe what she was hearing. She wondered why Lillian hadn't said anything about this incident. As soon as the thought came to her, Althea knew that her friend couldn't have known anything about the incident.

"That's what folks are saying. They say the girl wouldn't even tell them that she wasn't white till they had beat Jonah half to death."

Bess went on talking about other neighborhood gossip but Althea couldn't hear her anymore. All she could think of was telling Lillian and wondering how Lillian would take this terrible news. She knew that Rebecca was foolish enough to want to be white but this was something else altogether. As far as Althea was concerned, to actually let a man be beaten by white folks and not try to save him by just admitting that you aren't white, was just unthinkable. She couldn't wait to tell Lillian what she learned from Bess.

That evening Lillian and Rebecca casually walked the few blocks home from where Mr. Briggs dropped them off. It was a warm spring evening and they were enjoying the night air as they slowly walked and talked about the Wallingford's. Lillian noticed Althea sitting on her front steps as she came near the house. "Hey, Althea," she said, but as soon as she looked at Althea's face, she knew that something was wrong. At first, she thought that Bernie was back. "What is it? What's wrong Althea?"

Rebecca knew exactly what was wrong with Althea. She knew that someone would eventually tell and the entire sordid story would get back to her mother. She didn't even bother to speak to Althea. She left Althea and her mother standing on the sidewalk while she hurried to get indoors.

"Jonah Mason was beat nearly to death at that picnic with Rebecca," Althea began.

"What?" Lillian said. She twisted her head to the side, eyes wide as shock spread across her pretty face.

Althea told Lillian everything she knew of the incident and Lillian listened with growing outrage. Eventually, Lillian sat her bag down and sat on the steps as she listened. By the time Althea finished, Lillian had dropped her head into her hands and was shaking her head. She couldn't believe what she was hearing even as she knew that what Althea said about Rebecca was true.

When Althea had finished, Lillian didn't know what to say. "Thank you, Althea," was all she said. Althea sat down beside Lillian on the step and they both sat quietly for several minutes. Lillian continued to shake her head as she tried to understand her daughter and wondered what she could say or do that would change Rebecca's attitudes about passing for white. Finally, she confessed that she didn't know what to do.

"There ain't much you can do," Althea said. "You have already told the girl how dangerous her thinking can be and now she got to see it for herself."

"No, she didn't learn anything. I can't believe she didn't tell me about this. How could she let that boy suffer such a beating when all she had to do was say that she wasn't white? I hope Jonah will be all right."

"I'm sure he'll heal but I am just as sure that he won't want to court Rebecca anymore."

"I'll have to send a card to his parents to tell them how sorry I am about this."

"I'll pray for them both," Althea said as she stood to go into her house.

Lillian sat outside a while longer before she went into the house. Rebecca was waiting for her and stood as soon as Lillian entered the house. "I know what you're going to say Mama, and I don't want to hear it. Jonah did not take that beating because of me, no matter what Miss Althea says. I didn't say anything because I was afraid. There was nothing I could say that would have stopped those men from beating Jonah. It isn't my fault if they thought I was white. Now, that is all there is to it and I don't care what other people are saying about me."

To Rebecca's surprise, Lillian didn't even answer her daughter. She calmly hung her shawl and bag on the hook by the door and went into the kitchen to make a cup of tea. Rebecca followed close on her heels.

"Well, aren't you going to say something?" Rebecca said indignantly.

"I thought you already knew what I was going to say. I don't see the need for me to say anything. Besides Rebecca, I really don't know what to say to you. What I do know is that the next time you play this little game, it could be you taking the beating."

"No one is going to beat me Mama. Men think that I'm beautiful. They can't take their eyes away from me. Why on earth would anyone want to beat me?"

"Because, Rebecca, you are not white!"

With that, Rebecca stormed up the steps to her room.

Lillian decided that in light of everything that had happened, she couldn't bear to face the Mason family. She took the time to write out a card expressing her regret for the entire incident and Rebecca's improper behavior. She said how sorry she was that Jonah had suffered such brutality and hoped that he was healing. She did not, however, ask for forgiveness, as she didn't believe it could sincerely be offered under the circumstances. She ended by asking them to accept her sincere sympathy and an offer to help Jonah in any way they deemed necessary. She sent the card but she did not expect a response and there was none.

As spring moved into summer, the incident in the park became the talk of the community. Althea assumed that Lillian would be embarrassed by all the talk but she was wrong. This was not the first time Lillian had to endure being the subject of gossipers. She was able to resurrect the self-confidence she had worn so easily during her days on Gloria. Lillian walked with her head held high as before, but this time she continued to be kind to everyone she encountered. She would not be embarrassed or feel responsible for something she could not control. She had done her best to teach Rebecca. All she could do now was pray for her.

Rebecca tried to get out of going to church but Lillian wouldn't allow her to stay at home. "If you think that you are going to hide here at home so you won't have to face what you've done, you are mistaken. You are going to church and you are going to endure the whispers and gossip about you. It is time you learned to be responsible for what you do and say."

If the stares and whispers bothered Rebecca, she gave no clue. The only thing she dreaded was seeing Jonah again.

Althea's prediction couldn't have been more right. Jonah's wounds did heal, even his eye. Though he could eventually see out of the injured eye, his face was marred for life. However, the budding relationship between him and Rebecca was broken beyond repair. He never called on her again. The first time they came face to face after the incident in the park was after church one Sunday. He walked right up to Rebecca.

"Hello," he said.

Rebecca stood starring at his scarred face and she tried not to seem shaken at the sight of him. "Hello, Jonah," she said in a low voice. For a few moments, they just looked at each other. "How are you doing?"

"Oh, I'm strong. I'm getting better every day."

The silence between them extended longer than was comfortable for either. "Well, take care of yourself, Rebecca." Jonah tipped his hat and walked away.

"Yeah," was all Rebecca said as she watched him walk away. She did not see his mother, Mrs. Mason approaching from behind. When Rebecca turned around to look for her mother, Mrs. Mason was standing there looking at her.

"We've never met," she said softly. "But I feel as if I know you as well as my son because, until that picnic, he talked about you so much that my husband and I couldn't wait to meet you. He really loved you,

you know? He wanted to marry you, said he wanted to spend the rest of his life with you." She waited a few moments to see if her words had touched the young woman in any way. "That's all over with now. He's right, you know. Jonah is a strong young man and his body is healing but I fear his heart will take a little longer to heal."

"I am so sorry, Mrs. Mason."

Mrs. Mason smiled. "No you aren't. You think that you are better than my son, because you look white. That's why you wouldn't tell those men that you were colored. Well, you are colored and no matter how much you wish it weren't so, it is so. You are not white Rebecca Vance, and you never will be white. I know that my son will get over you but if you don't get over yourself, you are heading for a lifetime of trouble. Good day to you, Miss Vance." She walked quickly passed Rebecca and caught up with her husband and Jonah.

Rebecca and Jonah would run into each other from time to time, but their exchanges were no more than cordial chitchat.

CHAPTER 10

"Therefore shall a man leave his father and his mother?
And shall cleave unto his wife:
and they shall be one flesh." Genesis 2:24 KJV

Though Beth was miserable without Jefferson, her note to him was not exactly an apology. She really felt that she was doing the right thing when she spurred his advances. Now she thought that she may have over-reacted. She couldn't help but remember the time when she had let herself be led by the physical urges of her body and the damage those decisions had caused. She had lost the only child she had ever conceived and betrayed the husband that she had so desperately wanted to win over. This time Beth was determined that if she married, it would be for love. Jefferson would just have to be patient because she had no intention of giving herself to him on the mere promise of love and marriage.

Patience had never been one of Jefferson's characteristics but he was ecstatic to hear from Beth. He had missed her more than even he thought possible.

He'd gone on with life as usual but he found himself thinking of Beth often. His mind would suddenly think of her at the most inopportune times. He thought of her during important business meetings, during dinner with his mother or business associates, and even in church. He could not deny that he was truly in love with Elizabeth Gable Vance. Their trial separation was over and he was eager to make amends. He waited for what he considered to be a reasonable amount of time before asking Beth to accompany him to a fine dinner and the theater. The couple easily resumed their relationship, almost as if there hadn't been a separation and Jefferson was understandably trying to be on his best behavior.

Beth was still determined to move slowly, though she could hardly deny that she adored Jefferson Miller. He had an easy way about him and he was not one to take himself or life too seriously. He was charming, attentive and a jokester, of sorts. Sometimes just a look from him could bring a smile to Beth's face. Her needs and desires were always uppermost in his mind and he proved it with every action. He would produce a small rag before the sneeze; wrap her shawl around her shoulders before the chill if the wind picked up on a cool evening; or just simply give her a hug when she most needed to be hugged.

They saw each other often and had settled into a period of calm anticipation. At the beginning of February, Jefferson invited Beth to have dinner with him and his mother, Clarisse at the old farmhouse.

To call the Miller home a farmhouse is a bit deceiving. It may have been a farmhouse at one time, but the renovations and additions had transformed it into a charming Victorian style stick house. It was a two-story wooden house with an attic. There were six bedrooms and two recently installed water closets. The wooden façade was painted an odd shade of gray and all the windows, except the attic windows, were shuttered in a dark burgundy color. There was a large porch at the front of the house and a smaller one on the side. There was another porch or deck right above the smaller porch, which was off the master bedroom. The inside of the house was dark, almost gloomy. It was decorated with thick wooden tables and cupboards and the sofa and chairs in the front room were all in overstuffed brocades. Heavy velvet drapes hung at the windows and Beth wondered if the luminous rays of the sun had ever been allowed to grace these ominous rooms. Everything was old and in dark burgundy, gray, or a very, muted beige. If ever given the opportunity, Beth knew that she would discard almost everything she saw and bring color and brightness to the inside of the house so as to match the beauty of the architecture and grounds on the outside.

Clarisse Miller was a woman of small stature but broad, giving her the shape of a box from shoulders to hips. She had dark eyes, thin pink lips, and the sharp nose like one of the ancient Greeks. Her hair was completely gray and pulled back from her face into a knot at the nap of her neck. Jefferson hung their coats in the small hall just off the foyer. Taking Beth by the hand, they moved down a narrow hall that lead to the dining room. The Miller's employed only three servants. There was the cook, the housekeeper, and a nurse for Mrs. Miller. The table was beautifully set with an old eight-candle candelabrum at the center. In keeping with the dark ambiance, only four of the candles flamed. With the help of her nurse, Mrs. Miller stood as Beth and Jefferson entered the room.

"So," she said in a frail voice. "You must be this Elizabeth that has finally stolen my son's heart?" She smiled as she held out her hand for Beth's greeting.

Beth took the pale, delicate hand into her own. "Yes, I'm Elizabeth Vance and I am so happy to finally meet you, Mrs. Miller." Beth gave the nurse a nod to acknowledge her presence and to allow her to help Mrs. Miller to sit again. "Mrs. Miller, I must dispute your assumption that I have somehow stolen your son's heart."

"Really," the old woman said as Jefferson bent to kiss her cheek.

"Yes, I have never stolen anything in my life. Jefferson gave me his heart most willingly. In fact, he came just short of demanding that I take it in exchange for my own. It was a mutual exchange and I have yet to decide who has been awarded the better deal."

Clarisse eyed Beth suspiciously at first but then she smiled broadly. "I think I like her, Jefferson."

"I was sure the two of you would get on splendidly," he said.

Beth breathed a sigh of relief. The ice was easily broken and the fluttering in the pit of her stomach had been successfully staunched. Dinner was delicious and the three of them participated in light conversation. Beth revealed very little of her life in Virginia and Mrs. Miller was kind enough not to ask too many questions. After about an hour, it became obvious that Mrs. Miller was tiring. "Well, Miss Elizabeth, it has been my pleasure to spend this delightful evening with you. I must say, I haven't seen Jefferson this happy in many years. I wish you both the best but for now, I must retire. It seems the older I get, the more sleep I need. I hope you won't hold it against me if I leave you two now?"

"Of course not," Beth said. "This has been a lovely evening and I'm sure we will enjoy many more in the future. It was my pleasure to make your acquaintance, Mrs. Miller."

The nurse helped Clarisse to her feet then she stopped and turned to face Beth. "I share that pleasure, Miss Elizabeth."

"Beth. Elizabeth seems a bit formal. Just call me Beth."

She nodded. "All right, then I suppose it would be better if you called me Clarisse." She smiled as they turned to leave the dining room. "Good night Beth," she called as they moved toward the steps.

Jefferson informed the cook that he and Beth would have coffee and cake in the sitting room before he took Beth by the hand and lead her to the front of the house. "Well, well," Beth said. "Your mother is an enchanting woman."

"She used to be as feisty as a caged cat but she has mellowed somewhat with age."

"I can tell."

"It seems she likes you also."

"That's a good thing. I plan to be around for a while."

Jefferson suddenly turned silent and his expression became serious. Beth knew right away that there was something on his mind but she didn't want to pry. They sipped hot coffee and nibbled on the small fancy cakes the cook brought in, but there was very little conversation. Finally, Beth feigned sleepiness and stretched her arms out in an exaggerated yawn. "I'm a little tired," she said through her yawn. It was such bad acting, that they both had to laugh.

"Why would you pretend to be tired?" Jefferson asked when the giggling finally subsided.

"You seem to have gotten so serious that I thought I should go home."

"You're right. I was thinking of us, wondering if this was the right time to talk about our future together." Beth didn't answer. Her mind whirled with questions. She didn't want to appear too anxious so she tried to appear patient and nonchalant but when Jefferson went down on his knees, all questions were answered. "Beth," he said in a low voice. "I've loved you from the first moment we met and I know that we haven't known each other very long." He was looking so serious and unlike the fun-loving Jefferson she had come to know, that Beth had to stifle a giggle. "Oh, come on now, Beth. This is hard. Let me be serious for just a moment."

"I'm sorry," she said. "Go on."

"I want to marry you."

Beth giggled again. "Is that your idea of a proposal Mr. Miller?"

"Elizabeth Gable Vance, I love you and want to spend the rest of my life with you, if you will have me. Will you consent to be my wife?"

Beth stood and pulled Jefferson up from his kneeling position to meet her. He took her into his arms and kissed her passionately until she almost lost her breath. "Jeff," she whispered.

"Anything," he said. "I will give you anything your heart desires."

"I haven't said yes, yet." Jefferson tried to pull away but Beth held him close. "I am not saying no, either."

At that, Jefferson whirled out of her arms and took several steps away. "What are you saying, Beth."

"I'm saying that I think I'm in love with you and, right now I'd like nothing better than to be your wife but . . ."

"But what?"

"I'm just a little scared. We've only known each other for four months. . . FOUR MONTHS, Jefferson. I need a little more time to be sure."

"But if you love me, time will not change that fact. We will be wasting time that we could spend together."

"I do love you Jeff, but my first marriage was a compulsive decision and it turned out to be a disaster. I want this marriage to be for life. I want to feel secure in our love. We need to wait. I need time."

"That doesn't mean we cannot be engaged for a while."

"No, it doesn't," Beth conceded.

He fished into his jacket pocket and produced a little black velvet box. When he opened the box, Beth gasped. It was the largest, most brilliant diamond she had ever seen. It was round and set in white gold and surrounded by tiny pearls. "It's beautiful," she said.

Jefferson pulled the ring from the box and placed it on Beth's finger. "I ask again, Miss Elizabeth Gable Vance, will you marry me? I don't care if it is tomorrow or a year from tomorrow, just say yes."

"Yes," Beth whispered. Again, she was enveloped in Jefferson's arms and she did not resist. He kissed her hungrily and Beth returned his passion.

Happy and content, that night Beth slept as she hadn't in years. Though they had agreed not to set a date until they thought the time was right, Beth felt that she had finally come to a place of peace and serenity in her life. She had good friends, charitable actives that she enjoyed and a man that she adored. She was happy until she received a letter from Virginia.

⤳

February 10, 1840

My Dearest Elizabeth:

It is with an over-whelming joy that I received your letter of January 15th, 1840. Thoughts of you, Lillian, and Rebecca have rarely left my mind over these past six months. I am happy to learn that you have managed to secure a comfortable life for yourself and that you are well in spirit and body.

However, I cannot deny that I am concerned for the well-being of Lillian and Rebecca. It saddens me that you have lost touch with them. I pray that they will seek you out sometime in the near future.

Thoughts of our last days together have also been heavy on my mind. I regret to tell you that I was not completely honest with you at the time that I shared the contents of my father's journals with you. There was one journal in particular that I did not share. I am uncertain of the reasons why I kept these findings to myself. It could be that my shame out weighted my feelings of duty.

However, after much thought and a generous amount of regret, I now share the contents of the final journal with you.

In this journal, my father recorded the details of the birth of yet another son, which was conceived sometime after my birth and my mother's death. The boy was conceived with another slave woman by the name of Martina. Soon after the child was born, my father sold Martina to a planter in Louisiana.

I must tell you that this entire matter has left me with this inexplicable sense of guilt, shame, and bewilderment, so much so that I spent some time investigating this matter. I finally found this half-brother, Louis Bissette, and he now serves as Gloria's new Overseer.

The information I share with you now, is in no way meant to be a burden to you. I still consider you the only family I have left and I share these things with you in that regard. As strange as it may seem, I also recognize that Rebecca is my blood relative and she is never far from my mind.

I will keep you informed of the happenings here on Gloria and I hope you will keep me informed of your life in

Philadelphia. Please know that you will always have a home here, should you decide to return.

With Love and Respect,
Yours Always,
James Vance

Beth was dismayed by James' letter. She was saddened that James had somehow developed a sense of guilt over all of the damage caused when Big Bill's journals were discovered. The news of a third brother was shocking and left Beth with more questions than answers. She was also sorry that she could not tell James that Lillian and Rebecca were well. However, she was still happy to hear from him and vowed that she would keep in touch with James. She wished she could report some news about Lillian and Rebecca that would ease his mind but could she ever hope to find them in the expanding metropolis of Philadelphia?

March 1, 1840

My Dear James,

It saddens me to hear that you are having such difficulty moving past the tragedies that recently befell the Vance family. Though I know that it may do little to ease your conscious, I assure you that you have no reason to feel guilty for no grievous deed was by your hand.

The four of us are simply victims of circumstances set in motion long before any of us could have possibly imagined such disaster. I have stopped grieving for your brother. My cares are with you, Rebecca and Lillian. I no longer harbor any ill resentment against Lillian for I know that she, as we all are, is a victim.

It is my sincere prayer that you are able to right yourself in this matter and realize that you are in a position to move past the dark legacy of the Vance family and build a new, lasting legacy of which you can be proud.

It does not surprise me that there is another Vance brother, born to a slave woman. There could very well be many more whose births were not written in those God forsaken journals. In any case, I am proud of you for reaching out to this brother and bringing him to Gloria. In this effort, you have already begun a new legacy.

I am sorry to tell you that I still have not heard from Lillian or Rebecca. I will keep a watchful eye as I too am concerned for how they are faring in this very violent city. I will write again as soon as I have anything to report.

Until our next communication, be well brother. Your strength and moral fortitude has always been your most admiring characteristics. I look forward to hearing from you soon.

With Love and Admiration,
Beth

In the months that followed, Beth began to spend a great deal of time at the Miller house. Though she and Jefferson had not yet set a date, the marriage loomed large in Beth's thoughts. She knew that she would be expected to move into the Miller house and with every visit; she tried to imagine herself living in the house with Jefferson and his mother. Her frequent encounters with Clarisse Martin often reminded her of the old adage about first impressions. It didn't take very long for Beth to discover that her soon to be mother-in-law, was in no way the woman who had been presented to her the night of her engagement. Clarisse was exceptionally skilled at hiding her true self behind pleasant small talk and mock expressions of comfort and sympathy, when in truth she was an over-bearing, stubborn woman prone to tantrums when she could not dictate to the people in her presence. Jefferson was either afraid or simply unwilling to confront his mother on any subject he thought might upset her in any way. Though she loved Jefferson dearly, Beth was soon having second thoughts about marriage.

It quickly became apparent that Clarisse Martin did not want her son to marry. Beth was sure that Clarisse's aversion to Jefferson marrying was not directed at her. Clarisse would be opposed to any woman Jefferson loved. The woman was a skilled manipulator when it came to her son. According to Jefferson, his mother was sixty-four years old and in good health for a woman of her age. She suffered from the usual ailments common to a woman in her sixties but she often professed to have a weak heart. Whenever the subject of Jefferson and Beth's marriage came up, she would begin to pant as if she couldn't catch her breath. She would clasp one hand over her heart and say, "Not now Jefferson. I don't feel well enough to talk about this now."

Jefferson and Beth began to see each other less. It appeared that the only time they could spend together was at his home. Whenever they planned an outing, his mother would become ill and Jefferson would be obliged to stay at home. He was oblivious to his mother's manipulative tactics but Beth saw right through Clarisse. Beth kept her feelings to herself. How could she tell him that his mother was manipulating him?

"Your mother appears to be ill much of the time. Why don't you have her seen by a doctor?" Beth finally said.

"Mother hates doctors,"

Of course, she hates doctors, Beth thought but she said no more on the matter. She made up her mind at that moment that if Jefferson was so attached to his mother, there was no room in that relationship for her now or in the future. She had shared one husband and she did not intend to share another.

CHAPTER 11

May 1840

Gloria - The Vance Plantation

As Europeans began to manufacture cigars, their demand for American grown tobacco began to rise. Production on the Gloria plantation had always been able to keep pace with the demand for tobacco from the northeast and abroad until recent years. In the last couple of years, production had fallen far short of expectations and James knew that it was partly because his own melancholy may have prevented him from conducting business, as he knew he should. Reaching out to Louis was the first step in righting the wrongs of the past and bringing Gloria Plantation back to the prominence it once enjoyed.

James and Louis sat on their horses at the top of the hill where they could look out and survey the fields. The neat symmetrical rows of budding tobacco plants made James smile. It had been a couple of years since Gloria's fields had looked so good and James was more grateful to Louis than he could express.

With his easy-going personality and genuine kind-heartedness, Louis was able to slowly develop good working relationships with the field hands of Gloria. He never pushed, demanded, or threatened. When problems arose, he used a sort of gentle persuasion to expose the folly in disobedience. Most of the slaves liked and respected him, which made the plowing and planting as easy and orderly as James had ever witnessed.

"You've done a great job," James said. "I knew from the moment we met that this arrangement would work out for both of us."

"Yes," Louis said. "I've come to love Gloria. I've never seen land so fertile. Beautiful landscapes, friendly cooperative field hands, and the great house staff, make this a wonderful place to work. I have absolutely no complaints."

James laughed aloud. "Well, I'm happy you've been able to fit in so well here."

"There is one thing that puzzles me, James." Louis said.

James eyed him suspiciously before pulling the reins of his horse and turning to go down the hill toward home. Louis followed a few paces behind. "I know what you want to know," James said without turning to face Louis. "We'll discuss it over lunch. I'll tell you the whole story but be aware; you might not feel the same about Gloria once you've learned of your connection to this plantation."

A young slave boy in ragged clothes came running up to take the horses back to the stables. He walked with a pronounced limp, favoring his left leg while stepping lightly on the right leg. He couldn't have been more than twelve or thirteen. "Mornin, Massa," he said as he took the reins from James and Louis. "Mornin, Boss," he said to Louis who nodded his greeting.

"Good morning, Manny," James said. "What's wrong with your leg? Why are you limping, boy?"

"Oh, it ain't nothin sir. I just got a little piece of tree wood stuck between my toes."

Both men looked down at the boy's dirty bare feet. Louis turned to look at James and the expression on his face was unmistakable contempt. He couldn't help wondering why this boy had no shoes, but he said nothing.

"Where are your shoes, boy?" James said.

"They hurt, sir. I think my feet just got too big for them shoes."

"Let me have a look at that foot," Louis said as he motioned for the boy to sit on the step." Between the caked on dirt and dried blood, Louis could clearly see a large splinter wedged between the boy's great toe and the second toe. Louis took a sharp knife from his belt. Manny's eyes stretched wide open at the sight of the knife. Louis straddled the boy's leg with his back blocking his next move. With the tip of his knife, Louis was able to pluck the splinter from Manny's foot in a matter of seconds. It was so deep into the boy's flesh that once removed, blood sputtered forward.

"Ouch!" the boy yelled.

"Hey, it's all over now," James, said. "Now, you go on and wash all that dirt and blood from your feet and I'll see what I can do about getting you some shoes that fit properly."

It was a warm day in May and James decided that they would have lunch in the garden. Nan and

Denny served them cold honey ham slices, potato salad and biscuits with lemonade. As Nan placed a large pitcher of lemonade on the table, James said, "Why doesn't Manny have shoes that fit?"

At first, Nan looked surprised. "I didn't know Massa. His Mama didn't tell me the boy needed shoes."

"See that he gets a pair of shoes that fit by the end of the day."

"Yes Massa," was all Nan said.

Louis had wrongly assumed that Manny's dirty bare feet was an indication of James' disregard for his slaves. He was hardly surprised though. James would not have been the first southern planter with such attitudes. However, as he watched James interact with Manny and then Nan, he was forced to change his mind. He saw compassion in James' face when he learned that the boy did not have well-fitting shoes.

Louis had been a free man most of his life but he did grow up on a plantation and counted men both free and slave as friends. Though he had been able to escape the burdens of slavery, he was not only familiar with the hardships; he was unabashedly opposed to the institution of slavery. Once satisfied that he need not worry about Manny, he sat down with James and realized that he was famished. He wasted no time stuffing his mouth with ham followed by a gulp of the cool lemonade. James watched him for a few moments without speaking. Then he cleared his throat and took a sip of the cool lemonade. "Before you received my letter, had you ever heard anything about Gloria Plantation or the Vance name?"

Louis thought for a moment. "No," he said. "I don't think so. Should I have heard anything?"

"I thought there was a possibility that your mother might have mentioned something about this plantation. After all, she was a slave here before you were born."

Louis stopped chewing and turned his full attention to James. "I knew my mother was a slave before she came to the Bissette Plantation but she has never mentioned Gloria or the Vance name. The only thing that I remember her saying about her life before the Bissette Plantation was that no one had bothered to give her a last name before Jon Bissette."

James smiled at that but he didn't want to diminish the seriousness of their conversation. "I suppose she had good reason for not wanting to remember her stay here on Gloria," James said.

"Her stay?" Louis repeated. "You say it like she was on holiday. My mother was a slave, for God's sake!"

"I apologize. You are right, of course." James was silent and thoughtful for a moment.

The look of apprehension Louis wore seemed to implore James to move on and get to the point. "I'll not drag this on." James said. "To put it simply, Louis, you are my half-brother. Your mother was sold to the Bissette Plantation as soon as you were born." James watched Louis closely but his expression never changed. He didn't seem surprised. He just continued to look at James as if he wanted him to hurry and get on with it.

"I did not know your mother. My father never spoke of her to any of us but he did write about the whole matter in his journals. He's been dead for a quite a few years now but his journals were found only about a year ago. That's when I found out about you and your mother."

Again, James waited for a reaction but there was none. Louis continued to eat, looking up at James every few minutes. He shook his head a few times to indicate that he understood. "You are certainly welcomed to read the journal for yourself, but I'm not sure if learning all of the shameful details would make this any better."

They were both quiet for a few moments. Louis seemed to have suddenly lost his appetite. He dropped his fork, pushed his plate away and folded his hands on the table in front of him as he stared off in the distance. Louis had known that his father was a white man but he never had any desire to know who the man was or how his mother came to have a child by the man. "I have no interest in the details," Louis said softly. He sat there looking at James as he wondered now what possible reason James could have had to bring him here to the place where he was conceived in shame. He watched James fidget uncomfortably, pushing his potato salad around his plate nervously, he felt that there was something James was not saying. "And what was it that made you reach out to me? Were you just curious, wanting to see your half-black brother? Have I met your expectations, brother?" Louis said sarcastically.

"I won't lie. That was certainly part of my motivation." James paused, wondering just how much of the Vance story he should reveal. "You see, my older brother committed suicide leaving me sole owner of Gloria Plantation. The adjustment has been difficult, to say the least."

"I understand. Grief is always difficult."

"Thank you, but you really don't understand. My brother was also half-black and none of us knew anything until we read my father's journals. It seems my father was a bit of a cad when it came to his female slaves."

"You're right, I don't understand. What about your mother, wouldn't she know if the boy was not her son?"

"My father wrote that my mother's son was still born. A slave named Mamie bore my father a son within hours of my mother's child. Rather than tell my mother that her child died, my father switched the infants and kept the secret the rest of his life, nearly thirty years. This news devastated my brother and within days, he took his own life. Whether it was because he couldn't live with knowing that he was half black or that he wasn't the rightful heir to Gloria, we will never know."

James had not eaten a bite from the food on his plate. In his stress, his stomach churned and twisted. He glanced down at his plate and decided that he could not consume a morsel. He dropped his fork and it clanged loudly against the plate. It was obvious to Louis that James was in some emotional pain. He was reminded of the pain and hopelessness he'd felt not long ago at the loss of his family and he empathized with James. "You and your brother must have been very close," Louis offered.

"Not as close as you might think. When we learned about David's true parentage, he was shattered but I also felt ashamed. I was ashamed of my father and what his actions did to David, to us all. I wished that there was something I could do to atone, but there was nothing to be done. We'd all been living a lie our entire lives and after the truth came out, there simply was nothing to be done. I assured my brother that it made no difference to me and that we could go on running the plantation just the same. I thought he was in agreement until I had to cut him down from the tree at the front gate."

When Nan returned to clear away the dishes, she noticed that neither of the men had eaten very much. "Shall I clear table, Massa?"

"Yes, Nan," James said without looking up. Both men were quiet as she cleared away the dishes and uneaten food. James did not speak again until Nan was far enough away not to overhear him. "There is more, much more. But now is not the time to discuss these things."

Louis was still confused. "So, am I to understand that your desire to find me is because you lost your brother?"

"Yes, to a point, but more than that, I don't have an heir. I have a half-black niece in Philadelphia but I have no wife and no children. In truth, you are my only male relative."

"But that's ridiculous," Louis said. "You are still a young man. Who's to say you won't marry in the future?"

"I suppose you're right but I've only ever loved one woman and she was forbidden to me. I don't expect I will ever love another." James sighed loudly. "Don't get me wrong. I've had my share of women but I knew a very long time ago that I could never love another woman."

"Who? Who was this forbidden woman?"

James did not answer right away. He had only recently admitted this to himself and he had never voiced it aloud to anyone else. Finally, he whispered, "My sister-in-law, Beth."

"The dead brother's wife?"

"Yes."

"A white woman, yes?"

"Yes. My brother treated her awfully and I could only stand by and watch as the love she had for him slowly destroyed her. She even turned to me once. That's when I realized that I was in love with her but what could I do? I shunned her advances for my brother's sake but I love her no less now than I did the one time I was able to hold her in my arms."

"Wow," Louis said.

"As I said, there is more but nothing that needs to be discussed now. So, in the event that I do not marry and eventually have children, I want to be comfortable knowing that a blood relative will inherit this land. If you are worried about legal matters, rest assured that I have looked into it and learned that it is not illegal for a black man to own a plantation and slaves. As quiet as it is kept, there are many black plantation owners. There is no one to oppose my will so there will be no legal issues to stand in the way of you taking possession after I've passed on."

Louis got up and thrust his hands into the pockets of his trousers as he paced around the table. James just sat quietly. "Well, that is quite a story, brother. But, before you go giving away your inheritance, I think you ought to find this sister-in-law and tell her how you feel. She just may come running back to Virginia, marry you straight away and give you a house full of heirs before you know it. Then again, she may spurn you, in which case, you should be able to move on with your life."

"Louis, I have given this a lot of thought and I'm not sure telling her would make much difference. She lives in Philadelphia. She is a beautiful, sensitive woman and I'm sure she has many suitors by now."

"You're putting an awful lot of stock in assumptions. You don't know what her life in Philadelphia is like, do you?"

"No, I don't. Her letters reveal very little of her life in Philadelphia." James stood up to leave, indicating that he'd had enough of this conversation. "Look Louis, think about what I've told you. We'll talk about this again soon. Until then, I suggest you spend as much time as possible learning all you can about the plantation that you may one day own." With that, James strode off, leaving Louis with more questions than answers about this new brother.

As soon as James was alone in his study, he found the letter from Beth that he received back in March. He was appreciative of her attempts to lessen his feelings of guilt and it only served to make him love her more. She was a compassionate woman and it pained him to think of the life she'd been forced to live with his brother. David did not deserve a woman like Beth and he knew it, which was probably why Beth was duped into marrying David.

Louis had given him a few things to think about. He now wondered if he could somehow persuade Beth to return to Gloria. The circumstances that led to her fleeing to Philadelphia no longer existed. Even if he could persuade her to return, now was not the right time. There needed to be more time away from all the things that had made her life on Gloria so difficult. She would surely be reminded of those things if she returned too soon. James vowed to keep in constant communication and to wait for the right time. Louis had given him hope that he could one day have Beth as his wife and mistress of Gloria. But unlike David, James would be honest with Beth about everything. He dreamed of the time when he could confess his love for her and promise to make her happy for the rest of her life.

"Hope," James said the word aloud. What better feeling than hope to replace the heavy burden of despair. He smiled to himself knowing that at that moment, he felt better than he had in many months.

CHAPTER 12

Wolves and Lambs

The Black Empress, the Wallingford's merchant ship, was scheduled to set sail on Sunday, June 15, 1840. Mrs. Byrne planned to sail with Mr. Wallingford to England; from there she would take another voyage to her beloved Ireland.

The entire house was in an uproar as they were all expected to help in preparation for Mr. Wallingford's departure. Mrs. Wallingford was an emotional wreck, barking orders and stamping her cane on the floor to indicate her displeasure at the smallest infraction. It was on Saturday that she had instructed Rebecca to lay out her outfit for Sunday. It was a navy blue dress with white corded piping around the waist and cuffs. She wanted her blue caplet and hat and dark blue boots. She would accept nothing less than perfection when she went to the docks to see her husband off on his trip. Unfortunately, Rebecca couldn't find the boots.

Rebecca searched frantically. She looked in Mrs. Wallingford's closet but the boots were not there. She even looked in the boxes that had been packed away in the attic, but she still could not find the boots. She did find a very stylish pair of black leather boots, which were laced with shiny black ribbons. She thought they would be a lovely substitute, so she brought them down from the attic. She then, cleaned and shined the boots to perfection. She hung the entire outfit from the closet door and placed the boots on the floor below, so Mrs. Wallingford might see how well the boots went with the rest of her outfit. When Mrs. Wallingford came in from the sitting room, she took one look at the black boots and went into a rage.

"What is this?" she screamed. "I distinctly told you to find the blue boots." Her rage boiled but her stare was icy as her face turned crimson. "Why can't you follow simple directions? You stupid, stupid, girl! Don't you know the difference between dark blue and black?" She banged the cane on the floor with every word.

Rebecca wasn't given a chance to explain that she hadn't been able to find the blue boots. Mrs. Wallingford was so angry that Rebecca just wanted to leave the room as quickly as possible. This was not the sweet old lady that had been so kind to her when she'd first come to Wallingford House. This was a woman Rebecca had not seen before this moment. As Rebecca slowly backed toward the door, Mrs. Wallingford picked up the black boot and threw it at her head. Rebecca quickly turned to avoid the flying boot, but not quickly enough. The boot hit her on the side of her face above her right eye. Before she could recover from that blow, Mrs. Wallingford crossed the room with uncommon speed and slapped Rebecca hard across the face.

Rebecca's hand went instinctively to her painful cheek. She was stunned. She hadn't believed Mrs. Wallingford capable of such cruelty. Rebecca again tried to leave the room, but Mrs. Wallingford raised her cane high above her head as if she were going to strike her with the cane. Rebecca stopped and just stared at the woman. It was as if she were suddenly possessed by a demon.

The commotion brought Lindy running down the hall with Mr. Wallingford a few steps behind her. Lindy stopped just inside the bedroom door just as Mrs. Wallingford lifted the cane above her head. "Mrs. Wallingford, put the cane down," she said softly. "You are upset but you don't want to hurt Rebecca. Just, put the cane down and I'll get your medicine. Everything will be all right, Mrs. Wallingford. Just put down the cane." Lindy spoke as if talking to a small child.

By that time, Mr. Wallingford was there. He just walked into the room and took the cane from his wife's hand. He led her to the chair by the window, where she usually sat. "Calm yourself, Ella," he commanded. "You're under some stress because I'm leaving," he said in a softer, more soothing tone. "Everything will be all right, Dear." He nodded his head at Lindy and she knew to get the vial of medicine.

"You're leaving me again," Mrs. Wallingford said tearfully. "I just wanted to look good for you, so you would think of me while you were away."

"I know," he said soothingly. "I know."

"But this girl, this stupid girl, would not do as I told her. She was trying to sabotage my plans. She's wicked."

"No, no, Ella. You don't mean that. Rebecca was just trying to help."

Rebecca stood stock still while red welts were rising on her forehead and cheek. Lindy returned with the vial of medicine and Mr. Wallingford put a couple of drops of laudanum on his wife's tongue. Within minutes, she seemed to have folded in on herself and was suddenly as dossal as a toddler.

"What's wrong with her?" Rebecca asked.

"She's just upset because I will be going away for a while. She'll be fine. Don't worry." Lindy eyed Rebecca as if she could add to Mr. Wallingford's explanation but she said nothing. "That will be all, Lindy," Mr. Wallingford said and Lindy turned and quickly left the room.

As Mrs. Wallingford began to relax, her head fell back, her eyes fluttered, and her arms went lax like a ragdoll. "Rebecca, help me get her into bed."

Rebecca rushed to help. She turned down the covers on the bed while Mr. Wallingford lifted his wife and laid her down on the bed. She was almost unconscious when Mr. Wallingford helped her into bed. Rebecca helped him undress her and put her nightgown on, even though it was two o'clock in the afternoon. Once Mrs. Wallingford was in her bed, Rebecca waited, hoping to be dismissed.

"Thank you Rebecca," he said. When he turned to face her, he seemed shocked to see the bruises on her face. "Oh, you're hurt," he said as he ran his fingers down the side of her face. Rebecca stepped away. "What happened?"

"Mrs. Wallingford hit me with her boot then she slapped me."

"I'm sorry," he said as he stepped closer to her.

She didn't know why, but she wanted to move away from him. She stood where she was and he walked right up to her and ran his hand down her bruised cheek again. She stood there, feeling very uncomfortable but not afraid. After several moments he whispered, "Have you dusted my study yet?"

"No sir."

"Then I suggest you do that now."

"Yes sir," Rebecca said as slipped around him and left the room.

She headed for the back staircase but before she could get there, Lindy pulled her into one of the empty bedrooms. "That woman is unstable," Lindy said. "Always has been, at least since I've been here."

"But she seemed perfectly normal for months. I've been here since September and she has never acted this way before now."

"That's because she's been taking her medicine but every time Mr. Wallingford comes home, she stops taking her medicine. I don't understand why but that woman should be in a hospital where they keep crazy people."

"I've got to go Lindy. He wants me to clean the study."

"Hum," Lindy said with a smirk.

"What's that supposed to mean?"

"Nothing, I just know Edward Wallingford more than any girl should." Rebecca didn't have a clue what Lindy was talking about and her placid face revealed as much. "You just watch out for him."

"Why?"

"Come on Rebecca. Do you really think he loves that old lady?"

"I never thought about it at all."

"Well, no honey. He loves her money, which is the only reason she hasn't been put away somewhere yet. He also loves going after the help. Just watch yourself."

"Thanks," Rebecca said, but she hardly needed Lindy's advice. She was already watching Edward Wallingford. Though it had been her naive dream to have a white man fall madly in love with her, and marry her, she was smart enough to know that her dream did not include Edward Wallingford. There was something about the man that just seemed dangerous. Though he was tall and good looking by any woman's standards and he even resembled her father, but there was something sinister in his dark eyes.

In the study, Rebecca tried to tidy up as quickly as she could. After speaking with Lindy, she had a feeling that Mr. Wallingford had planned to follow her to the study. After she had dusted the entire room, she used a solution of vinegar and water to clean the windows. As she wiped vigorously at the windows, she heard the door close behind her and knew that she had run out of time. She turned slowly but Edward Wallingford moved quickly and was only arm's length away by the time she saw him. "My, my," he said. "That is a nasty bruise. I do apologize for my wife. She sometimes has these episodes. She really doesn't mean you any harm." Rebecca did not answer but watched him as he slowly closed the distance between them.

Lindy was just leaving the guest room when she saw Mr. Wallingford slip quietly into the study. She didn't have to guess what his intentions were as it had only been a year since she had experienced an unwelcomed meeting with Mr. Wallingford in the study. Lindy hurried to the dining room where Lillian was busy polishing the silver. Lindy came over to the table and announced that Rebecca was in the study. Lillian thought her announcement was curious until she looked at Lindy. Although she wore a smile on her face, Lillian detected some sort of warning in her hazel eyes.

"What is it?" she said to Lindy.

"I think you should go to the study now."

"What on earth for?"

"Just go, Lillian. Hurry."

As Lillian rose from the table, Lindy quickly took her place and began polishing silver. She took one last glance at Lindy who nodded her head slightly. Once out of the sight of the other house staff, Lillian lifted the hem of her dress and ran to reach the study as quickly as she could.

Rebecca had not been afraid of Mr. Wallingford until that moment. She knew what he meant to do and she felt powerless to stop him. She began to shake.

"You're trembling. Are you catching a chill?"

"No, sir."

"Then why are your hands shaking so, are you afraid of me?"

"No sir," Rebecca said. She turned away from him and continued to wash the windows, trying hard to hide her apprehension. In the next moment, she felt him. She felt his hands resting on her trembling shoulders and she felt him through the layers of petticoats and her woolen dress as he pressed against her back. She felt his hot breath on her neck and she could smell him. The pungent smell of cologne with a mixture stale tobacco and lye soap assailed her. Rebecca didn't know what to do so she just stood there as still as if she were rooted in that spot. He began to kiss her neck as his fingers started to probe up her dress.

"Please," she whispered. "Don't do this."

"Why do you resist me? I know that this is what you want. I'm sure that you've done this before, a pretty little country girl like yourself."

"No, sir," Rebecca said with as much force as tiny voice could muster, as she tried to wiggle out of his grasp. "I ain't ever been with a man and I'm begging you not to do this Mr. Wallingford."

"I won't hurt you, I promise."

As soon she felt him move, she swung around and tried to side step him, but he was much too fast and far stronger than she was. He grabbed her by the wrist and turned her around in one swift motion. Before she knew it, she was face down on the window seat, his body covering hers as his hands pulled at her petticoat. She felt his fingers caressing the soft folds between her legs. Rebecca began to cry softly.

Edward heard her sobbing but he chose to ignore her. His heart pounded and his breath came in quick gasp as he undid his trousers. He wanted this girl from the first moment he saw her and he meant to have her. He had come this far and he saw no reason why her tears should stop him from fulfilling his need. He wanted Rebecca more than he could ever remember wanting another woman, but she continued to sob. With one swift movement, he parted her legs. Rebecca was still struggling to free herself when she felt her petticoat rip up the seam. She was exposed now and it was only a matter of time before he would enter her. Again, his hands were probing and his breathing was heavy. Desperation forced Rebecca to struggle even harder and then they both heard the loud clap of the study door as it slammed against its jam.

Edward jumped to his feet, exposing himself to the intruder. Rebecca quickly got to her feet, trying unsuccessfully to adjust her torn petticoat she ran behind her mother. Lillian didn't say a word but her eyes narrowed and fury blazed in her face. For one brief moment, she didn't see this rich northern man about to rape her daughter, she saw Big Bill forcing himself on her as a young girl. She grabbed the poker from the fireplace and approached Edward as if she meant to bring it down on his head but Rebecca stepped in front of her.

"No Mama! No! Let's just go!"

There was no explanation or apology Edward Wallingford could offer that would appease this situation. As he continued to adjust his clothing, he looked at Lillian and Rebecca with a spiteful expression on his face and finally said, "Your daughter is right. I think it best if you both just leave."

Lillian put her arms around her daughter. "Did he hurt you?"

"No. I just want to leave this evil house, Mama." Arm in arm, they moved toward the door and Edward sat down at his desk as if nothing had happened. At the door Lillian turned to face him again.

"Why?" she said.

"Excuse me?"

"Why do white men think that black women are just there for the taking? Why are you not satisfied with your own women?" Lillian knew even as she asked the question that he would not, in fact could not answer the question.

The question both shocked and outraged Edward. "Get out!" he yelled. "Leave my property immediately or I will have you both arrested."

Lillian knew that he meant what he said. Though neither had committed a crime, Lillian also knew that the constable would believe any lie Edward Wallingford could spew. "I don't doubt for a second that you would have us both arrested. I do not plan to stay in your house any longer than necessary. I pray that one day you will burn in hell for your secret crimes." Lillian then softly closed the door and wasted no time gathering her and Rebecca's things and leaving Wallingford House.

In the kitchen both Mrs. Byrne and Della wanted to know why they were leaving but Lillian gave them no explanation. Della shook her head and grumbled something under her breath. Lillian had the feeling that she knew because it had happened before. Lindy gave a sympathetic nod to Rebecca to indicate that she had a good idea of what happened.

It was near four in the afternoon and Mr. Briggs and his wagon would not be by for at least a couple of hours. Lillian knew that they could not wait for him on Wallingford property, so they began the long and dangerous walk back to the city.

Just as they had when they had escaped from the Gloria Plantation, they kept off of the main roads and traveled under the cover of deep foliage until they came to the bridge. There was only one bridge over the Schuylkill River and the women would have to be very careful when they chose to cross. They would be completely in the open as they crossed the bridge, a very dangerous situation.

By now, the bruise over Rebecca's eye was a large knot and the bruise on her cheek was more obvious. "Did he do that to you?" Lillian asked.

"No. Mrs. Wallingford hit me with her boot then she slapped me. Lindy says that she's not right in her head. She says she belongs where they keep crazy people."

Lillian just shook her head. She wanted to say that they would be better off not working in that house, but all she could think of at that moment was that she needed to get another job. How would she manage now that she would not have money to pay for their care?

They had been walking for what seemed to be nearly an hour before they heard the sound of a horse and buggy behind them. There were only two estates that far up the hill so the rider would have to be from Wallingford House or their neighbors. "Shssh," Lillian said. "There's someone coming." Lillian and Rebecca moved back further into the woods so as not to be seen. The elaborate bronzed "W" on the side of the carriage told Lillian that the carriage was definitely from Wallingford House. However, she was happy to see that it was Gabriel at the reins and not Edward. Lillian stepped from behind the bushes and waved down the driver. Gabriel jumped down from the carriage and ran to them. Genuine concern was on his face as enveloped both Lillian and Rebecca in his arms. "Lindy told me that Mr. Wallingford fired you both. Why, what happened?"

"Let's just say that I caught Mr. Wallingford doing something that he would not want known. And now that I know who these people really are, I would not spend another moment under their roof." Lillian said.

"I am sorry to see you leave," he said. "I left as soon as Lindy told me you had gone. I couldn't let you two walk all the way back to the city. These woods are crawling with slave catchers. Come on, I'll take you into the city."

"Thank you, Gabriel," Lillian said.

"Did he give you permission to take the carriage out?" Rebecca wanted to know.

"No, but I don't think he will miss it. He's probably still in his study trying to figure out what he'll tell Mrs. Wallingford about your sudden departure."

Gabriel took Lillian and Rebecca to the house on Lombard Street. Before leaving, he promised to keep in touch and that he would visit whenever he was in the city. Lillian and Rebecca both thanked and hugged him before he climbed back into the carriage to head back to the estate. "Oh, and Gabriel," Lillian said. "Tell Lindy I said thank you." He nodded and then snapped the reins and horse lurched forward.

Inside her small bedroom, Lillian went down on her knees and prayed. She thanked God that she had not hit Mr. Wallingford with the poker as she had wanted to do. She also thanked God for Lindy who led her to the study in time to save Rebecca. In the nine months that she had worked for the Wallingford she had been in the study only once before. She had no reason to be there until today. She had no idea how or when she could find work, so she prayed that God would take care of her and Rebecca.

Once inside the house, Rebecca moved through the house as if in a trance. She sat down at the kitchen table, a blank expression on her face. Lillian wanted to say something, but what could she say that would change what Rebecca was feeling? She wanted to assure her that everything would be all right, that it wouldn't ever happen again; but how could she say those things when she knew that it could *very well* happen again. Women had little protection from the lust of men and black women had no protection. Lillian moved around the kitchen making tea and tiding up an already clean kitchen. Finally, Rebecca said, "Why, Mama? I thought they liked me."

Lillian sat down beside Rebecca and took her unblemished hands into her own. She didn't know what to say.

"I really thought that Mrs. Wallingford liked me. I knew that Mr. Wallingford thought I was pretty because I would catch him staring at me, but I never thought he would try to hurt me."

"I knew that there was something strange about Ella Wallingford from the beginning but I had no idea about Edward Wallingford. He seemed so reserved, so dignified. I never would have guessed that he was the kind of man to take advantage of the help." Lillian said in a low voice.

"But why, Mama? He said he knew that I had been with a man before. He didn't believe me when I said that I hadn't and I begged him not to do it, but he just wouldn't stop. Thank God you came in when . . ."

"Rebecca," Lillian said. "Try to put it out of your mind. I can't explain what makes men do such things, just know that it happens and especially to black women. We have no protection against such men so we must protect ourselves. Now, no more talk of the Wallingford's. They served a purpose for a time now we've got to move on with our lives."

Rebecca's bruises healed but her encounter with Edward Wallingford had changed her in ways that were not readily visible. She kept more to herself and was quiet much of the time. Lillian hoped that the incident had changed her desire to live as a white woman, but she feared that the entire matter had strengthened Rebecca's determination to become a part of the race she thought would award her a measure of respect. Lillian knew her daughter well and she knew that Rebecca, with her limited knowledge of the world, would convince herself that Edward Wallingford would have never forced himself on a white woman. However, Lillian knew that men like Edward Wallingford had no such limits on their lust.

With no work and no money, Lillian again turned to the church for help. She checked with the church office at least three times a week looking for work. The clerk was very helpful and supplied her with information about several places where she could apply for work. For three weeks she walked the streets of Philadelphia, took rides from Mr. Briggs and others, applying for work everywhere she was told to go. She even applied for work in a textile factory outside the city. Each time she was turned down. Either the jobs had been filled or she wasn't exactly the person the employer was looking to hire. Frustrated and near broke, Lillian sought to make money in other ways. She watched Althea tend the small garden in the back of her house and take her baskets of fruits and vegetables to

New Market every weekend. She knew that Althea wasn't making a lot of money with her small garden, but it seemed a far better choice than starving.

That May Althea helped Lillian to turn over the soil in the small space behind her house and prepare it for planting tomatoes, peppers, and a host of herbs. She had become handy with a needle when she was on the plantation so she began to make modest cotton dresses which she would then sell to some of the shops along the east end of Market Street. Although meager, it was a living. She could barely pay Althea the rent and there was never any extra money. Althea was sympathetic and did not pressure Lillian for the money she knew she didn't have. "Don't worry," Althea would say. "We'll manage and maybe next week will be better."

In the weeks that followed, Rebecca was able to get a job at the only African American Library in the city, which was run by the Pennsylvania Abolition Society on Front Street, below Chestnut. The pay was measly but the benefit was that she could read as many books as she liked.

It was August 1, 1840, a day of celebration in the African American community. The Freedom Day Jubilee was a celebration of Britain's emancipation of the slaves held in the West Indies. However, though the emancipation went into effect in 1834, Blacks in America were not quick to participate in the celebration because they viewed the emancipation as bogus. Besides the fact that the institution of slavery was still active in the Americas, the slaves of the West Indies were still in bondage until they passed through a required period of apprenticeship. The holiday didn't really take hold in the United States until the end of the apprenticeship period in 1838.

On this day, the streets were teaming with thongs of people. There were sidewalk vendors of all manner of foods. There was fried chicken and fish, salads, and sausages for sale. People were selling crafts, quilts, flowers, herbs, and vegetables. People were singing and dancing.

Lillian was in no mood to celebrate but on this sweltering hot day, when even the air seemed to be charged with the sounds of celebration, a soft knock on Lillian's door brought her running from the back of the house. Lillian opened the door casually. She caught her breath when she saw Lindy standing on the stoop outside her door. Lillian's hair was tied up in a rag and her face and clothes were smudged with soil when she opened the door. She was so happy to see Lindy standing there that she gave no thought to her soiled clothes and hands as she hugged the girl happily. "Oh my God, Lindy! I can't believe you're here." As she embraced the girl, she saw Gabriel standing a few feet away on the sidewalk. "Gabriel, you too? Come in, come in, I am so glad to see you both. Make yourselves at home while I clean up a bit."

Lindy and Gabriel had wisely used the Freedom Day Celebration as an excuse to go into the city and to the Lombard Street house for a visit. As the three sat at Lillian's small kitchen table sipping homemade lemonade and munching on cold chicken and biscuits, Gabriel told Lillian why she was having such a difficult time finding work.

"Old Edward had no problem cooking up a lie that would satisfy Ella." He spoke of his employers with a familiarity that was steeped in distain. "While her mind was still in a laudanum induced haze, he told her that you were the worse housekeeper Wallingford House had ever hired and that Rebecca was a fast little tart who continuously made sexual advances toward him and Charles."

Lillian was not surprised. "Well, I was sure he would say something to cover his behind."

"Yeah," said Lindy. "Mrs. Wallingford did not question what he said. She was so distraught over his leaving that she could hardly think of anything else. But once he was gone, she had no problem spreading the lie to all of her friends and neighbors. You and Rebecca were the talk of the Overbrook mansions for weeks. Mrs. Wallingford wanted to make sure that you wouldn't find work in Overbrook ever again."

Lillian thought for a moment, her expression bland. Then she shook her head. "I don't understand how people with so much can be so hateful."

The three of them talked for a while longer and Lillian noticed for the first time how Gabriel looked at Lindy when she spoke. Then she saw him cover Lindy's hand with his own. "So," she said smiling. "How long have you two been a couple?"

Lindy blushed and hide her face behind her hands while Gabriel beamed with pride. "Is it that obvious?" Gabriel said.

"Well, not at first but I couldn't help noticing how you both seem so happy with each other. When did all this happen?"

"Gab and I have been seeing each other for more than a year now but we didn't want anyone to know until we are able to leave Wallingford House."

"You're planning to leave? But, Gabriel, you've been there since you were a boy."

For a moment, Lillian thought she saw a look of sadness on his handsome face. "Yes, I have. As a child I had the protection of Captain Todd Phillips, Mrs. Wallingford's brother. It wasn't until his death, when I was fifteen that I became Mrs. Wallingford's ward. I have never liked the woman. Captain Phillips treated me like a son. Mrs. Wallingford never let me forget that I was no more than a charity case for her and that she expected some divine blessing for her charity. I have been saving money since I came to Wallingford House and in a year or two, I think I will have enough for Lindy and I to open a little shop and move into the city."

Lillian couldn't have been happier for Lindy and Gabriel. The three of them laughed and talked for a while longer before Gabriel said they should be getting back to Overbrook. Lillian embraced them both, thanked them for coming, and wished them well.

As summer wore into the hazy, sweltering heat of August, there came a time when the cupboards in Lillian's kitchen were bare. The tomatoes, vegetables, and herbs were not yet ready for harvest and Lillian's orders for cotton dresses were few. Over the past few months, Althea had given Lillian so much that her pride would not allow her to ask for more. She had been rationing their paltry food supplies for weeks. Both she and Rebecca had lost weight but Lillian hardly noticed her own change in appearance while Rebecca's weight loss seemed stark. She was a slightly built girl to begin with, and now she looked dreadfully thin with sunken dark eyes. Lillian's heart ached every time she looked at Rebecca.

One day when Rebecca came home from her library job, she brought a half a loaf of fresh baked bread, wrapped in paper. "It was all I could afford," she said apologetically. They silently ate bread and drank warm lemonade.

It had become customary to sit on the front steps in the evenings because it was too hot to stay indoors. She and Althea could talk a while as the heat of the day evaporated and cooler winds blew in from the Delaware River. One evening as the three sat outside, Rebecca talked about books and the library and Althea talked about church events planned and her garden but her friend Lillian had little to say. Finally, Lillian complained of a headache and left Althea and Rebecca on the steps as she went to her bedroom. There was a small wooden box hidden under her bed soon after she and Rebecca had moved into the house. Lillian took out the box and gingerly opened it and removed the folded heavy sheets of paper that certified that she and Rebecca were no longer slaves. In the bottom of the box was a small folded piece of paper that Lillian couldn't even read the day she had placed it in the box. She unfolded the paper now and read, *"I will always be here for you Lillian. If you ever need anything, come to me at 924 Walnut Street, Philadelphia. Elizabeth Gable Vance."*

"Huh," Lillian said. She was surprised that it had been almost a year and she had no idea that she and Beth were living only a few blocks away from each other. She sat there a few moments as she contemplated reaching out to Beth for help.

Suddenly there was a loud scream. Lillian jumped to her feet, dropping the contents of the box on the floor. Another scream and Lillian knew that it was

213

Rebecca who screamed. She gathered the hem of her dress ran down the steps. Before reaching the front door, there was another scream. This time it was Althea. When Lillian reached the front of the house she saw Rebecca standing on the sidewalk with her eyes wide and both hands covering her mouth. "What is it," Lillian asked. She followed Rebecca's gaze and saw that Althea's door was wide open.

"He's back," was all Rebecca said. The screams were so loud and so alarming that other neighbors had begun to gather outside Althea's door.

Lillian tore into Althea's house while Rebecca tried to rally some of the men to intervene. You could clearly hear Althea's screams now as she begged her husband to stop hitting her. No one moved to help.

Once inside the house, Lillian looked around for anything she could use as a weapon. She could smell the alcohol before she even saw Bernie. She took the small shovel from the fireplace and moved slowly toward the kitchen. Althea was on the floor and Bernie held her by her hair. "Give it to me," he snarled.

"I swear Bernie, I don't have any money." Althea said and he punched her in the face again. Blood spurted from her nose and she coughed and spit a stream of fresh blood. "Please, Bernie, please," she begged.

"Let her go," Lillian said in a hoarse, almost growling voice.

"Look lady. You ain't got no right to come between a man and his wife. Mind your own business."

"I said, let her go," Lillian said again.

He did let Althea go, but only so, he could come after Lillian. "Oh, so you want some of this?"

"Yeah, Lillian said. " I'm not afraid of you. You're a coward." He stumbled forward. "Get out of here Althea," Lillian yelled.

As soon as Bernie was close enough, Lillian brought the shovel down on his out stretched arm and he winced as he snatched his arm back. In the next moment, he was on her, landing his fist on her face with such forced that it knocked her back and the shovel flew from her hand. She scrambled on her hands and knees to retrieve it, as he lumbered forward. He reached down and grabbed one of her feet and Lillian began to kick him in the face with her other foot. He reeled backward but quickly regained his footing and came forward again. Lillian was on her feet again. She drew back and threw the only punch she had ever thrown in her life, hitting him square on the jaw. Surprised and encouraged by her own strength, she then flung herself at him, hitting him hard and furiously. But she was hardly a match for his strength. With one arm, he flung her across the room. She landed on her bottom and slid across the wooden kitchen floor. As Bernie staggered forward, Lillian got to her feet and grabbed a knife from the sink. "Take one more step and I swear I'll plunge this blade so far into your gut that you will surely meet God before the sun rises."

The moonlight that streamed through the back window made the blade twinkle as Lillian waved it in front of Bernie's swollen face. He took one look at the blade and began to back away. Lillian let out a breath of relief and relaxed her shoulders sure that Bernie was finally leaving. But as soon as she dropped the knife down to her side, he was on her again, punching her hard in the face. She dropped the knife and Bernie kicked it out of reach as he continued to strike her over and over again.

Rebecca had run the few blocks to the constable's office and returned with two large policemen. They rushed into the house just in time to stop Bernie from landing another punch on Lillian's already swollen face. The two policemen grabbed Bernie and wrestled him to the floor. As they shackled him and lead him from the house, he spewed obscenities to both Lillian and Althea, promising to kill them both the next time.

Althea was on her knees in the front room shaking uncontrollably when Lillian went to her. She took one look at Lillian's swollen face and began to cry. "Oh my God! He hurt you."

"I'll be alright," Lillian whispered. "We will both be alright. The police took him away."

"He'll be back, Lillian. I've been through this before. They are only gonna keep him until he sobers and as soon as they let him go, he'll be back."

Rebecca came in with a pan of water and some rags to clean away the blood from the faces of both women. Lillian was quiet as she dabbed at her swollen and bruised cheek but Althea talked on nervously. "I know he meant what he said. He really will kill us both. It's only a matter of time before they let him go and he comes for both of us. You should have stayed out of it Lillian. I have survived worse from him, now you are right in the middle of my problem."

Suddenly Lillian was angry again. "Why, Althea?" she screamed as she got to her feet.

"Why? I don't know what you mean."

"You said that you have survived worse. I want to know why. Why do you allow this man to beat you and you just wait for the next time?"

"What else am I going to do?"

"Leave!"

"But where would I go? What about my houses, they are all that I own?"

Lillian thought for a moment. "Listen Althea. We are all going to leave in the morning. Whenever they let Bernie go, we won't be here."

"But what about my houses?" Althea said.

"I don't know. Maybe we can sell them later."

"Where will we go?"

"I know someone that I think will help us."

Rebecca just listened to the conversation, for the first time feeling sorry for Miss Althea. She couldn't understand any more than Lillian could, why Miss Althea would just let this man hurt her whenever he took a notion. Then, when she heard her mother say that she knew someone who could help, Rebecca knew she spoke of Miss Beth. Just the possibility of moving away from Lombard Street was appealing to Rebecca. She had not been able to shake the stigma left in the wake of the incident that left Jonah Mason scarred for life. People still stared at her, pointed, and whispered behind her back. She was the tart that got Jonah hurt and the neighborhood made it clear that they did not intend to forgive her. Moving away was more than appealing to Rebecca.

"Lillian, I can't leave everything that I own. I just can't go."

"Are you telling me that these two houses mean more to you than your own life?"

Althea was quiet for a moment. "I don't know," she finally said.

"Look Althea, just leave for the time being. Maybe you can come back later or maybe you can sell these houses and buy another far away from Lombard Street. But you cannot stay here and just wait for the next beating."

Minutes passed as Althea tried to come to terms with leaving home. "Yes," she finally said. "You're right of course. I don't want to be here when they let Bernie out of jail."

∽

The next morning, shortly after sunrise, the three women left Lombard Street loaded down with their few belongings in backpacks and carpetbags. Their injured faces looked even worse in the light of day. Both had black eyes and the bruise on Lillian's cheek was swollen to the size of a small lemon. Althea had a busted lip and Lillian was sure that Bernie had cracked a few of Althea's ribs. She could hardly take a deep breath without pain.

The three women looked as if they were refugees from war, as they stood on the sidewalk in the affluent neighborhood in front of 924 Walnut Street. Lillian looked up at the property in awe. *It seems Miss Beth did very well for herself, she thought.*

"You two wait here," she said. The Iron Gate clanged loudly as she opened and closed it behind her. *What a beautiful house*, Lillian thought as she lifted the heavy doorknocker. She tapped it three times, took a step back and then waited. There was a peep through the window and then the door was cracked open slightly.

"Yes?" came the familiar voice.

"Miss Beth?"

"Yes?" It was early and Beth was still in her nightgown.

"It's me. It's Lillian."

With that, the door swung open wide. "Oh my God! Lillian I didn't recognize you. What on earth happened to your face?" In the next moment, Beth threw her arms around Lillian's neck. "All these months, I've wondered what happened to you. Where is Rebecca?"

"There," Lillian pointed. "Miss Beth, you said to come if I ever needed you,"

"Yes, yes," Beth said as she motioned for Rebecca and Althea to come closer.

"Well, I'm in a bit of trouble and I need your help."

Beth reached out and hugged Rebecca as if they had loved each other Rebecca's entire life. "Come in; come in, all of you." Beth eyed Althea and immediately noticed that her face was as battered as Lillian's was. "Oh my," she said.

After Beth had relieved them of their heavy bags, they sat around the table in her spacious kitchen and Lillian told Beth everything. She told her about the Wallingford's and not being able to find work after leaving the Wallingford's. She also told her of her friendship with Althea and Althea's contentious relationship with her husband Bernie. Rebecca and Althea just listened, seldom interjecting.

"Well, you've had quite a year but not to worry. I'm sure we can work something out. If you remember, before we left the hotel I offered you the position of housekeeper here with me. That offer is still open. I would be happy to have you run my house, for a wage, of course. I'm sure you know that Rebecca is also welcome to stay here." Beth then turned her attention to Althea.

"I am happy to meet you, Althea and I am really sorry for your troubles. I don't know you but I know that making friends has not been one of Lillian's best qualities. That is why I am sure that if Lillian befriended you, you must indeed be a very special lady."

"Thank you, Miss," Althea whispered.

"I'm not sure what you can do here, but you are welcome to stay. We will work out something."

"Thank you," she said again.

Beth showed them all around her house and they each picked the room they preferred. Beth brought rags and helped Lillian to wrap Althea's bruised and maybe cracked ribs. Althea winced with every touch and every breath. However, even in the midst of her agony, she smiled for the first time in a couple of days.

"Oh," Lillian said. "Looks to me like you are feeling a bit better?"

"Maybe a little," she said.

"That's because you know that you are safe."

"She's right," Beth said. "But this is only the beginning. You will flourish when you realize that you have nothing to worry about now. You'll see. I'm sure."

By evening, Lillian had familiarized herself with all the modern conveniences of Beth's kitchen and was comfortable preparing the evening meal.

After supper, the women sat in Beth's spacious garden at the back of the house. Beth was delighted to learn that both Lillian and Rebecca had learned to read and write. She was even more overjoyed to realize that reading had become a passion for Rebecca.

The cool breeze that usually came with the setting of the sun was absent on this August evening. Instead of a breeze, the air was heavy with heat and so much moisture that it seemed to weigh everything down. The women talked most of the night. Beth told Lillian how James worried about her and Rebecca.

"You look surprised," Beth said.

"I am. Though I've thought of Gloria a lot, I never had a single thought about Massa James."

"Just James, Lillian. He isn't your master anymore and he thinks of himself as family. He recognizes that Rebecca is his niece and he is concerned for her. I can't wait to write and tell him that you two are here with me. I think he will be pleased."

Lillian didn't answer but she wondered why James would be pleased that she and Rebecca were living with Miss Beth. He'd never shown a bit of care or concern for her in all the years she'd known him.

Over the next few weeks, the women settled into a comfortable routine. Althea and Lillian's wounds healed but Althea had nightmares about her ordeal at the hands of her husband. She still jumped at the slightest noise. She also had a bit of a problem taking orders from Beth and Lillian. After all, she had never been a slave and had never worked as a domestic in the home of a white family. She still saw herself as a free black woman, even as she knew she could probably never go home again.

Althea also worried about her property and expressed her concern to Lillian one evening. "Don't worry. Tomorrow I will walk down to New Market and try to see Mr. Briggs. I'm sure he will be able to tell us what to do and I'll also ask him to keep an eye on the property." That seemed to satisfy Althea.

The next morning, Lillian kept her word and made her way down the route where she knew Mr. Briggs would travel on his daily run to Overbrook. She waited only a few minutes before she saw the familiar wagon and two nags plodding over the hard earth. Mr. Briggs saw her right away and reined the nags to a stop. "Climb up," he said urgently.

"Well, good morning," Lillian said cheerfully.

"Climb up, I said. It isn't safe for you to be standing out in the open. Climb up."

Lillian did as she was told and took a seat right behind Mr. Briggs. "Why is it not safe for me? What are you talking about?"

"Althea's husband Bernie. The constable released him just a few days after you three disappeared. He's living in Althea's house and he's been going around telling the whole neighborhood that he's gonna kill her and you if he ever sets eyes on the two of you again. Now, I've heard men talk like that most of my life and usually, I think it is all just a bunch of talk. But, there is something about this man that makes me believe him. He's had a bad life and in his sick mind, he wants to lay the blame square on Althea and now you."

"But, that's Althea's house. He can't just move in and take it over, can he?"

"He's her husband. Ain't no law gonna put a man out of his wife's house. You tell her to stay as far away from that house as she can. It might be better if she were to leave Philadelphia altogether."

They rode in silence for a little while. The wagon took passengers on and let some others off before Mr. Briggs turned the wagon and headed back to the city. "Where you all living, anyway?"

"We're all working for a lady named Elizabeth Vance up on Walnut."

"Vance? She kin?"

"No. She used to own me."

Mr. Briggs raised an eyebrow but did not pry further. He dropped Lillian off just where he'd picked her up. "I'll find you if I get good news to report but until then, you two stay away from the city."

"Thank you, Mr. Briggs."

Althea did not take Beth's news well. She was sickened by the thought of Bernie living in her house and the news that he'd shared his sinister intentions to kill her with the entire neighborhood. This brought on another series of nightmares and daytime fears. Althea became an emotional wreck for the next few weeks.

CHAPTER 13

The Lioness

Jefferson had arranged for Beth and his mother to lunch together and Beth reluctantly agreed. The mid-September afternoon was warm and the sky was clear blue and cloudless. However, the inside of the Martin house was cold and dark. You could almost feel the melancholy. One step inside that house was akin to passing from one season to the next. The darkness was almost morbid. Clarisse's nurse opened the door, and then discretely disappeared to leave Beth and Clarisse time alone. Beth hung her straw hat and purse on a hook in the entry hall and proceeded slowly toward the dining room. The table was set and Clarisse sat in her high backed chair at the far end of the table. "Good afternoon," Beth said trying to keep the uneasiness she felt from her voice.

"Good afternoon," Clarisse said. "It was good of you to accept my invitation. My son insisted that we get to know each other better."

Beth took a seat on Clarisse's left and she instinctively looked toward the empty chair on Clarisse's right. "Oh," Clarisse said apparently reading Beth's mind. "Jefferson will not be joining us today." At that moment, their cook came in bearing a tray of finger sandwiches, crackers, and cheese. She poured tall glasses of lemonade. "So, dear," Clarisse said as she unfolded her napkin and placed it in her lap. "Tell me a little about your life before Philadelphia."

Before Beth could answer, Clarisse had begun to say a blessing over the meal. Beth waited patiently. "I was raised here in Philadelphia," she said. "Well, just outside of Philadelphia."

"And you traveled to Virginia with your husband?"

"Not exactly. We did not wed until we were in Virginia."

"Ah, right. So you've said. Now tell me about your life in Virginia."

Beth took a bite from one of the sandwiches on her plate and when she looked up, the look on Clarisse's face was a scowl. "There isn't much to tell. I lived on a tobacco plantation until my husband died and then I returned to Philadelphia."

"According to what I've heard, you were married for seven years. Are you telling me that there was nothing in those seven years, worth sharing?"

Beth could feel heat rising in her face and knew she was likely flushed. "Just what is it you would like to know, Clarisse?

Clarisse smiled. It was an empty smile, void of any warmth or compassion. "You seem a little defensive, dear. I'm just trying to get to know the woman my son has chosen to marry." She continued to smile at Beth as she waited for a satisfactory answer, but Beth did not feel the need to give her an answer. Whatever appetite Beth had for lunch was lost in Clarisse's interrogations. Determined not to be goaded into saying something that she may later regret, Beth ignored Clarisse's question and quietly sipped her lemonade as she tried desperately to understand what Clarisse was searching for in this strange conversation. Several uncomfortable moments passed before Beth spoke. "So, it seems that you have some reservations about Jefferson's plans for us to marry. If that is so, I'm sure that Jefferson will happily ease your mind if you tell him of your misgivings. He is a grown man, after all. That is why I don't understand this cat and mouse game that you are trying to play with me?"

Clarisse's face gave away more than she would have liked. She seemed genuinely shocked at Beth's candor. "I did speak with my son but he is so smitten with you that he is unable to see what is plainly before him. I know exactly what and who you are, Mrs. Vance."

"Oh! And what am I, Clarisse?"

"You, my dear, are an opportunist, using your beauty and refinement to climb Philadelphia's social ladder which we both know would not be available to you without the right man at your side."

Beth laughed.

"No?" Clarisse said. "Then tell me dear, what exactly do you bring to this marriage? You have no property, no recognizable name, no family, and I presume no money."

Beth pushed her chair away from the table and stood. She took a deep breath, willing herself to control her anger and reminding herself that this was Jefferson's mother. "You're right," she said with a smile. "I have none of those things. It might surprise you to know that I didn't come to Philadelphia looking for a new husband. In fact, I was quite happy as a young widow without the fetters of marriage. However, your son fell in love with me, pursued me, and never once questioned me about my marriage or the time I spent in Virginia. I can assure you, Clarisse, I have no wish to climb social ladders. Furthermore, I want you to understand that this little party of yours will not dissuade me in the least. Jefferson is not your little boy anymore, he is a grown man and if Jefferson and I choose to marry, we will do so, and you will just have to learn to live with your son's decision." Beth took a sip from her glass and then placed it back on the table. "The only thing that you have accomplished this beautiful afternoon is revealing what a manipulative witch you are and the lengths you are willing to go to have your son unhappily tethered to your hip for the rest of your life."

"You know, you aren't the first woman Jefferson thought he wanted to marry."

"I don't doubt it and I am sure you were successful in scaring each one of them away."

"I did not scare them away. I only made Jefferson see those women for what and who they were and he chose to let them go."

By this time, Beth had retrieved her hat and purse and stood just inside the dining room. "Yes, I'm sure. I'm also sure that it would be easier for Jefferson to think that these women just weren't right for him than to believe that his loving mother was scheming to keep him all to herself." Beth turned and strode toward the door, yelling over her shoulder, "Enjoy the rest of your afternoon Mrs. Martin. We will see each other again sooner than you think."

⁓

Jefferson was not happy with Beth's new house servants. She supplied only a minimum of detail regarding the relationship between her and Lillian, which left Jefferson finding it difficult to understand her obvious devotion to an ex-slave.

Both mother and daughter were stunningly beautiful. Lillian was olive skinned, tall, slim, and carried herself with an elegance that was rarely seen in a woman of her station. Jefferson couldn't remember ever seeing a Negro woman with such dignity and presence. She moved about the house with an easy confidence that was hard to ignore. He found himself just staring at the woman on more than one occasion.

Her daughter, Rebecca was equally as beautiful. If he didn't know that Lillian was her mother, she could have easily been mistaken for a white woman. However, unlike her mother, Rebecca's eyes rarely met his eyes. Most of the time she greeted him silently with a bow of her head or a whispered greeting.

It was obvious that Lillian and her daughter were mulatto or quadroon and with Vance as their last name, Jefferson couldn't help but wonder if they were somehow related to Beth. He was offered very little explanation for the other woman, Althea, who appeared to be the oldest of the three. She was a big woman, tall and thick with a reddish complexion. She was scarred and solemn. She only spoke when spoken to, often with her hand trying to cover her scars.

He did not voice his objections to Beth's new house staff because he could not deny that Beth seemed happier with these women around. Beth was more than comfortable with Lillian and he had often caught snippets of their conversations. These were not the conversations that one usually heard between slave and mistress or employer and employee. They actually seemed to be friends. This was more than a little baffling to Jefferson, especially considering that Beth referred to Lillian as her former slave. Jefferson had assumed that after he and Beth married, she would move into the house with him and his mother, but it quickly became apparent that their planned nuptials would not take place any time in the near future and now Jefferson worried if they would ever take place at all. Beth was too comfortable in her own home with her own staff.

Beth's relationship with his mother posed an additional problem for his plans. He was learning that their easy association was little more than a sham for his benefit. Clarisse had begun to drop subtle hints that she didn't exactly agree with his choice for a mate. "But, mother, I thought you liked Beth," he'd said to her.

"I think Elizabeth Vance is a lovely woman and a good friend to you Jefferson."

"Mother, don't act as if you don't understand me. You know very well that Beth is much more than a good friend to me. You know of my intentions to marry Elizabeth."

"Oh," she feigned surprise. "I had no idea you planned to marry this woman. If you told me, it must have slipped my mind. I was under the impression that you two were friends. Had I known, I would have been obliged to inquire more of her background."

Jefferson knew his mother well and he knew that there must have been something Beth said or something someone else said about Beth, that caused this sudden change of heart. Whatever it was, Jefferson felt no obligation to appease his mother concerning his choice for a wife.

A couple of weeks later, Beth attended church services with Jefferson and his mother. The women barely spoke two words to each other. It would have been impossible for Jefferson not to notice that there was some umbrage between his mother and Beth. He waited until he and Beth were alone in the carriage before he brought up the subject. "I take it that lunch with my mother wasn't as pleasant as you led me to believe?"

Beth smiled. "No Jefferson, but I learned more about Clarisse in that half hour then I could have ever expected."

"Oh?"

"Look Jefferson, she's your mother and I don't want to disrespect either of you."

"Yes, she is my mother and I know her better than you think."

Beth sighed. "I think that she is a very smart woman but she is manipulative and uses her age and feebleness to keep you close. She even admitted that she has sabotaged previous relationships when she thought you might marry again."

Jefferson eyed Beth with a raised brow. "I see," he said. He was silent for some time as he thought about the things Beth said about his mother. "She means no harm," he finally said.

"I know Jefferson. She is trying to do whatever she can to keep you all to herself. How do you feel about that, though? Don't you think that you deserve a life? For God's sake Jefferson, you're close to forty years old."

He chuckled a little. "Beth, you give me no credit what so ever. As I said, I know my mother. If she has you believing that she can control what I do or who I marry, then you *are* the one who has been manipulated. I love my mother but she does not control me. Remember that Beth. She does not control me."

Jefferson may have sounded confident when speaking to Beth but he knew that no matter how much he wished it to be so; these two very strong willed women could not exist under the same roof. He didn't know how, but somehow he would have to make this work if he intended to keep the love of his life. He didn't want to lose Beth. He briefly considered leaving his mother in his house and moving in with Beth after their marriage. Now, with her new house staff, he thought that both scenarios were unlikely.

❧

It was a cool September evening and Lillian sat reading her Bible while Beth worked lackadaisically on her embroidery. She couldn't seem to keep her mind on the tedious stitching. She glanced over at Lillian who appeared content. Rebecca had not yet come home from the library and Althea had gone to her room hours ago.

"Do you still think of him?" Beth asked without warning.

Lillian looked up, startled, as much by the question as she was that Beth had asked it. "Yes," she whispered as she closed her Bible and turned her attention to Beth. "I don't want to think of him, but I can't seem to stop. I still see him. I think of other things of the past but nothing of the past is without David." She waited a few moments to see Beth's reaction to her confession but there was none. "What about you? Do you think of him?"

Beth was thoughtful for a few moments. "Well, it's like you said," she answered. "Nothing of the past is without David. We may both think about him but I'm sure our thoughts are much different. You still loved him."

Lillian thought she may have offended Beth by asking her the same question. But when she looked at the expression on Beth's face, she knew that there was a light heartedness in her statement and she began to laugh out loud. Beth laughed too for a few minutes. "Really though, don't you miss having a man?" Beth asked.

"No, I don't think I will ever love a man again. I don't feel quite right saying this to you but I loved David, practically all of my life. When he told me what Big Bill's journals said, it made me feel dirty. Oh, I don't mean just not clean. It made me feel dirty on the inside. I felt like I carried the smell of incest and no matter how many times I washed, I just could not get rid of the smell. Do you know what I mean?"

"Yes, I think so, but it sounds like you are blaming David. It wasn't his fault any more than it was your fault. With me, it was all David's fault because he knew that he was still in love with you when he brought me to Virginia. But with you, if you must blame anyone, it was Big Bill who kept David's birth a secret. David was just as devastated as we all were to learn the truth."

"Do you think that's why he killed himself or do you think it was because he found out that he wasn't white and he wasn't the true master of Gloria?"

Beth picked up her embroidery again. "I never thought about it," she said.

"Maybe," Lillian said thoughtfully. "I think that he couldn't bear to be master of Gloria once he found out that he could have been a slave just like me."

Both women were quiet for a few moments. It wasn't until that moment that Beth realized that David's true identity really meant she had actually been married to a colored man. The thought was startling and she gasped. *'Why didn't she think of this before now?'* Her embroidery dropped into her lap again. Her eyes stared but she saw nothing as her mind raced. Several minutes passed before she realized that Lillian was watching her.

"Miss Beth," Lillian whispered. "Are you all right?"

"I'm fine," Beth said. "I saw him after he read the journal and he was hurt and as upset as I've ever seen him. James and I tried to persuade him that no one need ever know that he was Mamie's son. He was still Big Bills first born and James was so ashamed of his father's actions that he was willing to go on keeping the secret. But David just couldn't bring himself to live with the lie any longer. It wasn't just about his relationship with you; it was also about learning that he wasn't the man he thought he was."

Lillian listened and was then quiet for some minutes before she whispered, "I don't think that I will ever be able to trust a man again."

Beth was surprised. "Lillian, that's foolish. You're still a young woman. You have many years ahead of you."

"I know, but I really think that I will spend them alone."

Lillian was content running Beth's house. After all, she was doing the same things she had done all of her life. However, conditions in Philadelphia were much different than they had been in Virginia. Beth hired a young woman named Hilda, whom they called Sweet, to help with the cleaning. Sweet's job was to keep the bedrooms clean and anything else Lillian deemed necessary. Lillian spent most of her time in the kitchen. She cooked all of the meals and did most of the shopping. Both she and Sweet saw to the laundry. Beth paid her well and as long as she was able to fulfill her responsibilities, she could come and go as she pleased.

Beth was right when she said that Lillian was still a very beautiful woman. She carried herself with her head held high and her back straight. What was seen as haughty in Virginia was confidence in Philadelphia and she turned many heads, both male and female. The one thing that was different was her attitude toward the women she met. Her demeanor was not spirited, but she was cordial and friendly. She had been invited to join virtually every group within the church and she politely declined each invitation. It was only a matter of time before she received an invitation from one of the single men of the church. Lillian knew that she would decline that invitation as well.

Lillian knew that Althea had not adjusted well to her domestic duties within Beth's household. She seemed to have changed since leaving her Lombard Street home. She was quiet most of the time. Lillian and Beth had tried unsuccessfully to coax Althea out of her melancholy but her sadness was so profound that nothing Lillian could do or say could reach Althea. That is why it did not come as much of a surprise when Althea appeared at the door of the sitting room dressed in her shawl and hat with her packed carpetbag in hand. Lillian looked up from her Bible and Beth dropped her embroidery into her lap yet again.

"Althea," Lillian said. "Where are you going?"

"I'm sorry Lillian, but I've got to go home, to my own house."

"Are you sure that is what you want to do?" Beth asked.

Althea turned her attention to Beth. "Miss Beth, you've been very kind to me and I thank you, but this is not the life for me. I need to be in my own home. I hope you understand."

Beth nodded. "Yes Althea, I understand."

Lillian did not understand. "What about Bernie? " He is a dangerous man Althea. What will happen the next time he wants to hurt you? I know you want to go home, but it just isn't safe."

"Yes, I know what kind of man Bernie is and there was a time when I loved that man. I married him. Bernie is mean because he is just so full of hate from all the hurt that he's suffered. Maybe, with God's help, I can find the man he used to be and help him with his drinking and all the hurt he feels."

"And what if you can't help him? He could kill you the next time. In fact, he's already promised to do just that."

"Lillian, I love you. You have been the best friend I've ever had and I thank God for bringing you to my door that day but I've got to do this, I've got to go home. As far as Bernie beating me again or killing me, well I'm just gone leave that in God's hands."

Lillian went to Althea and embraced her. The two women held on to each other for several minutes. "I'll be all right, Lillian. I promise."

"I'll worry about you."

"I'll come back for a visit and you'll see."

Lillian walked Althea to the front gate and with tears in her eyes, she waved goodbye to her friend as Althea moved quickly down the street.

Back in the sitting room with Beth she said, "I got a real bad feeling about Althea going back to that man."

"You've done all that you could possibly do for her Lillian. Althea is the only one who can decide what is right for her and apparently, she thinks that going back to her husband is the right thing to do."

Lillian said no more on the subject but the thought of Althea being back with Bernie would weigh heavily on her for several weeks.

CHAPTER 14

The Glory Plantation
Virginia

Brother to Brother

It was the last week of August and harvest season on Gloria Plantation. Because this was his first experience growing tobacco, Louis knew that he would need to rely on the expertise of others who had gone through the process before. James readily gave him the names of field hands who he thought would be worthy assistants to the new Overseer.

In the past, James had gone out to the fields every day to evaluate the process and Louis knew that most planters kept a watchful eye on the harvest. But James was curiously absent on this day. In fact, it had been a couple of days since Louis saw James.

The heat began to rise almost as soon as the sun began its slow eastern climb and by midday, it was unbearably hot. Louis was use to the heat of southern climates but this day was by far the hottest weather he'd ever experienced. He allowed more than the usual number of water breaks for the field hands, but even that wasn't enough. Two field hands already passed out due to the heat and he was sure that there would be others before the end of the day. If time were not of the utmost importance, Louis would have gladly called an early day, but there were acres to harvest and he was told that harvesting too late could result in poor quality tobacco.

It was early afternoon when he decided that he would go in for something to eat and a cool drink. Hopefully, he would be able to speak with James. "Afternoon," Nan said as Louis came into the kitchen house.

"Afternoon, Nan."

Sliced ham and biscuits with a tall drink of lemonade waited for him on the table. "Thank you," he said as he sat and began to devour the small meal. "Massa James been around?"

"Massa James never left his room today."

"Didn't come down for breakfast either," Inez said.

"Is he ill?"

"I don't know. He didn't say he was feeling poorly when I saw him last night and I ain't seen or heard a thing from him today."

Louis stuffed the last of the ham into his mouth with a big bite from the biscuit. "I'm going up to check on him," he said. Nan handed him a towel and he hastily wiped his mouth and hands and then headed for the main house.

He encountered Sally upon reaching the landing of the second floor. She looked as if she had swallowed her tongue. "Oh!" she said as she jumped back. "Massa Louis you scared me."

"Sorry," he said softly. "I didn't mean to scare you and remember, Sally. I'm just Louis. I am not your Master. Just Louis."

"Louis," she repeated.

"Have you seen Massa James this morning?"

"No sir. He wouldn't even let me come in to tidy up and change the linen. He said, 'not now Sally.' I just closed the door. And . . ." Sally would have gone on for several minutes had Louis not stopped her in mid-sentence.

"Thank you," he said. Louis moved passed Sally who still stood with her back against the wall as if she thought he would bite her. He tapped lightly on the door of James' bedroom and waited. There was no response and he heard no sound coming from the room. He knocked again and softly called out James' name. There was still no response so Louis slowly turned the knob and went inside.

James was lying face down, across the bed. His head hung over the side of the bed. He did not move or give the slightest indication that he knew someone had entered the bedroom. Louis rushed over to him and turned him over on his back. His body was burning with fever. He had obviously spit up some blood as his nightshirt was streaked with blood. "James, James," Louis said as he shook his brother and tried to revive him. At first, James eyes seemed to open but simply rolled back and he seemed to have lost consciousness again.

Louis called for Sally and told her to fetch Nan. He managed to pull James into the center of the bed, putting several pillows under his head. Briefly, James opened his eyes and uttered a few incoherent words before he slipped back into the haze of fever. His body was clammy and seemed to be drained of all color. Louis pulled off his soiled nightshirt and scoured the drawers of his bureau until he found a clean nightshirt.

A moment later Nan was there. "Oh my God," she said when she saw James.

"Get some cool water and rags," Louis said. "I'll wipe him down while you send someone for the doctor. Do you know who his doctor is, Nan?"

"Yes. Dr. Winston."

"How far away is Dr. Winston?"

"I don't know but I know it ain't as far as Richmond."

Louis frowned. This was a problem that only he could solve. There wasn't another white man on the plantation and to send one of the slaves would just be foolish. They could be stopped on the road and detained or captured if they couldn't produce a pass signed by James. "All right, change of plans. I will change James and then you and Sally take turns keeping his head cool while I ride for the doctor."

"Yes, but how will you find Dr. Winston?"

"I'll find him. You just get some cool water and rags and hurry."

When Nan came back with a pan of cool water and rags, Louis asked the two women to wait in the hall while he wiped James down and put on the clean nightshirt. Dazed, James managed to open his eyes briefly before consciousness slipped away again. After calling the women back into the room, he pulled open the curtains and raised the three windows that were shut tightly to keep out flying insects. "I will be back as soon as I can. Just try to keep his head cool."

"I will," Nan said.

Louis ended the harvesting for the day and his decision was met with shouts of joy as most of the field hands were near to passing out after toiling under the hot sun most of the day. As soon as they were dismissed, Louis saddled his horse and went to find the doctor.

The road was virtually deserted and Louis pushed his stead as hard as he'd ever ridden. It was nearly an hour before he encountered another person on the road and he quickly asked to be directed to Dr. Winston's house. He was only a few miles away.

An elderly woman whom Louis assumed to be the doctor's wife answered the door and went to get the doctor. Louis explained that he was there on behalf of James Vance and beckoned the doctor to come to the Gloria plantation as soon as possible. Dr. Winston did not hesitate. After a few words with his wife, he and Louis set out for Gloria with all haste.

As soon as they arrived, the doctor immediately went in to see his patient and was with James for more than thirty minutes while Louis nervously waited in the downstairs parlor.

When Dr. Winston finally emerged, he asked to speak with the next of kin and Nan lead him to Louis. His skepticism was written in his eyes as he said, "YOU are the next of kin?"

"Yes," Louis said. "I am his brother. My name is Louis Bissette."

"I've known this family most of my life. I knew Big Bill since we were both boys, skipping stones at the river's edge but I don't know you, sir."

Louis did not answer right away. Then with a calm voice that he struggled to keep even, he said. "Well sir, if you knew my father then I'm sure you are aware, as we have recently learned, that he had many children, some of which were unclaimed before his death."

"And your mother?" the doctor asked.

"A slave girl named Martina."

That name obviously meant something to the old doctor because the expression on his face went through an obvious change and he asked no more questions. He turned his back on Louis and began to pace around the room as he spoke. "Well Louis, I have unfortunate news to report. Your brother seems to have Pneumonia. In fact, I believe that he has been ill for quite some time and likely just ignored the symptoms." He went into his bag and handed Louis two bottles of medicine." Make sure he takes a generous spoonful of the red one twice a day and a spoonful of the yellow liquid before bed. It will help him sleep."

"Will he be all right, Doctor Winston?"

"Though it is known that Pneumonia kills hundreds of people each year, I believe he will recover in time. My fear is that because he had this infection for some time, he may be left with some permanent damage to his lungs."

"Is he awake now? Can I see him?"

"Yes, but the medicine will keep him pretty much out of it for a few days. He'll sleep quite a bit but he needs the rest."

"Thank you," Louis said.

Louis was unable to speak with James that day or for the next few days. Just as Dr. Winston said, James was out of it for a couple of days. Nan, Sally, and Denny kept cool rags on his head and back until his fever broke. Once the fever left his body, he seemed to recover quickly. When Louis was finally able to speak with James, he was happy to report that the harvest was complete and all the plants had been hand hung from sticks and were drying in the curing shed.

The entire house seemed to be affected by James' mourning and then illness. The mansion had been dark and quiet ever since David's death and Beth took Lillian and Rebecca with her to Philadelphia. It seemed to Nan that all the happiness that had ever graced these darkened rooms had died on that same fateful day. Now, with Massa James always in a state of depression, the mansion seemed to grow even darker and more sullen with each passing day.

Before Massa David died, the end of harvest season had always been cause for a celebration in the mansion and in the slave quarters. Gloria's field slaves were already celebrating. You could hear the faint sounds of laughter, singing, banjo music, and drums. Louis had allowed a few more chickens to be slaughtered for the occasion but there was no celebration in the mansion. There was just an eerie quiet. The slaves only spoke in whispers so as not to disturb James. Louis came to the mansion at least twice a day to check on James.

More than a week after James' recovery, the brothers enjoyed an after supper glass of brandy together and some very expensive cigars in the parlor. Though James assured Louis that he was more than pleased with the tobacco crop and his handling of the harvest, he did not look as if he was pleased. He said all the right words, but his demeanor was still disheartened, sad even. Was this a remnant of his weeklong suffering with illness or was there something deeper that he was unwilling to share with Louis. "Is there something else on your mind, brother?" Louis asked cautiously.

James looked up in surprise. "I'm sorry Louis. If I seem distracted, it is only because there is so much on my mind these days."

"Anything I can do to help?"

"No. I'm afraid I'm on my own with this one. You see, I can't help but wonder if this sudden attack is evidence that I may have inherited the same lung ailment that took Big Bill's life."

Louis took a sip from his drink as he eyed James. "That's quite a leap, don't you think? I mean, you were diagnosed with pneumonia, a very common illness. You were not diagnosed with a life threatening lung ailment."

"I know, I know. I guess I'm just taking everything a little more serious these days. Yeah, that's it. You're right, of course. I am over reacting." He drained the rest of the brandy in his glass. "Forget about it. Let's talk of other matters"

Neither spoke for several minutes, each lost in their own thoughts. Finally, Louis spoke in soft tones. "No James. I think we need to talk about exactly what you're thinking and feeling. I've only known you for a few months and you seem to be changing before my eyes. I want to know where the self-assured, determined man that I met in that terrible tavern in Richmond has gone."

James chuckled. "All right. You win." He put his glass down and stood. Thrusting both his hands into the pockets of his trousers, he began to pace. "I am worried about inheriting the same lung disease that killed Big Bill, but there are other things on my mind as well. We've spoken about this before, although not in great detail. I just can't stop thinking about the past. I cannot stop thinking about Beth and the terrible way my brother treated her when she was here. I thought about telling her how I feel and asking her to come back to Gloria. I even went so far as to write and tell her that I am planning a trip to Philadelphia in the spring. But then I got this pneumonia and all sorts of things ran through my mind. In my fever induced delirium my mind was fixed on the past. It was like it was all happening all over again. I could see Beth's tear stained face as she read my father's journals. I could see the look of utter shock on Lillian's face when she realized that she and David had the same mother."

"Go on."

"I had a cough and a scratchy throat and I ignored it, thinking it was just a cold. I don't even know when the fever took hold. I just know that I woke up feeling that I could not breathe. I fell back to sleep and I guess the fever just took over. My dreams took me to the front gate, right to the base of that 200 year old Live Oak where David chose to end his life. My body would not let go of David's body swinging from a low branch. Once the medication let my mind return to reality, all I could think of was bringing Beth to Gloria and then not living long enough to make her happy."

"Wow! That is quite a fiction brother."

"You're laughing at me."

"No. I'm just wondering why you are so pessimistic. From what you've already shared with me,

Beth doesn't have a clue about your feelings. And you have no clue about her life in Philadelphia. It seems to me that you are just lonely. A little female companionship will, no doubt, chase away some of those bad feelings."

"You know Louis," James said with a lifted eyebrow. "I could say the same about you."

"Yes, and you would be right, but brother, I am still mourning but you are sulking."

"Yes. I suppose I am. I just need a little more time."

"Who were you seeing while Beth was with your brother?"

James smiled. "I courted one of the Whittaker daughters from York for a time. It was short lived, though."

"What happened?"

"She was no different from any other southern lady. She was looking for marriage and I just couldn't go on deceiving her into believing that marriage was a possibility."

"All right. What about less formal relationships?"

James looked puzzled for a moment. As realization came to him, he couldn't help but smile. "Oh, well brother, I've had my share of the brothels and flop houses but they seemed to lose some of the allure as we mature. I could easily spend a night or two in Richmond but I'm just not interested. I'm also not interested in following in the footsteps of Big Daddy or David."

"So, you seemed to be saying that there is only one woman in the world for you and she just happens to be about 250 miles away and doesn't have a clue about your feelings."

"All right! All right! You've made your point. I just need a little time. Maybe I'll feel differently in a few months and when I do, you will be the first to know."

October was still very warm in Southampton County, Virginia. Mosquitoes were still in abundance along the banks of the James River and the heat of the day lingered after the sun set. The work on Gloria Plantation was about preparation for the coming winter. Work hours were shorter, which gave Louis more personal time. Since his arrival on Gloria, there was so much going on, that he had little time to dwell on his life and recent losses. Now, with the sound of crickets chirping and the wind rustling through the trees, Louis sat on the front porch of his cabin smoking his Cobb pipe and reflecting on the changes that had taken place in his life.

All the people that he loved were taken on one fateful day. 'How does a man get over such loss,' he wondered. He told himself that he had no choice but to move on with his life. He was determined to do so without bitterness or malice. He would put that day out of his mind and only reflect on good memories. He was happy here on Gloria. There was nothing here that would remind him of his life in Louisiana. However, after his talk with James, he realized that he was lonely.

CHAPTER 15

Innocence Lost

In the few months since Lillian and Rebecca had come to live with Beth, Rebecca had become friends with Mary, the Nottingham's nanny. Lillian, who had spent most of her life without a friend or anyone with whom she could confide, was absolutely thrilled that Rebecca now had a friend and she encouraged her daughter to visit with the young woman whenever possible.

Though a few years older Mary was no less naïve. The daughter of a born free Baptist Minister father and a devoutly religious ex-slave mother, Mary was far from a worldly young woman. She was a slim girl of average height with long thick hair, which she wore in a French braid down the back of her head. Her brown, almond shaped eyes were surrounded by a dark chocolate colored, unblemished complexion. She was a cheerful girl with an outgoing personality, but in the presence of white people, she seemed to fold in on herself, becoming docile and shy. Rebecca was surprised to learn of what a chatterbox Mary could be when they were alone. Both girls had grown up spending much of their time in the presence of adults rather than girls their own age. From their first meeting, there was an immediate affection for one another. As teenagers everywhere, the girls could talk for hours. They talked about the fashions of the day, new hairstyles, and of course, boys.

It was the fall of 1840 and the Pennsylvania foliage had begun to transform into beautiful shades of orange, yellow, and fading shades of green. The October air was cool and crisp, but not cold. On this chilly October afternoon, Rebecca and Mary sat talking in the rear garden of the Nottingham home. Mary was supervising the two Nottingham boys in her charge. Daniel and Harry were six and four, and content to lay in the grass and stage imaginary scrimmages between their red and blue coat wooden soldiers while Mary entertained Rebecca with the details of her recent outing with a special young man.

At first, Rebecca listened intently, hanging on every word as if Mary's story was right out of a great romantic novel. In dramatic fashion, Mary prattled on about her new beau as if he were a gift from God.

"Oh Rebecca, he is the most handsome man that I've ever met. I would love for you to meet him. He's kind and attentive, a real gentleman. He's studying to be a mortician. My mother says that being a mortician is a worthy profession and he is sure to make a good living. She says that one day this young man will make some lucky young woman a wonderful husband. All I could think was that I wanted to be that lucky young woman."

"Where did you ever meet this man?" Rebecca wanted to know.

"At church, of course," Mary said excitedly. "I don't really go anywhere else."

"Do you think that he will ask you to marry him?"

"I don't know, of course, but there is no harm in wishing it were so."

When Mary began talking about her new beau, Rebecca was as eager to hear Mary's story as Mary was to tell the story. But the more Mary talked, the less interested Rebecca became. Her self-absorbed personality did not allow her to dwell on anything that did not directly involve her for too long. After a while, Rebecca's mind began to wonder and she was only pretending to listen.

Mary talked on, completely unaware of Rebecca's disinterest. "He is so handsome. He would be even more handsome if he hadn't had an accident earlier this year and injured his eye. Now he wears an eye patch over his injured eye. I have to admit, the patch makes him look a little dangerous. You know, like a pirate or something. I don't mind, though. I like it because, even with the patch, he is still quite handsome."

With that, Rebecca's attention was brought immediately back to the conversation. "Which eye?" Rebecca asked bluntly.

"His right eye."

Rebecca stiffened while her eyes became wide in disbelief. She didn't know if she were jealous, envious, or remorseful. What is his name, Mary?" Rebecca's tone was harsher than she would have liked, but she was unable to hide the feelings that suddenly surged through her with the realization that Jonah was Mary's new beau.

"Jonah Mason," Mary said. "Do you know him?"

"Yes," Rebecca whispered. She was still experiencing a bevy of emotions and was unsure of how she should handle these new feelings.

Mary watched Rebecca suspiciously, wondering what she'd said that could have changed Rebecca's mood so quickly. She didn't know Rebecca well enough to be able to read the change in her disposition, so she was quiet for a few moments as she studied her friend. Realization came slowly but as Mary stared at Rebecca's face, she suddenly realized that her friend was the girl that had been whispered about throughout the church community. Rebecca was the girl who stood by while Jonah took a severe beating because she refused to tell his attackers that she wasn't a white woman.

Mary's scrutiny had settled on Rebecca like a bright light causing her to move about uncomfortably. Twisting in her chair and turning her face away from Mary's gaze. "Is there something you want to tell me about Jonah?" Mary asked softly.

"No," Rebecca said. "I know Jonah from church too. He's a good man and I hope you two will be very happy together."

The girls were so intent on their conversation that they didn't hear the side gate as it clanged shut. "Hello," said a male voice and both girls were startled at the sound.

"Oh, Mr. Colbert," Mary said as she jumped to her feet. "I didn't hear you come in."

A young handsome white man, dressed in a crumpled suit, stood at the gate. He carried a leather case under his arm. "That's all right, Mary," he said cheerfully. "No one answered the door and I heard voices coming from the back. Mr. Nottingham should be expecting me."

Mary quickly started for the door. "I'll let him know that you are here, sir," she said over her shoulder as she moved quickly toward the door.

"Thank you," the man said. Mary had been sitting in such a way that she blocked the full view of Rebecca. Once she got up and went for the door, the man seemed to notice Rebecca. He stood there staring at her as uncomfortable moments passed in silence. He took note of her smooth creamy complexion and piercing green eyes. *She is absolutely exquisite*, he thought.

He smiled and Rebecca couldn't resist the urge to flirt with this handsome young man. She pushed her full cherry colored lips into a pout before she smiled and turned her head away with a flutter of her full lashes.

As Mary disappeared behind the back door, the man took a few steps closer to Rebecca. "Hello, my name is Garrett," he said as he extended his hand. Again, Rebecca immediately knew that he thought that she was white. He would never have offered his hand to a Negro.

"Hello," she said in her sweetest voice as she took his hand and smiled coyly. "I'm Rebecca" she said as she bowed her head slightly.

"I'm very happy to meet you Rebecca. Are you related to the Nottingham's?"

Rebecca continued to smile while Garrett began to look a bit uncomfortable. "No, the Nottingham's are neighbors." She waited a full minute before she said, "So you work for Mr. Nottingham?"

"Well, not exactly. Mr. Nottingham is my client. I am his accountant."

Rebecca had no idea of what an accountant was or what they did. "That must be interesting," she said.

"Not at all. It is a very tedious and time consuming endeavor but it's also a good living."

"How long have you been an accountant, Mr. Colbert?"

"Garrett," he corrected. "Just Garrett. I've only been doing this a couple of years."

"Garrett," Rebecca said as she left her chair and moved closer to the accountant. "What if I needed an accountant? How would I get in touch with you?"

"Do you own a business, Miss Rebecca?"

"No. Not now, but who's to say that I won't own a business one day?"

A shy man by nature, it took Garrett a few minutes to realize that Rebecca was flirting with him. "Oh," he said with a smile. He fumbled for a moment in the leather case and presented Rebecca with a card. "My office is only a few blocks away, on Market Street," he paused. "If you find yourself in need of an accountant, you are welcomed to stop by the office at any time."

"Thank you, Garrett," Rebecca said as she pushed the card into her ample cleavage in the front of her dress. Again, Garrett smiled nervously.

Mary came back. "Mr. Nottingham will see you now, Mr. Colbert. Follow me," she said as she walked back toward the back door with Garrett following.

When she returned, Rebecca showered her with a barrage of questions about Garrett Colbert.

"Do you know if he is married?" Rebecca wanted to know. "How old he is, I wonder. Do you think he has a girl, maybe a fiancée?" Rebecca could hardly contain her excitement.

"How should I know, Becca? The Nottingham's don't tell me their personal business," Mary said as she looked at her new friend in wonderment. "Why are you asking all these questions, anyway?"

"He's awfully cute, don't you think?"

"Yes he is, but he is also awfully white!"

Mary just stared at Rebecca for a few moments. She couldn't believe what she was hearing. "He's white, Rebecca. I don't think anything about him and I'm wondering exactly what you are thinking asking about a white man. You are treading on dangerous ground and you don't even seem to know it."

Rebecca only smiled as if she knew something that Mary could never know. "Like I said," she said as she sashayed toward the back gate. "I think he's awfully cute."

"Well I think you're crazy," Mary said as she followed Rebecca to the gate. "This ain't Virginia Miss Rebecca. If you go messing with that white man and he finds out that you are colored and done tricked him, there is gone to be hell to pay." By now, Rebecca was on the other side of the gate. Mary stood there a moment holding onto the gate as four-year-old Daniel ran up and smothered his face in her skirt. "I'm telling you Rebecca, don't do it. You're playing a dangerous game. Just don't do it." Mary pleaded. Rebecca just smiled back at her as she disappeared behind the hedge that separated the two homes.

For the next couple of days all Rebecca could think about was Garrett Colbert. Night after night, she imagined the two of them walking hand in hand through the market or in the small park across from Rittenhouse Square. She even dreamed of their wedding. Though it was obvious to her that the young man had mistaken her for a white girl, Rebecca convinced herself that she could enter into a relationship with this man and keep her heritage a secret until he had fallen in love with her; and then her heritage would not matter. She never gave any thought to what would happen if he found out who she was before he fell in love.

Though at the time of their first meeting, Garrett was taken with Rebecca's beauty but had not given her any thought since that day. Their next encounter happened one evening when he and a few of his friends stopped to have a couple of beers at their favorite tavern.

Rebecca left her job at the Pennsylvania Abolition Society later than usual this evening. As October was coming to an end, the icy winds of winter blew into the city from the river, once the sun had gone down. Rebecca wrapped her shawl tightly around her shoulders as she began her walk up Chestnut Street. As she moved toward Second Street, she saw a few men gathered on the sidewalk outside of a well-known tavern. She considered crossing to the other side of the street, as she did not enjoy the catcalls and jeers that sometimes came from men who'd had too much to drink. It was unusual to see an unaccompanied young woman on the street after dark and she knew that she would be assumed to be a woman of low virtue. However, as she came closer, she decided that the few men looked well behaved and harmless. They appeared to be engrossed in conversation and Rebecca was sure that none would notice if she quickly passed them. She kept her head down, kept close to the curb, and tried to scurry passed the group unnoticed. She let out a sigh of relief once she'd moved past the men. "Rebecca!" The sound of her name stopped her and she turned to see Garrett hurrying toward her.

"Oh my God" he said. "Why on earth are you on the street at this hour?"

"Oh, Garrett," she said as she tried to think of an appropriate lie to explain why she should be out at this hour. "Hello," She graced him with one of her most disarming smiles. "How lucky am I to have run into you this evening."

"I was thinking the same thing," he said honestly. "But it is awfully late for you to be out on the street. Is there something wrong?"

"Not at all," Rebecca tried to be nonchalant. "I had some errands to run and it just took me longer than I had planned. Time just seemed to get away from me.

"I see," he said. "I will be happy to escort you home. I would not feel comfortable letting you walk alone at this hour."

"That really isn't necessary. I'll be fine."

"I'm sure you will because I insist on accompanying you right to your front door." With that, he turned to his friends on the sidewalk and said his farewells. He gently lifted Rebecca's arm and linked it with his own and they began to walk up Chestnut Street.

After a few minutes of walking, he said, "I was just thinking. Might I ask your father for the privilege of calling on you?"

Rebecca looked up in surprise. "That's very sweet Garrett, but my father is long dead."

"Oh, I'm sorry. Well, shall I speak with your mother?"

"Oh no," Rebecca said. "My mother is quite ill. She rarely takes visitors."

"Oh," Garrett said soberly.

They walked in silence for a few minutes. "Garrett, there is no one you can ask. I don't need my mother's permission. I am a grown woman and in charge of my own life."

"Really," he said in a questioning tone.

"Yes, really. My mother has been ill for a long time and our roles have somewhat reversed. I take care of my mother." As her lie began to expand, Rebecca began to feel that she may have given Garrett a little too much incorrect information.

Garrett was asking too many questions, probing into her upbringing and background and Rebecca gave him vague answers as she tried desperately to think of a reason why he should not come to her front door. If Lillian were to open the door, or if he were to learn that Lillian was her mother, all of her plans would fall apart. As long as she could keep Garrett thinking that she was a young white woman, Rebecca believed that she had a chance. She acknowledged to herself that this was going to be harder than she had anticipated.

They were on Walnut Street now, just a few doors away from Beth's house. Despite the chill in the air, Rebecca's palms began to sweat. She became flush and color brightened her cheeks. Garrett stopped walking and turned her around to face him. "Are you all right?" he asked.

"No," she said honestly. "I think that I may be coming down with something. I'm suddenly not feeling very well. I hope you won't mind if I leave you here." She quickly unlinked her arm and began to walk quickly down the sidewalk.

"Rebecca!" Garrett called after her. "We've less than a block to go."

Rebecca stopped. "I know. I'll be fine."

"Can we meet tomorrow for lunch?"

"Yes," she called over her shoulder. "I'll meet you at your office, if that's all right." She turned again and began to walk away, leaving Garrett no time to respond. He stood there watching her walk away for a few minutes while Rebecca silently prayed that he would turn and walk in the other direction. When she was finally in front of the house, she turned again, but Garrett was gone.

✧

After a harried morning of dusting bookshelves and logging mounds of dusty old manuscripts at the Pennsylvania Abolition Society, Rebecca feigned illness saying that the dust was not only making her sneeze, but also making her dizzy and giving her a headache. Her performance gained her a sidelong glance from Mr. Rogers who supervised the library. "You may go, if you must, but your wage will reflect the time missed, Miss Vance."

"Thank you," she said as she gathered her things and slipped away before Mr. Rogers could change his mind.

Rebecca was grateful that Lillian was not at home when she entered the house through the kitchen door. She heard the muffled voices of Miss Beth and Mr. Jefferson coming from the front sitting room as she slipped up the back staircase. In her room, Rebecca dressed carefully for her lunch date with Garrett. She chose a yellow and blue cotton dress with matching wrap. She pinned her hair up and used decorative combs to hold it in place. She surveyed herself in the full-length mirror and smiled, satisfied that she could have easily been taken for one of the white ladies from the upscale neighborhoods of Philadelphia. She left the house quietly, the same way she had come in and made her way to Garrett's Market Street Office Building.

She waited for Garrett, pacing up and down the sidewalk, but there was no sign of him. She couldn't help but wonder why he kept her waiting. With each minute that ticked by, her ire rose. Finally, after more than thirty minutes, Rebecca could not stand waiting anymore and decided to go directly to his office.

An older white woman with hair streaked with silver sat at the desk. "Miss Rebecca Vance to see Mr. Garrett Colbert," she said with confidence. The woman never even lifter her head from her work. She just pointed to one of the doors directly behind her. "Thank you," Rebecca said. She stood for a moment outside of the door to smooth her dress down and give her hair a final pat. She knocked softly before she opened the door and went inside.

Garrett's head jerked up at the intrusion. For a moment, he didn't seem to know who she was and he just sat there with a confused look on his face. "Have you forgotten me so soon," Rebecca asked playfully.

"Absolutely not," Garrett said as he rounded the desk to embrace Rebecca and place a light kiss on her cheek. "I could never forget you but I did forget our lunch date. You look beautiful, Miss Rebecca."

"Thank you," she said as she perched on the corner of his desk.

"Just give me a minute or two to clean up and we can go."

He took her to Joseph Head Mansion's House on Spruce Street, one of the better restaurants in Philadelphia. Rebecca had never been to such an elegant restaurant and she was in awe. They talked quietly and Garrett was again asking too many questions about her family and background. And again, Rebecca did her best to deflect while pursuing her own inquiries about his family and background.

Garrett was a very tall man. In fact, Rebecca had to tilt her head back to look into his eyes. He was well over six feet with large hands and a robust barrel chest. He was blonde and sporting the barest hint of a beard. He likely thought that the facial hair made him look closer to his twenty-two years. He was from a good family, but not a wealthy family. He was the youngest of six siblings, all girls. His mother was a homemaker and his father was a family lawyer. The senior Mr. Colbert had expected his son to share his interest in the law but from the time Garrett was old enough to understand what his father did for a living, he'd wanted nothing to do with the law. He wanted to do anything but be a family lawyer. Though he'd had no great interest in accounting, it came easy to him and did not require him to spend many years in school. It seemed to be the obvious choice of a profession that would allow him to leave the shelter and security of his parent's home and begin a life of his own. He landed a job with the Franklin and Bosch Accounting Firm shortly after finishing school. Franklin and Bosch was a well-established firm and offered him a good salary. He was able to rent a small house in the city and was quite happy living on his own.

They got on well together and Rebecca decided that Garrett was more than just a handsome face. He was charming and interesting and he treated her as if she were special. After that first lunch, they began to meet regularly. He took her to the theater, for long walks in the park, to lunch and sometimes dinner. With the exception of Jonah, Rebecca had never spent time with a young man before Garrett. Everything felt right about this new relationship. Rebecca was falling in love and she was convinced that Garrett shared her amorous feelings. After all, Garrett would certainly not spend so much time and care with her if he did not share her feelings.

However, it was becoming increasingly difficult to get out of the house. Though tight lipped about everything, Lillian knew that Rebecca was keeping a secret. Also, Garrett never stopped asking questions. He wanted to meet her mother but curiously, he never offered to introduce Rebecca to his family.

When she was finally able to share her secret with Mary, her friend was horrified. "I don't believe you," Mary said. "Mr. Colbert is a respectable business man. Why on earth would he be interested in you?"

"He thinks I'm white. He's just courting a young lady as most young men do before choosing a wife."

"But you aren't white! He will find out eventually and what do you think will happen then?"

"I've just got to make sure that he doesn't find out until he realizes that he just can't live without me."

"You're crazy Rebecca."

"No," Rebecca said. "I am in love with a wonderful man. I'm not even sure I can wait for a wedding. I want to give myself to him every time I feel his strong arms pull me to him. I know he feels the same."

Mary just shook her head in dismay.

"I was afraid of Mr. Wallingford," Rebecca went on. "And I just wasn't interested in the one young man that wanted to court me." Rebecca was careful not to mention Jonah's name. "But with Garrett, he rings every bell and I just shiver with desire every time we are together. It is going to happen and I'm looking forward to my first taste of love making."

"Now I know you're crazy. What if you become pregnant and then he finds out that you're colored? He'll kill you Rebecca. Do you realize the danger you are courting?"

"Oh Mary, don't worry. It will all work out. I know it."

But Mary did worry. Even if Rebecca was so blinded by her desire to be white that she was separated from reality, Mary knew that her friend was playing a dangerous game that could eventually get her killed and she wanted so much to share Rebecca's secret with someone.

Their secret rendezvous had been going on for more than a month and Rebecca couldn't help but notice that the places he took her to were less upscale than in the beginning of their association. Some places were downright shabby. Rebecca thought that Garrett may be having financial trouble but that did not deter her in the least.

Finally, Garrett suggested that they meet in a more private setting and Rebecca readily agreed. After lunch one day, he rode to a two-story house in the Kensington section of the city. "Is this where you live?" Rebecca wanted to know.

"No," Garrett said. "This is the home of a friend but no one is at home now. We can spend the rest of the afternoon here and no one will disturb us." The furnishings were shabby and sparse. The windows were clouded with yellow grime and the wooden steps creaked and whined as they climbed to the second floor. He led her to a front bedroom with tattered curtains and an iron bed with an old straw filled mattress. Rebecca stood leaning against a wall as Garrett covered the bed with a clean sheet. She had no illusions about his intentions though she hadn't expected to him to be so bold.

Her thoughts and emotions were whirling so fast that she literally felt as if she were losing her breath. She wanted to give herself to him with every fiber in her body but she was not sure if that was the right thing to do? This could be the thing that seals their bond to each other and forges a life-long devotion or it could be what ends the relationship. If this was all Garrett had wanted from her, he would be finished with her as soon as his conquest was over. *'Garrett loves me. I know he does,'* she thought.

Rebecca lost her virginity to Garrett that afternoon. Her inexperience was evident, which both surprised and angered Garrett. He raised himself on his elbow and looked down at Rebecca. "You've never done this before, have you?"

"No, but it's all right. I wanted to."

He hesitated for a moment but thought, *'if not me, it would certainly be some else in a short time.'*

They met at the Kensington house at least three times a week and each time was the same as the last. He no longer took her to the theater or fancy restaurants. There were no more walks in the park or even polite conversation. Rebecca knew that she had made the biggest mistake of her life but she couldn't take it back and she refused to give up hope. She was convinced that Garrett would love her eventually and she could have the life she dreamed. The dream was shattered one afternoon when she innocently asked him again about his family.

"Why do you care so much about my family?" he wanted to know.

"Well, we're a couple. Why shouldn't I want to meet your family?"

Garrett laughed outright. "Are you daft?" he said mockingly. "I'm not taking you to meet my family. You're a whore, for God's sake!"

WHORE! The word hung in the air like the stench from the gutter. Immediately tears began to burn at the back of Rebecca's eyes. She struggled to keep them from spilling onto her cheeks. "Why do you say something so cruel?" she muttered. "I am not a whore. I have only been with one man. You, Garrett. And only because I love you. I thought you loved me too."

"Oh come on Rebecca. I am only the first and you practically threw yourself at me. I'd have been a fool not to see that this is what you wanted. You said so yourself. After the first time, you said you wanted to do it."

"That's because I thought we loved each other but I guess I was wrong," she said as she bounced out of the squeaky old bed and began to dress quickly. "I'm a good girl Garrett. I was just stupid enough to fall in love with you."

"No Rebecca. Good girls don't get into bed with a man they hardly know to get to know him. In fact, good girls wait until they are married."

"But I thought you loved me. I thought you would one day marry me."

"Marry you?" Garrett laughed again. He could not believe that she was so naïve and he turned over as if he were finished with the conversation.

Garrett had done more than just hurt Rebecca he had destroyed all of her hopes and dreams. With those few words, Garrett had been able to do what Lillian had not been able to do in months of talking to Rebecca. He was able to reveal just how ridiculous her plans to assimilate into the white world were and how foolish she was to think that it would be so simple to carry out her plan.

Rebecca continued to dress with hot tears streaming down her cheeks while Garrett lounged in the bed with a single sheet covering his nakedness.

Watching Rebecca in such a state touched something in him and he began to feel somewhat sorry for his harsh words. He realized that he had misjudged her to some extent. While he did think that she was little more than a hot little vamp, he also knew that her feelings for him were true and she was trying to cultivate a relationship. There was little he could do about it now though, he thought. "Rebecca, I'm sorry. I thought this was what you wanted."

"You thought that all I wanted was to give myself to a man who cared nothing for me? You thought I wanted to give myself to a man who thought of me as a whore?"

"Well, you *did* come on very strong. What was I to think?" He regretted those few words as soon as they left his lips.

"I don't know Garrett. It seems to me that you may have thought that I was attracted to you, that I wanted to get to know you better, or that I wanted you to get to know me better. I don't know but I know it wasn't this."

Garrett chuckled again. "Really Rebecca? Proper ladies don't throw themselves at a gentleman to get to know him and you had no objections about spoiling yourself for me."

"I wanted you to love me." She said more softly.

"Love?"

"Yes Garrett, Love. But don't worry. Now that I know that you are no gentleman, I have no desire for you. I just want to go home."

Garrett swung his legs over the side of the bed and began to pull on his trousers.

"It doesn't matter now," Rebecca said. "Now that I know that you think of me as a whore, there is nothing left." She gathered her things and left the house, slamming the door behind her. Once on the street she was filled with shame and regret. Then she realized that she had no way to get home and she began to cry. With tears streaming down her face she began to walk.

A moment later, Garrett came out of the house. When he realized that Rebecca had begun to walk home, he jumped into his carriage and caught up with her. "Walnut Street is a long way from here. Were you planning to walk?" Rebecca didn't answer. "Come on," he said. "I will take you as far as Market Street."

They rode in silence for the entire ride. Once the carriage was close to Market Street, Rebecca asked that he take her to the Nottingham's house. She waited until Garrett's carriage was completely out of sight before she went into Beth's house from the back door.

Garrett's rejection had destroyed Rebecca's spirit. She now felt only shame and regret. She was depressed and kept to her bedroom for a couple days complaining of a stomach ache. The next few weeks went by with her hardly aware of anything or anybody around her. She went to her job in the library and right home afterwards. Most of her time at home was spent in her bedroom. After nearly a week, Lillian demanded that Rebecca come down for dinner. One look at Rebecca's tear-swollen face and Lillian knew that something awful had happened but Rebecca would reveal nothing. "Are you still feeling ill?" she asked.

"No Mama. I'm fine."

"You are not fine. I can see that something is wrong. If you don't want to tell me now, I will wait until you are ready to talk to me but don't sit here and tell me that there is nothing wrong."

As the weeks went by, Rebecca slowly returned to herself and began to spend more time with Miss Beth and her mother. She even ventured next door but she told Mary nothing of her failed relationship with Garrett Colbert.

Lillian still waited for Rebecca to open up and talk with her about whatever it was that had made her so sad. Rebecca remained silent but Lillian knew that whatever it was it had changed her daughter profoundly.

‿

The weather was unusually raw for November. It began to rain before dawn and as the sun rose behind a dense cloud cover, temperatures plummeted. The rain turned to slivers of ice. Despite the gloominess of the day, Beth was in high spirits when she came looking for Lillian in the kitchen.

"Lillian, I've got some amazing news." She carried a letter in her hand.

Lillian was sitting at the table with a cup of tea. Her mood was more reflective of the overcast weather but she did her best to hide her anxiety from Beth. "What is it?" she said as she stood to pour a cup of tea for Beth. "Did you get another letter from Virginia?"

"Yes, and you will never guess what James says in his letter." Lillian was in no mood to guess and it didn't take long for Beth to recognize the sadness in

Lillian's subdued demeanor but she chose to ignore it for now. "James is coming to Philadelphia in the spring. Can you believe it? He is actually coming for a business meeting but he will certainly make time for a visit. He expresses his desire to see both you and Rebecca."

Lillian was puzzled. Why James would want to see her was a wonder. After all, she had been his slave. There was never any relationship between the two of them. "Why?" was all she said.

"With David gone, Rebecca and Louis, his recently discovered half-brother, are his only living relatives. He hasn't explained why but I know that he feels an obligation toward Rebecca because she is David's daughter."

Lillian's smile faded. She could not at first find the words to express her true feelings. When did James begin to care about Rebecca? Where was his concern when we were there on Gloria? "Why does Massa James suddenly care about Rebecca?"

"I think he always cared about Rebecca but once he read Big Bill's journals, he was affected in ways that we may never understand. I think that he may finally see slavery differently."

"I don't understand."

"Slavery was all James knew. He could not see anything shameful or sinful in it because he has never known life without slavery. It was a way of life. But something happened to him when he saw how Big Bill had so easily destroyed lives with a lie. He was ashamed. But when David killed himself, James was overcome with grief and anger at Big Bill. I know that he has thought of little else since we left for

272

Philadelphia. He thinks that he can somehow make better the lives his father destroyed."

Beth watched Lillian as she quietly sipped her tea. Her face gave no indication of what she was thinking but Beth could not help but notice the sadness in her face. "Is there something else bothering you Lillian?"

"Yes, I'm not really good at hiding my feelings." Tears filled her eyes but she quickly blinked them back and fought hard to keep them from spilling onto her cheek. "I haven't heard from Althea since she left here and I just want to know if she is all right."

"Well, that's easy enough to find out."

"I'm also worried about Rebecca. She has been staying out late and sneaking off whenever she got the chance, then it all stopped suddenly. Now she is so sad. She won't tell me where she was going or who she was with."

"That sounds to me like there is a new beau about."

"Yes. I've thought about that but why is he a secret?"

"Why don't you just ask her? She's a teenager, Lillian. They often keep secrets, especially from a parent. I'm sure she confided in Mary."

"I have asked her. She hasn't given me a good answer yet." Lillian was thoughtful for a few moments. "Miss Beth, there are things about Rebecca that you may not know."

Beth looked up but she did not answer. She waited for Lillian to tell her more. After what seemed like a full minute, Lillian blurted out, "Rebecca wants to pass for white."

Beth was shocked into silence so Lillian went on. "She seems to think that she looks white enough to pass and if she can get a white man to fall in love with her and marry her, she will be able to easily slip into a white world and no one would ever know that she is colored."

"Oh my!" Beth said. "I'm sure you've told her how dangerous that kind of thinking can be?"

"Of course, but why would she listen to me when she knows of the relationship I had with her father. So you see, it isn't just that she has been untruthful to me or that she may have feelings for a young man. I am so afraid that she has somehow begun a relationship with a white man. If I'm right, her life could be in danger."

"Do you think it would help if I spoke with her?"

"I don't know but I would like that very much."

"I will speak with her at the first opportunity."

Then Beth convinced Lillian that going to check on Althea at the Lombard Street house could be dangerous for both she and Althea, so they decided to send Sweet. Lillian's instructions to the sometime flighty young woman were very specific. On her way home from the market, Sweet was to stop by the house on Lombard Street. If a man answered, Sweet was to pose as a newcomer to Philadelphia and ask for directions to the church. If she were lucky enough to see Althea alone, she could tell her that Lillian wanted to know how she was doing. Lillian told Sweet that she was not to mention her name unless the man was nowhere around.

Now Lillian waited anxiously for Sweet's return. Beth sat at the small desk writing a letter while Lillian paced the short space of the sitting room, wringing her hands and nervously massaging the nap of her neck. When finally, she heard the latch on the back door, she was there in a second. Sweet took her time hanging up her shawl and feigning exaggerated exhaustion. "Whew," she said as she reached down and took the handles of the two shopping bags.

"Well?" Lillian said impatiently.

"It's getting really cold. I think we might have snow before the night is out," Sweet said as she made her way into the kitchen. Lillian followed.

"Was she there?" Lillian wanted to know.

Sweet was dragging this out as long as she could, obviously enjoying Lillian's anxiety. She began to unpack the bags. "It's so cold out that some of the stands began closing up early. I got what I could, though."

"Enough!" Lillian said as she grabbed the girl by her shoulders. "Did you see Althea or not?"

Sweet stopped what she was doing and thrust both hands into the pockets of her skirt. "Well, not at first. I did what you said. A big man answered the door. As soon as he opened his mouth, I could smell the liquor. I told him that I was lost and asked if he could direct me to the church. He took a long swig from the jug he held, wiped at his mouth with his sleeve, and then said no. Said he didn't know where no church was and he slammed the door."

"Oh my God!"

"I stood there for a minute then I heard tapping on the window from the upper floor. I looked up to see Miss Althea at the window."

"Was she all right?"

"I'm not sure. I only saw her for a moment but I could see that her face was bruised. She lifted the widow and dropped this out." Sweet produced a small crumbled piece of paper.

Lillian unfolded the paper and read.

Lillian,

> *I know that you must be worried but I'm all right. Bernie still drinks too much and wants to fight when he is drunk. But I am always aware and most times, I can get out of his way. He still goes off for days at a time and I am able to get a break until he comes back. More and more he seems restless and I think it won't be long before he runs off again.*
>
> *I am alright. Don't worry about me. I will come and see you soon.*

Althea.

Althea's note did not ease Lillian's concern because it confirmed that Bernie was still there and still abusing her friend. Lillian went through the rest of her day feeling an overwhelming sadness and helplessness.

CHAPTER 16

SACRIFICE

Over time, Jefferson and Beth had developed a Sunday routine. They attended Church Services with Clarisse, then brunch at the Maximilian Restaurant, after which they usually returned to Jefferson's house until Clarisse was ready for her afternoon nap.

From the moment Beth settled into the carriage, she knew that something was wrong. Jefferson exhibited his usual disarming charm while Clarisse, who always found a reason to be unhappy, scowled. She sat stiffly with her head tilted backward as if a foul order hovered above.

"Good morning," Beth said cheerfully. "It is a bit too cold for November."

Clarisse smirked and turned her head away from Beth.

"Maybe," Jefferson said. "But the chill is exhilarating. Kind of wakes you up."

The remainder of the ride was in silence. It was obvious to Beth that Jefferson's mother was upset about something and Beth suspected that she was that something.

As soon as she and Jefferson were alone in the carriage, Beth confronted him with her suspicions. "What is it this time, Jefferson? Am I too old? Is my virtue in question? Your mother has had something against me from the beginning. I've tried to be understanding. I've even tried, to no avail, to win her over, but she is just determined to doom this relationship and frankly, I am tired of the fight."

"I know," was all Jefferson could say. They rode in silence for some time before Jefferson would speak again. He took a long deep breath, trying to settle his obvious frustration. Jefferson found himself in a most precarious position between the two women that he loved most. He knew that his mother was possessive and jealous but she had stood by him through all the hardships of life and he would do nothing to hurt her.

On the other hand, Beth was a rare treasure and he'd fallen in love with her the very first time they met. She had been lighthearted and happy then but he was to learn that there was much more to Elizabeth Gable Vance. She did not share much of the details of her first marriage or her life in Virginia but Jefferson knew that whatever happened in her past had made her a strong and independent woman. He appreciated her independence. He marveled at the way Beth could go from carefree happiness to serious and forthright in the blink of an eye and he didn't want to lose her. Beth was the one woman with whom he thought he could actually build a life. His feelings notwithstanding, he knew that he was losing her.

"My mother is very jealous," he finally said. "I've known for some time now that she doesn't really want anyone to love me and she is not happy when she believes that I love someone other than her. You should know that you are not the first woman that she has tried to drive away. Believe me Beth, I know how this sounds, but it's the truth. It took a while for me to see what was happening but I see now. I don't understand it, but I do see now."

"Jefferson, I know how much you love your mother and I would do nothing to change that but I also know that we will never find happiness as long as she stands between us."

They were both quiet as the carriage rumbled forward. Beth had not given much thought to her feelings. She was speaking out of the vexation that she often experienced whenever she was put under Clarisse's scrutiny.

Finally, Jefferson turned to look at Beth. His expression was grave, his eyes dark and brooding. "So what are you saying Beth? Are you going to leave me because of my mother?"

The carriage came to a stop in front of Beth's house. "No Jefferson. I am not leaving you because of your mother. Your mother is pushing me away. As I said, I am just tired of the fight. Sometimes your mother is exhausting."

"Oh come on Beth. She's an old woman. It is my duty to see that her last years on this earth are happy and peaceful. Can't you understand that?"

"Of course," she said as she opened the door. Jefferson made no move to come around to help her down so Beth jumped down on her own. "Jefferson, I understand more than you know. I just think it is a shame that your mother's happiness depends on you sacrificing your own happiness."

"I'm not sacrificing anything Beth."

"And I'm not willing to share the man I love with another woman, even if it is his mother."

They were both silent as Beth closed the door softly and began to walk to her front door. "I'm not giving up Beth." Jefferson called after her.

She stopped and turned to face him. "And I can't promise you that I will be waiting when you are finally free of those maternal ties." She moved quickly up the path and was inside the house before Jefferson could think of a suitable reply.

It was still early afternoon when Beth came home and she was grateful that no one else seemed to be at home. Lillian and Rebecca were likely still in church and there was no telling where Sweet was hiding. After making a cup of tea, Beth settled herself in the sitting room. Even though it was not her plan, she'd just broken up with Jefferson and she now wondered why she felt no regret. Had she even been in love with Jefferson or was she just bending to his will and not her own heart. All she could feel was sorrow. She was sorry for Clarisse and Jefferson. How could a man as wise as Jefferson have such difficulty breaking away from his mother's grip? Maybe I'm just destined to be alone, she reasoned.

Supper that evening was unusually quiet. Lillian and Sweet prepared a sumptuous dinner of roast duck, candied yams, mashed potatoes and creamed corn pudding. Even Rebecca had come to dine with the other women. Though each of them had their own individual problems, they were set aside while they enjoyed a meal and each other's company. The topic of conversation was the two different sermons preached in their respective churches. It was ironic that their churches could not be more different but they somehow preached on the very same topic, forgiveness. Sweet and Rebecca were quiet as they paid close attention to the discussion between Beth and Lillian on the subject of forgiveness.

Their conversation was interrupted by an unexpected knock on the door. Sweet hurried off to answer the door and soon came back to the dining room door. "Gabriel and Lindy, for you Miss Lillian," she said.

Lillian was surprised but overjoyed at the visit. She introduced the young couple to Beth and Sweet and then asked Beth if they could use the sitting room for their visit. She readily agreed.

"So, how are you both?" Lillian said.

"We're great," Gabriel answered.

"How did you find us?"

"Mr. Briggs, of course?" Lindy answered.

"Well, you both look great," Lillian said.

"What news do you bring from Wallingford House?" Rebecca asked.

"Nothing much has changed, Becca." Lindy said. Miss Ella is still throwing tantrums when she doesn't get what she wants and Mr. Wallingford hasn't returned from his voyage overseas.

Both young women laughed. "Yeah, Mrs. Wallingford keeps asking about her companion. She doesn't even remember why the two of you left Wallingford House and she thinks that Rebecca was her companion. Keeps asking where is the pretty girl with the green eyes that looked so much like my Amy?"

Gabriel announced that he and Lindy planned to be married in the spring and he planned to work as an apprentice in the haberdashery he intended to purchase as soon as he learned the business. They laughed and talked for nearly an hour before Gabriel announced that they should be getting back before too late. "It was very sweet of you to visit," Lillian said. "We will see each other again really soon. I promise."

No sooner had Gabriel and Lindy left, then there was another unexpected knock at the door. It was Ellen Nottingham.

∽

The Nottingham's were hosting another dinner for Mr. Nottingham's business partners and associates. However, an unanticipated problem arose when a member of their staff, Leola, suddenly took ill and could not help in the preparation or on the night of the festivities. Ellen thought nothing of asking Beth if Rebecca could help. However, Beth politely informed Ellen that Rebecca was not her servant or her slave. Ellen did not hide her confusion. She got a puzzled look on her face and then said to Beth, "Then why is she here?"

"It is a long and complicated story that I will share with you at some point but not today. Wait here while I ask her mother before asking Rebecca if she is available.

Lillian saw no harm in Rebecca helping out the Nottingham's for an evening but when she informed Rebecca, she immediately objected to the idea.

"I am not a maid mother," she said when Lillian approached her on the subject.

"Oh?" Lillian was shocked at Rebecca's outburst. "What are you Rebecca?
Are you a schoolteacher or an opera singer? You are not a maid, so what are you, Rebecca?"

"That's not what I mean, Mama."

"Well, it doesn't matter what you mean. The truth is, you are not a slave, but you were a maid at the Wallingford's and you will likely be a maid again and sooner than you think."

"But I work in a library."

"Oh, so you think that because you are dusting book shelves and old books that you are something better than a maid? Well I'm here to tell you that you are a maid even if it is in a library. Look around you girl and open your eyes. White folks are not exactly bending over backwards to give spoiled little black girls from Virginia a profession." Rebecca was silent. "Besides, I think it is about time you start to learn how to keep a proper house. Miss Beth has been real nice letting you skip out on the housework around here but eventually you are going to have to learn how to support yourself and being a maid is how you will do it. Working for the Nottingham's a few days is as good a start as any."

Rebecca was not happy but she kept silent and did not complain any further. The only thought that crossed her mind was that her dreams of a grander life were dashed the moment that Garrett called her a whore.

Rebecca silently sulked around the Nottingham house, following orders as they prepared for the next night's festivities. On a few occasions, she and Mary passed each other and Rebecca was sure she detected a slight smirk on Mary's face. When they finally met face to face, Mary couldn't help throwing a dig at her haughty friend's predicament. "Guess you didn't get the marriage proposal you were hoping for, huh?"

Rebecca just glared at her.

The next evening Rebecca was dressed in a simple black dress with a white apron. Her hair was pulled tightly back from her face and pinned under a little white cap. With a stoic demeanor, she moved around the Nottingham dining table, serving their guest but never offering even a hint of a smile. There was only one empty chair at the table and Rebecca heard Mr. Nottingham say that Garrett Colbert would be joining them later.

Rebecca had not given any thought to the possibility of Garrett being among the Nottingham's guests and now she knew, not only that he was coming, but also that he would see her as a maid and know that she was a Negro. Her heart began to beat more rapidly. The palms of her hands began to sweat while her stomach started to twist into a knot and she was suddenly sick to her stomach. As soon as the last plate was served, she escaped into the kitchen. By now she was visibly shaking.

"Child, are you all right?" the cook asked.

"No, I'm not feeling very well. May I be excused?"

As she spoke, she heard the door chime and everything seemed to stop. She stood there with her hands covering her mouth. From what seemed like a great distance away, she heard the cook again asking if she were all right. Then she heard someone calling her name loudly. "Rebecca, Rebecca!" It took several seconds before she realized that it was Mrs. Nottingham and that she expected her to answer the door. Rebecca took a deep shaky breath, brushed her hand over her hair and apron, and went to answer the door.

She knew that Garrett stood on the other side of that door and that one look and he would know who and what she was, a Negro. If she didn't know it before now, she knew that the dream of being Garrett's wife was a childish fantasy. Rebecca opened the door slowly and Garrett stood there in his finest suit and tie and his hat in his hand. He was more handsome than ever. Their eyes met for only a second and Rebecca felt as if her legs had turned to water and she struggled to stay on her feet. However, Garrett didn't seem to recognize her at that moment. She was invisible as most servants are to the people they serve. He saw her, but just as the maid who was there to serve him in some way. He did not see the Rebecca who he had held in his arms and made love to for several months. She was just the maid and Rebecca immediately lowered her eyes.

"Good evening, Mr. Colbert. May I take your hat and coat?" she said in a voice that she didn't even recognize as her own.

He looked down, their eyes met again and the light in his eyes seemed to darken as recognition slowly crept across his face. This this time he did not look away, he stared in disbelief, unable to turn his head away and Rebecca quickly took his hat and coat and hurried away.

"So, you've made it?" Mr. Nottingham said as he came forward to greet his associate.

"Yes, I made it, though the roads have become quite treacherous," he said as he thrust his hat and coat at Rebecca. He and Mr. Nottingham proceeded into the dining room. Rebecca stood there watching the guests as they chatted with one another. Seeing Garrett was humiliating and knowing that she would never be a part of such a group was heart breaking.

Eventually, Garrett leaned closer to Edward and asked, "Who is the young woman that answered the door? She is quite beautiful."

"Rebecca? Oh, she is quite stunning and so is her mother. She's the daughter of one of our neighbor's servants. I'll tell you, that woman could turn more than one head."

"I don't remember seeing her before. Is she new to Philadelphia?"

"Yes. They've been here about two years now. As I understand it, their master set them both free after his marriage ended. The Misses elected to bring them both back to Philadelphia with her."

"So they are Negros?

"Well, isn't it obvious that they are both of mixed blood? I think they call that colored these days."

Rebecca was devastated but there was no escape. For the rest of the evening, she made certain that she did not look directly at Garrett. She kept her head averted as she served dessert and he seemed to do the same.

'I need to explain,' she thought. 'I don't know how or when but I need to explain.'

CHAPTER 17

Revenge

Philadelphia was in the midst of a brutal winter. The first snow of the season fell just before Thanksgiving on November 15, 1840 and since then the wintry weather only paused periodically. Day after day, the snow fell and temperatures plummeted, shrouding the city in an unmovable ice and bringing the hustle and bustle of the city to little more than a crawl.

As the New Year dawned, wind whistled as it careened around three-story buildings and through the alleys of center city Philadelphia. Most everything was covered in ice and the cold wind promised to blow in a new storm.

There was a temporary pause in falling snow and most people used this lull to venture out of their homes and stock up on needed supplies. The Vance household was no different. Lillian sent Rebecca to a small market on Market Street for bags of rice, flour, and sugar and other essential food items. The market was virtually empty and there was little left on the shelves.

Rebecca bought what she could and with the heavy bundle strapped to her back, she started for home. As she slowly made her way up Market Street she eventually passed the building where she knew Garrett worked. She had not thought of him since that evening at the Nottingham's house. She glanced up and saw that a candle burned in the window. Briefly, she considered going in to talk with him, maybe give him some explanation for what he saw the last time that he saw her at the Nottingham's. The thought died almost as quickly as it came to her because she knew there was no explanation that he would accept. She tucked her head down against the wind and moved past the building quickly.

She walked a few blocks before a carriage came to a stop beside her. It was Garrett. "Rebecca!" he yelled. He jumped down from the seat and stepped in front of her blocking her way.

"Garrett," she said. Rebecca was startled. "I'm glad you're here. I wanted to . . . ." was all she said before he punched her square in the face. She reeled backward and the heavy bundle on her back carried her to the icy ground. She slid her tongue over the split in her lip and tasted blood.

Garrett bent down close to her face. "You're not only a dirty little whore, you're a nigger! I should kill you for your trickery." he said and then he punched her in her face. After the second punch landed over her nose she tried to shield her face but it did little good as Garrett just kept punching her over and over again. Eventually Rebecca fell to the ground and began to crawl toward the wall of a building, trying to escape the blows. She struggled to get to her feet again. "I'm sorry

Garrett. I only wanted you to love me." Huddled against a wall, she looked up at Garrett. The rage in his face was frightening.

He punched her again, even harder and it sent her sprawling to the ice again. While she was on the ground he kicked her, his boot heel smashing into her forehead and dragged down the side of her face, leaving a terrible gash. Again, his boot made a hard contact with her head, which hit the icy ground hard with a thud. He kicked her again, this time in the stomach. There seemed to be no end to his kicking, all the while he called her vile names. Rebecca rolled over onto her stomach and lay there on the ice, consciousness slowly ebbing away. Just as her eyes began to close, she saw Garrett's boots walk back to his carriage. She heard the wheels crack and creek over the frozen earth as he drove away and then the whole world went black.

Rebecca didn't know how long she had been laying, unconscious on the ice. She opened her eyes and tried to lift herself from the frozen ground but all she could do was moan. Every inch of her battered body throbbed with pain. She lifted a shaky hand to the lump that was quickly forming at her temple. The spot was wet and sticky with fresh blood. She moaned again as she struggled to get to her feet. On unsteady legs, she tried to make it to the alley behind Market Street where she knew she was less likely to be noticed. She slipped and fell on the ice, losing consciousness again. She had no idea how long she lay there on the frozen ground but when she next became aware, she was being dragged by her arms over the ice. Rebecca immediately began to struggle, thinking Garrett had returned to inflict even more horror.

"Let go of me," she tried to yell but her voice was little more than a hoarse whisper. "Help, help me please."

"I'm trying to help you," said a man that tried to move Rebecca.

Rebecca vaguely recognized the voice but her mind was in such a muddled state from the attack that she couldn't place the voice. "Do you think you can walk?" the man asked. "Let's try to get you on your feet."

The man bent close to her face and as she wrapped her arms around his neck, she recognized Benjamin from the hotel. As soon as she was on her feet, Rebecca knew that she could not walk, her right leg was broken. She leaned heavily into Benjamin.

"I can't walk. It's my leg. I think it's broken."

"I got you," he whispered. Then he swooped her up into his arms and Rebecca threw her arms around his neck. He carried Rebecca nearly three blocks to a small house on a tiny little street on the North side of Market Street.

"Where are you taking me?" she asked. "I want to go home."

"You can't walk that far on a broken leg and I sure as hell can't carry you that far. I'm taking you to my grandmother's house. It's just a little further."

By the time they reached his grandmother's house, Rebecca was woozy and felt as if she would pass out again. Benjamin pushed open the back door to a warm and spacious kitchen. A short stout woman with long gray hair met them at the door.

"Oh my God Benny! What happened to her? Have you lost your mind? You can't bring that white girl here."

"She ain't white, Nana," he said as he helped Rebecca to a cot against the wall. "Somebody tried to beat the hell out of her."

As soon as Rebecca was lowered onto the cot, she closed her eyes and was out again. "She looks white to me," Benjamin's grandmother, who was called Miss Kathy, said.

"She ain't white Nana. I know her from the hotel. She may look white, but she's a colored girl. That might be why someone beat her up like this."

Miss Kathy moved closer to get a better look at Rebecca. "Benny, heat some water and get me a cloth so I can clean some of the blood off of her. I can't even tell how bad she's hurt with all this dried blood."

Benjamin hung a kettle of water over the fire and went to get the cloth. Miss Kathy removed Rebecca's boots. As she went to pull the right boot off, Rebecca winced. Once the boot was off, Miss Kathy could see that the leg was broken right at the shin. Rebecca's left eye was black and a long gash was above the right eye and another along the side of her face. Her lips were swollen and bruised.

When the water was heated slightly, Miss Kathy began to wipe away the blood. "I think she needs a doctor," Benjamin said.

"Yeah, but where you gone find a doctor in this weather? I guess we gone have to do the doctoring."

"What about her leg?"

"You go find me two pieces of wood, thin and flat. I'll set it the best I can or else she'll be limping the rest of her life."

Benjamin did as he was told. Miss Kathy moved Rebecca's leg until she felt the bone move into place. Rebecca woke up and began to scream. Benjamin tried to comfort her as Miss Kathy placed the wood strips on both sides of the leg and then wrapped it tightly with fabric torn from a bed sheet. Then she got her sewing basket and found the smallest needle she could find. With patience and precision, she stitched close the gash above Rebecca's eye and down the side of her face. Rebecca winced with every stitch. She then placed ice over her wounds to reduce the swelling.

Rebecca's head throbbed as she lay back on the bare pillow and closed her eyes. After a few minutes, Benjamin came back. He held up Rebecca's head and forced her to drink a bitter brown liquid. As soon as she tasted the foul drink, she turned away. "No," he said. "Drink this tonic down. It will make you feel better."

"What is it?"

"It's a potion Nana mixes for pain."

"What's in it?"

"I don't know. I just know that if you drink it straight down, you'll feel much better. It will help you sleep too."

Rebecca did not protest further. She downed the liquid in one gulp, frowning at the horrible taste of it. Within minutes, she was asleep.

〜

Lillian's concern mounted as the afternoon moved into evening and then the stars overtook the night sky. It was long pass the time when Rebecca should have returned. Lillian was sure something must have happened to her. Wringing her hands, Lillian began to pace between the kitchen and dining room. Finally, she could take the waiting no longer and she called for Sweet.

Lillian had noticed some time ago that Sweet was lazy and would hide to avoid extra duties. When she didn't answer Lillian's call, she knew that the girl was somewhere in the house hiding. "Sweet!" she called again, but it was Beth who came into the kitchen.

"My God," Beth said. "What is all the yelling about?"

"It's Rebecca, Miss Beth. She has been gone since early afternoon. Something awful must have happened to her. I just know it."

"Where did she go?"

"I sent her for a few bags of flour, rice and sugar on Market Street. She should have been back long ago."

"All right, Lillian, don't panic. We'll find her."

"I was just about to send Sweet to look for her."

"Well," Beth looked puzzled. "Where is Sweet?"

Lillian did not want to tell Beth about Sweet's laziness because she didn't want Beth to fire the girl. "Oh, she'll be down in a few minutes."

"Let me know if she finds Rebecca," was all Beth said. Lillian may have thought that Beth hadn't noticed Sweet's neglect of her duties but very little got by Beth's notice. Although there were few conversations between Beth and Rebecca, enough was said for Beth to know that Rebecca was far from grounded. She thought herself above those around her, much the same way her mother had while on Gloria. However, Beth did not know the motivation of Rebecca's lofty impression of herself. Sweet on the other hand, besides being lazy, was a very sweet girl and Beth felt that Rebecca needed to spend time with girls of her own age and station in life. Beth knew of Sweet's laziness and only kept the girl around because she and Rebecca had become close friends and Beth thought that may help Rebecca to get her head out of the clouds.

"Yes, I will." Lillian said.

Lillian searched every room in the house. It was obvious that Sweet had not completed the cleaning chores for the day, but the girl could not be found. Frustrated and afraid, Lillian began to wring her hands again as she stood in an upstairs hallway. The house was completely quiet and as she stood there pondering what she should do next when she heard the soft murmur of snoring and knew that Sweet was sleeping in the upstairs linen closet. Lillian silently moved towards the sound. When she was positively sure that Sweet slept inside the closet, she slapped her hand hard on the bottom of the door and Sweet popped out like a wooden toy.

"Oh Lillian," she said. "A funny thing happened while I was straightening out this closet. I just got so sleepy and the next thing you know, I was sound asleep on the floor."

Lillian crossed her arms over her chest. "Sweet, that's the biggest lie you ever told but I ain't got time for your foolishness now. Rebecca is missing. I want you to wrap up, warm as you can, and take a walk to the

Market Street Vendors. See if you see Rebecca anywhere. She might have fallen on the ice or worse."

Sweet stood there torn between defending her lie and going to look for Rebecca. When she looked into Lillian's worried eyes, she knew she had better go and look for Rebecca. "Yes Ma'am," Sweet said and immediately made ready to leave.

As Sweet walked north on Seventeenth Street, the wind began to pick up drastically, almost pushing at her back as she tried to maneuver over the ice and trudge through high snow drifts. By the time she got to Market Street vendor's stands, it had begun to snow again. At first, it was just tiny little flurries dancing on the northward wind. In less than an hour, the city was covered with a new layer of snow. Sweet searched alleys and tiny streets, but there was no sign of Rebecca. The market was closed and there was hardly a soul on the streets. An old white man was behind the market stacking the wood from broken produce crates. He was stacking them into and old sleigh hitched to an old hag of a horse. Sweet thought he was probably stealing the crates for firewood. "Excuse me, Mister," Sweet yelled.

He immediately stopped what he was doing and looked around before looking at the girl, but he didn't answer. "How long as the market been closed?" she yelled.

"Since early this afternoon," he yelled back.

"Thank you," Sweet yelled. If Rebecca were out in this cold since early afternoon, she would be frozen to death, Sweet thought. As she started for home, she realized that the wind blew harder and now she would be walking into the storm instead of away from it. The snow was no longer flurries, but a heavy wet snow that was blinding. She could hardly see three feet in front of her and she kept her head tucked because the snow was blowing right at her. It took much longer to get home and walking was difficult. It had taken Sweet a little more than an hour and she was met at the door by both Lillian and Beth.

"Did you see her? Had anyone seen her?" Lillian asked.

"I'm sure the market was no longer open in this weather."

Sweet struggled to shed her wet clothes and boots. "No. There was no sign of her. A man outside the market told me that they closed early this afternoon."

Beth watched as Lillian's face seemed to melt. Tears welled in her eyes and she quickly covered her mouth with her hand and began to sob. "Alright now Lillian, don't jump to conclusions. We don't know what has happened. Maybe she fell and someone took her in or to the hospital. Let's just wait a few days until the weather is better, and we'll look again. We can check the hospital. When more people are about we can ask if anyone has seen her or she may send us word."

"You're right, of course Miss Beth. It's just that I am so worried."

"Worrying has never accomplished anything. I'm sure she is just fine. Try not to worry."

The snow didn't let up for two and a half days, covering the city with twenty-two additional inches of snow. It was a Thursday afternoon when the snow finally stopped and the sun began to shine again. People began to slowly, emerge from their forced hibernation to clear away as much snow and ice as possible in the hope of returning to some sense of normalcy. The sun was high in the sky and very bright, but it was bitterly cold.

Rebecca slept through the storm, only waking to take a little chicken broth and Miss Kathy's special tonic. She finally awoke on Thursday evening. "What day is it?" she mumbled.

Benjamin was by her side in a moment. He kneeled down and whispered to her. "It's Thursday. You've been asleep for a four of days."

It took time for his words to penetrate. "THURSDAY!" she said with alarm as she tried to sit up. "I've got to go. I've got to let Mama and Miss Beth know that I'm all right."

"You can't go anywhere Rebecca. You can't even stand. You have a broken leg. It will be weeks before you can walk on that leg. Unless your Mother can send a carriage for you, you will be here with me and my Grand for a while."

It was as if she didn't even remember. She stared at Benjamin for a couple of seconds as she slid her hand over the boards and bandages around her leg. "You've got to go and tell them what happened."

Benjamin smiled. "Rebecca, I don't even know what happened. All I know is that I found you badly beaten and lying in the snow. Who did this to you?"

Rebecca didn't answer right away, but Benjamin pressed her. "I mean, you were really beaten up. My Nana stitched the gash over your eye and she set your broken leg. Who would do this to you?"

Her hands touched the bandages around her face and eye, as if she doubted Benjamin's words. "It was a thief," Rebecca whispered as she fell back onto the pillows.

"A thief?"

"Yes, he tried to steal my package of rice, flour, and sugar."

"Uh-hu," Benjamin said, but he didn't believe she was telling the truth. Why would someone who didn't even know her, give her such a beating? No, this was done by someone who knew Rebecca and wanted to hurt her, Benjamin thought, but he would not press her further.

"Benjamin, you have to go to my Mama and tell her about my leg. You have to tell her that I am well and I'll be coming home as soon as I can."

"I will," he said. "You lay back down and rest. I promise, I'll go to them as soon as I can. What's the address?"

"1105 Walnut Street; Can you go today?"

"No, but first thing tomorrow, I promise."

"Thank you." Satisfied that Benjamin would go to her mother and Miss Beth, Rebecca was asleep again within minutes.

It was Sweet who answered Benjamin's knock at the back door. "Miss Lillian," she screamed. She left Benjamin standing in the foyer as she went screaming into the kitchen. "Miss Lillian, there is a man say he got news bout Rebecca!"

Lillian dropped the dough she was kneading and ran to the door. Beth came running from the front of the house. "Benjamin," Beth said in surprise.

"You know where my Rebecca is?" Lillian said.

"Yes Ma'am."

"Come in, come in," she said. Lillian helped Benjamin out of his heavy coat and scarf. "Sweet," she called. "Get Mr. Benjamin a cup of tea."

"Yes Ma'am," Sweet said.

"Where is she?"

"She's staying at my grandmother's house. She was hurt really bad and with the storm and all, I couldn't get her here."

"Hurt? What happened to her?" Lillian led Benjamin to the kitchen table and Sweet sat a steaming cup of tea on the table and motioned for him to sit.

"Well, Ma'am, she says that a thief beat her up and tried to take her package."

Lillian weighed this information skeptically. "You sound as if you don't believe her," she said.

"Well she was beat pretty badly. Someone took their fist to her face and then stomped her in the chest and stomach. Her leg was stomped so hard that it broke. She suffered a gaping gash down the side of her face and another over her eye. Whoever beat Rebecca, knew her. It really looked kind of personal to me, Ma'am."

"But Rebecca doesn't know anyone who would do such a thing."

"Well, it's for sure someone did beat her up. Maybe they even thought they had killed her."

"Can I see her?"

"I'm sure my Nana wouldn't mind if you come by to see her, but it will be sometime before she can come home. I mean, with all the snow and ice, she can't walk. I'm going to see if I can get her some crutches but until the snow and ice have melted away, she won't be walking too far."

"Do you think I could go with you now?"

"Yes Ma'am. That would be just fine."

Sweet brought Benjamin another cup of tea while Lillian dressed to walk with him to his grandmother's house. She hadn't seen Rebecca for four days and she was anxious to see her.

As Benjamin and Lillian walked the short distance to his Grandmother's Lillian asked many questions, most of which Benjamin could answer. He told her that his Grandmother was known as Miss Kathy and that she wasn't a real doctor but had been practicing medicine in the Negro Neighborhood for as long as he could remember. He told her that Miss Kathy had set Rebecca's broken leg and sewed up the gashes in her face. Other than that, he could not tell Lillian how or why Rebecca had been attacked.

Once they reached the small house, Miss Kathy and Benjamin were kind enough to leave Rebecca and Lillian alone for a few moments. Rebecca tried to sit up with some difficulty. "Mama, you're here. I wanted to come home but I couldn't."

Lillian was not prepared for what she saw when she looked at the face of her once beautiful daughter. She pulled a chair close to the cot and sat down. "It's all right baby. I can see that you couldn't get home. What happened? Who did this to you?"

Rebecca was silent. She turned her head away from her mother but not before Lillian saw the tears that welled in the corners of her bruised eyes.

Rebecca attempted to tell the same lie about someone trying to steal her package but Lillian cut her off. "That isn't what happened, Rebecca. No one is going to beat you like this for a couple of sacks of rice and flour, so don't tell that lie again. All right," Lillian said. "You don't want to tell me now. I will wait until you feel ready to talk but, know this Rebecca, you will have to tell me and soon. I can't help but wonder who could hate you enough to do this to you." Rebecca was still silent.

Lillian ran her hand over Rebecca's hair. She took her chin in her hand and Rebecca winced. Then she turned her face from side to side as she inspected her wounds. Still, Rebecca was silent.

Lillian placed a light kiss on the unmarred cheek then stood to leave. She put the chair back and called for Miss Kathy and Benjamin. "I don't even know what to say to you. I am so thankful that you found my daughter, Benjamin. She may have lay on the ice and died if not for you. And, Miss Kathy, I am sorry that we had to meet over such a terrible thing but, I am grateful that God has blessed you with the gift of healing and you were here to take care of my daughter. Thank you Miss Kathy."

Lillian embraced them both as Rebecca watched from her cot without saying a word. "I will come again soon, if that is all right with you Miss Kathy?"

"Rebecca's wounds may take quite some time to heal, especially her broken leg. She is welcome to stay as long as necessary and until then, you may come whenever you like. You are welcome here, Miss Lillian."

CHAPTER 18

Humiliation

Beth and Sweet met Lillian at the door when she returned from seeing Rebecca. Her expression was severe. They knew that she was pleased to finally see Rebecca, but there was no joy in her expression. For as long as Beth had known Lillian, she had walked tall with a regal stature but now her shoulders were rounded and her head hung low. Her heart was heavy. The injuries Rebecca suffered would be heart wrenching for any mother to see.

"Well, how was she?" Beth wanted to know.

"Bad, Miss Beth. It's very bad." Lillian said while shaking her head. She seemed to run out of breath and she slumped down in a kitchen chair and dropped her head into her hands. "I'm sure Rebecca doesn't know it yet but she will never be beautiful again. She is scarred for the rest of her life and I know that this was no accident."

Sweet ran over and began to softly massage Lillian's back in an effort to console her.

"What are you saying?" Beth asked as she sat opposite Lillian at the kitchen table. "You think someone did this to hurt Rebecca? Who would do such a thing?"

Lillian raised her head slowly and looked into Beth eyes. "Someone who felt wronged by Rebecca. I begged her but she wouldn't tell me so I can only guess."

"What about that young man that was hurt in the park with Rebecca?"

"Jonah? Oh no, Jonah loved Rebecca before he was hurt. This was done by someone who hated her. Whoever did this, wanted to destroy her, they wanted to kill her." Lillian shook her head as if in disbelief. "Only hatred could do this kind of damage."

Beth didn't know what she could say to Lillian that would make her feel any better. Both women were silent for some time until Lillian stood. She splashed some cool water in her face to wash away her tears. She dried her hands and face on a towel and began to prepare supper without another word. Taking Lillian's lead, Sweet fetched a few sweet potatoes and began to prepare them for baking. Beth slowly walked from the kitchen and they each went about the rest of their day as if everything was normal.

Lillian walked to Miss Kathy's at least twice a week to visit with Rebecca. Most of the time, Benjamin was not at home. Miss Kathy was always nice and polite. Lillian would sometimes bring food and at other times she gave Miss Kathy money to help and to thank her for caring for Rebecca. One day in February, Miss Kathy met Lillian outside the door. It was a blustery cold day snow flurries danced on the wind. Miss Kathy stood shivering a couple of doors away from her house. At first Lillian thought something dreadful must have happened to Rebecca. "Oh my God, Miss Kathy! What's happened?"

Miss Kathy waved her arm and shook her head. "Nothing has happened to your girl since the last time you saw her, but what did happen was likely before she got the crap beat out of her."

Lillian just stood there, their warm breath making puffs of smoke in the cold air. "I don't understand," she said.

"I think she's carrying a child," Miss Kathy said.

"Pregnant? Oh my God!"

"Yes Ma'am. She has been puking in a bucket for the past two days. She can't keep a crumb down. She looks a bit bloated too."

"Oh my God!" Lillian said again.

"I thought you should tell her."

"I will. Thank you Miss Kathy. Now, let us get out of this cold." Lillian linked her arm through the old woman's arm and they went inside.

Rebecca lay on the cot with her leg propped up and her face turned toward the wall. She snored softly. Lillian was content to sit with Miss Kathy and sip hot tea until Rebecca woke.

It was nearly an hour before Rebecca was roused from her nap. "Mama?" she said.

Lillian pulled her chair close to cot. "How are you feeling, honey?" she asked.

"I've been sick to my stomach lately."

"Miss Kathy told me. Do you know why?" Rebecca shook her head. "I think you might be with child," Lillian said. Rebecca just glared at her mother as if she didn't understand. "You are going to have a baby, child," Lillian said. "Do you understand? Now do you want to tell me who did this to you?"

Rebecca's eyes seemed to stretch open but she shook her head again to say that she would not tell. Then she turned her face away from Lillian and began to softly sob into her pillow.

Lillian wanted to take Rebecca by the shoulders and shake her until she would tell her what happened to her. Was she raped the same night she was attacked or had the attack had something to do with the child she carried. There were so many questions and Rebecca would not answer any of them.

Lillian's visit with Rebecca was short that day. She couldn't bear to look at her daughter without feeling a simmering rage in her spirit. She thanked Miss Kathy as usual and promised to return in a few days.

Weeks later, Philadelphia was still covered in ice and was experiencing intermittent bouts of freezing rain. However, feeling sick of being shut in, Beth decided to have lunch with her neighbor Ellen in the Nottingham's small sitting room. Beth was excited to tell Ellen of her brother-in-law James' expected spring visit. She hadn't seen James in more than a year and she was excited for his visit. After a while, the conversation turned to Rebecca, and Beth shared with Ellen all that she knew of Rebecca's injuries and subsequent recovery. She also told her that Rebecca refused to tell anyone who had attacked her.

"Oh my God," Ellen said sympathetically. "Why do you suppose she won't tell?"

"I probably shouldn't say this but Lillian has had a difficult time with Rebecca ever since we arrived here in Philadelphia. As you can see, the girl is really fair and she's got it into her head to pass."

"Pass?" Ellen repeated. "What does that mean?"

Beth looked at her naïve friend in disbelief. "Pass for white, Ellen. Very fair skinned blacks have been doing it for years and most of the time we whites are none the wiser."

The look on Ellen's face was pure shock. "And what does this have to do with Rebecca?"

"Rebecca has had it in her head for some time now that she believes she is fair enough to pass. Oh, Lillian doesn't know that I am aware of these things but I have heard her mother warn her of such thinking a number of times. Now, I'm sure that beating she took has something to do with her trying to pass for white."

"So you think that a white man found out that he had been tricked by Rebecca?"

"Yes, of course I don't know the details of what happened but I wouldn't be surprised if that was the truth of it." Ellen was shocked and Beth realized that she had said too much. However, neither of the women knew that their conversation was being over-heard by Mary, the Nottingham's nanny.

As soon as she was able to get away, Mary went to the back door of the Vance house and asked Sweet if she might speak with Miss Lillian. Sweet took Mary by the hand and led her into the warm kitchen. Miss Beth was napping in her bedroom so Lillian was the only one in the kitchen.

"Miss Lillian," Sweet began. "Mary has something she would like to tell you about Rebecca."

Lillian was rolling out dough to cut biscuits for dinner. Her hands were covered in flour and her eyes were moist with unshed tears. "Hello Mary," she said as she wiped the flour from her hands onto her apron.

"Hello," Mary said timidly.

"What is it, Dear?" Lillian wanted to get to the meat of this conversation quickly.

"I think I know who beat Rebecca," she said. "Well, I don't really know if he beat her but I know who Rebecca was seeing."

With that Lillian grabbed the girl by the hands and they both sat down. "Tell me all that you know, Mary."

Mary shook her head before she began. "Rebecca was seeing one of Mr. Nottingham's associates. He is an accountant, Mr. Garrett Colbert, and they saw each other in secret most of the summer. But when Rebecca came to help out at the Nottingham's dinner he was there and saw her in her maid uniform. They didn't see each other after that, even though Rebecca wanted to see him one last time to explain."

"An accountant," Lillian repeated in disbelief.

"There's more, Miss Lillian." Mary paused to make sure she had Lillian's full attention. "About a month ago, right after Christmas, I heard Mr. Colbert speaking with Mr. Nottingham about a woman he was seeing. He told Mr. Nottingham that he found out that the woman was a Negro and that he gave her what she deserved. He never said that it was Rebecca but I know that was who he talked about. I'm sure Mr. Nottingham didn't know either but he agreed that Mr. Colbert had done the right thing to teach these women to stay in their place."

Lillian just sat quiet for several minutes. Finally, she said, "Thank you, Mary. You have been very helpful."

∽

March winds blew a promise of the coming spring but spring did not appear until well into May. When the temperatures finally did rise above freezing, the Delaware and Schuylkill Rivers began to thaw and thick slabs of ice broke off, allowing water to pour into the city. The streets of the city and the roads west of the Schuylkill were covered in wet mud. Travel under such conditions was as troublesome to maneuver through as the snow had been.

However, nothing would deter Lillian from seeing her daughter once she knew where to go. Lillian continued to walk several blocks to Miss Kathy's house twice a week. She was saddened every time she looked at Rebecca's marred face and rapidly swelling belly, but she learned to smile as if nothing was wrong.

Rebecca's wounds healed nicely and Miss Kathy was praised for her wonderful handy work with the needle. However, it did not matter how neatly the stitching, Rebecca's scars, both physical and psychological, would not be so easily hidden. Rebecca's left eye was partially closed and would likely never open as before the beating. Though her wounds were healing, Rebecca was not the same person. Sometimes when Lillian looked at her daughter, she could not help but be reminded of Jonah's injured to eye and the words of a sermon she heard would come to mine. "*An eye for an eye,"* the minister's booming voice had shouted over the hushed congregation. Lillian would remember those words for years to come.

Benjamin spent many hours working at the hotel, but when he came to his grandmother's little house, Rebecca took every moment of his attention. He doted on Rebecca, seeing to her every need or want. He would help her to exercise her leg and she could now walk with some difficulty. He would assure her that her scars did not diminish her beauty. Even though he had not confided in anyone, his grandmother knew that he was falling in love with Rebecca. Miss Kathy eventually told Benjamin of Rebecca's condition and he seemed to take it all in stride.

It had been four months since the incident and still Rebecca refused to name her attacker. Lillian eventually told Beth about Garrett Colbert but Beth could offer no advice in the matter. She would only say that it was best that Rebecca not be anywhere near this man again.

It was the middle of May when Lillian paid Mr. Briggs to bring Rebecca home. Though Beth knew everything there was to know about what happened to Rebecca, she was not prepared for the girl she saw emerge from the carriage on that sunny May afternoon. Rebecca was pale, her body was round with child, her head hung, and her shoulders slumped as if the burden of shame was too great. Benjamin was at her side, his hand around her waist as he led her into the house. She greeted Beth warmly but she hardly lifted her head.

After only a few days, Rebecca finally opened up to her mother, telling her everything that had happened between her and Garrett. Lillian peeked into Rebecca's bedroom to check on her and without warning, Rebecca just blurted out, "I thought I could make him love me," she said through tears.

Lillian went into her room and wrapped Rebecca in her arms as she whispered in the girl's ear. "You made two mistakes. I tried to warn you about trying to pass for white. That was your first mistake. The second was thinking that you could make any man love you, any man. It doesn't work that way."

"But my father loved you."

Lillian released her and sat back on the bed. "Your father knew who and what I was. I was his slave. I never once tried to make him love me. We were simply drawn to one another. We now know it was a love that should have never been. Look what his love did. It not only destroyed him, he took a little piece of all of us when he died." They were both quiet for a time. "Rebecca, your life will never be the same but you are a free woman. I know that this freedom hasn't been as great as we thought it would be but we have something that we never had as slaves."

"Yeah, Mama? What? We still work for white people, cleaning and cooking and doing their bidding. They still treat us as if we're dirt or pets. It makes me sick that Miss Beth keeps trying to act as if we are family. We are not family. She is still white and we work for her. So what good is freedom? I almost want to go back to Gloria. At least there I knew it was no use dreaming of something better."

Lillian sat down again and took Rebecca's hands in her own. "Everything you say is true but as free people we have choices that we didn't have on the plantation. You can't go back to Virginia as a free woman. If you go back, you will be a slave again."

"But I don't want to stay here. I hate going to church because of what happened to Jonah and now this. I'm carrying a child with the father nowhere around. I want to leave Philadelphia. All the Negros live together, just like on the plantation. Everyone knows everything about you and they judge you and talk about you."

"All of that is true but you brought all of this on yourself. You were pig headed and stubborn and now you have to live with the choices you've made. Yeah, people will stare and people will talk, but you will get over it and so will they."

Rebecca pulled away and threw herself on the bed in tears. Lillian stood to leave but once at the door, she turned to her daughter again. "You might hate church, but that is where you need to go. The same people that you think will talk about you, will also pray for you and hold your hand in time of trouble. You might want to try talking to God about all of this. Pray Rebecca. It works."

Rebecca did pray and when she wasn't praying, she was in bed. Both Lillian and Beth agreed that Rebecca would need a few days to settle in, accept her plight and bear up in strength.

"Yes, just a few days," Lillian confirmed. "But I have no intention of allowing Rebecca to wallow in her misfortune."

"I agree," Beth said as if Lillian needed her approval.

For four days Rebecca did not leave her bed. Lillian sent up plates of food which Sweet returned to the kitchen uneaten. On the fifth day of Rebecca's self-imposed exile, Lillian stormed into her room at sun rise. "Get up," she said in a low voice that was simmering with anger.

Surprised, Rebecca sat up with wide eyes. "I don't want to get up."

"I didn't ask you what you wanted. I said, get up."

"But I don't feel well, mother."

"That is because you want to waste your days feeling sorry for yourself but I will no longer allow you to wallow in self-pity. Yes, you suffered some hardship but as I told you before, you will get over it. So get up and get dressed. You have chores to do." With that, Lillian turned and stormed from the room, not leaving Rebecca any chance to response.

Minutes later Rebecca appeared with red-rimmed sullen eyes and a downcast expression. Lillian rattled off a list of chores that she expected Rebecca to complete. Lillian had instructed Sweet not to feel sorry for Rebecca and to let her complete her chores on her own. Then she and Sweet gave no special notice to Rebecca until the end of the day.

CHAPTER 19

CONFESSION

During the waning days of his recovery, James thought a great deal about his feelings for Beth. Why had he not recognized how deeply he felt for her before now? He hadn't even admitted to himself how he felt before he shared his feelings with Louis. He thought about all the times he had witnessed her being hurt by David and how he had wanted to embrace her and console her. He also remembered the one time she had come to him broken and hurt and he couldn't bring himself to betray David. Talking with Louis had awakened all of those feelings he thought he had successfully subdued. He had spent so many years trying to deny his feelings for Beth that now that he had acknowledged how he felt, there was no turning back.

Beth was all he could think of as he went about preparing for his trip to Philadelphia. He was now anxious to see her and for her to meet Louis. Although he had scheduled several meetings in the city, he had planned to be there for at least a week and would have ample time to spend with Beth.

James and Louis arrived in Philadelphia late on the evening of Sunday, May 16, 1841. Recent floods had left the streets and even some of the sidewalks covered with thick mud. They immediately checked into the City Hotel on Market Street.

With Louis' olive colored skin and shock of curly charcoal hair, he could have passed for a Cuban or a dark Italian but because he had traveled with an obvious southern planter, his Negro heritage was assumed. He was not allowed to eat in the hotel dining room or come and go by the front entrance. In fact, the only eating establishments where he was welcomed were those owned and run by Blacks.

James apologized as if it was all his doing and Louis just shook his head. Nothing happened that he hadn't expected.

Louis accompanied James to several meetings on Monday morning. His presence was never questioned by the other business men in attendance. However, when James and Louis met with a New England merchant, the man was obviously impressed with Louis' knowledge of European supply and demand. Louis had just eloquently explained the reason for the rise in European demand for Virginia tobacco when the man interrupted saying, "That's a damn smart nigger you got there, fellow."

Neither of the brothers were surprised at this but it seems that they both wanted to further shock this racist merchant. James cleared his throat loudly. "Yes, Mr. Bissette is quite intelligent but he's not my nigger.

Mr. Louis Bissette is a free man of color, and my half-brother."

Louis stood and put his hand forward to shake the hand of the merchant who stood there looking as if he'd been caught in something nasty. "So, do we have a deal?" James asked. "You won't get better prices anywhere on the east coast."

Reluctantly, the merchant agreed to the terms James set forth but refused the hand shake from Louis and their last meeting was concluded.

They returned to the hotel in late afternoon to prepare for dinner at Beth's house.

❧

Beth was so excited she could hardly contain herself. Lillian and Rebecca could not understand her excitement. Lillian really had no feelings toward James whatsoever. She knew him first as a spoiled kid and then as a kind hearted master. She didn't miss him or anyone else on Gloria. She only felt curiosity about his sudden concern for her and Rebecca.

Even though Lillian had prepared the meal, Beth had instructed her that they would all have dinner together in the drawing room that evening. She hired a woman to help Sweet in the kitchen and with the serving. Beth was anxious to show James that they were living as a family.

When the knock on the door finally sounded, Beth froze. "Oh my God, they're here!"

"They?" Lillian questioned. "I thought it was just Massa James."

317

"He isn't your master anymore, Lillian. He is Mister James and he is bringing the brother I told you about."

Lillian just looked at Beth in wonder. She didn't remember any conversation about another brother. "Sweet," she called. "Fix your hair then open the door."

Sweet opened the door and before James could cross the threshold, Beth came running and James opened his arms to receive her. With very little effort, James lifted Beth in a crushing embrace and swung her around before he gently set her back on her feet. "Oh my God, are you really here?" she asked breathlessly.

"Yes, I'm really here." He held her away from him for a moment. "Look at you. You haven't aged. You are as beautiful as you were the first time I saw you." He pulled her to him again and as they embraced the smell of lilac in her hair heightened his senses as did her soft touch on his hand. *Oh, if he could only hold her in this embrace forever he would finally know happiness, he thought.*

Beth could not return the compliment as James was little more than a shadow of the man she remembered. He was noticeably thinner and his handsome face seemed gaunt and colorless. They embraced again and held on to each other for a little longer than was customary.

Louis had handed off his jacket and hat to Sweet and stood patiently by the door waiting to be noticed. Likewise, Lillian and Rebecca stood waiting a few feet away. Finally, James pulled away. "Beth, here is someone I'd like you to meet." He motioned for Louis to step forward and he did so. "This is Louis, the brother that I wrote you about."

Louis bowed deeply. "Hello," he said in his most gallant voice of a southern gentleman. In keeping with that persona, he brought Beth's hand to his lips and kissed it ever so gently.

Lillian glanced at Louis and her legs seemed to weaken. She couldn't believe what she was seeing. He was younger and darker but he had the same mass of charcoal curly hair and green eyes. His hair was long and he had it pulled back and tied. The man who stood only a few feet away looked like a younger, slimmer version of the man she had loved her entire life. She wanted to reach out and touch him to prove that he was real and not a ghost from her past. She hadn't even realized that she had whispered his name. "David."

Louis took a step closer to Lillian and bowed deeply. "Louis Bissette, Ma'am," he announced as he presented his hand.

"Oh," Lillian whispered as she bowed her head slightly and placed her hand in his. "I'm happy to meet you." To her amazement, Louis kissed her hand.

"Lillian," James said. "I am so happy to see you. I can see from the look on your face that you've noticed how much Louis looks like David." Lillian nodded in affirmation. "Well," James went on. "Louis is my younger brother. I couldn't believe it when we first met." He paused a moment to look Lillian up and down. "You look well. You are still a beautiful woman, Lillian."

Her view seemed to ripple as if she were looking through a water filled glass. She opened her mouth to speak and found that the words would not come out for several seconds. "Thank you," she managed to whisper. Besides the fact that this man was standing in front of her looking like David's twin, she really didn't know what to say to her former master.

"Where is Rebecca?" James asked.

An eerie silence descended over the entry hall and Rebecca, who had been standing beside her mother now hid her face behind her hands. "Here she is," Lillian said as a firm hand on the small of Rebecca's back guided her over to James. The uncomfortable silence lasted for a few more moments as James took in the scars on Rebecca's face, the closed eye and her round belly. He looked toward Beth as if he expected some explanation from her.

Rebecca performed a clumsy courtesy. "I'm happy to see you again," she said hesitantly. "Mr. James."

"Mr.?" He questioned. "I know that it is all a bit confusing but I would really like it if you called me Uncle James." With that he pulled Rebecca into a firm embrace which took her completely by surprised. Beth, Lillian, and even Louis could not hide their shock. This was not the James that the women knew when they were on Gloria.

With introductions and pleasantries out of the way, Beth led James and Louis into the sitting room. Rebecca escaped into the kitchen with Sweet and Lillian would have done the same if Beth had not stopped her. "Lillian," she whispered. "I would like you to join us in the sitting room."

James and Beth chattered on as they tried to catch each other up on the past two years. Then Beth explained to James everything she knew of Rebecca's ordeal and although he couldn't have been more shocked by the entire sordid matter, he showed genuine concern for Rebecca. "Where on earth would she get the idea of passing?"

"I don't know but Lillian has been trying to set her straight ever since our arrival in the city. She is free here in Philadelphia, without the constraints of plantation life. Here she could feel that anything is possible. I'm sure she thought that if she could pass for white and escape the scourge of racism, it would be the ultimate freedom."

James just shook his head in disbelief. "So you have no idea who attacked her and left her battered, scarred, and pregnant.

"We have an idea but there isn't anything we can do about it. He is a prominent citizen, a well know accountant. The authorities would never arrest him. Besides, any attention to the matter would only serve to drag Rebecca's name through the mud again."

"I guess you're right."

"Lillian is worried what might happen if Rebecca was to run into this man again or if he learns that she is carrying his child. Lillian has not let her stray far from the house since her return."

"Don't worry, Beth. I will see to her safety."

Lillian sat across from Louis feeling uncomfortable and confused. "I take it no one has bothered to explain how James came to have another brother?" he said.

"Miss Beth mentioned it, but she didn't give much detail."

"Well, I've heard a lot about you. It is only fair that you know my story as well." Lillian eyed him suspiciously but she said nothing. "My mother was once a slave on the Gloria plantation. Same as many, Big Bill took advantage of her and sold her soon after I was born."

"What is your mother's name?"

"She is passed on now, but her name was Martina?"

"Martina?" Lillian repeated. "I remember my Mama talking about a Martina." Lillian was thoughtful for a few moments and Louis gave her time. "So, if Big Bill sold off your Mama, how did Massa, I mean Mr. James, find you?"

"My Mama and I were sold to the Bissette Plantation in New Orleans. We were manumitted by Master Bissette on his death bed so I've lived most of my adult life as a free man in New Orleans."

"Oh," Lillian said, not bothering to hide her surprise that Louis had been free for so long. "So, that is where Massa, I mean Mister James found you?"

"Yes, but not before I experienced some terrible misfortune."

"Oh?"

"Yes. Unfortunately, I lost my mother, wife, and two daughters to a suspicious fire. I was more than devastated and didn't know if I would ever get over the loss. I had made up my mind that I had to leave New Orleans. Living there was a daily reminder of my devastation. I didn't know where I was going, I was just going and that's when a letter arrived from James Vance of Virginia. He didn't, at first tell me that we were kin. He offered me the job of Overseer on Gloria and I took it."

Lillian was touched by the ordeal Louis suffered and she suddenly felt the need to comfort this beautiful, strong man. She reached over and placed her hand softly over his. "I'm so sorry," she said.

"Don't be. I believe that the trials we suffer only serve to make us stronger. I will never stop loving my family but I am still here and I'm sure that God has wonderful things in store for me."

Lillian only smiled. She had no words to express the warm feelings she felt for this man she barely knew.

Supper was very pleasant. Louis regaled the family with humorous stories of mishaps and confusions from his experience with growing tobacco for the first time. Rebecca and Lillian were both quiet. They were having a difficult time with this new family atmosphere that Beth wanted to present to James. They spent most of their lives as his slaves with James as their Master. It was not easy to suddenly see James as a kindly uncle. However, Beth and James seemed to be getting on very well. Lillian couldn't remember when she had seen Beth so happy.

Once the meal was consumed, Lillian rose to help Sweet clear away the dishes but James stopped her. "Wait Lillian. There is something I'd like to say." They all stopped and turned to James. "I know this all may seem very strange to you so I would like to explain a few things. First, you should know that when Elizabeth first arrived on Gloria she would often lecture my brother and me on the evils of slavery. She was convinced that it was a vile system and a sin against God. However, slavery was all we knew and our very way of life depended on slavery. "He paused as if to reflect on this before going on. " A great deal has changed since those days. "Up until my father banned my brother from the plantation, I looked up to David. He was my big brother and I loved him unconditionally.

"When I found Big Bill's journals, it was shocking to all of us. I know that you have all been dealing with David's death. Beth, I'm sure you have been mourning your marriage." Beth did not answer. "And Lillian and Rebecca, I know that you are both mourning David's death as you come to terms with your new found freedom. But me, I have been struggling with a whole host of things. First, I was raised to think that blacks were beneath me. Once I learned that David was half black, it destroyed everything I knew about the races of man. What Big Bill did by switching David with the deceased Vance son, destroyed our entire family. Yes, I said our family. David was my half-brother, just as Louis is my half-brother. Rebecca that makes you my niece."

Rebecca looked up but said nothing. "James, it isn't necessary for you go on like this." Beth said.

"I know," he said. "Rebecca, I would love to take you away from everything that has ever hurt you but, the truth is I can't take you back to Virginia as a free woman. If you come back, you will be a slave again."

"I know. That's what Mama says."

"You are my blood and I will do everything in my power to see you safe and happy wherever you chose to go. We are family."

"Thank you," Rebecca mumbled. She was still very confused.

"I know that the society may not see us as family but I do and that's what is important."

The room went silent and Beth reached over to pat James on the hand as if she understood. Lillian again turned to leave the room.

"Wait," James went on. "Beth, I have loved you since the day you yelled at me for not coming when we both heard little Maggie screaming. Do you remember that day?"

Louis looked up just in time to catch Lillian staring at him. He smiled back as if to say, I caught you. At this point, Lillian looked toward Beth who nodded her consent for Lillian and Rebecca to leave the room. Louis feigned disinterest and began to fidget in his chair before he got up and left the room. He went to the front parlor. "Of course I do," Beth said.

Lillian stopped just inside the kitchen door. She listened for a few minutes.

"I loved you even then but you were David's wife. Every time he hurt you, I hurt for you but there was nothing to be done. Now, I am all alone. Besides the Beaufords of North Caroline, which I have never seen, they disconnected from the Vance's when my mother passed. You all are all the family I have. Beth, if you will come back to Virginia with me . . ." James next words were smothered away by an attack of coughing that seemed to leave him spent of all energy. Minutes passed before he could speak again.

Beth was visibly shocked and heartbroken as she witnessed James cough blood into his handkerchief, then discreetly tuck it into his breast pocket. She looked down to hide her face. When she finally lifted her head, she was met with and expression on James' face that she had never witnessed before now.

James was not just physically ill, he was heart sick as well. He had confessed his undying love but then stopped cold. His intention was to ask for her hand in marriage then punctuate the moment with a tight embrace and a passionate kiss. However, just as he reached for her, his throat constricted and an attack of the familiar dry hacking cough ensued, this time bringing up a spattering of blood on his handkerchief. Beth may have been expecting a proposal but none came. He was sure that their talk had left Beth more confused than ever.

"James, I tried to stop you," Beth whispered. "I really didn't want you to reveal all of your feelings."

"Why not. This is new for all of you but I have been struggling with this for quite a long time."

"James, you can't expect me to just pick up and leave Philadelphia," Beth said. "Please don't forget that I've done this before."

"I am not David. Gloria needs a mistress and I need you. It isn't as if we don't know each other. You hardly knew David when you married him."

Lillian had heard enough and she moved away from the door and began to help Sweet and Rebecca with cleaning the kitchen.

"That isn't fair James. The circumstances were different."

"I am not here to pressure you, Beth. I have been miserable, thinking of you and all that has happened. It took time and a considerable amount of thought to come to this. Now, I have laid my soul bare. It is . . ." Another attack of coughing ensued and James wondered even as he tried to catch his breath, how could he ask for Beth's hand in marriage when there was the chance that he may not live long enough to make her happy. When he was able to speak again, in a raspy voice he said, "We are here for the next week so I'm sure we will speak of this again."

"Where are you staying?" Beth wanted to know.

"We are in the City Hotel on Market Street."

"You are welcome to stay here. I have plenty of room."

"That sounds wonderful. Louis and I will retrieve our belongings from the hotel and return as soon as we are able. Is that all right?"

"Yes, of course," Beth said.

"I will not speak of this again unless you are ready."

"James, I don't mean to hurt you but I do need time to think. Please say that you understand."

"I do. As I said, I've been struggling with this for months."

"It is obvious that you are ill."

"Yes," he somberly confessed. "I can't seem to get over this cough," he said between coughs. When the coughing finally stopped again and he could catch his breath, Beth insisted that he see a Philadelphia doctor before returning to Virginia, and he agreed.

Once the kitchen was tidy and Rebecca and Sweet had retired to their rooms, Lillian wanted to wait to see if Beth needed anything else before she retired. However, she and Mister James were still deep in conversation in the drawing room. Lillian found Louis in the front sitting room.

"Well," he said. "This has been quite an evening." Lillian gave him a half smile. "Is there something wrong, Lillian?"

"No, I just didn't expect any of this, none of us did. Especially Mister James asking Miss Beth to move back to Virginia."

"Oh, you heard that, did you? Well, I knew he loved her. He told me so but, if it makes you feel any better, I didn't know he planned to ask her to move back to Virginia so quickly."

"Though he didn't say it, I'm sure that he will ask her to marry him and if she accepts his proposal that will mean that I and Rebecca will be uprooted once again. We can't go back to Virginia and I would die before I went back there."

"Don't worry Lillian. I'm sure it will all work out."

As the week wore on James spent less and less time with his business associates and more time trying to woo Beth into moving back to Virginia. This also forced Lillian to spend more time with Louis who she found to be as charming as he was handsome. They easily developed a friendship void of any sexual tension. He was easy to talk with and Lillian found herself looking forward to their meetings.

As he promised, James saw Dr. Albert Burke, who was a well-known and celebrated internist from the University of Pennsylvania. James thought his examination was thorough and he was confident, although grieved at the doctor's diagnosis. He was diagnosed with a rare lung disease that the doctor predicted would take his life in a few years if he were lucky. The doctor also confirmed that it *was* very likely that he had inherited the disease from his father.

At first James just wanted to be alone. He needed time to reconcile himself to the reality that he may not even live another five years. He left that office feeling like he carried the heaviest burden of his life. The knowledge that he was responsible for the lives of so many people was foremost in his mind. Besides the love and responsibility he felt for Lillian, Rebecca, Louis, and Beth, there were the slaves to think about. If he died without an heir, his slaves would be sold at auction. There were at least sixty slaves on Gloria, many of them he had known most of his life and were sometimes connected to one another by family. He did not want to leave their lives in the unpredictable hands of fate.

After strolling around the city for what seemed like hours, he returned to Beth's house still not knowing how he would go on. He had planned to return to Virginia on Sunday and he needed to make ready. It was a struggle to keep Louis and Beth from worrying too much about him so he only gave them vague answers to their questions about his health and his visit with the doctor. However, his heart was heavy with many regrets and sorrows as he packed his bags to leave Philadelphia.

In the space of just a few hours everything in his life had changed. He now knew that he and Beth would never marry and he will likely die soon and alone.

In the guest room of Beth's house a Bible lay on the table and although James was never a very religious man, he felt an unusual compulsion to touch this book of many wonders. He had not read the Bible for many years, on this night he opened the book and read from Second Kings.

"And the prophet Isaiah the son of Amoz
came to him, and said unto him, Thus saith

> *the LORD, Set thine house in order; for thou*
> *shalt die, and not live."* (II Kings 20:1)

As he pondered those thoughts, he is somewhat removed from the conversation in the sitting room that evening. Louis and Lillian sat together on the small sofa in front of the window while he and Beth sat in chairs on either side of the fire place. Beth talked about how fond she has become of her charity work but James hardly heard a word. The scripture he read earlier that evening played in his head while a new plan suddenly became clear to him. He now knew what he must do to put his house in order.

CHAPTER 20

THE GIFT OF FRIENDSHIP

Spring had finally arrived in Philadelphia. A brisk wind blew dusty clouds toward the river and ushered warmer weather into the city. After such a long and brutal winter the citizens of Philadelphia were eager to enjoy the outdoors and warmer weather. Miss Kathy decided that it was a good day to tidy up her small two-room house. She opened the only two windows in the house to let the fresh air blow through. Her kitchen had served as a make shift hospital room for nearly six months and she was anxious to clean away the smell of medicine and the hoard of bottles and bandages.

Benjamin had been sleeping at a friend's house, after Rebecca had taken over his cot in the kitchen. He was back now and Miss Kathy noticed that he had begun to spend almost as much time in the cot as Rebecca did during her recovery. He rarely left the house except to go to his job at the City Hotel.

It was obvious to Miss Kathy that something was bothering her grandson but he was silent on the matter and she did not want to pry.

"Benji, the bed clothes on that cot have to be washed."

Benjamin did not hear Miss Kathy because his mind was some place far away.

"Benji!" she yelled.

"Yes, Ma'am," he answered.

"How is Rebecca doing?"

"I don't know. I haven't seen her since Mr. Briggs took her home."

Miss Kathy swung her arms wide, a gesture that told Benjamin to move away from the cot. She then proceeded to gather the soiled bed clothes from the cot. "I don't understand," she said. "You were watching over that girl like she was a new born babe and now you act like you don't even care how she is getting on."

"It ain't that Gran," he said as he dropped into one of the wooden chairs at the table. "Rebecca acts as if she doesn't even want to look at me. She acts like I did something to her and she still won't tell me what happened the night she was hurt."

"Well," Miss Kathy began. "We all know that something terrible happened to that girl and it's my guess she is still hurting and confused."

"Yeah," Benjamin said and then he was lost in his thoughts again.

"You love her, don't you?" his grandmother said.

"What, why, yes! How did you know?"

"I've known for a while. I never saw you take care of anything like you took care of that girl."

"Huh, there is no fooling you, Gran."

"Have you thought about the fact that she is carrying another man's baby?"

"Of course, but she just won't talk to me."

"She is just as confused as you are, son. Benjamin, if you love the girl you have to let her know."

"I know Gran. But I just don't know when or how."

"Well it is for sure you ain't gone make no progress sitting here feeling sorry for yourself. Go see her."

Benjamin took his grandmother's advice and showed up to Beth's backdoor on a warm May evening. Sweet opened the door. "Hey, Miss Sweet," Benjamin said shyly. "I need to speak with Miss Lillian if I may."

Sweet knew Benjamin had come to see Rebecca but she could not resist a little flirt with this handsome young man. "Sure," she said as her eyes moved over his young strong body. She smiled and winked at him but Benjamin kept his gaze as steady as an arrow. He resisted the impulse to return her flirt and tipped his hat instead. Sweet was disappointed that she could not get a rise out of Benjamin and turned and went back into the kitchen. Lillian soon appeared at the door.--

"Oh Benjamin, come in, come in" she said. "We missed you. Why haven't you come to see us before now?"

"I wasn't sure Rebecca wanted to see me," he said as he moved into the kitchen.

"Nonsense, why would she not want to see you?" She led Benjamin into the kitchen as she called for Rebecca who came slowly from the front of the house with her limp more pronounced than usual. "Benjamin is here to see you."

To the surprise of all of them, Rebecca's face seemed to light up at the sight of Benjamin. "Hello, Becca," he said softly. Lillian noticed that he had addressed her by a name that she hadn't heard in years.

"Hey," Rebecca whispered. They stood just looking at each other for a few moments. "Mother," Rebecca said. "May we sit out back for a while?"

Lillian nodded her approval and the two slipped out the back door quickly and quietly. They sat until well into the evening. Benjamin talked about his plans to resurrect his family's name in the catering business. He told Rebecca that he had been saving since he started his first job. He wondered why he chose to tell Rebecca so much. Was he trying to assure her that he would be financially able to care for her and her child or was he just trying to impress her? It really didn't matter. He just knew that he felt comfortable and easy in her presence.

Rebecca still wore the scars of her night of terror but when she smiled her beauty was still visible behind the scars. Benjamin had to resist the urge to just envelope her in his arms and assure her that nothing would harm her ever again. The two were quiet for a few minutes.

Benjamin could hold back no longer. "When are you going to tell me about that night, Rebecca?" He had to know.

Rebecca stiffened at first. Then she exhaled deeply and lifted her head to face Benjamin. "I'm going to tell you Benji because I know that you care about me, but you have to promise me that you won't tell another soul."

"I promise."

"I was seeing a young man that I met at the Nottingham's house. I fell in love with him and I thought he loved me. I gave myself to him because I loved him so and I was sure that he would propose marriage."

Now it was Benjamin who stiffened but he said nothing.

"Well," Rebecca paused. "He had no intention of proposing to me. He thought that I was a woman with no morals, a whore. I felt like such a fool but I could live with my mistake even if others could not."

At that point she stopped talking leaving Benjamin with more questions than answers. "The beating you took from this man was brutal. You offended him in some way. I've never heard of a man being that offended because he bedded a whore. What are you not telling me, Rebecca?"

Rebecca quickly got to her feet and walked away. She couldn't bear to look into Benjamin's face as she revealed her deadly secret. "He thought that I was white," she whispered. "When he found out that I was a Negro, he wanted to kill me. I'm pretty sure he thinks he did kill me."

"Does he know about the baby?"

"No. I'm not sure what he will do when he finds out."

Benjamin stood and embraced Rebecca. "We will just have to make sure that he doesn't find out."

They were quiet for a time and Rebecca seemed to relax into his embrace. Benjamin felt comfortable and she felt unburdened after telling the secret that she had kept for so many months. "I love you, Rebecca and I will do anything I can to protect you."

Rebecca did not confess her love for Benjamin but she did acknowledge to herself that she felt very comfortable with him.

After that day Benjamin came every couple of days and each time Rebecca seemed genuinely happy to see him.

 ⤳

It had been months since anyone had seen or heard from Althea and Lillian was beginning to worry again. When she had gone to hire Mr. Briggs to bring Rebecca home, she'd asked him to check in on Althea and report back to her.

Mr. Briggs informed Lillian that Althea had not been seen by anyone at church since early January. Now it was spring, a time when people were used to seeing Althea sprucing up the outside of her properties and tending to her garden. However, Mr. Briggs reported that the garden was overgrown and unkempt as were both her properties.

Everyone was so consumed with Rebecca's return and the visit from James and Louis that Lillian hadn't even thought about Althea. Now she was all she could think about.

On a sunny afternoon in the middle of week while James and Louis visited, Louis asked Lillian if she would like to take a walk. "Yes, I would love to take a walk with you, if you don't mind my checking on a friend while we are walking."

"Sure. I don't see why not."

Lillian was finding Louis very easy to like. They had begun to spend time together in the evenings after the house had settled down. He talked about the family he lost and Lillian learned that Louis loved music and reading. Before he left Louisiana he attended a Methodist Church with his family regularly. He also told her how he came to know Louis and become the Overseer on Gloria. Lillian thought he was fascinating and when he spoke, she was mesmerized by his voice and the things he said. The more time Lillian spent with Louis, the more she liked him. Besides being handsome, smart, and attentive, he was sometimes funny with a quirky sense of humor.

As soon as they left the front of Beth's house, Louis presented his arm and Lillian gladly entwined her arm in his. They moved slowly down Chestnut Street making a right turn on Seventh.

Althea's two houses on Lombard Street looked as if they had been abandoned. Large planks of wood had been nailed over the windows and doors. As Lillian stood there on the sidewalk, she was suddenly gripped with fear. She pulled her arm away from Louis and took a step toward the house. "Oh my God," she whispered.

"This is your friend's house?" Louis asked.

"It was the last time we spoke. I can't imagine what has happened to her."

"Why not ask one of her neighbors. I'm sure someone will be able to tell you what happened."

Louis hadn't even finished speaking before Lillian ran to the nearest house on the block. It was the home of an elderly black woman who Lillian remembered had always been kind to her and Rebecca. She knocked frantically on the door and in minutes, the woman cracked the door open just a fraction and peeped through the small opening. "Mrs. Winter, do you remember me?" Lillian asked. The woman shook her head yes but she said nothing. Lillian didn't wait for her to speak. "I'm looking for Althea Brown. Do you know what has happened to her or her husband Bernie?"

Several seconds passed before Mrs. Winter responded. She slowly opened her door and came outside, all the while shaking her head as if in disbelief. Finally, she said, "Althea is in Penn Hospital. Folks say she lost her mind after her man Bernie drank himself into a stupor and froze to death this past winter. The city was gonna take the houses any ways cause that no good man drank up all her money and she couldn't pay the taxes. Then he up and dies and I guess it was just too much for her to take. When the constable came to evict Althea, she was in there talking out of her head, you know, crazy like. The constable sent the head doctors and they wrapped her in that funny looking white coat and took her away. That was some time ago, maybe March."

Lillian's eyes filled with tears as she and Louis listened to Mrs. Winter tell her what happened to her only friend. Louis could see the pain in Lillian's eyes and he slid his arm around her as he thanked Mrs. Winter and apologized for disturbing her.

"Let's go, Lillian. Maybe we can see your friend at the hospital."

∽

The Pennsylvania Hospital consisted of a couple of beautiful red brick buildings surrounded by neatly trimmed hedges and lush green grass. A stone path was cut through the landscape and lead to the grand white doors bordered on each side by tall pillars. Inside the nurses wore dark blue gowns covered by pristine white aprons and white caps under which their hair was neatly hidden. Men in white coats hurried back and forth through the foyer. Louis took Lillian by the hand and hurried up to the front desk. A young white man sat behind a large desk in the center of the foyer. "Excuse me sir," Louis began. "We are looking for Mrs. Althea Brown who may be a patient in your mental ward."

The young man eyed Louis suspiciously but said not a word. He retrieved a note pad and jotted down a message before ringing a desktop bell. "You may have a seat," he said to Louis and Lillian as he inclined his head toward a group of chairs against a far wall. Within minutes another young man appeared in answer to his ring. He handed over the note and quickly dispatched this new young man on a mission. Lillian and Louis sat quietly as they watched hospital workers walk back and forth through the foyer.

After what seemed like an hour or more, they were approached by an older white man. "Hello," He said cheerfully. "I understand that you are inquiring about Miss Althea Brown?"

"Yes, sir," Lillian said as she stood. Louis stood too.

"Well, yes. Miss Brown is a patient here and has been for more than a month now. Are you a relative?"

"No. I'm her friend. What's wrong with her, why is she here?"

"Sit, please," he said as he pulled up a chair to sit opposite Lillian and Louis. It is my understanding that Miss Brown had been evicted from her house but she refused to go. She was found in the house, talking to herself with the decaying corpse of her husband lying just a few feet away. When her only response to the officers was uncontrollable sobbing, the hospital was summoned and she was admitted here."

"Oh my God, how is she now?"

"Much better, however, she has no place to go and we are concerned that if discharged she would be homeless. We are trying to place her with family or a fellow church member but have had little success in finding a place to send her."

"She has no family, sir."

"So I have learned."

"May we see her?"

"Yes. Follow me," he said. He stood and moved quickly through the foyer to a narrow arched passageway. Lillian and Louis had to walk fast to keep up with the doctor as he moved through one passage way after another, a maze of archways and whitewashed washed walls. "This way," he said as he moved through a narrow door and up a flight of stairs. It turned out to be four flights of stairs that finally opened into the mental ward of Pennsylvania Hospital.

The pristine walls were lined with old metal beds, at least half of which patients occupied. Some patients sat on their beds talking to figures only they could see. Other patients seemed in a daze as they rocked backward and forward in those strange white jackets with sleeves that wrapped completely around the body. The doctor called them straight jackets and assured Lillian and Louis that they were for the protection of the patient as well as the staff. Althea sat in a chair in front of the window and Lillian saw her even before the doctor pointed to where she sat. "There is your friend. As you can see, she is much improved from the woman that came here months ago."

Louis waited at the door while Lillian and the doctor moved slowly down the center of the room. The doctor warned Lillian not to make any sudden moves that might startle the patients. "Miss Brown," he said.

Althea, with her eyes cast downward slowly turned toward the voice.

"You have a visitor," the doctor said.

With that Althea looked up and as soon as she saw Lillian, she leaped from her chair. Lillian received her with open arms and the two women embraced, tears filling both their eyes. "I thought you were dead," Lillian sobbed. Dr. Wilson quietly walked away and left the two woman to their visit.

"I was Althea whispered. Inside I was dead." Shaking her head in despair, Althea sat down again. "I've lost everything. Bernie spent every dime I could make and I couldn't keep up the houses. When the city came to evict me that was just the last straw. I couldn't take any more and I thought that I would die." Tears still filled her eyes as she spoke and Lillian just stood quietly and listened to her friend. "Bernie is dead," she said as if defeated. "Do you know how many times I've wished him dead?" She shook her head again. "But not like this. He took everything I had and left me with nothing."

"You've still got a friend Althea. Why didn't you come to me? I would have helped in any way that I could and you know that I would."

"I heard about Rebecca and I knew you had your own problems to deal with. I didn't want to add to your burden."

"Are you open to living with Miss Beth again?"

"Maybe, at least until I can do better for myself. I'd live anywhere to get out of here. These people are crazy. I was sad, not crazy." They both laughed and embraced again.

"Althea, I'll be back in a few days, after I've had a chance to speak with Miss Beth. You will be fine until then, won't you?"

"Yes. Thank you for looking for me, Lillian."

"Are you joking with me? I love you Althea Brown. You are my best and only friend."

"Really? What about that handsome man waiting by the door. He hasn't taken his eyes from you since I looked up."

Lillian chuckled. "Well, yes. He's my friend too."

Talking with Beth wouldn't be as easy as Lillian anticipated. James concluded his business in Philadelphia by midweek and now spent all of his time with Beth. It was nearly four days later when Lillian found Beth alone in her sitting room.

She tried to tell Beth all that she'd learned about Althea's situation, but after only a few minutes it became obvious that Beth's mind was far away. "Are you all right, Miss Beth," Lillian asked.

At first it seemed that Beth didn't even hear Lillian. Then she seemed to snap back. "What? Oh, I'm fine. Why do you ask?"

"I've been trying to talk with you about Althea but your attention seems to be elsewhere."

"I'm so sorry Lillian. It's just that James has made a proposal that has stunned me. I just can't stop thinking about the things he said."

"Proposal? Has he asked you to marry him?"

"Not exactly, but I think that he will eventually and I can't believe that I'm even considering such a thing. He wants me to move back to Virginia."

Lillian was quiet for some time as many questions ran through her mind. Finally she said, "What about us, Miss Beth. You know I can't go back to Virginia. Even you told me that a freed slave cannot return to Virginia."

Beth looked stunned. She hadn't even considered Lillian and Rebecca and she didn't know how to answer Lillian now.

"And, what about Mr. Martin, I thought you loved Mr. Martin?"

"Huh, Mr. Martin will never be able to take a wife as long as his mother lives and I'm not willing to wait the old witch out. Evil like her can live forever."

Lillian didn't want to talk anymore. Her mind raced far ahead as she considered where she would go if Beth went back to Virginia. "What were you trying to tell me about Althea?" Beth wanted to know.

"I wanted to know if she could come back here to work, but I see now that it really isn't a good idea. Don't worry. I'll figure out something, for all of us."

Beth was so deep in thought that she hardly heard a word from Lillian. "Fine," she said but she really had no idea what she was responding to.

∽

With the help of Ellen Nottingham, Lillian was surprisingly able to secure housing for Althea in a Quaker owned boarding house in Manyunk. It was located on a quiet, tree lined street. Its owner, Miss Martha Jenkins, did not require that Althea be a Quaker but she insisted that her residents be practicing Christians. Althea would not be the only border but she was the only female.

It was the day before Louis and James had planned to return to Virginia. Louis graciously offered to rent a carriage to transport Lillian to the hospital to pick up her friend and then take them both to the house in Manyunk. As they rode along, Lillian silently watched Louis. This wasn't the first time. She often caught herself observing him when he was unaware of the attention.

The time Lillian spent with Louis offered a new and different kind of freedom, one that she had not experienced before now. As slave and master, she and David's association was often in secret, precious stolen moments in time. They could never have shared the kind of open intimacy she shared with Louis. At that moment, Louis turned to face Lillian. He didn't seem surprised that he caught her staring at him. He smiled and reached for her hand which she surrendered willingly.

Lillian was simply fascinated by Louis. It wasn't just that he looked so much like David. She loved to hear his slow speech with its New Orleans accent. She was surprised at how attentive he was when she spoke and she loved how gentle his touch was when he took her hand or put his arm around her shoulders. Lillian did not know if she were falling in love with Louis but she did know that she was happy in his presence and when they were not together, she could hardly wait until she saw him again.

Althea was ready and waiting in the lobby when Louis and Lillian arrived at the hospital. Lillian assumed that Althea would be happy to be finally leaving the psych ward of the Pennsylvania Hospital but she sat on the straight back wooden bench with her hands folded in her lap and her eyes downcast. Sadness filled her face. Louis graciously waited as Lillian approached Althea.

Althea stood as Lillian approached and the two women embraced. "What troubles you, Althea?" Lillian asked bluntly. "I thought you would be happy to be leaving this place?"

Althea responded with a weak, unconvincing smile. "I am happy Lillian."

They joined Louis and began to walk toward the carriage. "You don't look happy. Tell me what troubles you, Althea?"

"I'm sorry. I do appreciate what you do for me but I just can't stop thinking about the houses I've lost. My parents worked so hard all their lives to own and keep their home and I've lost the only thing they were able to leave me."

"Look Althea," Lillian said rather sternly. "I'm sorry that you lost your houses. But now that you are well again, we can see what we can do to get them back."

"How, Lillian? I have no money to pay the taxes."

"You will have to work for the money and save until you have enough. I will help you. I promise,"

"I know that you mean well Lillian but those houses are not going to wait until I have the money."

"You don't know that Althea. Look, when I came here I didn't know what my life would be like. I had left everything I had ever known and you taught me how to trust God. Now, I'm asking you to trust God. We will take this to God in prayer, just like you taught me, and we will wait and trust God."

Althea was silent for a few moments before she whispered, "Thank you, Lillian," as she climbed into the carriage.

The boarding house was an old Victorian Stone house with white washed shutters and heavy doors. The furniture inside was heavy and dark though the rooms were filled with sunlight. It was clean and orderly. They were greeted by a bright faced young woman with rosy cheeks who wore a gray wool dress and white cap. She was pleasant but not overly social as she led the way to the room that would be Althea's home for a time.

Louis stayed in the carriage while the two women said their goodbyes. He marveled at Lillian's devotion to her friend. In only a few minutes he and Lillian were on their way back into the city. They rode in silence for a short time but both felt as if they needed to share their feelings before Louis and James left Philadelphia.

"Lillian," Louis said softly, his eyes looking forward on the road ahead. "I want you to know that I have enjoyed these past few weeks more than I could have imagined."

"Me too," Lillian said. She wanted to say so much more but it was as if her tongue was stuck in her mouth. A stream of loving words ran through her mind but she was unable to utter any of them. Suddenly Louis turned to face her. Maybe it was because her response was so vague or maybe he just wanted to look into her face. Whatever the reason, those intent green eyes caused Lillian to flush from her hairline to her chin and she turned her head to hide her own emotionally filled eyes. She wanted to beg him not leave Philadelphia when they were just getting to know one another. She wanted to confess that she thought she was falling in love with him, but she said nothing.

"I really wish I didn't have to leave," he said. "I will admit that I am feeling a growing affection for you Lillian. I haven't been this happy in a long time."

Lillian didn't respond to that and in the next few minutes he was pulling the horses in front of Beth's house. He reached over and put his hand over Lillian's hand. "I am feeling that same growing affection for you, Louis," she whispered. He smiled and Lillian felt her heart flutter. "Well," she whispered. She was going to bid him farewell until later but before she could get out the next word, Louis slipped his hand behind her head and pulled her to him. His kiss was long and passionate and Lillian was grateful that she hadn't been standing. Surely a kiss such as this would have knocked her off of her feet.

With his beautiful mouth he smiled and with his eyes he promised love like she has never known. "I'll be back in time for supper." He helped her down from the carriage and kissed her forehead before he jumped back into the carriage and snapped the reins, spurring the horses forward.

∽

That evening Beth couldn't help but feel a bit of sadness as the Vance's enjoyed the last supper before Louis and James were to return to Virginia. As she sat across from James she wondered what could have happened that change him so quickly and profoundly. He at first seemed just on the brink of a proposal and then stopped suddenly as if he had run into an unmovable wall.

James did the honor of blessing the table. Then light conversation about the weather, Rebecca's health, and the coming of the baby commanded the evening. Lillian informed Beth and the others about Althea's dilemma and her new home in the Quaker boarding house. When supper was over Lillian went to the kitchen, Beth and James took to the sitting room and Rebecca went to her room.

Louis followed Lillian into the kitchen where she and Sweet began to clean the dishes. He stood by the door, quite unnoticed at first. Sweet was the first to see him and he winked an eye and tilted his head. A gesture that told Sweet he wanted to be alone with Lillian. Sweet quietly slipped out of the door and into the drawing room. Lillian chattered on, talking to Sweet, unaware that she had left the room. Louis came up behind her and slipped his arms around her waist. She was startled and jumped at his touch. He quickly turned her around and kissed her passionately. Lillian returned his passion until she felt her legs could hold her upright no longer. His kiss left her breathless. As his lips left hers, he continued to stare down into her eyes. "I think I'm falling in love with you Lillian Vance," he said.

"Wow," she said playfully. "That is quite a leap, Mr. Bissette."

"What leap do you speak of, Miss Vance," he said willingly participating in her little game.

"We have leaped from a growing affection to love in the space of one afternoon."

"Well, what can I say? I am completely smitten with you Miss. Vance." Then he kissed her again.

"I'm sure that I am falling in love with you also, Louis, but you are going back to Virginia. What am I to do?"

"I'll be back. I'm not sure when but I cannot leave James now. James is very sick. I'm not sure what is to become of it but I can't leave him until I know that he is well. I hope you understand."

"I do."

"I will stay in touch until we see each other again but right now, Lillian, all I can think about is spending more time with you. I want to hold you in my arms and make love to you, kiss you all night."

Lillian stiffened. "Did I say something wrong?" Louis wanted to know.

"No," Lillian whispered.

"James told me about you and David. I hope that won't cause you to reject me."

"No. But you must understand Louis. I am not the same person I was when I was in love with David. Then I was a slave and a heathen. I didn't know or ever experience the love of God. Now I am a free woman, Louis, and a Godly woman. When I think of the things I did before knowing God, it makes me cringe."

Louis just stood there looking down into her eyes and Lillian thought that she had said the one thing that would send him running. She lowered her head and looked away, sure that the dream had died before it had a chance to live. Louis put his hand under her chin and lifted her head so that he could look into her eyes again. "I won't lie to you Lillian. I fully expected a night of passionate love making before departing for Virginia. In fact, I was looking forward to holding you in my arms as I said."

"So, is that why all this talk of love? You just wanted to get me into bed?" She placed both hands on his chest and tried to push him away but he didn't budge.

"No. In fact, I think that knowing that you are a Godly woman makes me love you even more."

Lillian lost her breath for the second time that night and she reached for the edge of the table to steady herself. Louis took her into his arms again. "We will be together, Lillian. Remember, I can offer you something that David could never offer. You will be my wife and I your husband and we will both give thanks to God for making it all possible." He kissed her again and Lillian began to cry as she returned his kisses.

"Oh, Louis, you continue to surprise me."

"Don't worry. This will all work out for us. Let's keep this to ourselves until I figure out when I can leave James."

The next day, shortly after sunrise, James and Louis took a carriage to the train that would take them back to Virginia.

CHAPTER 21

FOR EVERYTHING THERE IS A SEASON

With James and Louis on their way back to Virginia, Beth's Spruce Street home seemed extraordinarily quiet. Although the late May sun burned warm and bright outside, the inside was as overcast as if storm clouds gathered in the rafters of the house.

Beth was in an uncharacteristic bad mood that seemed to affect everyone in one way or another. She actually yelled at Sweet for being lazy, something she hadn't done since hiring the girl though her laziness was no secret. Lillian noticed Beth's bad mood early that morning and decided that she would talk with Beth as soon as the opportunity presented itself. Lillian knew that after James and Beth spoke, she was left even more confused than ever.

Late that afternoon Lillian found Beth alone in the sitting room. She entered the room as quietly as possible so as not to startle Beth who seemed to be deep in thought. Lillian sat down across from Beth and waited patiently to be noticed. Several minutes passed before Beth even looked up. "Oh, Lillian. I didn't hear you come in. Is everything all right?"

"As far as I know," Lillian said. "What about you? You don't seem yourself today."

"Oh, I know. I can't explain it. I don't know what I'm feeling. I just know that James leaving has left me with a very strange feeling. I'm not really sad but I'm far from happy. Like I said, I don't know what I'm feeling."

"Do you love him?" Lillian asked bluntly.

Beth took about a half a minute to answer. "No. I don't think I do."

"Then why the confusion?"

"Oh, I don't know. After Jefferson and his mother, I think that I was just happy to have someone love me."

"I understand that but I think James wanted more than just you returning to Virginia. I think that he really was going to ask you to marry him and return to Virginia. The only reason he didn't ask was he's so afraid of this sickness. He believes he's going to die soon."

"Yes, I understood that, but even that doesn't make sense to me." She paused and was thoughtful for a moment. "Did you know that I went to James once when I was back on Gloria? I was feeling really lonely and hurt and I looked to James for comfort."

Lillian did not hide her shock as her eyes opened wide in amazement. "What happened?"

"He turned me down. He didn't want to hurt David. He was loyal to his brother which is why I don't really understand his infatuation now."

"But, what would you have said if he asked?"

Beth was thoughtful again. "I don't know. I guess I just got caught up in his fantasy. I really have no desire to return to Virginia and to be honest with you, I still love Jefferson. I just don't want to deal with his mother. I suppose it is a good thing that James never really asked. I know that he wanted to but once he started coughing and he lost his breath, he seemed to change his mind. When I think about it, I'm not sure he really loves me as he says. I think that this is all out of some guilt he is feeling."

"Yes," Lillian agreed. "Maybe it's that guilt that also explains his devotion to Louis." Lillian was silent for a moment as she considered what Beth said. "But if you had refused his proposal, it would have hurt him deeply."

"I think that James has been hurting ever since he read Big Bill's journals. Everything else that happened, has just thrown him deeper into depression."

∽

Beth could not have known how right she was about James. He was indeed depressed but he was also physically ill. The dry hacking cough got even worse on his return trip to Virginia. He took the medicine prescribed to him by the Philadelphia physician as directed but it seemed to do very little to alleviate his symptoms. By the time they reached Gloria, James was wet with perspiration, red faced and burning with fever. With Nan's help, Louis helped James to bed where he stayed for the next three weeks.

It took a few days before things would settle back into a normal routine but Louis had no difficulty handling the responsibilities of the running the plantation.

He even made some crucial decisions without the approval of his brother.

Louis took the liberty of moving Moses and his wife Geri in to the cabin that he'd built for himself. He told Moses that the move was only temporary, just in case James voiced any opposition to the idea. Moses and Geri were delighted with their new accommodations.

Louis took a suite of rooms on the second floor of the mansion. He wanted to be near James in case there was a change in his condition or he needed to be moved for any reason.

Of course, the slave chatter was alive with the news that the half black brother was actually living in the mansion. "I bet Big Bill is turning over in his grave," Inez whispered to Denny as they cleared the dishes from the table.

"Shush. Nan don't like gossip. If she hear you talking like that there'll be hell to pay," Denny said.

James knew that he was being talked about but he didn't care. Although Nan would never speak of her objections to Inez and Denny, she did tell her husband Jacob that she thought Louis didn't know his place. Those feelings were hard to keep to herself and she appeared to Louis to suddenly be a little cold.

One morning, a couple of days after he moved into the mansion, Nan asked Louis if he would move James into the chair so that the bed linen could be changed. He readily obliged, lifting James and depositing him into the arm chair in the master bedroom.

"Is there something wrong?" he asked Nan.

"You mean besides Massa being so sick?"

"I mean, with you and I. You don't like me very much, do you? Did I do something to offend you?"

"I don't offend easily," was Nan's curt answer.

"I'm not your enemy Nan."

With that remark, she glanced up at him. "I know who you are Louis. You're Massa's half-brother, showing up here all of the sudden. Massa is kind enough to give you a good job as Overseer and you wait till Massa is too sick to say anything and you move in the big house like you the Massa. I know exactly who you are Louis."

The hate in her eyes was unmistakable but Louis took it all in stride. He smiled at Nan as she went about changing the bed linin. "Well, well. I guess I was right. You don't like me much." Nan did not respond. "Well, most of what you say is true Miss Nan but there are some things that you could not know. I am James' legal heir. Do you know what that means, Miss Nan?"

She shook her head, "No."

"It means Nan, that unless James has a son, when he dies I will inherit Gloria."

"And I'm sure you can't wait but, you're half black, a mulatto, a Negro. How can you be Massa of Gloria?"

"I am all of those things and the legal heir to this plantation. First, you should know that there are many plantations in this country owned and run by black men and mulattos." Louis waited for the shock of this information to take hold of Nan. "Secondly, Miss Nan, I did not just suddenly show up. James searched for and found me. He invited me here. He knew we were half-brothers before I knew anything about the Vance's or this plantation."

By now the bed was made and Nan threw the covers back for Louis to deposit James into the bed. "I'm sorry," Nan stammered. "I didn't know."

When James was securely lain in the bed and a cool towel was placed on his feverish head, Louis turned to Nan who stood by the door watching Louis with his brother. "I forgive you because as I said, you could not have known. I hold nothing against you Nan."

"Thank you."

"Just keep this bit of information to yourself. The entire plantation will be made aware in due time." He excused himself then and walked passed Nan.

Louis ran the plantation as best he could while looking in on James at every spare moment. The doctor from Richmond had come three times in the first two weeks of James illness. Again, he assured Louis that James would survive. It was only a matter of time before he would be up and about again. At the end of the third week, the fever broke. However, the man that emerged after those three weeks was a very different man. Although James was still coughing, it was no longer a dry hacking cough. Now he coughed up several clumps of blood and phlegm continuously. He'd lost a great deal of weight and was visibly smaller in stature.

His hair seemed thinner and he couldn't seem to concentrate. He sat staring into space as if he was unaware of where he was or what he should be doing. Louis tried unsuccessfully to engage him, asking questions about the running of the plantation but James seemed uninterested. It seemed to Louis that James was falling deeper into depression.

"Just give him time," was the doctor's advice. "He'll bounce back, I'm sure."

Louis wasn't so sure.

∽

It had been more than a couple of months and Lillian had not heard anything from Louis. She missed him more than she thought possible. She thought of him often. Sometimes she would think of him when she was doing the most mundane chore and her mind's eye would see his lazy smile and bright eyes and she couldn't help but smile to herself at the image.

Beth's mood had not improved much over the past couple of months and Lillian spent more time than usual away from the house. She would meet with Althea and they would walk in town, go to the church or just sit and talk. Lillian could tell that Althea was getting back to herself but very few conversations ended without Althea crying about her lost houses.

With the help of the church, Althea was able to get a job selling produce at New Market for a couple of the Quaker farmers in Overbrook. She didn't make much but it did wonders for her self-esteem and was enough to take care of herself and even save a little.

CHAPTER 22

NEW DAY, NEW LIFE

It was late August and the temperatures soared even after the sun went down. Benjamin couldn't wait to be released from his job at the City Hotel. He hurried from one task to the next with one eye on the big clock that hung over the desk in the lobby. He had made an important decision about his life and he was eager to share his good news with Rebecca. The two of them had grown quite close during Rebecca's recovery and now Benjamin knew that he loved Rebecca more than anyone knew.

After years of saving, he decided that he had finally saved enough to start the business he always wanted to start. Rebecca was never far from his mind during the decision making even though she has never given him the slightest encouragement. Benjamin wanted to ask her to marry him and assure her that his business as a caterer would provide a comfortable living for them. He fully expected Rebecca to turn him down but he loved her and he had to at least try to make her his wife.

He had become a constant presence at the Vance house and it was therefore no surprise when he appeared at the door on this particular August evening. He was greeted warmly by all of the ladies including Althea who was visiting with Lillian. Lillian happily introduced them before calling for Rebecca.

Still walking with a limp and wearing the scars of her ordeal, Rebecca slowly descended the steps. She was close to the end of her pregnancy now and quite large. Her small frame was reared backward with the weight of the baby. The larger Rebecca's belly grew the more Benjamin doted on her. To Benjamin, Rebecca was still the most beautiful woman he had ever seen. Benjamin has told Rebecca that he loves her often and Rebecca has never turned him away but she also never tells him that she feels anything more than friendship.

"Why, you are positively beaming," Beth says to Benjamin. "What's got you so happy?"

"I'd rather not say, at the moment, Ma'am. If all goes well, you will all know by the end of the evening."

That was enough to send Beth's mind in a whirl. She glanced at Lillian who did not look surprised or concerned. She only smiled at Benjamin and nodded her head. "Where are the two of you going this evening?" Lillian asked.

"We're going to have supper with my granny, take a walk and I'll have Rebecca back here before you know it."

The three ladies smiled at Benjamin but Lillian was the only one that looked as if she were truly happy.

With arms linked, Rebecca and Benjamin walked to his waiting carriage.

Miss Kathy had prepared a nice supper for the young couple. The aroma of roasted duck wafted through the windows and Rebecca could smell the delicious food as soon as the carriage came to a stop. Miss Kathy had also prepared mashed sweet potatoes, green beans, buttermilk biscuits, and gravy.

Rebecca was genuinely happy to see Miss Kathy. She'd missed the old woman's jubilant spirit. Miss Kathy was one of the few people who seemed happy most of the time and this evening was no different. She enveloped Rebecca into her ample arms as soon as she stepped over the threshold. "My, my," she said. "Still as beautiful as ever, come on girl and give Granny a hug."

The three laughed and talked as they ate the sumptuous meal. Of course, Miss Kathy knew her grandson's plans to ask Rebecca to marry him but she never gave anything away. "Your time is getting near," Miss Kathy said. "How are you feeling?"

Rebecca smiled and rubbed a hand across her ample belly. "I'm just tired, Miss Kathy. At first I was afraid, thinking of all the pain and everything. But now I just want to hurry up and have this baby. It seems like it gets heavier each day." They both laughed at that statement.

"Thank you, Gran. Dinner was great but we should be going. I want to show Rebecca something before taking her home."

After heartfelt goodbyes and warm embraces, Benjamin and Rebecca climbed into the carriage. But to Rebecca's surprise, Benjamin did not turn the horse in the direction of Miss Beth's Spruce Street home.

"Where are we going Benjamin?"

"I want to show you something?"

They rode only a short distance from Miss Kathy's house. It was a storefront building on North Broad Street. There was gold lettering on the glass but it looked as if the lettering was in the process of being removed. "Here? This is what you wanted me to see?" Rebecca asked.

"Yes. I know it doesn't look like much but this is my dream and I finally think that I can afford to rent the space."

"Oh, the catering business you're always talking about." She smiled.

"Yes. This was once an eat-in restaurant. There are two stoves and a stand-alone oven so I won't need to do much renovation."

"Wow. That sounds great. Can we go inside?"

"Yes, but only by the side door."   They walked a few feet away to the alley between buildings but it was filled with debris and garbage apparently thrown out from the previous renter. "You wait here," he said. "I'll go in and unlock the front door." Then he disappeared.

Rebecca waited in front of the building on Broad Street. She heard Benjamin moving debris around as he tried to reach the side door. Suddenly she heard carriage wheels rumbling on the cobbled street. She looked up just as a black carriage came to stop right in front of the store. Rebecca stared wide-eyed as Garrett jumped down from the carriage. Instinctively, she began to back away. "Garrett," she whispered. His unmistakable long strides moved fast, gaining ground at an alarming rate. Rebecca was in disbelief as she continued to back away.

"So Rebecca, did you think that I wouldn't find out about your bastard?" Garrett said as he approached. His blonde hair was longer than Rebecca remembered but the look on his face as he came closer was frightening. One look at his face and she knew that his rage boiled.

"Who told you?"

"Only a few people knew about you but they've all seen you lumbering around town with your big belly. You know that you will never have that bastard," he warned through clinched teeth. "Do you hear me? You will never have that baby, you lying black whore." His raised voice and offensive language caught the attention of other people on the street and a crowd slowly began to gather.

By now the two were face to face and they could both hear Benjamin as he rummaged through displaced furniture inside the building as he tried to make his way to the front door. Benjamin had no idea what was happening on the sidewalk just a few feet away and Garrett did not know that the man behind that door would come to Rebecca's defense.

"Garrett, I mean you no harm," Rebecca whispered as she put up an outstretched hand to stop his advancement. "This is my baby." Rebecca pleaded as she took another step backwards. "I don't want anything from you. I mean it Garrett. I don't want anything except to be left alone. You leave me alone and I swear you will never have to even look at the child. I promise, I will never ask for anything." Murmurs went through the crowd.

That did not satisfy Garrett and suddenly he lunged forward punching Rebecca hard in the face. She lost her footing and her head slammed into the plate glass window of the front of the store. The crowd gasped.

Benjamin's head sprung up at the sound of Rebecca's head smashing into the plate glass window causing it to shatter. All he could see was the blood on the back of Rebecca's head. He began to throw furniture out of the way as he moved to the front door. Just as he swung the front door open, Garrett punched Rebecca hard in her belly causing her to double over and go down on the sidewalk in a heap. Garrett then lifted his foot, intent on stomping Rebecca in the stomach and causing her to lose the child she carried.

However, while his foot was raised in the air, Benjamin hit him with such force that both his feet left the ground. His body came down on the sidewalk a few feet away and he quickly scrambled to his feet. When he regained his footing he came at Benjamin with a vengeance but Benjamin was taller, bigger and stronger and easily landed another punch square on Garrett's jaw. He went down to the sidewalk with a thud and before he could get to his feet again, Benjamin was lifting him off the ground by his neck. He hit him again, and again, until another man pulled Benjamin away. Garrett's unconscious body fell to the ground with blood running from his nose and mouth.

Benjamin went to see if Rebecca was all right. As he helped her get to her feet, he could feel that she was shaking violently. He took a rag from his pocket and placed it over the cut on the back of her head. Then he pulled her to him and held her tightly. He could feel the beat of her heart as well as the movement of the infant she carried. That small movement reassured him of the baby's well-being and he couldn't help but smile. "I love you, Rebecca. I will never let anyone or anything ever hurt you again."

Her knees buckled but Benjamin held her firmly. "I love you, too," Rebecca said hesitantly.

"Don't say it if it isn't real," Benjamin warned.

"It is real, Benjamin. I do love you. I just wasn't sure at first but I love you Benjamin. I really do."

At that moment, they were pulled apart by the same intervening white man. "Take your hand off the white lady boy." He was a large man and he looked around at his fellow citizens wondering why no one else came to the rescue of this young woman.

People who had watched the fight, both black and white, pointed to Benjamin as the man who had knocked Garrett out. Some people were even kind enough to inform the man that Benjamin was protecting the young woman who was being assaulted. "I am not interested in the details," he said. "I need one of you men to help me hold onto this boy while someone goes for the constable," the man yelled. "You can't assault a white couple on the street and just walk off."

Benjamin could have pulled away at any time but he didn't want to cause more trouble. He just wanted to take Rebecca home. "That man was hitting the lady," he told the man.

"I was not with that man, sir," Rebecca said. "And I'm not white."

He turned and looked at her as if he could not hear what she was saying. "What's that you say?" He squinted and pushed his round head forward.

"I say," Rebecca said a little louder and more clearly, "I am not white and that man was trying to hurt me."

The white man was shocked. This girl, this beautiful young woman looked as white as his own sister, he thought. He pushed his round head forward to get a better look and Rebecca's green eyes twinkled under in the light of the moon. He'd never seen a Negro with green eyes. Whether it was her beauty or her admission that she was not white, no one will ever know but the shock of it made him relax his hold just enough for Benjamin to pull away. "I've broken no law here, Mister and if you don't mind, I am going to take my girl home. As you can see, she is in a delicate state."

The man was still trying to make sense of what was happening. He was so sure that the woman was a white lady that now he just stood there with a stunned look on his face. Benjamin ushered Rebecca into the carriage as quickly as he could and climbed in after her. Out of the corner of his eye, he saw that same man was now bending over Garrett and Benjamin snapped the reins and moved the carriage forward quickly without appearing as if he were running from anything. As soon as he knew that they were out of sight, he snapped the reins again to spur the horse into a speedier trot.

"So, I take it that was the man who fathered your child? Is he also the one who tried to kill you?"

"Yes," Rebecca whispered through a groan.

"Are you all right?"

"No. It hurts Benjamin. It hurts really badly."

"Hold on. We will be at Miss Beth's house in just a few minutes."

They rode in silence for the next few minutes as each silently prayed that the baby had not been injured during Garrett's assault.

Outside of Beth's house, "Can you walk?" Benjamin asked.

"Yes, I think so."

After securing the carriage Benjamin helped Rebecca to the door. Sweet opened the door and Rebecca quickly announced, "I think the baby is coming now."

Everyone came running. It was a good thing Althea was there as she knew where to get the local midwife and Sweet was dispatched on that mission immediately.

Lillian noticed the blood as she began to help Rebecca into the bed to prepare for the delivery. "Oh my God!" she said. "There's blood. What happened to you?"

"I was punched in the stomach. The labor started as soon as I hit the ground."

"Oh my God," Lillian said again. Her questions were written on her face.

"Yes, mother. It was him, the father of the baby. He did try to kill me before and he tried again tonight but Benjamin saved me."

Althea looked stunned while Lillian shook her head as tears rolled down her pretty face. "What happened?" Lillian asked but she knew Rebecca could not answer her as she moaned and groaned in pain.

The midwife arrived within a few minutes and they were all ushered from the room except Sweet who stayed to help. Downstairs in Beth's sitting room, Benjamin told the ladies what happened. "Who is this man? Did she ever say his name?"

"I think she called him Garrett. He was a tall, blonde white man."

That comment brought on gasp from everyone except Lillian. "I'm not surprised. I tried to warn her but she just would not listen to me."

Twelve hours later, after Lillian had prepared breakfast and they all sat around the drawing room table, Sweet came and announced that Rebecca has successfully bore a healthy baby boy and was now resting comfortably. They all ran to get a look at the baby.

After a while Lillian thought that she might be taking advantage of her position as grandmother and she quietly left the room so that Beth and Althea could marvel at the perfect little sleeping boy. She went to the kitchen to make some tea and Benjamin followed.

"She told me that she loved me," he whispered so low that Lillian thought she didn't hear him right.

"What? She did what?"

"She loves me."

"She actually said that?"

"Yes. She actually said that."

Lillian went to Benjamin and gave him a hug.

༄

Unbeknown to any of the people in Beth's house on that same August morning in 1841 when David Benjamin Bowman came into the world, across town in a renovated Victorian style-stick house in Manayunk, Clarisse Martin, whose health had been failing for some months, was gripped with a sudden pain in her chest. She tried to pull the cord which would ring the bell for her nurse who was taking a much needed break from her duties. However, as Clarisse lifted her left arm, the muscle in that arm was suddenly seized by a cramp. Her efforts to scream were choked away and she unfortunately took her last breath while trying to call for help. When the nurse returned she found Clarisse hanging out of the left side of the bed with an outstretched arm. Her cold eyes were wide open and a look of terror was on her face.

As anyone could have predicted, Jefferson was devastated. He wanted to send a card to Beth and inform her of his mother's demise but decided that such an action would be the height of poor taste so soon after his mother's death. He would make the necessary arrangements and Beth would be informed the same as everyone else.

Beth received the card a few days later as did her neighbor Ellen Nottingham who immediately came over to chat. After ordering Sweet to bring in a pot of tea, the two ladies settled down in Beth's cozy sitting room for a long chat.

"Have you heard from Jefferson?" Ellen wanted to know.

"No and I don't expect I will until after the services and burial. It just wouldn't be right. He knows I'm here. There is nothing to do but wait."

"I'm sure you are right," Ellen said.

"On a brighter note, Rebecca delivered a heathy baby boy just four days ago."

"Oh my God, how is she?"

"She and baby are doing well."

"Did you ever find out who attacked her?"

"Well," Beth said as she scooted to the edge of her sofa. "He attacked her again but this time Benjamin was with her and I'm told that Benjamin really gave him a beating."

Ellen's face changed and a look of concern creased her brow. "Did Rebecca ever tell you or her mother who this man is?"

"Benjamin said she called him Garrett."

Ellen gasped. "What is it?" Beth wanted to know.

"I think I know who he is. My husband's accountant is Garrett Colbert. Last year he told my husband about a girl he'd been seeing. She was a very beautiful girl who threw herself at him. His only interest was to bed her and move on but then he found out that he had been tricked. She turned out to be a Negro. He even told Stuart that he'd given the girl the beating that she deserved. I had no idea he was talking about Rebecca." Tears filled Ellen's eyes as she spoke.

"Stop," Beth said. "I love Rebecca but I can't deny that she likely brought some of this on herself. Now, what can you tell me about Garrett Colbert?"

Ellen sniffed back her tears. "I never thought him a violent man until now. He's just an accountant."

"What about his family? Are they rich or average?"

"I don't know but I know that his father, Frederick Colbert is active in city government and he is a close friend of Major Swift."

"Well, that isn't good news."

"Why? What are you thinking, Beth?"

"Benjamin gave him a good beating to get him away from Rebecca. I'm just wondering if he will retaliate in some way."

"There isn't any way we could know that so you might want to tell Benjamin to leave town for a while."

"Yes. I agree."

The ladies went on chatting about other things and Beth took Ellen up to see the baby.

Later that evening, Beth shared what Ellen told her with the rest of the family and Benjamin. "Do you think he'll try to have me arrested?" Benjamin wanted to know.

"No. If the authorities get hold of this, he would have to tell why he assaulted Rebecca. He wouldn't want to do that in open court. However, according to Ellen, his family is well connected and he may want to come after you in other ways. He has political connections in the city that could make life very difficult for Benjamin, especially if Benjamin is planning to do business in Philadelphia."

"But where would he go?" Rebecca said.

"It isn't just Benjamin," Lillian said. "I think the two of you should leave Philadelphia as soon as possible. There is no need to take the chance on running into this man again."

"Mother!" Rebecca's alarm was evident. "I have a new baby. Where could we go with a newborn?"

"I don't know but we've got to find some place and soon."

"Pack," Benjamin said to Rebecca as he stood. "I'll be back in a couple of hours. I need to get my money back from the man who was going to rent me the store and I need to speak with my grandmother. By the time I come back I will know where we're going. So just pack."

Benjamin was true to his word and he returned in two hours with his grandmother, their minister from the Presbyterian Church, and a plan.

It was Saturday, August 29, 1841 and life was about to change forever for the three Vance women.

CHAPTER 23

CONFESSIONS

Miss Kathy put a hand to her chest and made a long purring sound. "Hummm," she whispered. "I knew that girl would come around," she said. Now she noticed that Benjamin was moving about her small house erratically grabbing clothes and shoes at will and stuffing them into a cloth bag. Her smile was replaced by a look of concern. "What is it?" she asked. "You should be happy. The woman you have been sweet on for more than a year just confessed her love for you." She was following behind Benjamin now. "Benny, what is it? What is wrong? Stop. Talk to me." She grabbed both his hands to still him.

"All right," he said. He plopped down in a chair, as if giving up. "Gran. I didn't tell you everything. That night, the man that had beat up Rebecca back in January showed up in front of the store. While I was inside, he tried to beat her up again. Somehow he learned that she was having his baby and he was determined that he would stop the baby from being born, not even caring if he killed her in the process."

"Oh my," Miss Kathy said.

"He was a white man, Grand. He was a white man and I hit him more than once."

"Oh my God!"

"Now, Miss Beth tells us that his family is connected to some powerful people who may want to strike back against me and Rebecca may still be in danger. We have no choice. We have to leave Philadelphia as soon as possible."

"Yes," Miss Kathy said as she sat across from her grandson. "Miss Beth is right. You must leave as soon as possible. They will either kill you or throw you into prison. You have to leave."

"Yeah, but where do we go? Neither Rebecca or me has family in New York or further north."

"I don't know but I'm sure Reverend Pickett will know something. You keep packing. I'll be back in a little while."

Reverend Henry Pickett was a well-known abolitionist and one of the Associate Pastors of the Presbyterian Church in Germantown where Miss Kathy worshiped but he lived just a few blocks away. It was rumored that he had helped several fugitive slaves on their way to safety in Canada. Miss Kathy was sure that he would know what to do and she was right. Reverend Pickett had the perfect solution. He told her of a village in New Jersey called Timbuctoo, named for the Timbuktu of Mali, Africa. The village was founded by fugitive and freed slaves with the help of some Quaker abolitionist back in 1820. "It is a self-sustained, all-black community," he'd said. "Black people own everything there except there is a Quaker church and boarding house. No one would look for Benjamin and Rebecca in Timbuctoo."

Benjamin was overjoyed when his grandmother returned with the news. He grabbed her and swung her around. "Thank you Grand. You are the best."

"Don't thank me Benny. You need to spend some time getting your knees dirty and thank God. Only way you gone get out of this mess is with God."

"Yes grandma. I know that you're right but we've got to get away first." Then he lifted his eyes toward heaven and whispered, "thank you God."

As Benjamin continued to pack, he noticed that his grandmother seem to be packing her own clothes into an old beat-up leather bag. "What's going on Grand? Why are you packing?"

"If you're leaving Philadelphia, I ain't got no reason to stay here. Besides, that girl is gone need some help with the baby." She didn't wait for him to answer. She kept packing and kept talking. "Reverend Pickett is going meet us at Miss Beth's house as soon as the sun goes down. He'll bring all the papers we need to travel and if you like he can marry the two of you."

Benjamin stopped suddenly. "Marry?" he questioned.

"Yes, marry."

"That girl foolishly got herself in a family way. It ain't gone help her situation to go on living in sin with you. You say you love her and she loves you so, marry her."

Benjamin was quiet as he thought about what his grandmother was saying. Finally, after several minutes he said, "Right again, Grand, if she will have me."

"If she'll have you? Ah, what choice does she have?"

Miss Kathy and Benjamin's arrival at Beth's house was bitter sweet for Lillian. She was happy that Miss Kathy was able to find a place for the young couple to go but she couldn't help feeling that in only a couple of hours she would be losing her only daughter. As she helped Rebecca pack, she tried to offer every morsel of motherly advice she could think of. "Mother, don't worry. I will be fine and I will write you as soon as we are settled."

As Lillian looked at Rebecca she noticed that her daughter no longer looked like the innocent naive young woman with her head in the clouds that had traveled to Philadelphia with her just three years ago. Rebecca actually looked grown up. Her scars, although still visible, did not look so prominent anymore. Her brow was no longer creased with the lines of anxiety. Lillian could see that her daughter was no longer a pretty girl. Even with her scars, she was now a beautiful woman. Her encounter with this Garrett Colbert, though heartbreaking, had matured Rebecca in ways no one could have predicted.

"What about the baby, Rebecca. You haven't even given him a name."

Benjamin came into the room at that moment. He hadn't expected to see Lillian there and he paused for just a moment. Rebecca reached out and took his hand.

"I know mother," she said. I thought I would name the baby David. How do you feel about another David Vance?"

Lillian was stunned and speechless. How could she tell Rebecca that she hoped that there would never be another David Vance? Fortunately, she didn't have to tell her anything.

"You can certainly name him David, if you wish," Benjamin said. "But my son's last name will be Bowman. He will be the next in a long line of proud Bowman's." Both women were speechless now. Benjamin went down on one knee as he took Rebecca's left hand in his own. "Rebecca Vance, will you marry me?"

Tears streamed from Lillian's eyes and Rebecca uttered a barely audible, "Yes."

Benjamin placed a beautiful gold ring with a small diamond surrounded by tiny pearls on the third finger of Rebecca's left hand. "This was my mother's wedding ring," he said. "My grandmother was kind enough to save it for me until I found a woman worthy enough to wear it. I love you Rebecca." Benjamin got to his feet and Lillian gave him a hug.

"I knew that you were an honorable young man the first time that I saw you at the City Hotel."

"Let's go down stairs. I want to tell the others," Rebecca said.

"Sure. I just need to tell you and your mother a couple of things. First, my grandmother is coming with us and second, the Reverend Pickett is going to marry us before we leave."

Lillian patted him on the back. "You have thought of everything Benjamin."

"I would love to take credit for being so thoughtful but it was Grand. She thinks of everything and she thought that Rebecca would need some help with the baby."

"She's right, again," Rebecca said.

As promised, the Reverend brought all the necessary traveling papers, directions to the Timbuctoo Village, and a marriage license.

Benjamin and Rebecca said their wedding vows in Beth's beautifully decorated parlor with Beth, Lillian, Althea, Sweet, Miss Kathy and Ellen Nottingham as witnesses. After they were pronounced man and wife, the Reverend graciously agreed to pray for the baby and he was christened David Benjamin Bowman.

It was close to eight when the sun finally began to set. Everything was packed into the small wagon given to the newlyweds by the Reverend Pickett. Little David was packed securely in a wicker basket with a sugar rag to suckle. Lillian embraced her daughter and held on for a little longer than necessary. "I will miss you so much."

"I'm going to miss you too Mother, but I don't want you to worry."

"I'm not worried Rebecca. I trust Benjamin because I know just how much he loves you. He put himself at risk for you. I know he will not let anything or anyone harm you. I hope you know how lucky you are to have a man love you so."

"I do mother. I really do."

Beth gave Rebecca a beautiful shawl to take with her. She also had Sweet pack some food in a basket. She hugged Rebecca and told her that she loved her. "Remember the first time I saw you. You were about ten and you were hiding under the stairs with a broken doll. Do you remember?"

"Yes, I remember."

"I've watched you grow and learn to deal with some situations that most adults would find difficult. Your mother and I use to worry for you constantly. I'm no longer worried. I guess you had to learn some things on your own. I am so sorry the lessons had to be so harsh but you were determined to have things your own way. Now I know that you have finally learned that you cannot be anyone other than who God made you to be. There is something in your eyes that tells me you are finally proud to be Rebecca Vance Bowman. You have grown up Rebecca." Beth embraced her again. "You know that I will have to tell your uncle James of this so don't be surprised if he looks you up in New Jersey."

Reverend Pickett stressed that the traveling Bowman's must arrive at Popular Lane in Kensington for the William Ridgeway ferry which would make its last run of the evening to the Camden shore at about half pass eight. After all the goodbyes, hugs, and kisses they didn't have a minute to lose.

Benjamin snapped the reins and they moved forward at a steady pace. The trip went as planned until they reached the Trenton train tracks in Kensington. No one expected to see the crossing being patrolled by armed guards.

Rebecca noticed Benjamin tense. "What is it?" she asked.

They were still a block and half away but they could see that guards walked back and forth across the intersection. "Guards," Benjamin said. "But I don't know if they are militia or police."

"It doesn't matter." Miss Kathy whispered from the back of the wagon. "I doubt if they're looking for you. They are probably looking for fugitive slaves. Just keep a cool head and don't act like you've done something wrong."

As they approached the intersection, one of the guards put up his hand to halt the wagon. Benjamin pulled back on the reins bringing the nag to a stop. He didn't say anything. He breathed a sigh of relief when he realized that the guards were Pennsylvania Militia and not Philadelphia Police. The guard, a fairly young white man, didn't address Benjamin at all. He tipped his hat to Rebecca. "Evening, Ma'am," he said and straightaway they all knew that he thought Rebecca was white.

"Evening," she replied hesitantly, at first. Then without any prompting Rebecca quickly assumed the identity that the young man thought he saw. "What is the problem here?" she said with some authority.

"Oh, there is nothing for you to worry about, Ma'am. There has been some talk about trouble on the railroad. We have to stop anyone crossing."

"I see. Well, let us hope that there is no trouble. We've had quite enough unrest lately, wouldn't you say?"

"Yes, Ma'am."

"Well," she waited for a few seconds. "May we pass?"

"Oh, yes," he said a little flustered. "Good evening, Ma'am"

As soon as the guard stepped back Benjamin snapped the reins and the nag moved forward. When they were far enough away not to draw any suspicion, Benjamin snapped the reins again to force the nag into a faster trot. They all laughed then. "You were great,"

Benjamin said. He was both surprised and somewhat in awe.

"I've had plenty of practice," Rebecca replied. "I wanted to be white so badly that I would practice the way they spoke and moved." One look at Benjamin's face and she knew she had said too much. His expression, barely visible in the moonlight, had changed. He was no longer smiling.

"And now?" he questioned. "You don't want to be white anymore because a white man beat you up, is that it?"

"No," she said emphatically. "Those months that I spent on the cot in your kitchen you all thought I was mending from my wounds but the truth is I was mourning the Rebecca that I use to be. Garrett Colbert taught me that I would never be accepted in his world no matter how light my skin or how green my eyes are. I may not look like a Negro, but that is who I am deep inside. I use to wear my shame at not being white like a cloak. I needed to shed that cloak of shame and fall in love with the Rebecca that I am and not the one I imagined."

"Amen," Miss Kathy whispered.

"You all helped. Even Miss Beth helped. I resented her because she was white and she was the woman who my fathered married. My mother was just his slave."

This was a revelation to both Benjamin and his grandmother as they never knew the real circumstances of Lillian and Rebecca's lives before Philadelphia. Miss Kathy patted Rebecca's back as if to console her and Benjamin kept his eyes on the road ahead.

"One day I just realized that Miss Beth loved me too, even though she knew who I really was and where I came from. The more time I spent in her house, the more I realized that she loved my mother too, even though they had once shared David Vance. I can't explain any of this. I just know that it made me feel very foolish to wish I were white."

They reached the ferry just in time. It took less than an hour to cross the Delaware River. Before they knew it Benjamin was pulling the wagon ashore from the ferry boat. They were now in Camden, New Jersey ready to make their way across the state to the Timbuctoo Village.

Once they were all settled into the wagon again, Rebecca continued her confessions. "I want to apologize for the way that I treated you those few days we stayed in the City Hotel. I was really mean to you and I'm sorry."

"I forgave you then. I think that I was falling in love with you even then." Benjamin put his arm around her shoulders and pulled her to him. Rebecca smiled and snuggled into his embrace.

After a while, Rebecca and Miss Kathy had to change places so that Rebecca could feed baby David. They passed several small towns before they reached Timbuctoo near dawn the next day.

Back in Philadelphia, Ellen informed Beth that although questions were being asked by the city police, no one seemed to know who the man was that assaulted Garrett Colbert. Weeks after the incident, a man came to Beth's door inquiring about a pregnant servant in her employ. He said that he was hired by the Colbert family to investigate the beating of their son on a city street.

Beth pretended she knew nothing of Mr. Colbert or the incident.

"Oh that girl," Beth said. "She was lazy and shiftless. I fired her months ago."

"Do you have any idea where she went," the man wanted to know.

"I just told you that I fired her. Why in the world would she tell me where she was going?"

"Well, Ma'am, I was led to believe that you and this young woman had some relation."

"What are you saying? That girl was a Negro servant who I fired. I can tell you no more than that. Good day, sir." Beth closed the door without any further explanation.

For weeks afterwards Lillian and Beth prayed that the investigation had come to an end. There were no more knocks on the door but it wasn't until months later that Ellen told them that the Colbert's had given up their search for the assailant. They all breathed a sigh of relief. Rebecca and her small family could go on living in peace in Timbuctoo.

⌒

Ellen and Beth attended Clarisse's funeral services at the Presbyterian Church. To their surprise there were not many attendees. With the exception of Jefferson and a few of the nurses he had employed over the years, there were mostly Jefferson's employees and only a few women from the church. The service and the eulogy were short and to the point. Jefferson walked behind the coffin as it was being carried from the church. That's when he saw Beth and Ellen. His eyes met

Beth's and he simply nodded his head to acknowledge them but made no attempt to speak to them.

"Well, well," Ellen said. I guess the break up was more final than you thought.

"I don't blame him." Beth said as she climbed into her waiting carriage. "I really was unkind to Jefferson. He really didn't deserve such treatment from me." She was reflective for a few moments, shaking her head as if disbelief. "It was just that I had already gone through a marriage where my husband cared more about another woman than he did me and I just wasn't happy with the control Clarisse had over Jefferson." Beth sighed and Ellen reached over and patted her gloved hand to console her. They rode in silence for a time. "If he never speaks to me again," Beth began. "I wouldn't blame him. I guess I wrongly assumed that he would run back to me after his mother died. Does that sound morbid to you, Ellen?"

Ellen frowned. "Yes, it sounds as if you were both waiting for this woman to die, but I know that isn't what you meant."

"Of course not! I didn't wish her dead or anything. In fact, I was sure she would go on living and running Jefferson's life for many years. I was as shocked as anyone to find out that she had died."

"Still," Ellen said. "It is much too soon for Jefferson to even think about a relationship. Give him time Beth."

They were both quiet for a moment. "I think you might be right, Ellen, but right now it doesn't feel so good. James wouldn't propose to me because he thinks his illness is fatal but I didn't mind that so much. I wasn't in love with James. It was different with Jefferson though. I loved him but I was so insecure about Jefferson's relationship with his mother that I've ruined that relationship. Jefferson has no plans to come back to me and I guess I will just have to go on with my life. Maybe my destiny was always to be a lonely old spinster."

"All right Beth, stop this. You are just feeling sorry for yourself now. You'll get through this, I promise."

Beth was quiet from that point on. Ellen talked and coaxed but Beth seemed to fold in on herself. Ellen couldn't have known but Beth was silently praying for a blessing. She would wait for Jefferson to come around and if he didn't she vowed to swallow her pride and reach out to him because she didn't want to think about living the rest of her life without him.

CHAPTER 24

THE INHERITANCE

Early September was harvest season on Gloria which required Louis to be in the fields from sun up to sun down. Though it was the waning days of summer, the heat held on well into the next month. It was hard work in sweltering heat and Louis came home in the evenings too tired to think of anything aside from filling his belly before falling into bed. Most nights, pure exhaustion allowed him to sleep soundly. However, there were also nights when he tossed and turned, his mind filled with memories of Lillian and worries for the future his new brother had planned for him.

When James first mentioned that because Louis was his only living relative, he intended to leave Gloria to him, Louis could find no fault with the idea. Besides, at that time he thought James was being overly dramatic. Yes, he was ill, but no one thought that he would die soon, least of all Louis. However, James also took great pains to tell him all about Big Bill, his lies, and indiscretions. Louis knew that James had no choice but to share. It was the only way to alleviate the guilt that seemed to consume his every waking moment. No matter what his reasons were for sharing, everything James said seemed to paint a really dark picture of the Vance family and especially Big Bill Vance. But now, with James becoming sick and finding out that he had likely inherited the lung disease that had taken his father's life, Louis was beginning to think that the Vance family was somehow cursed.

When that thought originally occurred to him, he was able to easily dismiss it as idle superstition. However, as James' health continued to deteriorate, Louis began to give credence to the idea of a curse, making him not want anything to do with being master of Gloria. He just hadn't figured out a way to tell James.

Though Louis did the best job he could for the plantation, he didn't have a passion for the work and he never felt as if it was his inheritance. Now James' illness seemed worse than ever and the possibility that he would pass on soon, could not be denied. Some days James would never even leave his room. When he did leave his room it was because of the barrage of solicitors and accountants visiting Gloria since their return from Philadelphia. He was truly getting his house in order, Louis thought.

It was just such a day when Louis came in from the fields to find James locked in the study with Mr. Wheaton, a solicitor from Richmond. Retrieving the mail from the table in the foyer, he saw a letter from Philadelphia. Once Louis read the return address and knew that the letter was from Beth, he was anxious to give it to James because of the possibility that there was news about Lillian. However, Nan informed him that James did not want to be disturbed. At this point in their relationship such an order would not deter Louis in the least. He tapped lightly on the door and James yelled, "Come in."

Louis was more than a little dirty and damp from the humidity and sweat but he presented himself to Mr. Wheaton as if he were dressed as proper as any southern gentleman. He handed over the letter before making himself comfortable in one of the leather chairs as if he had every right to be a part of their meeting.

Once James saw the return address on the letter, he seemed to forget Mr. Wheaton was even in the room. He anxiously ripped open the letter, his eyes quickly scanning the neat handwriting. The expressions on his face bore the emotions he felt as he read. He smiled and Louis thought it was the first time he'd seen James smile in a very long time.

Suddenly he was ceased by an attack of coughing. He made a futile attempt at covering his mouth with a kerchief but he was not quick enough to keep blood from sputtering forth with droplets landing on his desk and the front of Mr. Wheaton's white shirt.

Mr. Wheaton gasped as he pushed his chair backward forcefully. Louis was on his feet in an instant.

"I apologize, Mr. Wheaton," Louis said. "As you can see, my brother is ill. I think it might be best to continue this meeting another day." He assisted Mr. Wheaton to his feet with a firm hand on his elbow.

James got to his feet also. "I apologize, Mr. Wheaton. If you would be so kind," he said with a deep raspy voice, his kerchief still covering his mouth. "Please leave the papers with my brother, and I will sign them and have them sent to your offices in Richmond as soon as possible." Mr. Wheaton nodded his head in affirmation before he donned his hat and hastily left the study.

"What is it?" Louis wanted to know as soon as the study door closed behind Mr. Wheaton.

"See Mr. Wheaton out, please. I have news when you return."

Louis did as James said and returned to the study in minutes, documents in hand. He rushed into the study and gave James the documents. "What is it?" he asked.

"Beth writes that the man who attacked Rebecca attacked her again. This time, her friend Benjamin was there and apparently gave this man a beating."

"Well, well," Louis said. He smiled as he returned to his seat. "It isn't as if the man didn't deserve it. Good for Benjamin." When he looked at James he saw no trace of satisfaction. "Is that all, brother? Why do you look so distraught?"

"Well," James said between coughing spells. "This man, Garrett Colbert is a white man, a prominent citizen. His family is associated with the Mayor."

"Oh my," Louis said. "That certainly changes things. Where is Benjamin? Is he in the city jail?"

"No, thank God." James wanted to tell Louis the whole story but he was again ceased by an attack of coughing. This time it took his breath away. He tossed the letter across the desk at Louis so he could read the details for himself.

Louis read quickly, shaking his head in disbelief as he read. When he looked up from the letter, he saw that James was slumped over the arm of the chair. He looked as if he were ready to pass out. "James," he said firmly. "Shall I go for the doctor?"

"No," James whispered. "Just help me to bed. I should be fine in a couple of days." Louis did as he was asked and James took to his bed again.

After the first couple of days, Louis visited James and he requested that James bring him the documents that Mr. Wheaton had left for him to sign. James signed one document after another as he explained to Louis that in the event of his death, Louis would inherit everything, slaves included.

"No," Louis interrupted. "I don't want to own Gloria."

James was stunned. "Why ever not, Louis? It would make you a wealthy man."

"Brother," Louis said as he made himself comfortable on the foot of James' bed. "I don't expect you to understand this and believe me, I mean no disrespect. But I believe that this plantation is cursed as is the family. There has been too much tragedy here. It seems as if there is a dark legacy hanging over the place."

"I don't know what you mean." James was defensive.

"Really?" Louis said as he stood and walked closer to his brother. "I could be wrong but I think the darkness in this house is what's making you sick. You are so full of guilt that you think you should die because of things you could never have controlled."

"That's ridiculous."

"Is it? Isn't your guilt what led you to find me in the first place?" James didn't answer. "Big Bill may have fathered me, but I want no part of his legacy. If I am to believe all that you've told me, our father was not a good person. The things he did over his life have have continued to destroy this family after he is long gone. He has left a dark legacy and from what I've seen, it has damaged this family beyond repair."

" You're talking gibberish, Louis. People don't die from guilt," James finally said. "Isn't it more likely that I have just inherited the same lung illness that killed Big Bill? There is nothing weird about this. There is no curse, Louis."

"Really brother? Have you not considered that this disease is part of Big Bill's legacy?"

James head jerked up to gaze into the mossy stare of his half-brother. "From what you've told me," Louis went on. "The best thing that Big Bill ever did was to sell my mother to the Bissette's in New Orleans. I thank God every day that my mother saw freedom before she passed." He paused to see if his words had any effect on James. "You forget brother, I was emancipated as a youth but I've been in and around plantations all of my life and I tell you now that I have no desire to own a plantation or slaves."

James began to cough again and Louis waited patiently for him to catch his breath. "Look Louis, I don't want to hear all that nonsense. I don't want to hear anything else about Big Bill, curses or even legacy. You are my only living heir. When I die, Gloria will belong to you. Do with it as you will. I don't care."

Louis didn't argue further. He knew that leaving Gloria to him somewhat assuaged the guilt James felt.

James was up and about for a couple of days and this gave Louis hope. He was never far from his bed though. He moved from the study to the bedroom and back. He wrote letters and signed papers. It was as if the business of preparing to die was the only thing that was keeping James alive. However, once the plans were made and all the proper documents were filed, James began to fade. He took to his bed again. Days turned into weeks and weeks into a month and Louis began to worry again. He made sure that the very best Richmond doctor was treating James and he instructed Nan to take the room closest to James' room in the mansion so that she could be near if needed.

By October the harvest was complete and the weather had finally started to cool. This gave Louis more time to himself and more time to spend with James. He was convinced that James would not get better because he really didn't want to get better. His poor health was the price he needed to pay for surviving the death of his brother and surviving Big Bill's dark legacy.

On a cool November morning Louis was feeling a sense of accomplishment and freedom. There was very little work to be done and he could spend some time with James discussing the future he imagined for himself. Another letter arrived from Philadelphia and he took the letter with him to visit his brother.

James experienced spikes and lulls in his fever; he had little appetite and was constantly coughing up blood. Nan was sponging him down with cool water to bring down his fever when Louis came into the room. "Good morning James. Feeling any better?" A deep grunt was all James could muster for an answer. "I have another letter from Beth. Would you like me to read it to you?" Minutes passed before another grunt and Louis took that as a yes answer. He cleared his throat and began to read.

Beth wrote that she and Lillian finally heard from Rebecca and Benjamin. Their small family was doing well and Rebecca was happy that Miss Kathy had come along with them. Benjamin found a suitable building to rent with a large enough living quarters above the commercial space. He and Rebecca could finally start the catering business he always wanted. Money was tight but they were confident that it would only take a few months before they could start making a decent living. Rebecca never thought that she could love two people as she loved Benjamin and baby David. She says that she is truly happy.

By the time Louis had finished reading the letter Nan had finished her work and James was dressed in a clean night shirt and was now propped upon several pillows. "I want to write her back. Would you write it for me?" he asked.

"Of course." Louis quickly found paper, pen, and ink and made himself comfortable at the small table near the bed.

Dear Beth:

I trust that this letter finds you and Lillian well. I was happy to learn that Rebecca is no longer in harm's way, however, it sounds as if the newlyweds are too proud to admit that they are experiencing some financial difficulty. Please know that a considerable amount of funds will be deposited on Rebecca's behalf in The Bank of America. I'm sure there is one in New Jersey.

394

Please let me know if there is anything else I can do for her and her new husband. She is my niece, after all.

I was happy to hear that she and Benjamin named the baby after David. Though a flawed man, in his way, he loved you all.

I love and miss you dearly and I don't know if I will ever see you again. It is my prayer that you and Lillian will both find lasting happiness.

Please give Lillian my regards.
Sincerely, James

He drifted off to sleep almost as soon as he ended his dictation.

Louis included his own letter to Lillian before taking the envelope to the post master. This was not only the first love letter he had ever written, it was the first love letter Lillian ever received. Louis confessed that he first rejected the idea that he could be in love a second time in his life. After all, he and Lillian had just met and only spent seven days in each other's company. He went on to say that he could not stop thinking about her and whenever he closed his eyes, he saw her smiling face. He promised that he would come back to Philadelphia as soon as he could.

He also confessed that he really did not want to inherit Gloria. "*I don't know what the future holds for me but I know that wherever I am and whatever I do, you will be with me. We will do it together,*" he wrote.

After that first letter Louis communicated with Lillian regularly. He kept her aware of the slow deterioration of James' health. He also told her of his theory that James' illness was brought on by his extreme feelings of guilt. Louis saw James' illness as another symptom of the dark legacy left after the death of Big Bill Vance. He let her know that this was his sole reason for refusing to become master of Gloria.

Louis explained that there was another reason he didn't want to be master of Gloria. *I just don't want to own slaves,* he wrote. He had thought about it ever since James first proposed the idea of leaving Gloria to him. Now James knew too.

In the middle of November, Virginia was hit with an enormous snow storm. During those days of being house bound Louis became lonely. Even though there was no way to post the letters, he wrote to Lillian every night.

He visited James every day and every day he had less and less hope for his recovery. He burned with fever and his breath became more and more shallow. It was Thanksgiving morning and Louis went out to get a turkey. The snow was at least a foot deep as Louis trudged up the hill to the house with the turkey in hand. He dropped the bird off at the kitchen house before he went to the main house. Nan met him at the door. There were tears in the corners of her red eyes and her usual cheery smile was downcast. She didn't have to say a word. The brother who had found him just a year ago was now dead.

CHAPTER 25

THE BLESSING OF PROVIDENCE

In the second week of November Lillian received a letter from Rebecca and Benjamin. She could hardly hide her excitement as she ripped open the envelope as soon as she read the return address. Both Althea and Beth were equally as excited to hear from the young couple and Lillian read them the letter that evening as they sat by the fire in the downstairs sitting room. The Bowman family was doing fine. The money Rebecca received from James did much to improve their living situation and Benjamin could now look for a larger commercial space for his catering business. Of course, she ended with news of the baby's progress. *"Davey was only a few months old and already showing signs of inquisitiveness. He was already lifting and turning his head,"* she wrote.

Beth couldn't wait to pass the news on to James in Virginia. However she did not receive a return letter as she expected. When she finally did hear from Virginia, his letter was vague and kind of sad. The letter was filled with ruminations of the past and his apologies for tragedies for which he took no part. Beth could almost feel the sadness in his words which was all she needed to start worrying about James again. That was the last time she heard anything from James.

Lillian received a couple of letters from Louis and in December Beth received a letter from Louis telling her that the lung disease that had so worried James had finally taken his life as he slept the day before Thanksgiving. Louis explained that James was very generous in his will and had left a sizable amount of money for her. There was also an inheritance for both Lillian and Rebecca which his solicitors would be forwarding very soon. The rest of the estate was left to him. Louis also explained that he didn't want to be master of Gloria and would only stay in Virginia long enough to put things in order and sell the estate, including the slaves. After everything was settled, he would return to Philadelphia. He never said why he planned to return to Philadelphia and Lillian never indicated that she knew anything of his plans so Beth just assumed he must certainly be returning for Lillian.

Lillian was surprised at how much she missed Louis. After all, they really hadn't spent much time together but she found herself thinking of him often and especially over the winter holidays.

Christmas 1841 was unlike any Christmas Lillian could remember. It was her first Christmas without her daughter and she missed her dearly. She and Althea had bought gifts for Rebecca and her small family weeks ago and had them forwarded to Timbuctoo, but she still missed having Rebecca and her new grandson there with her. She missed Rebecca and she missed Louis. Althea would try to cheer her but for the first time in her life Lillian was truly lonely. She was grateful for Althea, but then Althea became ill with a winter chill. With a persistent cough and a fever, Althea took to her bed the day after Christmas. Without Althea, Lillian really felt alone. That's when she first got the idea of moving to Timbuctoo, although she kept it to herself. She couldn't leave now. Beth, who she had become so close to over the years, could not be good company as she was also in a very emotional state these days. She was in mourning for both James and her relationship with Jefferson and Lillian would not leave her in such a state.

On New Year's Eve Ellen invited Beth to dinner at her house to celebrate the New Year but Beth declined. Althea had not left her boarding house room for several days as she nursed a winter cold. Both Lillian and Beth were resigned to bring in the New Year alone and in sadness, however, that afternoon Lillian got an unexpected visit.

She heard carriage wheels on the cobbled street below and peeked through the heavy drapes that hung from the window on the landing of the stairs. She could see that the carriage bore the familiar gold embossed "W" of the Wallingford Estate which sent her running down the steps two at a time to the door. She opened the door just in time to see Gabriel helping Lindy down from the carriage. Ignoring the chilled air, Lillian ran forward and embraced them both.

"Oh my God," Lillian said. "I am so happy so see you both. You're looking well."

"We are well," Gabriel said.

"Come in, come in," Beth urged.

Once inside, she asked Sweet to make a pot of tea and to bring in some treats. Lillian took their coats before asking Beth to join them. Beth declined and remained in her sitting room alone.

"So tell me," Lillian said as she sat down at the table. "How are things on the estate?"

Gabriel and Lindy passed knowing glances at each other before Gabriel said to Lindy, "Tell her." Lindy just shook her head to indicate that she thought Gabriel should be the one to tell Lillian.

"All right, I don't know what's going on but one of you should tell me."

"Mr. Wallingford is dead. He apparently contracted some illness while the Black Empress was at sea and by the time their voyage ended, he was dead. They say that the doctor on board did everything he could, but could not save him."

"Oh my," Lillian exclaimed.

"There is more," Gabriel said. "We didn't get word for almost six months and when Miss Ella was finally contacted, she really went mad."

"She was already mad," Lillian said. They all chuckled at that statement.

"I know but she went into a rage almost daily."

"We got word to her doctors," Lindy added. "He came and gave me some really strong medicine that would make her fall into a stupor almost as soon as a few drops touched her tongue. I thought it was too strong but after about a week she started asking for it every couple of hours. The doctor told me that she wasn't to have the medicine more than twice a day and I was really careful not to give her more than he prescribed. I didn't even leave the medicine in her room. I kept it in my room in my drawer."

Sweet came in and poured the tea and after serving the guests she remained at the kitchen door. Apparently, this story was so interesting that she didn't bother to conceal her eavesdropping.

Lillian sat with a stunned look or her face as Gabriel went on with his story.

"One evening while everyone ate supper in the kitchen, Miss Ella went to Lindy's room and tore it apart looking for the drug. When she found it, she took entire bottle."

"When I came up to give her the second dose and put her to bed, I found her lying across the bed with her eyes rolled back into her head. She was dead." Lindy shook her head as if she still could not believe what happened. "I guess she just didn't want to live without her husband."

"Oh my God," Lillian said. "If she really knew that man she would have been better off without him."

"Yeah," Gabriel agreed.

"I guess her son Charles will take over the estate now," Lillian said.

Gabriel and Lindy exchanged knowing glances again. "Hold on to your chair, Miss Lillian. This news is even more shocking," Lindy said.

"Turns out, Charles was Miss Ella's son and not Mr. Wallingford's. No one knows who his father really is but he will inherit the textile business that was originally owned by Miss Ella's family but not the shipping business or the estate. Mr. Wallingford's solicitors tell me that a portion of the shipping business and the estate were always mine, left to me by Mr. William in a trust with his son in charge until I became of age. Since he is also deceased I inherited both the shipping business and the estate."

"Oh my God! Really? But you are a black man. Is it even legal for you to have such wealth?"

"Yes. The solicitor who came to see me said that it is all very legal. Believe me, he didn't look too happy about the news but there was nothing he could do about it."

"And Charles is not fighting you on this?"

"Charles wants no part of it but I'm trying to get him involved. This inheritance is both a blessing and a curse. First, I know nothing about the shipping business so until I learn, I will have to depend on the advice of others. I know that business deals may not be as profitable with my face as proprietor. I think I might fare far better with a white face in the forefront and I'm trying to convince Charles to partner with me for that reason."

"I think that is very smart of you."

"Lindy and I are still in shock by all of this. It seems to me that running a shipping business will be very hard for a black man but I'm going to give it everything I've got. If I find that it really isn't working for us, I will sell it all and move away."

"Whatever you decide, please keep in touch."

They stayed for a couple of hours and Lillian went on to tell them of Rebecca's ordeal, her marriage and new baby. "I would really like to see Rebecca again," Lindy said. Gabriel promised that they would find them in New Jersey when they could get away and they vowed to visit often and keep in touch.

By the time they said their goodbyes and headed back to Wallingford House it was close to supper time and Lillian went to check on Beth. She was sitting in the chair closest to the window with a knitted blanket over knees. Lillian watched from the door for a moment and thought for the first time that, Beth looked as if she were not only sad but defeated. She even looked older than her thirty-eight years. "How are you feeling?" Lillian asked before she came into the room and sat across from Beth.

"I'm not ill, if that is what you are asking."

"It isn't and you know it. I know that James' death was a great shock for you. You and Louis were both so sure he would recover but I'm guessing God had other plans." Beth smiled at that. "You have been moping around ever since you and Miss Ellen came back from Mrs. Martin's funeral. Does this have anything to do with Mr. Jefferson?"

Beth did not answer right away. "Well, I guess you will find out anyway. Jefferson barely looked my way. I stupidly thought that after his mother died, he would come running back to me. I was wrong. He wants nothing to do with me."

"That really isn't fair, Miss Beth. The man just lost his mother, at least give him time to mourn his mother."

With that Beth burst into tears. "You're right," she sobbed. "Ellen said the same thing." Lillian went to her, kneeling at her feet so that Beth could lay her tear stained face on Lillian's shoulder. They embraced until Beth was able to pull herself together.   Supper was just the two of them. Beth gave Sweet the day off and she went to spend time with her family. Lillian and Beth spent the evening in front of the fire sipping warm wine and reminiscing about the past. They both cried some and laughed some and after a few glasses of wine, the women said things that they would have never uttered with a sober mind. "When did you stop hating me?" Beth asked.

Lillian thought for a moment. "Do you have any idea how *much* I hated you?"

"Well, of course I knew. I tried to come between you and David, but I was his wife, after all. Now answer my question."

"I think that I let go of my hatred the day you handed me the freedom papers. I knew that if you really hated me as much as I hated you, you would have been content to let me and my daughter remain slaves on the Gloria Plantation. But you convinced David to set us free and that confused me. I didn't know what to make of it at first but I realized that you only hated me because of David. Once the truth came out there was no reason to continue to hate you," Lillian said. "Even so, when you offered to see Rebecca and me safely to Philadelphia, I was sure you had some trick up your sleeve."

"I know that's what you thought," Beth spoke softly. "But the truth is that when you and Rebecca ran away and David went to look for you, I knew that I could not compete with his love for you. I had given up at that time. There was no need to hate you. All of my hatred went to him at that point for bringing me into such a complicated family. And then James found the journals. That changed everything." She and Lillian were looking directly at each other and Lillian did not blink or turn away as she usually did.

"Yes. The journals set me free in more ways than one. I was not only set free from slavery, I was set free

404

from an incestuous relationship that neither of us knew about. Even now, when I think about it, I cringe. It took me a long time to forgive myself even though I know that I was not at fault. I think that may be why I embraced the church when we moved here. I needed to know that God would forgive me for all of it."

"We've come a long way, you and I," Beth said. "When I look at you I don't see a former slave, my former slave. I only see a dear friend and I am so grateful that God put us together again."

Lillian didn't respond right away. How could she tell Beth that she wanted to leave, not because of anything to do with Beth, she just really missed Rebecca. "Yes, we have been good for each other. I don't know what I would have done if you hadn't been here for me after getting fired from the Wallingford's and then having such a run-in with Althea's husband. I really didn't want to come to you. I thought you would think that I couldn't take care of myself and my daughter without you."

"Really? I never thought that. My only thought was being grateful that the two of you were all right, and here I could keep an eye on you both."

Both women were quiet for a while. They were each slowly coming to terms with their new reality in their own way. "Miss Beth, I wouldn't worry too much about Mr. Jefferson. He will come along in time."

Beth smiled. "What about you and Louis? I know that he is sweet on you but I don't know how you feel."

Now it was Lillian's turn to smile. Just the thought of Louis would bring a smile to her face. "I can't deny that I really like him a lot but I haven't thought any further than that. I'm almost afraid to call it love."

"Did he tell you that he is coming back to Philadelphia?"

"He mentioned it in one of his letters."

"I think that he is coming back to ask you to marry him."

"No. What would make you think such a thing?"

"I don't know. I just think he fell in love with you over the summer."

"Hum." Lillian grinned. "Well that is something to think about," she said.

"You want to know something else?"

"What's that?" Lillian asked.

"I think that it is time you stop calling me Miss Beth. We're friends Lillian."

Lillian just smiled. The clock began to chime the midnight hour. "Happy New Year," Beth said.

"Yes, Happy New Year to you also, Beth!" Lillian said and they embraced again. "I'm going up to bed now. I've enjoyed spending this evening with you Lillian. I think we have finally cleared the air about our feelings and that feels good."

"You could have always known how I feel. Once we left Virginia, there was no reason to hold anything back."

"I didn't really know you when we were in Virginia but I have come to know you since we've been here. Freedom has allowed you to become an amazing woman, a good mother, and a better friend."

"Thank you."

"I hope you're right about Jefferson. I miss him very much. Good night, Lillian."

"I am. You'll see. Good night."

The winter of 1841 brought abnormally severe storms of snow and ice to the eastern coast of the United States but the winter of 1842 brought less severe storms but well below normal temperatures. Beth and Lillian awoke on New Year's Day to temperatures in the teens, strong winds and steady snow. Sweet never made it back from where ever she had spent the night so Lillian made her way to the shed behind the house to bring in some additional logs for the fires. By the time Beth came down to breakfast she had a good fire going in the two largest rooms downstairs and the kitchen.

After breakfast, with a shawl tightly wrapped around her shoulders, Beth looked out of the front window at billowing snow and bare branches swaying in the wind. You could hear the wind whistle through the city. "I don't expect we will have any visitors today," she said before settling herself before the fire.

Lillian walked over to look out to see what Beth saw. To her surprise a wagon and horse had just stopped at the end of the walkway. "Oh, I don't know," she said. "I think we may have a visitor."

"In this weather?" Beth asked. "That isn't likely." No sooner had the words left her lips then she heard the door knocker bang against the door. She jerked her head up in surprised and her eyes went directly toward Lillian who had already slid off to the kitchen. "Aren't you going to get that?" Beth asked before realizing that Lillian was no longer there.

She opened the door just a crack as she wondered who in the world would be out in this kind of weather. When she realized that it was Jefferson that stood on the front step, she pulled the door open with such force that it banged against the wall. He was so bundled up you could barely see his eyes. "Come in, come in," Beth said. Once inside, she helped him shed his wool cape and beaver hat. She didn't wait for him to shed his gloves and scarf before she flung herself into his arms. "Jefferson, I can't tell you how much I missed you."

"I missed you too," he said before he devoured her in passionate kisses.

Jefferson was back, bringing balance, joy, and love to Beth's world. Jefferson didn't leave Beth's house for the next four days and neither of them made an appearance before noon each day. Jefferson coming back into Beth's life transformed her in a matter of hours. Her disposition became light and cheerful. She walked around the house singing or humming. Every time her eyes met Lillian's, she would smile the broadest smile Lillian had ever witnessed.

Sweet returned the day after New Years and was also shocked and happy to see Jefferson. "Wow, are they really back together again?" she asked Lillian.

"Yes and I don't know when I've seen her so happy."

Though temperatures stayed abnormally low, the snow began to clear by the middle of the month and Lillian was no longer house bound. Her first venture into the city was to visit with Althea at the boarding house. They drank tea and talked in Althea's small stark room. Lillian couldn't wait to tell her about the talk she and Beth had on the eve of the holiday and about Mr. Jefferson's return to Beth's life.

"All of that sounds so good so why do you look as if you are still so sad?"

"Well, I shouldn't be really. I've been thinking about moving to Timbuctoo to be near Rebecca and her family but Miss Beth was so depressed that I couldn't dare leave her. But now, with Mr. Jefferson being back in her life they're likely to be planning a wedding soon."

"And then you would be free to move to the Timbuctoo Village, is that what you're thinking?"

"Yes, that is exactly what I'm thinking." As soon as Lillian answered Althea she could see the sadness in her eyes. "You know that when I move, you can come with me. There isn't anything here for you anymore. Why not come with me? We can both start again. Rebecca says that everything in Timbuctoo is owned by Negro people. The village was settled by fugitive and freed slaves."

"You mean the whole town is black? There are no whites?"

"Some, but not many."

Althea was thoughtful for a few moments. "I don't know, Lillian."

"Well you don't have to make up your mind now. Just think about it."

"I will. I promise."

༄

Lillian's thoughtful prediction was more accurate than she knew. A May wedding was scheduled and Beth and Ellen were completely engrossed in the planning for the event. Beth was determined that this wedding would be entirely different from her first wedding. She and Jefferson had not yet discussed where they would live but she had made up her mind that if he wanted her to move into the mansion she would have no objection, as long as she could redecorate as she pleased. It turned out that since the wedding would take place at the mansion, the redecorating had already begun.

The heavy damask drapes were replaced with sheer curtains throughout the lower floor. Heavy wood planks were removed from the walls and replaced with lighter wallpaper. Beth chose almost white wallpaper decorated with tiny yellow roses. She hired landscapers to improve the grounds around the house as she planned an outdoor wedding. She convinced Jefferson to permanently hire a host of servants for the upkeep of the house and grounds and a cook.

She returned to her own house every evening after the work of the day had been finished which left Jefferson to return home alone and face all the changes Beth made. He never once complained. Beth could do no wrong. He was so happy to have her back in his life that she could do almost anything with his approval. He saw his dark and gloomy boyhood home transformed into a home that was bright and cheerful with an inviting ambiance. He could only smile in awe at Beth's efforts.

As the weather warmed Lillian thought more and more about moving to Timbuctoo but she needed to speak with Beth. However, everyone was so excited and so busy preparing for the wedding that Lillian rarely saw Beth alone. She decided that she would have to confront Beth even if it was in the presence of Mr. Jefferson.

One evening as Jefferson and Beth sat in the sitting room handwriting invitations, Lillian came to the door. "Excuse me," she began.

"Yes, Lillian. What is it?"

"I hate to disturb you but I was wondering if you and Mr. Jefferson are going to stay here in your Walnut Street home or move to Mr. Jefferson's home."

It was dead quiet for a minute. They hadn't discussed it and could not answer. "Well," Beth began. "Come in, come in. Sit with us."

Lillian made herself comfortable in a chair close to the window. "Why do you ask?" Beth wanted to know.

"I was just curious. After all, you have already hired servants for the mansion and if you aren't going to continue to live here, you won't need me."

"I see," Beth said. She was thoughtful for a moment and Jefferson leaned over and whispered something in her ear. "I don't know, Lillian. Truthfully, I haven't thought about it yet."

"Well, you know that I am so grateful for everything you've done for me but I have missed Rebecca so much that I am considering moving to New Jersey."

"Oh!" Beth could not hide her surprise.

"Well I think that is a wonderful idea," Jefferson said trying to hide his contempt for Lillian. She could never understand why he had such opposition to her being here with Beth.

"Lillian you know that you will have a place with me no matter where I am and for as long as you like but if you want to move to New Jersey I certainly can't stop you. I do understand how much you miss Rebecca."

Nothing else needed to be said. Lillian would move to the Timbuctoo Village in New Jersey as soon as possible. She wasted no time in writing to her daughter and son-in-law to tell them that she would be joining them in May. Rebecca wrote back immediately. She could not be happier to have her mother with her and her small family in New Jersey.

And so it was that on Sunday, May 8, 1842 Elizabeth Gable Vance was wed to Jefferson DeWitt Martin in a beautiful garden wedding attended by most everyone who was anyone in the County of Philadelphia. The bride wore an ivory silk gown embroidered with a flower design along the hem with a lace covering over the bodice and a charming satin bow at the waist. Beth looked as regal as a queen as she moved slowly down the path under artificial arches of roses. This was the wedding she had dreamed of when she was but a girl in Narberth.

It was the Wednesday after the wedding and Lillian was smartly dressed in traveling clothes as she sat perched on her packed trunk. She and Beth were waiting for Althea to be dropped off and for a carriage to take them both to the ferry dock in Kensington. The house on Walnut Street was empty except a few pieces of furniture that Lillian bought for herself and Beth promised to ship as soon as Lillian sent her an address.

Althea was late and Lillian worried that they would miss the next ferry to Camden and that would mean that they would have to wait at least two hours for the next crossing.

Finally, a buckboard wagon pulled by a pitiful nag came down the street and they knew it was Althea. But where was the coach Lillian had hired to take them to the dock. She helped Althea down from the wagon with her small carpet bag.

After a few minutes they heard another wagon rumble over the cobbled street. "Well, I guess this is it," Lillian said. She and Beth embraced for the last time. "I will miss you," Lillian said.

"I don't think you will," Beth said. "I expect you will be so busy with your grandson, that you will hardly give me a thought."

"No. I may be busy but I will still miss you."

"And I will miss you. Good bye to you both," Beth said. She embraced Althea. "I'm praying you both find happiness in New Jersey."

CHAPTER 26

END OF THE LEGACY

This was by far the worst winter that Louis could remember. The cold lasted well into March and those infamous March winds were brutal in their assault on the bare tree limbs of Gloria Plantation. Those cold and windy days in early March kept Louis inside more than he would have liked. His bags had been packed for weeks but he could not leave until all of the slaves had been settled with their new owner, which was proving more difficult than he imagined. Just as his conscious would not allow him to own slaves, neither would it let him sell Gloria's slaves to what he considered may be cruel taskmasters. Though there were countless offers from planters around the state, Louis wanted to choose carefully and wisely. He had no idea if black or mulatto planters dealt more even handedly with slaves than whites, but he knew that it was more likely than not so that is where he began his search.

After considerable investigation by his solicitors a black plantation owner was found in Alexandria, Virginia. The   solicitors reported that the planter was a Mulatto woman who had inherited her cotton plantation from her white father. Miss. Regina Hilliard was a fifty year old spinster, who was known to be compassionate and that made selling her Gloria's slave population to her a very attractive prospect.

Louis traveled to Alexandria in late February to meet with Miss. Hilliard. She was a big woman with a voice that was just as big, booming and the deepest Louis had ever heard from a woman. However, she was extremely pleasant and she let Louis know right away that she was a religious woman. He watched her interact with her slaves as they shared a sumptuous brunch together. They spoke of many things including slavery. "It is a horrible practice. If I could, I would free them all."

"Were you not born a slave yourself?"

"Yes," she said. "But, as you might imagine, my experience was much different than most." She shifted in her chair uncomfortably and leaned forward as if she spoke some confidence. "Still, if I could run this plantation with hired hands, I would certainly do so. As it is, I'm barely making a profit. If I had to pay for labor I'd be bankrupt within a few months."

"I understand but you do know that this can't last forever. It is an unnatural state of affairs. Oppressed people will eventually do whatever it takes to be free."

"No disrespect to you Mr. Bissette, but this unnatural state of affairs, as you call it, has gone on for more than a hundred years and I've been hearing murmurs of slave revolts my entire life. The only one that has come about was started by that preacher Nat

Turner. Every last one of those rebels was hanged or shot. If there were to be such a revolt," she said as she looked Louis right in his eyes. "Who do you think would stop at my door; the slaves or the white folks? I have no fear of slave revolts, sir. I don't have the luxury of dabbling in politics. I'm just trying to live day by day with the resources the good Lord has put at my disposal."

"I understand," Louis said. "My concern is that the slaves will be treated well."

"It is only by the grace of our Lord that you and I are not in their place. Understanding that fact is what guides my treatment of slaves. You can be assured that I will not tolerate mistreatment of any kind by my overseers."

By the time Louis was ready to leave Alexandria in late afternoon, he was sure that this was the best deal he could possibly make for Gloria's slaves. The bill of sale was signed and Miss Hilliard could expect delivery as soon as arrangements could be made. Louis did not want to transport slaves in the brutal cold so he waited for winter to loosen its grip on Virginia. There hadn't been any snow since the middle of February but March also brought icy rain, so he waited. The first sunny day would not dawn until the end of the month at which time Louis immediately arranged the transport of the slaves.

He had long ago decided that he would not sell Nan, Jacob and Denny. They had been the kindest to him since he first arrived on Gloria and he had grown very fond of the three of them. His solicitors presented him with documents of their enslavement with him named as their master along with emancipation documents which only needed his signature.

Nan and Jacob stood on the front porch waving and saying their goodbyes as three wagons packed with Gloria slaves made ready to leave. Neither could understand why they were not taken away with the others. Nan held her silence as long as she could and then confronted the young master that very day. "Why have you not sold my husband and me? Do you leave us here for the new owners? And what of Denny, is she to stay here too?"

"Not to worry," Louis said with a smile. "I mean you no harm and the three of you will know your fates soon enough."

It took Louis to the end of April to settle everything and in the last week of April he packed for the long journey to Philadelphia, Pennsylvania. His few slaves would not know that he planned for them to accompany him to Philadelphia until the day they left.

Denny was excited as she had never even been off the plantation in her life. Jacob and Nan were surprised but they could find no joy because as far as they could tell, they would just be slaves in a different town.

They arrived the second week of May. Louis hired a coach to take the four of them from the train depot into the city of Philadelphia and to the City Hotel on Market Street. It was the same hotel where he and James had stayed earlier that year. All three slaves were wide eyed and in awe as they looked around. They were standing on the sidewalk in front of the hotel. "Are they gone let us sleep here?" Denny wanted to know.

"Only if that is what you want," was the confusing answer Louis gave. "This is as far as you go unless you decide to stay with me." He reached inside his jacket and retrieved an envelope. "The documents in this envelope free all three of you. I signed them before we left Virginia." He waited while his words took hold and he was sure that they understood.

"Free?" Jacob said slowly and in a questioning tone. "Free? Did you hear what Massa Louis said? We're free."

"I heard him," Nan said but she didn't seem happy about the news. "What are we going to do? We don't know nothing bout being free. Where we gone go?"

Louis listened for a few moments before interjecting. "Nan, there is a whole community of free blacks here in Philadelphia. You will be fine. I will help you rent a place to live and after the three of you find work you'll be able to make money and take care of yourselves. I promise you, it isn't as scary as it might seem."

Denny was slow to understand but it finally hit her and she screamed as loud as she could, drawing the attention of some people as they passed by. "We're free!"

"Or," Louis went on. "You can all stay with me as my employees and I will pay you a living wage."

"What does that mean?" Jacob asked.

"It means that you will work for me and I will pay you money which you will use to take care of yourself. That doesn't mean that you won't be free. You can leave anytime you choose."

Jacob seemed confused but Nan understood perfectly. Denny was still letting it all sink in. "That seems like a good idea," Nan began. "It seems to me that we should take some time to get used to being free before we go off by ourselves."

"I think Nan is right," Jacob said.

"Excellent!" Louis said. "I will rent rooms in the hotel until I decide where I am going next." He rented a room for himself and one for his servants in the City Hotel. He had food delivered to them before he set out for Beth's house.

Once the carriage came close to the Spruce Street mansion, Louis was overcome by a strange feeling. As the house came into view he realized that it looked empty and his uneasiness increased. There were no coverings on the windows of the upper floor, and the front door stood wide open. Lillian and Althea stood there all dressed in traveling clothes with a trunk and a carpet bag. Miss Beth was hugging Lillian as if she were saying good bye. Louis swung open the door before the carriage had come to a complete stop. He swung his long legs down and leaped to the sidewalk. All three ladies looked up in surprise because they all thought the wheels they heard rumbling over the cobbled street were those of the carriage Lillian had hired to take them to the ferry. When she saw that it was Louis that emerged from the carriage, she nearly lost her breath. "Louis," she whispered.

"Hello," he said cheerfully. "Miss Beth, you are looking as beautiful as ever. Are you ladies planning a trip somewhere?"

"Why, thank you Mr. Bissette. I am not planning a trip but Lillian is . . ."

"What are you doing here, Louis?" Lillian cut her off.

With long strides they were face to face in a second. "I told you that I was coming back, didn't I?"

"That was months ago. I haven't heard from you since the first of the year."

He slid his arm around her waist and pulled her to him with one swift movement. Lillian had to grab hold of him to keep her balance. "I'm here now, Lillian," he whispered. "Where are you going?"

Lillian detected a hint of annoyance in his voice. "Was I supposed to wait for you?"

Althea just watched the three of them but she did not offer a word. Beth moved a few steps away from Louis and Lillian.

"Yes, you were but now I just want to know where you are going."

"Miss Beth got married," Lillian spoke quickly.

He turned to Beth but did not let go of Lillian. "Congratulations Miss Beth!"

"Thank you," Beth whispered. "Look Louis! I've moved in with Jefferson and closed the house. Of course I offered Lillian the opportunity to come with me but she is missing Rebecca dearly, so she and Althea have decided to move to Timbuctoo to be with Rebecca and her family."

No one said anything for a noticeable moment. Louis finally bent his head close to Lillian's ear. "I love you," he said. She smiled but did not answer. "I love you and I want you to be my wife. If Timbuctoo is where you would like to live, then that is where we will go if you will have me for your husband?"

Though he whispered, Althea and Beth heard every word. They both smiled and Althea looked as if she were going to cry. "She loves you too," Beth said a little too loudly. "Don't you Lillian? Tell him."

Now it was Lillian's turn to laugh. "Yes, Louis. I love you and I will be happy to be your wife."

With that he picked her up and swung her around while they both giggled like school children. When her feet finally touched the ground again, she had to grab hold to Louis again to keep her balance.

"Do you mind if we stay here in Philadelphia for another day or two. That will give us time to get married and then we can all make the journey to New Jersey."

"All? Do you mean us and my friend Althea?"

"Yes, of course, but I have some friends of my own that I'd like to take along."   He waited to see the expression on Lillian's face but the hack driver was ready to move on. "Miss Beth, if you need a ride home, you can certainly use the carriage." Louis released Lillian and went to Beth. He led her to the carriage and helped her to climb inside. As Althea and Lillian said goodbye, Louis paid the hack. Soon the carriage lurched forward and Lillian and Althea stood on the sidewalk waving to Beth.

"I ordered another carriage to take me to the ferry," Lillian said. "It should be here soon."

"Good. We will have dinner in town and then spend the night in the hotel. There are some people back at the hotel that I thought you might like to see."

Lillian couldn't have looked more confused. "You brought someone from Gloria Plantation?"

"Yes. I have emancipated three of Gloria's slaves. They were very kind to me when I came to Gloria and I have grown fond of them. These three have lived on Gloria all of their lives so I know you must know them.

I'm sure they will be as happy to see you as you will be to see them." He was all smiles as he spoke and Lillian had a strange feeling creep over her.

How could she tell him that she had no friends on Gloria Plantation? Most of the slaves hated her for her haughty attitude and she had no use for their condemnation and jealousy. Noticeable time passed as she contemplated meeting some of Gloria's slaves again.

"Lillian," Louis whispered. "Are you all right?"

"I'm fine. It's just that I didn't have many friends when I was a slave. I can't imagine anyone who would be happy to see me again."

"I see," Louis answered. "You think that you weren't liked because of your relationship with David. Is that it?"

Just hearing Louis refer to David was a shock to Lillian. In the distance she could hear the hired carriage approaching and she wanted to answer Louis but for some reason she just could not make a sound. The carriage came to a stop and Louis helped both ladies climb inside. He gave the hack instructions as their bags were loaded in the back of the carriage before he climbed in beside Althea. He and Lillian were face to face and he just waited patiently for her to speak. The carriage lurched forward and Lillian spoke so softly he could barely hear her. "Yes."

"There are a couple of things you should know. First, I know all about your relationship with David. Secondly, you are not the same person that was a slave on Gloria. James told me how impressed he was at your transformation since leaving Virginia. I'm sure that this isn't going to be a problem for any of us. But, if for any reason you are unhappy with them I will help them find employment somewhere else."

"Thank you." She didn't ask who they were because she no longer cared. It was enough to know that her happiness was important to Louis.

∽

Their rooms at the City Hotel were all on the lower floors and in the rear of the hotel because even free blacks were not allowed above the second floor. After a dinner at one of the many black owned restaurants in the seventh ward, Louis, Lillian, and Althea returned to the hotel. They entered through the back door. Louis knocked on the door of one of the rooms he'd rented. Nan opened the door. It took a couple of seconds before she recognized Lillian. "Lillian, is that you?" She didn't even give Lillian a chance to answer before she threw her arms around Lillian's neck and gave her a big hug. "Look, Denny, Jacob, its Lillian."

They came running and were obviously happy to see Lillian.

"Look at you Denny. You're all grown up!" Lillian said.

"And I'm free," Denny said. "We're all free now."

The reunion was exactly as Louis expected and he could not have been happier. Louis was busy over the next couple of days as he arranged for an impromptu wedding at the Bethel Church and the passage for the six of them to travel to the Timbuctoo Village in New Jersey. He provided the money for Lillian and Althea to shop for whatever they needed for the wedding, new clothes for Nan, Denny and Jacob, and for the trip. Once a date and time was settled, Louis made sure that Beth and Jefferson were notified without Lillian's knowledge.

On Saturday, June 1, 1842 in the presence of the few people Lillian and Louis called friends, Lillian became Mrs. Lillian Bissette. As she and Louis looked into each other's eyes on that warm June morning, Lillian knew that she and Louis would spend the rest of their lives together. She would never love anyone more then she loved Louis at that moment. She was wished well by all and when the hugs and kisses stopped, she thanked everyone present then said a prayer to thank God.

That evening Lillian and Louis spent their first night together. She had not been with a man since David's death over four years ago but she wasn't a bit nervous. He was gentle and patient as he touched every inch of her body. Lillian lost herself in his embrace as she tried to breathe in the very essence of this wonderful man. She didn't know how much she missed being loved until Louis took her that night. "Louis," she whispered close to his ear. "I don't ever remember being as happy as I am right now, laying here in your arms."

"You have good reason to be happy. Not only have we found each other but we no longer have to fear that Big Bill's dark legacy will reach out and touch our lives. It is finally over."

"I had not thought of that."

"It could have continued but before James died I told him that I wanted no part of Big Bill's legacy. That's why I sold the plantation. All of that misery is behind both of us and I promise to do my best to make you happy every day of my life."

Lillian and Louis did not leave the hotel room for an entire day. The next Monday, they loaded up the wagon that Louis bought and six people, all who had lived through tragedy, heartbreak, and loss, left the ghost of the past behind and began their journey to a new life in Timbuctoo, New Jersey.

THE END!